MW01518716

RANDOM
HOUSE

I write a new book every day
A love theme for the wilderness
Blue Nile

ASHRAF JAMAL

Love themes for the Wilderness

KWELA BOOKS
in association with
RANDOM HOUSE

For Randolph Hartzenberg,
Christine Solomon and André Vorster

The artwork on the front cover (a detail from "Sebastian",
pastel on paper, 1994, 1 120 x 820 mm)
is by Tracy Payne; the three photographs inside the book are
the work of Marina Umari; and the photograph of the author on
the back cover was taken by Nick Aldridge.

These works are reproduced with the
kind permission of the artists.

AUTHOR'S ACKNOWLEDGEMENT

I'd like to acknowledge a few sources, sounds and words, which over the years have stuck and found their way into *Love Themes for the Wilderness*. There's A. R. Ammons's poem 'Corson's Inlet' which, if it could have been believable to have Stoker remember it in full, I'd have gladly quoted verbatim. There's Mike Nicol's *The Waiting Country* which I had somehow to turn into an epidemic, get most of the characters to read. The chunk I've taken is pretty sizable! It includes a poem by Ingrid Jonker, a slice of Mandela's inauguration speech, and Nicol's appraisal thereof which had a lot to do with Phyllis's recovery. Then there's Lionel Abrahams's poem 'Retreat' (Snailpress), from *A dead tree full of live birds*. The lyrics from Robbie Robinson, Björk and Portishead. The lyrics come from 'Ghost Dance – Music for the Native Americans, Hyperballad – Post'. As for Portishead, I've hit a blank. As for whether or not *Love Themes for the Wilderness* is fictional or real? Let's just say that the places are mostly real, the people mostly fictional.

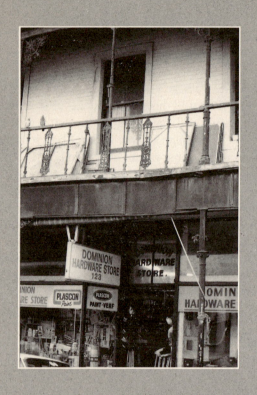

BOOK
ONE

CHAPTER ONE

Stoker stepped through the opened wedge of the circling door and into the street. There were other smokers milling about. He lit a Chesterfield Light and stared across the car park at the glittering city. Rain spat off the hoods of cars. Light from the bulging yellow eyes of a Citroën flashed momentarily across the huddled smokers, then died. Stoker smiled. Through the circling door others were stepping in and out of the gallery. Many of the people he saw he knew, some by name, mostly through faces.

Cape Town was a town in love with the idea of a city. All around him buildings reached into the sky, glowing with neon signs and liquid eye displays of construction companies advertising acres of prime office sites. To his right a highway curved and arched across a squat building owned by a shipping company. The building belonged to the age of girth, of space, to a time when the sky belonged to birds. A few feet above the building the highway stopped dead in its tracks. Rain poured in sheets from its blunted edge. Stoker pictured the pair of scissors, screened by the rain, which someone had painted across the edge. For years the highway had been this way. Now, with the new millennium about to pay its visit, with talk of athletes set to converge from the four corners of the world, there were plans to extend the highway. It needed to be done, it seemed. The highway stuck out like a sore thumb. According to Dean, the city's town planning department aimed to put a stop to the embarrassment. Stoker was sceptical. He liked the highway just the way it was, glittering blunt and grey in the sky above a busy intersection. A gorgeous blunder.

'Howzit Stoker.' He felt a hand press warmly on his shoulder.

'Howzit,' Stoker replied. 'Love the Citroën.'

'Yeah. You got a smoke?'

'Thought you'd never ask.'

Putter grinned. 'You give me a cigarette, I give you the future,' he said in a bad Chinese accent. He whipped out a pink business card. On the card was a photocopy of a muscle-bound hunk.

'A GQ Michelin Man,' Stoker said.

'You could see it like that.' Putter lit the cigarette.

Stoker flipped the card. It was blank. He read the words positioned next to the badly reproduced hunk. 'What's this?' he asked.

'It's the Locker Room Project.'

'And what's the Locker Room Project?'

'You tell me.'

'The future?'

'A beginning.' Putter flicked the ash into the street. 'Speaking of which, how's the opening?'

'Free wine. Lots of broke artists. Some suits.' They turned to look through the circling door.

'You never know. There might be a pretty red sticker where the sign reads PUTTER R1 500. Either that or my Citroën will end up languishing in storage.' And a tear fell from Putter's left eye. The tear was followed by a mock sniff, a flick of mittened fingers. 'Spot you later,' Putter said, crushing the cigarette with his heel, turning to enter the gallery.

Stoker lit another cigarette. He wondered whether or not to step back in. His wine glass was empty. He wondered whether he needed another drink. He wondered what he was doing outside. 'Smoking a cigarette,' he said. 'Waiting for a lift. That's what I always do. Smoke and wait.'

Stoker suddenly felt ridiculous standing in the rain, too stupid to think about getting wet. Through the circling door he saw people locked in conversation, grinning and hugging each other as they passed. The walls dripped with art, some of the works, such as his own, literally still sticky. 'If you're going to work in oils you'll have to plan better,' he said. He hoped no one would be curious enough to poke about his landscape with their grubby fingers.

4

'Smoke and wait,' he said. 'Smoke and wait.' Then he dug his hands into the torn pockets of his leather jacket and walked.

The Seeff Trust Gallery stood in a shrinking wasteland, dwarfed by mammoth fenced squares of poured concrete and girders. Part of a renovated Victorian building, the gallery overlooked the buried remains of the old harbour wall. Once a cold storage dock for cheeses and fish, the building now belonged to Seeff, a group of property brokers.

Stoker could picture the ocean lapping the shore where he walked, hear the creak of masts and hulls, the bleached sails of ships. Veering diagonally across the wasteland of rubble and mud he mourned the senseless loss of the power station which had once existed where he walked. With its angles and fluted towers the power station had always struck Stoker as a cross between an art deco jukebox and a chapel organ.

Was it the summer of '82? '83? Stoker couldn't recall. It must have been '83, he thought, when Dayglo, Joan and Waldo were caught red-handed in their surfing wetsuits, the snorkels, goggles and crayfish smuggled inside their backpacks. They'd discovered a major feeding area for crayfish in the canals and sewers linking the defunct power station to the ocean. On many nights in the summer of '83 they'd stolen through the fence around the power station in their wetsuits and industrial-strength gloves, to reach the access point to the sewers and feeding area. Once bagged, the crayfish would be sold to restaurants. Dayglo, Joan and Waldo must have been what? Nineteen? Twenty at the time? The fine didn't come cheap. Still, it was good while it lasted, Stoker remembered Waldo saying. He smiled, fancied he saw Dayglo, Joan and Waldo stealing through the pouring rain in black surfing wetsuits and backpacks. The visual was good while it lasted. The fact was Dayglo was drumming at the Seeff, Joan was in New York, Waldo in India. The power station was rubble, the sewers sealed. The crayfish had long since scuttled to different pastures.

Through the skeletal beginnings of buildings that broke through the rubble and mud, Stoker saw hulking ships cut out against a pouring sky. Two security guards huddled about a flailing fire, rain beating down on the low tarp that protected them. In the growing distance he could hear the rapid thudding of Dayglo's drums, the muted squeal of Percy's guitar, Jay's voice spiralling through the three floors of the gallery, still reaching him as he drifted away.

Stoker thought of stopping and warming himself by the fire, and nodded as he passed the cautious faces of the guards. He was not certain of where he was going, what he was doing. Was he walking towards the ocean? Going to stow away on a cargo ship destined for Taiwan? He reflected on the fact that he didn't have his passport. 'Always carry a passport,' he said. Then he pictured himself, his ID book, his thick glasses, his short red hair soaked beneath his peaked cap. He was going nowhere and he knew it. He was like the highway stranded in mid-air, sodden with arrested purpose, his oil painting as soaked as he was, as provincial, as banal, a haemorrhage of murk, bereft of line, of light. It was preposterous to assume that anyone would deign to touch a canvas as soiled, as incurious and blurred as his. Adrian Stoker – *Man in a Landscape* – R400.

He laughed as he veered away from the broken line of ships. Then, as he turned to go back to the gallery, he stopped. Why not? he asked himself. He was thinking of the Gideon Warehouse. Putter had recommended he have a look-see before the warehouse was finally demolished. Inside there was some gay graffiti worth the look. Why not?

Stoker stepped onto a narrow bridge of scaffolding. There was no guard in sight. Gideon's was not a space worth protecting. Inside it was black. He could hear pigeons in the rafting. Rain poured through the gutted roof and sides of the building. He lit a match and cradled the flame in the cup of his hand. The graffiti was on the far left wall, according to Putter. Stoker stepped diagonally into the blackness. His boots were soaked. Water sloshed in the hollows of his feet. 'Keep to the left,' he said, his arms outstretched, his feet inching forwards. Then he stopped, lit another match. In the distance he thought he saw a wall, thought he saw a painting. He moved closer, careful to ensure that he was on certain ground. Then he thought . . . there is nothing certain about mud. He was enjoying himself. There was a coherence to his actions. He was inching towards an exhibit. And then he slipped.

He sank to his knees into a pit of wet cement. For a split second he considered letting go, sinking deeper. His would be an insignificant absence, he thought. Another dead artist buried in the foundations of capital. Other than the two security guards no one would know where he was. Besides, were they actually looking when they looked at him? Stoker doubted it. He certainly had no idea of what they looked like. Surely others shared his disinterest? What were the traces which could lead an intrepid searcher to this vault of cement? None. His footsteps? A slither of mud. His last human contact? A brief hooded nod behind glasses which obscured his face. Glasses he was still wearing. In a moment of weakness he thought of flinging his glasses to a spot where they could be found. A last flicker of hope? A belief that he must be found? Then he remembered a photocopied pencil drawing he'd seen stuck to the window of the Bedroom Furnishings Emporium next to Dominion Hardware on Lower Main in Obs. LOOKING FOR THIS MAN. CALL 474809. The image he saw was that of a finely-bearded melancholy stranger, a chrysanthemum attached to a buttonhole of the stranger's dinner suit. The telephone number Stoker pictured was his own. He remembered how odd it had seemed to find the notice stuck to the lower section of the display window for children, dogs, dwarves and cripples to see. He remembered thinking that there should be billboards with giant pencil drawings and telephone numbers.

Stoker managed to pull himself away from the cement. When he returned to certain ground he discovered that he had lost his right Doc. He lit a match, saw the cement encrusted along his thighs. He'd sunk deeper than he'd thought. Breathing heavily, staring into the blackness, he wondered what to do next. His Docs cost six hundred rand. His sister had bought them for him in some fit of affection. Or was it despair? He'd only been wearing them for a month. It had taken him that long to break them in. What to do? He could come back tomorrow. Surely the cement wouldn't have hardened? And now? What about now? Now he was stuck in the pouring rain, weighed down with cement, with one cement Doc to show for it.

He removed his leather jacket and stuck his hand into the cold wet pit. It was here somewhere. He had to try and find it. He sank his thin bare arm deeper into the pit. He could feel the blood freeze. He dug deeper still, pushing his hand with all his weight in a slow steady arc, his fingers spread at acute angles. Had he touched the Doc and not known it? If this was purpose, if this was reason, then it was better to have none. He gave up. He doubted he'd come back the next day.

Walking through the wasteland he saw the Seeff Gallery in the distance. He was suddenly colder than he was able to admit. Colder than ice, colder than the ground on which he walked.

Outside the circling door he lit a cigarette. He noticed that now people were stopping to look at him.

'Stoker? What the hell happened to you?' It was Putter.

'I lost my Doc.'

Putter looked at Stoker's cement-encrusted jeans, his feet. 'That you have. How?'

'I'll tell you later. Right now I'm freezing.'

Taking Stoker by the arm, Putter drew him towards the gallery.

'What the fuck are you looking at?' Putter asked a group of well-heeled women. 'Art? You think you're looking at Art?'

'Fuck off,' all three women said in unison. Then one of the women lit a cigarette. The lighter stalled. Stoker walked up to her and struck a match.

'Thank you,' the woman said. They looked at each other. Stoker was smiling. She exhaled slowly, the smoke trailing across her eyes. Then, without shifting her gaze she passed the cigarette to her friend, took Stoker in her arm and led him into the gallery.

The marble foyer seethed with the heat of bodies. Putter cut a path towards the drinks and ordered a stiff whisky. Stoker and the woman followed. At the bar she bent down, lifted Stoker's foot and removed the right Doc.

'It's pointless staying attached to this,' she said, rising with the cement-encrusted Doc in her hand. Stoker gazed forlornly as she shifted a sculpture to make room for it on a plinth.

'There,' she said. 'Now at least it's found a decent fit.'

Stoker studied the bronze figure replete with cap and bells, the Doc a prehistoric mix of leather and stone beside it.

'Who knows, someone may decide to buy it? What shall we call it?' the woman asked.

Stoker mused. 'Lost my shape trying to act casual?'

'Too subjective'.

'Doc?'

'Too objective'.

'You decide,' Stoker said.

'Agreed,' the woman replied.

Putter arrived with the whisky.

'Thanks,' Stoker said.

'You want me to run you home?' Putter asked.

'Naah, I'll be fine.'

'Raindog,' the woman said.

Stoker and Putter stared at her.

'Why don't we call it Raindog?'

'Sounds fine,' Stoker said.

'That's a line from Waits,' Putter said.

'Good artists borrow, great artists steal,' the woman said.

'And that's a cliché,' Putter countered.

'Sounds okay to me,' Stoker said. He could sense that Putter and the woman didn't like each other.

'What's a Raindog?' Stoker asked.

'A Raindog is a dog that's lost its way in the rain,' the woman said.

'And the scent's been washed off the fire hydrants so the dog can't find its way home,' Putter chimed.

'That definitely sounds fine to me,' Stoker said.

'How much?' the woman said.

'How much?'

'How much you selling the Raindog for?'

'You kidding?' Stoker asked.

'It's got to have a price.'

'Six hundred,' Stoker said.

'Six hundred,' the woman said. 'I'll be with you in a minute.' Then she turned and, with a radiant smile, exited the gallery.

'Fuckin' suits,' Putter said, watching the woman as she disappeared. 'They come in here loaded, cause a stink and leave.'

'There's no need to get nasty,' Stoker said. 'You don't even know her.'

'And I suppose you do?'

'She seems fine to me.'

'Everything seems fine to you, Stoker. That's the problem.'

'That's bullshit, Putter.'

'Look, I'm not here to indulge your fantasies, okay? You want a lift or not?'

'I said I'm fine.'

'Yeah, sure.'

'You sell anything?' Stoker asked, cutting through the tension.

'Nope.'

'Let's just enjoy, okay.'

'Now you're talking.' Putter held out his palm. Stoker placed a ten rand note in it. They walked to the bar.

'So, you going to tell me about the Locker Room Project?' Stoker asked.

'There's nothing to tell.'

'What's with the cards?'

'Like I said, it's the future. Who knows what the future holds?'

'Here you go.' It was the woman. She was back.

Stoker looked at the gumboots and towel the woman was carrying.

'I found the towel and wellingtons in my friend's car. The towel's covered in dog hairs, but I'm sure it'll help.'

'Thanks,' Stoker said. Wellingtons? he asked himself.

'And here's the cash. One thousand rand.'

'I said six hundred. Besides, I was joking. The Docs cost my sister six hundred.'

'Well, here's six for the Doc and four for the painting.'

'You bought my painting?' Stoker was stunned.

'What do you think?' the woman asked. 'Do I look like a charity?'

'This is crazy,' Stoker said.

'You'll just have to get used to it,' the woman said. 'Take it, it's yours.'

Stoker stared at the wad of notes held before him.

'Take it,' Putter said.

'I can't, this is crazy,' Stoker said.

'Take it,' Putter insisted.

'You shouldn't attach a price tag if you don't believe in what you're selling,' the woman said. She couldn't resist smiling.

'Take the fuckin' money,' Putter whined.

Stoker turned to Putter and glared. Putter shut up.

'It's not the money,' Stoker resumed. Then he realised that words were starting to fail him.

The woman shoved the money into Stoker's jacket pocket. She started to laugh. Confused, Stoker followed the direction of her gaze. The money had tumbled onto the marble floor through the hole in his jacket pocket. He watched embarrassed as Putter and the woman gathered up the fifty and one hundred rand notes. The people in the gallery were paying him an abnormal degree of attention. He watched the woman as she turned to face him. He let her place the towel over his shoulder. He took the money.

'You'll catch your death if you don't do something sensible,' the woman said. 'The fact is I love your painting and I want it. As for the Doc, I've got my reasons. Besides, the transaction is perfectly legal. I've spoken to the gallery owners. Now I have to go. My friends are waiting for me. I've got an early morning. Cheers.' Stoker felt the warmth of her as she kissed his cheek.

'Cheers,' he said, as he watched her disappear for a second time. 'And thanks.' But the woman had vanished by the time his words could reach her.

'I guess we should have another round,' Stoker said to Putter.

'I guess,' Putter said. He was lost for words.

'Make it two triples,' Stoker said. Then he picked up the gumboots and walked towards the toilets. He noticed that the Doc the woman had placed on the plinth had gone.

Stoker filled the toilet sink with hot water. He removed his socks and wrung them out. Then he slipped into the gumboots. As he adjusted his feet he watched his face disappear in the steaming mirror.

CHAPTER TWO

Stoker sat up in bed feeling jittery, a tin tray painted with gaudy flowers balanced on his lap. The flowers failed to soothe his hangover. 'I must learn when to stop,' he muttered to himself, sipping his Milo and staring at a blob of margarine melting in a bowl of Jungle Oats, a cheese and tomato snackwich in his trembling hand. After a drinking binge he'd invariably be bedridden the following day. He'd already downed four Panados and a Grand-Pa headache powder, and the pain in his bracket felt as though it would take months to budge. He set aside the uneaten snackwich and picked up the spoon. Slowly he began to stir the porridge, scooped up a spoonful and steered it erratically towards his mouth.

Solemnly chewing his oats Stoker thought of restraint, of how he would marshal every shred of sense – a sorry store at best – and finally conquer his wilful ignorance of limit. I must learn when to stop, he mused, his jaw clicking noisily as he slid the porridge down his throat. Then, needing some variation from his monotonous pangs of guilt, he reflected on Robert Wilson's installation, *Memory Loss*. He'd only seen pictures of the intallation at Prue's, pictures of a man immersed to his shoulders in a blistering desert – the man and desert replicas in a vast room. According to the notes which accompanied the pictures, this was an ancient Mongolian form of torture. Horse thieves would have their heads shaved, the skin of a camel's neck strapped to their skulls. The skin would shrink, the growth of hair revert inwards. The combination of the sun, the compression of the skin and the inward growth of the hair follicles would result in memory loss. In this way thieves would be brainwashed and eventually become efficient citizens. Stoker presumed himself to be going through an equivalent torture. He hoped he'd eventually lose his mind – that squalid debauched side of it, anyway – and be redeemed from any future hangovers. 'Dream on,' he said. 'Dream on.' Then he polished off the Milo and the Jungle Oats.

On a blue plastic crate beside his bed lay the wad of rand notes which the woman had given him. The notes were spread like a deck of cards, the change mounted in towers of copper and silver. He'd drunk himself into a stupor because the absurdity of the situation had demanded it. He'd never seen so much money in one lump sum before, at least not a lump sum he could technically call his own. He related to money in dribs and drabs – the occasional handout from his sister, a hundred here, fifty for stretching a canvas, three fifty for painting a house, eighty for a logo, four fifty for spray-painting a car, one fifty for fixing and applying three coats to a fence. He'd never sold a painting before, let alone a Doc! The whole experience was too ridiculous for words. If the woman had just bought the painting he'd probably be feeling a lot better than he was feeling now. Feeling queasy and precious was not a healthy combination. His conscience was playing tricks with him, screwing him up even more. Who cared where and how the money landed on his bedside table? No one. No one cared. Besides, there was no doubt that he desperately needed it. Oil paints didn't come cheap. Not at the rate he was using them. Who the hell did he think he was? Anselm Keifer?! Besides, who the hell gave a fuck who he thought he was or wasn't? No one!

Okay, so he was feeling sorry for himself. He had a splitting headache. He was a nobody squeezing way too much money onto thick murky canvases, money he didn't have and couldn't afford to waste. His rent was overdue. The bank was hounding him over a debt he preferred to forget. He'd had it with trying to cover two rentals, was thinking of moving into his studio. Charming. At least he wasn't shoving his losses down other people's throats. He wasn't embarrassing himself asking for loans he couldn't pay back. The bank was one thing, friends another. He'd stripped his needs down to a minimum. He had a snackwich machine, he had groceries, he had a fuckin' studio!

Stoker suddenly realised that he was feeling a bit better. He'd cancelled work at Dominion Hardware, said he had a client to see. Olivieri, his boss, had said it was way-cool. Coming out of Olivieri's mouth the word had thrown him offbalance. The man was ninety years old for chrissakes, what was he doing mouthing off like some drugged-out inner-city technoid? Olivieri was constantly drumming up crazy words. It kept him young, he'd said. Sure. Olivieri wore a hairpiece and loafers. He kept his dentures in a Mickey Mouse jug. The freak was even thinking of piercing his navel! Stoker was convinced that Olivieri did these things to drive him crazy. Everything Olivieri did felt like a joke at somebody else's expense. His in particular. Still, Olivieri owned the studio above Dominion Hardware and charged him two fifty a month. Olivieri let him work three days a week as part payment, selling nails and junk – plastic teasets, bad reproductions of Jesus suffering on the cross, natty breakfast trays like the eyesore he had laid out on his lap. Olivieri was cool, that's for sure. Way-cool.

Stoker and Olivieri had hitched up a year and a half ago. Stoker had seen the ROOM TO LET sign and walked in and enquired.

'What do you do for a living?' Olivieri had asked him.

'I paint,' he'd said.

'Paint?' Olivieri had said. 'Paint?' Then Olivieri had leant over the counter in his pink satin bomber jacket, plucked a Camel plain off his hairy ear, lighted it with a Zippo, inhaled, paused, then furrowed his bushy grey eyebrows. With a soft meaningful whisper Olivieri had said: 'What do you paint?'

'Nudes,' Stoker had said loudly. 'I paint nudes.'

Olivieri had cast a searching look across the store. There was no one in sight. There rarely ever was.

'Women?' Olivieri had proffered.

'Women . . . men,' Stoker had ventured, keeping his options open.

'Why do you paint men?' Olivieri had enquired angrily.

'Mostly women,' Stoker had hurriedly replied. 'Lots of women. Fat ones, thin ones, brown ones, black ones.'

Stoker had wondered what the hell he was talking about. He'd never painted a nude in his life, but he needed the studio. If he'd said abstract landscapes he doubted Olivieri would have given him the time of day.

'Yes,' he'd said. 'I paint lots of women.'

'A noble pursuit, my boy. Noble. All the great artists have painted naked women. Degas, Courbet, Titian. We must forget about that faggot Michelangelo. His women were boys without cocks. Now Renoir, Rubens. Rubens knew how to paint women. Big bums, titties like ripe apples,' etc., etc.

Stoker thought he'd had the studio bagged, until Olivieri added: 'I must look. You paint, I look.'

'But the artist must respect a woman's privacy,' Stoker had said. 'Nude painting is a matter of the artist and his model.'

'But of course, my boy, of course. I will not disturb you. Come, let me show you the studio.'

Then Olivieri had taken Stoker up the rickety stairs to the studio. All it was was a storage space filled with boxes which hadn't been opened since before the Second World War. But there was light, lots of it, pouring in from a bank of filthy stained-glass windows overlooking Lower Main. If there hadn't been any windows Stoker would still have taken it.

'You paint in here,' Olivieri said. Then he took Stoker by the hand and led him to an adjacent room. 'Here,' Olivieri said. 'I will sit here.'

It took Stoker a ridiculously long time to figure out why Olivieri would wish to sit in the next room while he painted. And then he'd twigged.

'You mean . . .'

'Oh yes, oh yes,' Olivieri had said. 'I sit here and I look. You will have your privacy and I will have mine. The women won't know.' And then Olivieri had winked and sniggered.

The shock must have made Stoker's face drop, because Olivieri swiftly added: 'It will be cheap, my boy. Cheap cheap. Three hundred and fifty.'

Without flinching Stoker had said, 'Two fifty.' And that was that. The fact that he could pay the bulk of it in man-hours in the hardware store was a major plus.

Olivieri wasn't interested in the paintings. For all his talk of Titian and Rubens, Olivieri was interested in the women. Tits, bums, pussies, you name it. He was honest enough to add that it didn't matter what their faces were like. 'Faces are just faces,' he'd said. 'You see faces every day. Unless you live in Arabia. In Arabia faces are exciting because you don't see them. But here, here you see faces all the time.' Then Olivieri had graciously introduced Stoker to his store of porno pics and magazines dating back to the '20s. He was interested in the evolution of the female body, the width of waists, the size of hips, the design of pubic hair. He wished to have the women slightly covered and produced reams of diaphanous materials. 'They will not feel so ashamed,' Olivieri had said. 'They will trust you more.'

Stoker was flabbergasted by the direction his painting career had taken in the space of a few hours. Still, the prospect excited him. Olivieri's porno collection certainly did. He poured through racks of cards, hundreds of pages of sepia and technicolor, while Olivieri mused on the changes in photographic technology used for capturing the body, the true likeness of flesh. And flesh was Olivieri's principle theme.

It was Olivieri, proudly appraising his sultry aubergine Beetle and extolling Stoker's spray-painting skills, who had suggested that they go for a drive around the Peninsula. Stoker would drive.

The Sunday trip on a lovely sunny day had been a great break from dingy Obs. They'd started out early. Mrs Olivieri, whom Stoker had never seen, had packed a hamper filled with sausages and cheeses. Stoker had wondered why she hadn't joined them.

'She's too old,' Olivieri had said. 'She wants the spring chickens to enjoy themselves.'

Stoker had stared at Olivieri's baseball cap, Ray-Bans, crisp white shirt and acetate tie painted with the New South African flag. He'd wondered where Olivieri had bought his crazy tie.

'The station market,' Olivieri had said. He also sported an elegant wooden cane with elaborate African patterns carved into it. 'I got it for thirty.'

On closer inspection Stoker had discovered a dramatic convergence of snakes, cocks, cunts and bums. The man was definitely focused, he'd thought.

Stoker and Olivieri had crossed over the wooded hillsides of Constantia Nek, then cut through to Noordhoek. Stoker had suggested a walk along the beach, a visit to the wreck buried on the shore, but Olivieri didn't like Noordhoek beach. It made him feel old, he'd said. He'd been an extra when they'd shot scenes from *Ryan's Daughter* on the beach in 1940 something or other.

'There's another beach I'd rather visit,' Olivieri had proposed.

They'd travelled along Chapman's Peak, through Hout Bay and on to Llandudno. Olivieri had asked Stoker to turn left. It was then that Stoker had realised that the beach of Olivieri's preference was Sandy Bay, Cape Town's only nudist colony.

Before exiting the Beetle Olivieri had whisked out a blue sports bag and changed into what he'd called his *On Golden Pond* outfit. Very tweed, very geriatric. Then he'd whipped out his cane, adjusted his Ray-Bans, and stepped into the sunshine.

'What do you think? Just like Henry Fonda, ha?'

Stoker stared at Olivieri's rendition of blind decency. He was amused and astounded by the elaborate and crooked manner with which Olivieri had executed his disguise.

'Come. Now you take my hand.'

Grinning incredulously, Stoker had scooped up the towel

and picnic hamper, taken Olivieri in his arm, and ambled along the boardwalk into the kingdom of stark naked flesh.

'You should be at home in bed with a hot-water bottle, dreaming of your boyhood in Italy,' Stoker had said.

'Ag, dreams are for failures,' Olivieri had replied. 'See that woman over there! Isn't she marvellous!'

'You're supposed to be blind, for chrissakes. Don't go pointing your cane like that.'

'But I'm old, my boy. People respect old people.'

'Not dirty old men like you.'

'Do I look like a dirty old man? Do I? I'm Henry Fonda!'

'Henry Fonda is dead. And so will you be if you carry on like this.'

'Ag, the youth today. No fun. No fun at all. You should be taking all your clothes off and worshipping the sun. It's a beautiful day. A beautiful day to warm your willy.' And then Olivieri proceeded to undress. 'See, I'm not a pervert. I join in.' Layer by layer Olivieri removed his Henry Fonda gear. Stark naked, barring his dentures, hairpiece, Raybans and cane, Olivieri was a sorry yet noble sight. Inch by inch he pretended to walk blindly towards the ocean, paddled about the water's edge, then immersed himself, yelping and hollering, his cane swinging wildly in the air.

A stark naked blond with a Dulux dog hairdo raced up to Olivieri. 'Mr Olivieri,' she'd yelled. 'Mario!'

Mario? Stoker had stared as she held Olivieri in her arms, her tits still swinging, brushing against Olivieri's bony chest.

'Phyllis? Is that Phyllis?' Olivieri had enquired, feeling her all over as though in search of proof.

'Yes, Mario.'

'It's good to see you, Phyllis.'

'But you're blind, Mario!'

'It's an expression, my dear. It wouldn't be decent of me to say that it's good to feel you now, would it?'

'No it wouldn't,' Phyllis had said laughing. 'It's good to see you too.'

'Come, I want to introduce you to my nephew.'

Nephew? Stoker had pondered in horror.

'Adrian? Adrian, where are you, Adrian?'

'I'm right here,' Stoker had said, exasperated and pissed off. 'Meet Phyllis.'

'How do you do,' Phyllis had said.

Stoker had shaken her hand, tried to focus on the blazing horizon.

'Adrian brings me to Sandy Bay. But he never comes on his own. He is too shy. Adrian doesn't love the sun the way you and I do, Phyllis. It's his bad Catholic upbringing. His mother, my sister, sees the devil everywhere. Today I managed to get him here. It is because I am getting old, you see. I can't manage the way I used to.'

Stoker couldn't believe his ears.

'I must say, you've got a lovely uncle, Adrian. I'd be proud of him if I were you. He's fun, he's very respectful, not like those perverts hiding behind the rocks and flashing their hard cocks at you.'

Stoker had turned around and, lo and behold, there was a bald-headed man waving a huge dick at Phyllis.

'I'm used to it,' she'd said. 'Sun worship is still in its early days in South Africa.'

'Phyllis loves the sun,' Olivieri had confirmed. 'She loves it to warm every little inch of her. Tell me Adrian, is Phyllis a beautiful woman? She won't tell me. She says beauty is in the eye of the beholder, but alas I'm blind. So tell me Adrian, tell me what you think.'

Stoker had felt like punching Olivieri in the face. He'd stared fixedly at the horizon.

'Don't be silly, Mario,' Phyllis had said. 'You mustn't embarrass your nephew like that!'

'Embarrass! Embarrass! He must be embarrassed! He must wake up and smell the coffee!'

A waft of hot steam brought Stoker back to the present. He opened his eyes to find a mug of coffee held before him. Holding the mug was Phyllis.

'You haven't eaten your snackwich,' she said.

'I can't.'

'Would you mind taking this coffee? I've been standing here for ever.'

'I was just thinking of you. Of how we met. Olivieri.'

'That lump of depraved shit.'

'You certainly liked him at first.'

'Well I thought he was a harmless old man.'

'He still is.'

'You wish. When I think of how he used to accidentally rub his bony old chest all over me I get the shivers. The only reason he could get away with it was because he's too fucking old to get a hard-on.'

'Don't flatter yourself.'

'Oh. Thanks for the coffee Phyllis, thanks for the snackwich and the oats and Milo.' She was miffed.

'I'm sorry, love. I've just got an awful headache, that's all.'

'Well I'm sorry for not feeling sorry. The way the two of you bamboozled me, it's sickening.'

'It was Olivieri's idea, not mine.'

'Oh, so now you're just the innocent artist I suppose.'

'I needed the studio. The deal was I paint some nudes. Pretty harmless stuff.'

'So while I'm sitting there freezing my buns off, Olivieri's next door desperately trying to waken his cock from the dead.'

'It was your decision, Phyllis.'

'I did it for you,' Phyllis admitted. 'That day I saw you – so sweet and innocent with your skinny legs and red hair – I just couldn't resist.'

'And all the while I was trying to get a fix on the horizon and stop myself from getting a hard-on.'

'Little did I know your cock would be as splendid as that bald perv's behind the rocks.'

'You think so?'

'I still do.'

Phyllis gently removed the tray, then the bed sheet, and wrapped her mouth around Stoker's cock.

Dominion Hardware was out of bounds. As far as Olivieri was concerned Stoker had a client to see. Sure. Besides, the Seeff deadline had knocked out any desire to go to the studio. Today was his day off. Phyllis had wanted to spend it with him – she worked nights at Frogg Clothing – but Stoker needed to be alone. He had bills to pay, stuff to do. They'd meet for a late afternoon movie. Phyllis wanted to see *Pulp Fiction*, Stoker *Three Colours Red*.

Though Stoker liked Phyllis he was glad to see her leave. He'd felt fractionally uncomfortable about the blow-job. He hated using her, hated using anyone. Money was one thing, extorting pleasure another. He'd always felt superstitious about sex – you either did it with the person you were with or you didn't do it at all. It was a rule he liked to keep oiled, but the flesh was weak. Initially he'd been turned on by the way Phyllis's kimono flopped just below her tits, the pink-blue bruise of her nipples with their hard tips. She was meaty, beaty, big and bouncy, just like the Who said. He loved her fleshiness, her Betty Blue tummy, thighs, the works. She was extremely pleasant to be with, zestful, kind. In the year and a bit they'd been together they'd gotten along just fine. Stoker hated the thought of ever hurting her, which was why he'd cancelled the blow-job in mid-suck. It was the woman at the Seeff he'd been thinking about, her clothes he was tearing off, her inner thighs he was gnawing, her throat he was throttling the breath out of in an exquisite fucking fit.

'Stop,' he'd said. 'Please stop.' But Phyllis had taken him to mean she should go on. Eventually he'd had to force her off him.

'I can't,' he'd said.

'Looks like you can to me.'

'It doesn't feel right.'

'You've always liked it before.'

'I know, I know. Let's forget about it, okay.'

'You'll only end up wanking when I turn my back.'

'Stop being so paranoid.'

'Me? Paranoid? I could feel it, Stoker. I could feel your balls squirming. The pressure.'

The truth was he probably would have ended up wanking. 'I was thinking about someone else,' he confessed.

'Oh.'

'You know how it is,' he said, trying to soften the blow.

'Who?' Phyllis demanded.

'Just someone.'

'Who, Stoker?'

'Just someone, Phyllis. Not someone you know. Not even someone I know. Just a random combination. A tit here, a thigh there, an assemblage of body parts.'

'Thanks.'

'I don't want to hurt you, Phyllis, I really don't.'

'You're not, Stoker. Fantasies are fine,' Phyllis conceded.

'Bullshit.'

'I have mine and don't tell you.'

'You do?'

'Uh huh.'

'You think about someone else when you're fucking me?'

'Sometimes.'

'Who?'

'I can't tell you my secrets.'

'Come on Phyllis. Who? Olivieri?'

'Another Italian.'

'Someone we know?'

'Someone famous.'

'The Pope?'

'No.'

'That guy in *Johnny Stecchino*, in *Down By Law*. What's his name?'

'No.'

'Gina Lollobrigida?'

'There's a thought!'

'Marcello Mastroianni?'

'American Italian.'

'Al Pacino?'

'No.'

'Tintin Quarantino?'

'Not that grease ball!'

'I give up.'

'You sure?'

'I can't think anymore, I can't believe you've been cheating on me.' Stoker found himself getting more upset than he'd anticipated.

'Sylvester,' Phyllis finally confessed.

'Stallone?! You're joking!'

'No I'm not,' she said defensively.

'You fuck Stallone?'

'He fucks me.'

'I don't believe this!' Stoker started laughing.

'Well I think he's gorgeous,' Phyllis said.

'I always said you had a great taste in men, Phyllis. You see *Lock Up*?'

'Six times.'

'He was great in *Lock Up*. All that brooding masochism, I love it!'

'My heart goes out to him, Stoker. It really does.'

'I can see why,' Stoker gravely replied.

'He paints too.'

'I guess he can afford to.'

'Don't be such a cynic,' Phyllis said, slapping Stoker with a pillow, then adding: 'Sylvester means it, though. He's not doing it because he's rich and bored. It's a spiritual thing.'

'Phyllis, Phyllis, I love you, you know that.'

'I love you too,' Phyllis said.

Thanks to Stallone, Stoker was able to maintain an honest hard-on. Phyllis and Stoker fucked into the late morning, Stoker intercutting with scenes from *Cliffhanger*, *Demolition Man*, *The Specialist*, *Judge Dredd*, *Assassins*, then back to the golden age of *Rocky*. They lay sated, winter light splashing across Phyllis's flesh and Stoker's skin and bone. Phyllis eventually rose, stepped into her gold shoes with their crazy elevated cork heels, then slid into her dress. As she bent down to nuzzle Stoker, he slipped a hundred down her cleavage. 'For the petrol, movie and popcorn,' he said.

The day was grand. Summer in July. He wore a clean peach shirt with paint splodges – a present from Phyllis, electric green socks – from Lizzie, a pair of faded black denims, tight around the thighs and calves, and a pair of brown brogues – which he tended to wear for special occasions, occasions which were set to be permanent given the fact he'd lost his Docs. His hair, fresh and springy, blew about his head like the flailing flame of a brazier.

First Stoker stopped at the Farber's Sidewalk Grid for a steak roll and a Stoney ginger beer. He had three hours to spare before seeing Phyllis for the movie. He'd stop in at Dean's and pay him for the frame of *Man in a Landscape*, a crude affair, a mix of slivers of patterned aluminium and slats from a tomato box. Stoker loved the roughness, the feel of the south. Frames were mostly a rip off, he thought. An occupational hazard. They were always too glossy and pointless. Ideally he preferred plain old walls to frame his work. Still, he had to admit that Dean's frames were different. They had a life of their own, they were cheap, and they looked great. He'd contract Dean to frame some other work now that he was confident there was a market.

From Farber's Stoker took a back route down Nuttal to the bottle store on the corner of Trill and Lower Main, diagonally across from Dominion Hardware. There was no point in getting caught out by Olivieri. He bought a six-pack of Windhoek lager. Keeping a low profile he crossed Lower Main into upper Trill and walked over to Dean's on James Street.

Stoker opened the gate and scooped a yelping Perdita into his arms. Dean opened the security gate as Stoker crammed the remainder of his steak roll into Perdita's mouth.

'You got chilli on that roll?' Dean asked, swinging open the security gate. 'Don't go giving my dog chilli.'

'There's no chilli,' Stoker lied.

'Perdita doesn't like chilli,' Dean insisted.

24

Yeah, sure, Stoker thought, watching Perdita gobble away. Fuckin' dog owners, they've always got rules.

'Come in. Come in.' Stoker followed.

Stoker was tall. Dean was even taller. Stoker watched as Dean ambled down the corridor, all limbs and wires, like a giant mobile caught in a very faint breeze, all the parts moving in slow motion, out of synch, preferring to stay put.

Dean piled into the sofa. There were newspapers, books and magazines opened up all around him – *Interview, Face, Raygun, Mondo Madiba*. There was also a computer print-out of a novel in manuscript which Dean was most probably editing. The lounge was blitzed with images and print, the floor vaguely visible here and there. Stoker dropped Perdita and turned up the volume on the CD.

'What you doing that for?'

'So I can hear. What do you think?'

'You deaf or something?'

Stoker walked into the kitchen and switched on the kettle. He doled out the coffee, sugar and milk. Dean was a shitty host. Dean didn't do anything for anybody, if he could help it. For Dean even having a shit was a monumental effort. His whole life was an outer-body experience. Things happened to him, which made his fling with framing a sort of miracle. He'd found something he enjoyed doing. It wasn't much, he'd said, but it was something. He didn't mind decorating other people's efforts. The cynical fuck.

While the kettle boiled Stoker stepped into the toilet for a leak. Flox, the household rabbit, was on the tiled shower floor munching a lettuce leaf. There were pellets of shit everywhere. Stoker jauntily stepped through the minefield and pissed into the bowl. His brain, battered by nausea and a freak winter heat, was still throbbing. Needing to focus he steered his piss in neat concentric circles around the queasy yellow bowl. He needed coffee, he realised. Lots of it. He listened to Flox munching away and realised his hearing had radically amplified. Through the closed bathroom door Massive Attack slid into his brain with the intention, Stoker was convinced, of reducing it to soporific mush. No ways, he told himself. No ways. Then he zipped up his pants.

Stoker handed a coffee to Dean.

'So, tell me something,' Dean said.

Dean was curious. Very curious. If he could have it his own way, he'd just listen. You could say anything to Dean and he'd listen. And he actually did. Months later he'd tell you what you'd said. Dean kept tabs on people, indulged their efforts. He had a brain like a sponge.

Stoker handed Dean fifty for the frame. Dean stared at the cash.

'For the frame,' Stoker said, cracking open a Windhoek.

'You shouldn't mix coffee and beer.'

Stoker handed Dean a Windhoek. Dean drank.

'I see you haven't moved much since the last time I saw you. Maybe a few pages have been turned? Some stubble?'

'You come here to give me a lecture?'

'No.'

'So tell me something interesting.'

Dean didn't leave the house if he could help it, except to go down to the Spar and buy the papers and food. Or to take Perdita for walks down the Liesbeek River, past the madhouse and the squatters. Mostly Dean stayed at home proofing bad novels for which he charged thirty rand an hour, or listening to shitty music, or watching Sky News or documentaries on NNTV, or paging through magazines. The way Dean put it, he was in hiding.

Dean had an ex whom he couldn't bear the thought of seeing. Everyone who knew Dean knew the story of his break-up. It was one of those sordid little tragedies that movies were made of, packed with passion and hate and undying love. He could afford to continue feeling love-sick because he didn't have to pay for it. The house was owned by Dean and Waldo's dad, a loaded and extremely boring sports commentator. There were also two other tenants to foot the rental, a body-builder who worked for Health and Racquet and an art student-cum-waitress who worked at the Magnet. Fat Flox's daddy was the body-builder.

26

Stoker vividly recalled seeing the body-builder at the movies. It was at the end of a Health and Racquet Club trailer. The body-builder stepped into view just as the Health and Racquet logo was pulsing on the screen. He wore a blue Speedo, his black muscles glistening. It was pretty weird, watching all that aspirational brawn on the screen and seeing it live just a few feet away. The body-builder looked so coy and familiar it was depressing. Stoker had felt like strangling whoever it was who'd devised the promo.

'I sold the painting,' Stoker said.

'I gathered that.'

'Didn't you hear what I said? I sold a painting.'

'I know.'

'You're supposed to be impressed.'

'I'm impressed.'

'Thanks for the enthusiasm.'

'Okay hot shot, so you sold a painting. Now what?'

'Now I can do fuck-all like you is what I can do.' The way Stoker saw it, his retort held water even though it was technically inaccurate. Dean did things, he just kept them to a minumum.

Besides, Dean wasn't vaguely fazed. 'It's not that easy,' he said in all earnestness. 'It's never easy. You should try and do nothing some time. See what happens. You'd probably rush for the nearest paintbrush.'

'I guess,' Stoker grudgingly admitted.

'Look, it's great. You've sold a painting. So paint another. I love your work, you know that. You know I love what you do.'

'Yeah.'

'So, tell me something.'

'This woman who bought the painting . . .'

'Yeah?'

'She's something else . . .'

'Yeah.'

'She's . . . you know . . .'

'No I don't know.'

'I can't stop thinking about her.'

'What's she like?'

'Very aerodynamic. Her face has got these perfect angles. Her ears, nose and jaw fall in equidistant diagonals.'

'Sounds abstract.'

'She's got great ears. Her ears are like jewellery.'

'Next time I won't ask you to describe someone.'

'You want to hear or don't you?'

'Is she tall? What's her voice like? Has she got tits or is she flush? Is she a boy or a girl?'

'She's tall. She carries herself well. And she's got this smoky voice, really low, but not husky. She looks sort of Slavic, I don't know, her voice is sort of neutral, it's hard to tell. She's got tits, nothing overstated, they're just there, you know?'

'Pert?'

'Yeah, pert. And she's definitely a girl. There's nothing androgynous about her. Great hips. Like those women in the '40s movies, Joan Crawford say, bony around the ribs, fleshy around the hips. She had this *Achtung Baby* suit on, very '40s, like the women in the Wrens, very tapered, sheer. Blue.'

'She loaded?'

'She bought my painting for four. She even bought my Doc for six.'

'She bought your Doc for six?'

'It's a long story.'

'Tell me about it.'

'It's a stupid story.'

'The more stupid the better.'

Stoker and Dean polished off the six-pack while Dean listened.

'That's incredible,' Dean said.

'Weird, don't you think?'

'So who is she?'

'I don't know.'

'The dealer at the gallery should know.'

'I called. Nothing. Not a peep.'

'You're right, that's pretty weird. Some woman walks up and gives you a grand for a painting and a Doc Marten. That's weird. That's stranger than fiction. Stranger than CNN.'

Stoker showed Dean the wad of cash.

'She just give it to you like that. No cheque?'

'Just like that. Putter couldn't believe his eyes.'

'You saw Putter?'

'Of course I saw Putter. He's everywhere.'

'What's he scheming now?'

Stoker handed Dean Putter's card.

'The Locker Room Project?'

'He's on this whole Mother City queer trip thing. I don't think he knows what he's doing.'

'Sure he does. Putter's where it's at.'

'And how the fuck should you know? You never go any-where. You read the papers, watch TV.'

'And I suppose you do, right? I suppose the world opens itself up to you at Dominion Hardware?'

Stoker was pissed off. The truth was, Dean knew a lot. The whole world converged in Dean's lounge, except for the ex and the ex's faction. You just had to look at Dean's fridge to know. Dean had so many photos of friends and associates plastered over the fridge all you could see was the handle. Dean just had to sit and wait. Everybody came to see him. Dean was all ears. He probably knew more about the Locker Room Project than Stoker and wasn't letting on.

Stoker was usually the last person to hear anything about anything. He wasn't approachable the way Dean was. Dean in the middle of a depression remained a beacon of concern and information. Stoker on the other hand cared little, knew hardly anything. And he hated news. The people he met were people who took over, like Phyllis, like Olivieri, like the woman he'd seen at the gallery. Mostly he kept to himself. He wasn't part of the art mainstream. He didn't go to the right parties and restaurants. In most situations he was like a child on his first day at school – simultaneously intact and freaked because he didn't know anyone. He lived in his studio and painted land-scapes. He spent three days with Phyllis, three days at Domi-nion. The rest of the time he was either out walking in the woods around Kirstenbosch or Cecilia Forest, damming at

Rhodes Mem – a.k.a. the Newlands Reservoir –, hanging out at the river of rocks, or catching a train to Muizenberg beach. He collected debris, plant samples, bags of earth. He painted his landscapes from memory and the traces he'd collected. He painted at night in artificial light.

'What are you thinking about?' Dean asked.

'I'm thinking about what an idiot I am.'

'You're sore about something. I do something to offend you?'

Stoker wasn't. He was just hot and bothered and hung over. He didn't feel like hanging around at Dean's.

'Look, I've got to head off to Prue's,' Stoker said. 'Pay some bills.'

'Thanks for stopping in. Could use the fifty,' Dean said. 'Say hi to Bridge if you see her.'

'Here's another fifty,' Stoker said. Despite his shitty physical state he was feeling lucky. 'See it as an advance,' he added.

'Lock the gate behind you,' Dean said, not bothering to get up.

'I know the drill.'

Stoker caught the keys Dean tossed over to him.

'You hear anything from Waldo?' Stoker asked as he unlocked the security gate. Waldo had been away for months. Stoker was curious. He felt like talking to Dean about the vision he'd had, about the time Dayglo, Joan and Waldo were caught crayfishing in the power station. He could still picture the three of them in surfing wetsuits stealing across his line of vision, the inner-city night sky flashing yellow and amber across black rubber, rain pouring at an angle, soaking him through to the skin.

'I haven't heard a thing from Waldo,' Dean said. 'According to Joan he's on some camel safari in a desert up north, the Thar. Remember the baseball cap you left on the train the day we went to see Waldo off? Remember how pissed off you were?'

'Yeah?'

'According to Joan, Waldo's been wearing it. Just for the peak though. You know how he hates anything American. He camouflaged the whole thing with cloth. I guess it's Lawrence of Arabia shit he's into.'

'I guess,' Stoker said, his hands holding the bars of the security gate, Dean's story of his lost baseball cap travelling down the corridor, via Joan in New York. Joan and Waldo had to end on opposite sides of the world, Stoker thought. It figured that Joan would wind up in the one country Waldo hated. They were at loggerheads, had been for years. Stoker missed them both. Still, Joan was supposed to be flying back pretty soon.

'I'll keep you posted,' Dean said.

Stoker relocked the security gate and tossed the keys back in. Perdita squeezed through the grid and walked with Stoker into the garden.

'DON'T FORGET TO SAY HI TO BRIDGE!' Dean yelled.

'You look after Dean now,' Stoker said to Perdita. 'You can count on a chilli roll if you do.'

Perdita yelped enthusiastically as Stoker closed the garden gate behind him. His last image was Perdita's striped and dappled head bobbing up and down between a low brick wall and a wintry banana tree.

Blake Street was a few blocks away from Dean's. In Obs everything was a few blocks away. Prue ran a graphic workshop. This was where Stoker did all his photocopies – blown up colour repros of photos he'd taken, copies of paintings by the old masters, articles from Prue's stash of current art magazines. Stoker worked with references. William Turner was a major influence for *Man in a Landscape*, if only because he was trying to get the reverse effect. His studio walls were littered with details of city streets, skylines, close-ups of tree bark, earth. He had an account at Prue's. He owed her one fifty.

On the corner of Collingwood and Blake Stoker lit a Chesterfield Light. His head still throbbed with the swill of booze and heat. He pictured Waldo in his camouflaged baseball cap, his long pale nose and thin lips covered in green sunblock. He saw Waldo seated on a sluggish bony camel. The image made Stoker feel a little better. It was always good to know that his friends were battling with the elements.

Stoker pressed the buzzer and waited to be let into Prue's. While he smoked and waited he crushed a jasmine flower in his fingers and held the scent to his nose. He listened to machinery chugging away in the hosiery factory across the road. The chugging was the only sound in an otherwise quiet street. No one came to unlock the gate. He pressed the buzzer again. Nothing.

'Prue!' No answer.

'Bridge!' Bridge worked for Prue.

'Bridge! Prue!'

The door was unlocked as usual. The security gate was locked. Or was it?

Stoker walked in. The telephone rang. The fax kicked into operation.

'Hello?'

Prue's was usually a hive of activity. Bands copied posters for gigs at Prue's. Artists did flyers for exhibitions. Small business, the local art school, the Institute for Cancer Research, just about anybody who needed a Canon Colour Copier stopped in at Prue's.

The ringing stopped. The fax machine spluttered and died.

'Prue?'

Stoker stepped into the kitchen. And that was where he saw Prue, Bridge and Putter. They were sitting around the kitchen table staring at him imploringly. They were bound and gagged. In front of them was a mound of sliced avo, some nutty rolls and a slab of blue cheese.

It took Stoker a while to figure out that something was drastically wrong. If it wasn't for the pained expressions and writhing disjointed hands he would probably have stood staring at them a while longer, docked the situation as performance art.

Stoker ripped off the duck tape around Putter's mouth. With the knife on the table he cut the rope.

'What took you so long?!' Putter asked.

Stoker answered Putter's glare with a vague look, then cut

Bridge and Prue free. He let them remove the duck tape around their mouths.

'Thank you Stoker,' Prue said. She got up. Bridge remained seated and burst into tears.

'You can be such a moron, Stoker, you know that? A total fuckin' moron!'

'Putter, it's alright,' Prue said.

'ALRIGHT?! ALRIGHT?! THE BASTARDS!' Putter was livid.

'What happened?' Stoker asked.

'Bridget. Bridget, are you alright?' Prue gently stroked Bridge's hair as she burst into another fit of sobbing.

'THE BASTARDS!' Putter screamed. 'THE BASTARDS!' And slammed his fist against the wall.

Stoker watched as Prue exited the kitchen. He followed her at a distance. She stepped into the garden, breathed in the burst scent of jasmine as she stared up and down Blake Street.

It was best just to shut up, Stoker thought. He wished that the scene hadn't reminded him of a movie. He was truly sick, he thought. He stepped into the garden and stood beside Prue.

'They raped Bridget,' she said.

Stoker didn't know what to say. So he stood staring at the brick wall of the hosiery building. It didn't matter who had raped Bridge. The fact was enough. So he kept standing and staring at the brick wall, listening to the chug-chug of machinery.

Putter tore through the garden and into the street. Then he proceeded to run, screaming 'BASTARDS! YOU FUCKIN' BAS-TARDS!'

He'd best go in and talk to Bridge, Stoker thought.

She was still sitting in the kitchen chair, unable to move. He walked over to her and stared. He couldn't hold her, speak consoling words. He couldn't do anything. So he sat in front of her and applied some avo to a roll, some blue cheese. Then he started to eat.

Bridge slowly raised her head. Her face was wet with tears. Then, out of the blue, she smiled. Stoker smiled back. Smiling was the one thing he did with a complete idiotic sincerity.

'What do you think of the blue cheese?' Bridge asked.

'Delish,' Stoker said.

'Could I have a bite?'

Stoker passed the roll over to Bridge. He watched her eat. She seemed perfectly fine, but of course she wasn't. Stoker made another avo and blue cheese roll.

'There's some bacon if you want bacon. I fried some. Avo and bacon work well together.'

'You want some bacon?' Stoker asked.

'No thanks,' Bridge said. 'I don't eat bacon. I'm a vegetarian. I made it for Prue and Putter.'

How come he'd forgotten Bridge was a vegetarian? He should have known! He took Bridge by the hands. She gripped him tightly. She was shaking.

'We wondered who would be the one to save us. It's funny that it's you, Stoker.'

'Why's that funny, Bridge?' And he said her name with all the love he could muster.

'I was just writing a nasty note to you to tell you to pay your account when . . .'

'Guess what,' Stoker interrupted. He produced the one hundred and fifty he owed. 'It's a good thing I was so slack, don't you think?' Stoker realised that what he'd just said was inappropriate, off, but the words were out before he could censor himself.

Bridge took the money and got up. Stoker watched as she walked into the office. Through the open door he saw her put the money in the cash box. Then she came back and handed him a note of receipt.

'Now you're clear,' Bridge said. She made it sound like a bill of health, an acquittal.

Stoker took the receipt and placed it in his pocket.

'You want some coffee?' Bridge asked.

'Yes, please,' Stoker said. He was staring at Prue. She was on the phone to the police. Stoker felt hideously uncomfortable. He wanted to leave and felt he couldn't. He sensed that there was nothing he could do. Even relaying Dean's regards didn't make sense anymore.

34

Putter entered. He was exhausted.

'What are you looking at?' Putter asked.

'I'm looking at you,' Stoker said.

'Fuckin' moron.'

Stoker couldn't recognise Putter from the night before. He couldn't recognise him at all. Putter was possessed. He was out of his mind. He was so angry he could kill.

'Would you like a coffee?' Bridge asked Putter. He stared at Bridge, his face the picture of anguish and horror.

'I'll make you some. I think you need some.'

Then Putter slumped into the sofa. He didn't say a word for the next hour.

Stoker sipped his coffee. He watched as Prue put down the phone. Bridge walked in with a coffee and avo and bacon roll for Prue. Everyone sat in silence sipping and eating. And then Stoker noticed that the Canon Colour Copier was gone. He wanted to say something but there was nothing he could do, nothing he could say to correct the mess.

'Stoker's paid his bill,' Bridge said to Prue.

'That's good,' Prue said. She was so still it was terrifying. Prue had always exuded calm, but never a calm so acute, so harnessed. Stoker felt that Prue was holding on to every shred of composure she had left. This was why he had always loved her, he thought. He'd loved her because deep down he'd always sensed her resilience. She had a heart of gold. She was hard as nails. In a crisis situation she was the one who would save the day.

'They came in and stole the colour copier,' Prue said. 'They came in and raped Bridget.'

Stoker sensed that she was playing back what she was going to say to the police.

'They came in through the security gate. It didn't occur to me that they were evil. They pressed the buzzer and told me they were delivering artworks from the Linda Goodman Gallery in Jo'burg. I believed them. They came in carrying a crate. I thought the crate contained some pieces I'd exhibited in Havana, Aachen, then Jo'burg. I didn't think. I thought they were delivery men. One of them asked me to sign a form. I signed. The other two walked around. They saw Bridget and Putter. Bridget and Putter work here. This is an art studio and a graphic workshop. This is my place of business. What do I do? I am an artist. They stole my copier. They raped my daughter.'

Prue turned and looked at Stoker. Her eyes were the clearest blue. There was not a single trace of a tear.

CHAPTER FOUR

Phyllis was standing by the ticket desk. She was sipping a jumbo fruit cocktail, a box of popcorn in her other hand. Stoker didn't notice her at first. If it wasn't for the gold shoes he probably wouldn't have noticed her at all because Phyllis had cut and dyed her hair. Everything's happening too fast, Stoker thought. I can't take this any more. What's happening to me? It wasn't just what was happening to him that was bothering Stoker, it was the world. It was what was happening to everybody. The world wasn't a sick joke at his expense. The world was a sick joke – period.

'What do you think?' Phyllis asked, planting a juicy kiss on Stoker's lips, slipping her tongue inside, then pulling away and doing a twirl. Her hair was bright red and very short. 'Now we look like brother and sister,' she said.

Stoker noticed how lovely Phyllis's neck was. The blue vein pulsing beneath the pallor, the tattooed lizard slithering down the nape. She looked gorgeous and it made him feel very sad. People change, he thought. People change all the time. There was Phyllis looking gorgeous and all he could think of was Bridge sitting at the table asking him if he liked his avo roll. There was the memory so fresh that it hadn't started hurting.

'Since I was here first I thought we'd see *Pulp Fiction*. *Three Colours Red* is in French.' As if he didn't know.

'There's subtitles,' Stoker said.

'I forgot my glasses.'

Very convenient, Stoker thought.

Phyllis was vain as hell. The occasions she definitely needed her glasses, the movies and driving, were the occasions they were never available. Phyllis was so blind he had to tell her what was going on when they went to the movies. She always asked him questions in the middle of a scene, and not just because she was blind. She never really knew what was going on from one frame to the next, who the bad guys were, why a building exploded, who was connected to whom. He wondered why she even bothered going to the movies. She laughed at all the wrong moments, she cried when fuck-all worth a tear was happening. She went to the movies because he loved to go, she'd said. She went so they could cuddle. Phyllis was strange and he loved her. Right then she was just the lift he needed. And besides, though movies as a whole were Greek to her, she knew what was what when it counted. *One Deadly Summer*, *Naked* and *Bad Boy Bubby* were top of the pops for Phyllis. As was every movie that featured Sylvester Stallone. After all, there had to be a wild card.

Watching *Pulp Fiction* was a harrowing experience for Phyllis. For someone as supposedly blind as she was, she saw every gory detail and didn't like it one bit. Neither did Stoker, but for different reasons. *Pulp Fiction* was exactly the sort of sick infantile joke he'd had enough of. It was stupid and futile. He wondered what the big fuss was about. The movie had won the Palm D'Or, for chrissakes. If this was art then we were definitely fucked. Okay, so the acting was okay, so what? So casting Travolta was a stroke of genius. Still, the script was a piece of wilful arbitrary shit. Is this what people talked about? Is this what people did? He had to admit that his own life was as arbitrary, if not as bloody or as stupid. He wished he was watching *Three Colours Red*. He'd seen *Blue* and *White*. He couldn't figure out how *Pulp Fiction* could have beaten *Red* at Cannes. Europe is definitely fucked, he thought. Europe is so disgusted with itself that all it can do is wank along with Tarantino. The decadent thieving little cunt.

What pissed Stoker off even more was the hype. He could

forgive a puerile movie, he'd seen a lot of them. But the hype! There was nothing he could do about that. Some of his best friends had loved *Pulp Fiction*. Joan, for chrissakes! He was glad he was with Phyllis whose gut reaction was 'Yuck'.

'Next time I'll let you choose,' Phyllis said as she came out of the toilet.

Stoker bent down to kiss her.

'My breath stinks,' she said.

Stoker kissed her all the same. Right now I want nothing more than your smelly breath, he thought. Right now I need nothing more than you.

Phyllis popped a peppermint into her mouth. The fact that Stoker had kissed her with her vomity smell had meant all the world to her. They strolled through Cavendish Square looking at display windows. Phyllis saw a dress at Truworths and Stoker decided he'd buy it for her. He'd never bought her a dress before. Come to think of it, he'd never bought her anything special. Yup, he was definitely a self-centred little prick.

Phyllis wanted the dress because it was a summer dress and it was on sale. The dress was bright green with hibiscus flowers patterned all over it. Phyllis liked wearing summer clothes.

'Everyone looks so dull and boring in winter,' she said.

Stoker smiled. He liked her in her flowery dress with her short red hair and gold shoes. She was hardy, Phyllis was. She was stronger than he could ever be. He needed her, he knew. He needed her lightness, her humanity, her total absence of pretension. She could say the most ridiculous things and it didn't really matter. Conversation was an excuse she could do without, she'd said. She was happy to just be. And being for Phylis was being happy.

He watched her as he stepped out of the art store and walked towards her, a tube of cadmium red deep in his pocket. She was paging through a copy of *Elle* in the entrance to Exclusive Books.

'You got what you need?' she asked.

'Yeah. So. What do you feel like doing?'

'How much time have we got?'

'An hour and a half before you have to start selling.'

'Great,' Phyllis said with a sigh, then perked up. 'Let's eat.'

'You choose.'

'The Happy Wok?' she said.

'Claremont or town?' Stoker asked.

'Town,' Phyllis said.

Phyllis loved Chinese food. She ate it with chopsticks. Her mum's lover was Chinese. His name was Chan. Phyllis's mum was called Nellie. She and Chan had met years ago at a disco. He used to work in the boiler room of a ship. For years he and Phyllis's mum would meet off and on whenever he'd dock in Cape Town. Phyllis remembered him coming to her childhood home in Brooklyn with a basket full of crayfish tails. She'd never forgotten this detail. Somehow crayfish tails would always be more romantic to her than flowers.

After years of postcards and weekends, Chan had quit the sea and moved into Brooklyn with Phyllis and Nellie. For reasons unclear to Phyllis at the time, Chan had said he was Japanese, which was supposed to make a difference though it meant fuck-all to their neighbours in Brooklyn. Chan and Nellie took the flak and kept Phyllis clueless. Chan worked as an electrician. Phyllis's mum was a hairdresser – the genius behind Gloria's dye job. Chan had taught Phyllis to use chopsticks when she was a little girl.

'Open,' Phyllis said, holding a dollop of chicken chow mein between the chopsticks.

'Bridge was raped,' Stoker said. The chow mein fell to the table.

'When?'

'This afternoon, before I saw you. Some guys strolled into Prue's place. They were out to steal her colour copier. They saw Bridge and I guess one thing led to another.'

'Shit, Stoker.'

'Putter was there. And Prue. She saw the whole thing.'

'Oh my God, my God.'

'I had to let you know. I'm sorry I didn't tell you earlier. I didn't know what . . . I couldn't . . . I . . .'

Stoker started crying. He sat shaking and stifling his sobs. Phyllis walked around to the other side of the table and held him with all her heart.

'I don't know, Phyllis. I mean, she's such a good girl, she's . . . I was sitting there right opposite her. I didn't know what to say or do, I . . .'

'There's nothing you could do, Stoker.'

'The thing is I was dead, Phyllis, I was dead inside. It wasn't that I couldn't feel anything. It was as though there was no room inside me to feel. Like I'm dead, you know? All I could do was stare at her unbelievingly. I couldn't translate. I couldn't be where she was, feel what she felt. I couldn't, I . . .'

'Shhhh . . . It's alright. It's alright.'

'You should've seen Prue. Can you imagine what she felt, what she was going through? I couldn't, you see. I still can't. And I was thinking of you, of how much I loved you and what an idiot I've been.' He took a breath. 'This woman, this woman I've been talking about, the woman who bought my painting, I feel like a criminal lusting after her. I feel like a fool for not seeing what's right in front of me. I know I'm not the easiest person in the world to live with. I'm stuck up. Sometimes I think I'm smarter than most people. But I'm not. I'm just plain stupid. Sometimes I've wondered what the hell I was doing with you. I've even thought of breaking up with you. Now it all seems so stupid. The fact is I love you, Phyllis. I'd hate to have anything terrible happen to you. I . . .'

'Shhh. Relax. It's okay. It's over and done with. We'll just have to pick up the pieces. That's what we all do. Pick up the pieces.'

They hugged for the next half an hour, the food growing cold in front of them. Then Stoker dropped Phyllis off at Frogg Clothing on the Waterfront.

'Don't forget, twelve sharp,' Phyllis said. 'Maybe we could go to Robbie Tripp's or The Shakk if you're up to it?'

'How about the Magnet?' Stoker suggested. 'Jay, Dayglo and Percy should be playing. Dean's housemate's doing the door.'

'Magnet's fine,' Phyllis said. Right then she would have gone anywhere with Stoker.

'Thanks for the bakkie,' Stoker said.

'We won't make a habit of it, will we? See someone, get drunk. Forget about the studio.'

'Love your dress,' Stoker said.

'You'd better start loving what's inside,' Phyllis said. She bent down so Stoker could see her tits. Then she blew him a kiss and turned to walk into the east wing of the complex, her gold shoes with their crazy heels glittering against the stone paving.

Stoker drove past the Foreshore, past the Seeff Gallery and the Gideon Warehouse where he'd lost his Doc. He drove past the aborted highway jutting out in mid-air. He remembered thinking about driving off the highway. He'd pictured the car he was driving frozen in mid-air like the final frame in *Thelma and Louise*. Now he wondered how in hell he could have thought such a stupid thing. People change, he thought. Yes, people change. We pick up the pieces. Phyllis was right. That's all we do. We pick up the pieces, as though living was a gathering of all the scattered pieces that make a life, a gathering that was never ever finished. Even on one's death bed one was still gathering scattered pieces, Stoker thought. It never stops. We'll never be whole.

Stoker suddenly felt more alive than he'd felt in ages. Tomorrow he'd call Bridge. Right now he was going to forget about all the sad bad things that happened to people. Tonight he was going to enjoy.

As he drove out of the city centre he thought of Phyllis and smiled. He thought of her standing behind the counter in her hibiscus dress and beaming at all the prospective customers. He thought of her just beaming. A ray of sunshine for all to see and feel. Then he turned on the tape deck and drove past the harbour, the docks, past Brooklyn. He thought of Chan with his basket of crayfish tails. He thought of Phyllis's mother and how glad she was to have her Chan. Then he passed the Caltex oil refinery, flames leaping from the tower like a giant blowtorch.

He found himself driving on the old national road. He passed the West Coast National Park where he and Phyllis had gone when they'd needed to get away. He thought of the cottage that overlooked the Langebaan Lagoon, of the hundreds of sand-sharks he'd seen as he drifted across the shallow water. He was heading north listening to the Golden Palominos, the lead singer's voice keeping the thought of Phyllis in his head. As the sun set he realised he was heading way out into the country. He'd cut back to the N7. To his left he saw the first of the Eskom pylons that stretched all the way to the nuclear power station at Koeberg. Stoker was convinced he could hear the pylons singing. He passed Malmesbury and cut right on to the R46. He passed cows in fields, watched as they smudged in the inky darkness. He was heading for Riebeek-Kasteel. He was parking the car outside Dylan's.

CHAPTER FIVE

Stoker remained seated in the bakkie staring at the dark veranda. He had the window open. He listened to the night throbbing with life. The hooo-hooo of a nearby owl. The air was crisp and clean, the sky freshly laundered. The only light came from the tip of his cigarette, flashing off and on like a bleeper signal.

Stoker stepped out, pressed the small of his back, stretched. Then he stood staring out at the moonlit gravel road swooping down into blackness. A single light flickered in the distance. How near, how far, he couldn't tell. He was caught between stillness and movement, between the throbbing aromatic night and the city jammed inside his head. He heard the front door swing open and saw his brother cut out against the electric light of the hallway.

Stoker realised he was in darkness. He stared at the shadow of his brother's massive body consuming the length and breadth of the meshed threshold. Dylan looked indestructible against the blotted light. He was dressed in black. Stoker caught the glint of a rifle in Dylan's hand.

Stoker walked up the path without saying a word. Dylan stood watching the figure advance. Then he saw Stoker as he slowly entered into the dim light.

'Howzit Dylan.'

'You?'

'Yeah it's me. Surprise surprise.'

Dylan kept standing in the doorway behind the mesh. He leant the rifle against the opened door. Stoker stood on the veranda, his back to Dylan.

'What brings you here?' Dylan asked.

'Chance, I guess. I didn't think I'd end up here. I just did. I've brought the money I owe you.'

'That's good. I could use it.'

Dylan stepped onto the veranda. The floorboards creaked beneath his weight.

'You staying the night?'

'Nah. I've got to pick Phyllis up later.'

'You drive out all this way and you won't stay the night?'

'Maybe. Right now I've got a promise to keep.'

Dylan stepped off the veranda. 'Follow me,' he said.

They walked round the house, past the apple orchard, to the shed at the back. Dylan collected some logs and kindling and started making a fire. Stoker stood and watched his brother. This was always the way it was. Stoker watching.

'You been seeing Lizzie?' Dylan asked.

'Yeah. She's doing well.'

'Doing what?'

'Selling chemicals.'

'Chemicals?'

'Industrial cleaning chemicals. Some miracle Swedish product fronted by a British company.'

'She enjoy what she's doing?'

'I guess. She's on the phone all day. She makes around twenty grand a month doing reorders. Says she's gotten to the stage when she can tell from the first sentence whether the guy she's talking to is a whisky or brandy drinker.' Dylan chuckled. Stoker resumed. 'Initially she thought the work was stupid. She says it can drive you crazy working on the phone all day, that she has to wipe her brain clean after each call otherwise she won't cope. She knows exactly how to push the right buttons, how to pitch a sale. You know how it is, she's got this voice that drives men crazy. Very officious, witty and sexy. Guys in suits love it. They've got nothing better to do but to listen to her, what with being stuck in boiling prefab buildings in Springbok or Upington or wherever, pushing pens.'

Stoker paused. He was satisfied with the run-down he'd given on how Lizzie was doing. Dylan didn't care. Still, Dylan needed to know.

'I guess the whole world needs industrial cleaning chemicals,' Dylan said.

'I guess. The product's biodegradable.'

The fire burst into flame. Stoker watched his brother's pitted face glowing in the dark. He flicked his cigarette into the flame. Then he bent down and held his hands over it.

Dylan looked at Stoker. Dylan was grinning.

'It's funny,' Dylan said. 'I was just thinking about you.'

'What were you thinking?'

'I was thinking of paying you a visit. You still with that girl – what's her name again?'

'Phyllis,' Stoker said. He was pissed off that Dylan hadn't heard him the first time.

'It suits her.'

'What's that supposed to mean?'

Dylan didn't answer.

Still, the comment bugged Stoker. Dylan hardly knew Phyllis. He'd never even met her.

'When was the last time you were in Cape Town?' Stoker asked.

'A month ago.'

'You didn't come and see me then.'

'No time.'

Dylan never had any time. At least not for Stoker and Lizzie. Stoker had spent years wondering why, then given up thinking about it. Dylan had no time for anyone. He was cut off and he liked it that way. Dylan didn't have a phone because he didn't like talking. He had a fax machine. That's how Dylan conducted his business. On the fax machine. You can get to the point on a fax, Dylan had said. You can keep it short and sweet. Dylan was a poet. He'd spent the last three years working on a book that no one had seen or heard. Dylan didn't like talking about his work. He was superstitious. It was hard enough just to make the words stick, he'd said. If he talked about what he was writing, the words would get pissed off and disappear.

Stoker had to tread carefully. It was pointless asking Dylan anything about his work, he'd only end up talking about the weather, or the stoep he was fixing, the barbel he'd caught, a new cattle disease. *Farmer's Weekly* shit. The truth was, Stoker was interested. It was Dylan who'd taught him to see things. The way light fell, the different gradations of colour on a face, the way the temperature in the water shifted, the way everything was constantly moving. Stoker still remembered some of the lines from one of Dylan's favourite poems – 'Corson's Inlet' by A.R. Ammons. He mouthed the words in his mind:

by transitions the land falls from grassy dunes to creek
to undercreek: but there are no lines, though
                    change in that transition is clear
                    as any sharpness: but 'sharpness' spread out,
allowed to occur over a wider range
than mental lines can keep.

It was because of Dylan that Stoker started painting. Stoker had wanted to go to art school, Dylan had told him not to bother. Art school was a futile exercise, Dylan had said. You can go it alone, you've got the talent. Stoker had believed him. For years afterwards he'd wondered whether he'd made a mistake. He guessed it was because Dylan had never ever told him what to do before. The art school thing was an exception, and so he'd listened. Dylan was older. He'd gone to university. He'd regretted it ever since. His whole life had been an effort at forgetting. He wanted to be born again, to start afresh, he'd said. He was crammed with other people's ideas.

In his second year Dylan had quit university and joined the army. He'd fought in the Angolan war. He'd killed. He'd watched men in his platoon blown up by land-mines, seen bodies break into pieces, minds shattered. Dylan was a decorated hero when he'd left the army. He hadn't said a word. Who in their right mind would? He'd carried his shame in silence. Then everything had come out in the poems. Words had become his true place of war and atonement. Dylan Stoker became a name to be reckoned with.

And then he'd stopped publishing. He'd pulled out of Jo'burg and moved back to the family house in Riebeek-Kasteel. He'd spent the past three years fixing it up. He'd devised an underground insulation system to counter the damp and rot. Each day had produced something to do, he'd said. The house kept him busy. He enjoyed fixing things. At night he worked on his book. Neither Dylan, Stoker or Lizzie talked about why Dylan had chosen to return to the house in which their parents had been murdered. The murder had never been solved. There were theories of course, nothing more, although more than enough had been said in the papers. Dylan, Stoker and Lizzie knew that the only reason they'd been spared was because they were elsewhere at the time. The house had been standing empty for years. He'd needed a place to stay, was all Dylan had said.

'You eat?' Dylan asked, breaking the silence.

'Yes and no,' Stoker said.

'I guess you haven't then,' Dylan said.

Stoker felt like telling Dylan about losing his appetite at the Happy Wok, about Bridge, but somehow he couldn't drag the city, drag the pointlessness back. He watched Dylan as he walked through the back door into the kitchen. He realised he was happy right where he was, with the stillness, the fire. This was where he needed to be, in his brother's house, his house, the house where he was raised. The house in which his parents had died.

Stoker left the warmth of the fire and walked into the kitchen. Dylan was dipping a steak into a marinade. Stoker lit a cigarette and watched Dylan's slow steady movements, his quiet precision. Dylan inspired confidence in a way Stoker never could. Dylan was constant, methodical. Clear. He saw gradations in a blur.

'I sold a painting,' Stoker said.

'Good for you, Adrian. What's the painting?' Dylan asked.

'A man in a landscape. The painting's of you. You can't exactly see it's you. The likeness isn't photographic. It's more the angle of the body. The weight.'

'What's the man in a landscape doing?'

'I don't know.'

Dylan chuckled. 'I guess you wouldn't,' he said.

'It's a winter scene. The earth is solid. An icy glint bounces off the surface. But the sky is overcast. There's not much light. The sky is weighing down on you. The glint is barely perceptible. Everything's mostly murky. But nothing bleeds, you know. The earth doesn't drink the sky. Everything's solid, pure. There's a heat inside the man. He's the only beating thing in a dead season.'

'You should write,' Dylan said.

'I speak, I speak,' Stoker lied. Just because he liked talking to Dylan didn't make him a talker. He was grinning. Then his expression changed. 'I feel like I'm getting somewhere, Dylan. For the first time I feel as though I'm finding a language. It's nothing grand. Like I said – I don't know what the fuck you're doing there. You're just there, your face all pitted the way it is, like it's being eaten away. A quiver of light and dark. It's not especially flattering, but it's alive like I said.'

'Is that how you feel? Like you're being eaten away?' Dylan asked.

'I guess. We're each our own last supper, right?'

'What do you mean?'

'Just like I said. It makes sense to me, at any rate.'

'Put the grid on, would you.'

'Where is it?'

'Where do you think? Out back. In the shed.'

Stoker left the kitchen. In the shed he found the grid. He laid it over the flames. Dylan walked over with the steak. He lit a joint and passed it over. Stoker inhaled.

'Home-grown,' Dylan said.

'Another service industry you've succeeded in cutting out,' Stoker replied.

Dylan grinned. Paused. Then said: 'You never stop needing people.' It was a strange thing for him to say, considering all the bridges he'd burnt. 'No matter how hard you try, you never stop needing,' Dylan continued. 'This man in your picture, the man you say is me, you think he's alone but he's not. He's in the picture, know what I mean? It's good to know you're thinking of me, Adrian. Working with me. Working me through the surface of things.'

The flames died. Dylan laid the steak on the grid. The meat hissed and spat. Stoker passed the joint back to Dylan.

'It's a pity you can't stay,' Dylan said. 'I wanted to show you something.'

'You could show me now.'

'There's no time. We need time. I want to read to you.'

'The book?'

'Yes, the book. It's finished – if you can call it that. I'm done with it. It's over for me.'

'Now what?'

'Nothing. I told you I was in the city a month ago . . .'

'Yeah.'

'I dropped it off at the publisher.'

'And?'

'I've just got to wait and see, I guess.'

Stoker thought about Phyllis. He thought about staying. He watched Dylan turn the steak.

CHAPTER SIX

The drive back to the city was slow. Stoker cut away from the N7 into scrub country. In the distance to his right he could see the West Coast, the escarpment of dune, the pounding spray of a storm-tossed sea. Ahead of him stood Table Mountain, picture perfect in the winter light.

Stoker had decided to stick with Dylan. After supper he'd walked down to the local bar and called Phyllis at Frogg. He'd explained to her that he and Dylan were on a roll. She'd said it was okay, that she'd see him the next day. There were no questions, no talk of hijacking her bakkie. Before heading back to Dylan's Stoker had decided to shoot some pool, down a couple of beers. Dylan didn't drink.

Back at the house Dylan was still sitting by the fire. Stoker seated himself across from Dylan. There was nothing forced between them. Silence had become a living thing, as intimate as a heartbeat.

Eventually Stoker had called it a night. He was tired. The day had been long and stained. He needed to shut down, to rest and prepare himself for Dylan's book.

Lying in his bedroom, still exactly the way it was when he was a boy, Stoker could feel the momentousness of his life pounding in his chest. He stared at the plastic globe of the world swaying faintly above him, his places of preference, places he'd never been to – Murmansk, the Gobi Desert, Djibouti – marked with coloured pens. Watching the globe as it twisted in the faint breeze that stole through the bedroom window he thought of Phyllis's globe, so different to his own. Hers resembled a pumpkin. It was stuffed and made of dyed stitched cotton. There were no national boundaries. One night as they lay in her bed in the room on Long Street she'd pointed out the ley lines, the power points of healing. Table Mountain was one of them. Hug it, she'd said, holding the globe out to him. He'd thought of teddy bears and pillows and sleepless nights. It's for the inner child, she'd confided.

On the bookshelf before him stood the trophy he'd won for long-distance running. The trophy glinted faintly in the low lamplight. He'd been good at the long jump, triple jump and high jump. Unlike Dylan he'd never had the power or the speed for short distances. Marathon Man, that was his nickname at school. He had a capacity for endurance that was unbeatable.

Stoker smiled as he recalled a prowess long since faded. He realised that it was more than his capacity for endurance which had led his peers to compare him to Dustin Hoffman. He shared Hoffman's awkwardness. Like Hoffman he was always running. It didn't matter what the movie was, you'd always see Hoffman running. It was a talent Stoker had discovered by accident. Born with perforated eardrums, he was banned from swimming. As a consequence he was given the liberty to run. On Wednesdays, when the rest of his class converged at the pool, he would leave the school grounds and enter the veld. Now, so many years later, he was grateful for his ruined ears, grateful for the distance, the solitariness. He breathed in all the remembered space, the smell of earth and grass. Then he fell asleep.

In the throbbing blackness of a rural night he woke up with a jolt. He'd felt a sandshark brush against his leg, seen a flick of beige fin, a dust-cloud as the bed of sand broke, the shark swerving away. The sandshark was harmless. It was the sensation which had woken him. The brush of a fin as rough as a cat's tongue against his shin.

It had taken him a while to fall back to sleep again.

Dawn light broke through the chink in the blue curtains, yellow and red racing cars printed across it. Stoker could hear Dylan shuffling about below. He was probably back from his early morning walk, Stoker thought. No matter how late Dylan went to sleep, he always greeted the sun.

Stoker rose and stepped into his electric green socks and brogues, odd and ridiculous in this simple rural setting. He longed for his Docs, the one gone who knows where, the other sealed in a vault of cement. He realised that he must have been too numb to feel the cold the night before. Now he was freezing. He opened his cupboard and found a clean shirt, his duffle-coat and jersey. At the bottom of the cupboard lay the remote-controlled boat he'd built years ago. He read the name he'd painted on the side – Mira, his mother's. He was tempted to take the boat back with him. Then he changed his mind.

The stairs creaked more loudly now as Stoker descended. He realised that his senses were more acute. All of him felt charged with a rare keenness. Dylan was at his desk in the living room. His table light was on, softening the cold refracted brightness pouring in through the windows overlooking the bare branches of the apple orchard and the field beyond. Through the windows to the left Stoker saw that the driveway was misty, Phyllis's bakkie barely visible.

'There's coffee on the stove,' Dylan said, his back to Stoker as he riffled through his papers.

'Morning,' Stoker said. Dylan did not reply.

In the kitchen Stoker poured himself some strong black coffee. Then he lit a cigarette. He stepped out into the backyard, pissed into the dead remains of the fire and thought of Dean watching Sky News, of Phyllis fast asleep hugging her pumpkin globe, of Bridge . . . Prue . . . Putter. He thought of Olivieri, of the woman whose name he did not know. He thought of the city, of how he'd never been able to reconcile himself to living in Cape Town or living here. A procession of faces and passions flashed by in an instant as he stared out across the icy veld. Then he thought of why he painted landscapes by artifical light, of why he had a staged relation to things. And then he zipped up his pants and walked back in.

'You sleep well?'

'Yes,' Stoker lied, then added: 'I had a dream. I can't say if it was good or bad. I was standing in shallow water. I think it must have been the Langebaan Lagoon. I must have moved, stepped on a sandshark. The shark had recoiled. Then I'd looked down. There must have been about fifty of them writhing around me, beige against the beige sand.'

'You've always been scared of sandsharks,' Dylan said.

Was he? Was he really? 'It's creepy the way they blur into things,' Stoker said.

'It's a survival thing,' Dylan said. 'Cryptic coloration.'

'It's still creepy.'

'You were tired. Unsettled. This is no longer your home.'

Dylan was right. A sadness slowly began to grip Stoker.

As if sensing Stoker's pain, Dylan shifted the conversation back to a theme unmarred by ghosts.

'You always were unsettled by the way things blurred,' Dylan resumed. 'You've always looked for the slight differences in things. In colours. You've always wanted to isolate and catalogue the differences in things that looked the same.'

'You taught me that, Dylan.'

'I just showed you what I saw, Adrian. It was you who went further. You wanted to see what the eye refused to see. You frightened yourself with clarity.'

Stoker laughed.

'Why don't you pour yourself another coffee. Pour one for me,' Dylan said.

Stoker saw that Dylan was getting ready for the long haul. When he'd sat down, a fresh cup of coffee in his hand, Dylan had turned to face him and said: 'The book's called *Vertical Man, Horizontal World*.'

Stoker hadn't said a word. He'd sat and listened. He was nervous for his brother.

Dylan had spoken with his poet's voice, holding each word in a balance inaudible to the conscious ear. He'd paced himself well, breaking now and then to hold the silence, or to sip his coffee. For six hours Dylan had read, not once searching Stoker's face for signs of approval or disappointment. The whole was as solid as the man, the movement steady, incremental, a slow and certain surge. From start to finish it was as though nothing had happened, nothing that you could put your finger on. And yet there was a definite movement, a shift as final, as bracing and pellucid, as dawn. Stoker couldn't find the words to match Dylan's. It was best to shut up, smile his winning smile, look his brother clearly in the eye. The blood throbbed in his brain. Stoker realised that in the last six hours he had barely breathed, as though he'd forgotten he was alive. Dylan's book had taken him elsewhere, to another country within him, a country where words were fitted to things. Stoker thought of the strange power of words to move. A painting could never be the same, he thought. Words had the power to reach deeper, beyond sensation and idea. With words wielded in the way that Dylan wielded them, one could paint the soul.

Stoker realised that he did not quite understand what he was thinking. He loved his brother's book and that was that. He would wait and see what happened at the publisher. He realised also that he had to leave. Olivieri would definitely be ready to retrench him. He'd forgotten to ask Phyllis to cover for him. Somehow he didn't care. He was happy where he was.

Dylan's reading was more than he could have hoped for. He stared through the bare tangled branches of the apple orchard. The wisps of early morning mist had long ago evaporated. As his eyes clung to the tangled grey branches, penetrated into the dormant life within, he thought of a similar winter scene in Woody Allen's humourless and exquisitely stilted film, *Interiors*. In the scene Allen intercuts a poet's grappling hand with the knotted tangled branches of a tree outside the poet's window. Stoker pictured Dylan as Allen's poet. He saw Dylan's massive hand as it scratched then erased a word, then scratched again. The movement of the fountain-pen on paper was like the scratching of dead leaves. At every turn the words threatened to disappear. Words as knotted and entangled as the branches of the apple orchard he saw before him. The battle was worth it, Stoker thought. For now the battle had been won.

Stoker passed the pylons electrified with song. He passed the West Coast National Park, the lagoon which had triggered his dream of sandsharks. He passed the Caltex oil refinery with its pillars of flame, through Milnerton and Brooklyn. He cut off the national road, away from the sea. He turned left into Woodstock along Beach Road, a name which had long ago become a misnomer, containing only the memory of a dredged sea. Then he backtracked towards Obs.

On Arnold Street he passed the local mecca, a brightly painted house with each feature, each feasibly distinctive surface, a different colour – a railing, gutter, frame, section of fence. This was Obs, Stoker thought, with its motley flamboyance. The vibrant interplay of colours reminded him of a harlequin's coat. Whenever a customer stepped in at Dominion, unsure of what colour exactly they needed, Stoker would direct them to the harlequin house on Arnold. Take your pick and combination, he'd say, then let's look at the swatches.

Passing the harlequin house had perked him up. Stoker parked the bakkie outside his own bland rented spot and walked down to Gloria's Diner on Station for a late lunch.

CHAPTER SEVEN

At Gloria's you could eat an English breakfast for R7,50, a chicken pie or Cornish for R3,50. The walls were pink, the tablecloths were pink. The place had the allure of a defrosted salad but the food was good. Stoker ordered what he always ordered – a chicken pie and coffee. He'd missed the rush hour. The place was quiet. Across from him six marooned New Zealand rugby fans were piling into a second round of Gloria's legendary tipsy tart. Stoker opened a copy of *You* magazine and read an article on Hugh, Divine and Liz. He enjoyed reading up on the scandal. Hugh's indiscretion had restored his faith. The man was human after all. Besides, the scandal proved that blow-jobs sold more papers than Rwanda. He studied the snapshot of Hugh with his charming crow's feet wiped out by a magnesium glare, a serial number clenched in his panic-stricken hands. Maybe Hugh needed to destroy himself a little just to stay alive? Stoker thought. Morally upstanding pretty boys had an expiry date after all.

Gloria set down the chicken pie and coffee. 'You okay, Stoker?' she asked.

'Fine thanks. You?'

'Not good.'

'What's up?'

'Just getting old.'

Gloria hadn't been well lately. Her angina was playing up. She'd been robbed twice in the last month. Still, she looked good. Gloria was around sixty years old and looked fifty. Her eyes were painted like Cleopatra's. She had a hairdo you could hide a toaster in.

Gloria liked lots of people, Phyllis for instance, but she didn't care for Stoker. He'd asked for credit once and had lost her favour immediately. Gloria didn't believe in handouts. 'I've always paid for the food I eat,' she'd said. She was right of course. Just because Stoker ate there five days a week meant nothing. Gloria didn't believe in trust. Besides, Stoker had a definite feeling that he shouldn't be trusted. He believed that Gloria tolerated him because of Phyllis. Gloria was Phyllis's mum's cousin. He could see they were related. Stoker pictured Phyllis at sixty with a beehive and Cleopatra eyes. It would suit her, he thought.

As far as Gloria was concerned, Stoker smelt like old money but no money. He was mostly broke and an artist, the kind of lethal combination Gloria was hell-bent on staying clear of. Her best clients were ex-socialists with cell phones. Though she didn't care for him, Stoker felt sorry about the robberies and the angina. Maybe it was time for Gloria to quit working, but then again she liked the hustle and bustle.

Stoker ordered a tipsy tart with a double scoop of ice-cream. He listened to the New Zealanders rap on about the World Cup. They didn't seem to mind the defeat. He discovered they were bunking at the Rolling Stone, the hostel on Lower Main. They were planning a road trip across the Karoo. Stoker wondered whether they'd seen *Once Were Warriors*, a New Zealand movie which was on his hit list for the year, along with England's *Naked* and Australia's *Bad Boy Bubby* – suitably charming and fucked-up visions all, with just the kind of through-line into the future which Stoker could identify with. He wondered whether to tell them about Helen Martins and the Owl House in Nieu-Bethesda, since it sounded like they were heading in that direction. Would they be interested in some crazy old lady's sculpture garden, her walls of glittering crushed glass? He'd tell them anyway. People needed to know about crazy meccas. He thought of talking about Dylan's famous poem, 'The Ballad of Koos Malgas', then he decided he was pushing it. Most people didn't give a flying fuck that Koos had built all the sculptures in Helen Martins' garden. For most people, Fugard included, Koos was just the invisible nobody stoking the myth of the Owl House. At least Dylan's poem had helped to correct the mess.

Bored with *You* magazine, Stoker stared out the window. What he saw was the Heidelberg Tavern, except he was looking at nothing in particular. Visions from Dylan's book kept appearing before him, intercut with thoughts of Bridge, the gallery opening at Seeff, *Pulp Fiction*, Phyllis. Stoker realised that he was drifting. He was drinking coffee he didn't need, eating food he didn't want, spending money he didn't have. Worse, he was going nowhere. He was sitting at Gloria's because it was routine. He was caught between small certainties and arbitrary manoeuvres. Looking back over the last two days he saw his life as a series of accidents held together by a thin thread of routine. He needed to sort out his life, talk to Olivieri, maybe get another job, something more regular, more financially rewarding. He thought of finding work making sets for TV ads, talking to Joan when she got back from New York. He wondered whether he should quit painting.

He'd told Dylan that he was finally finding a language. Was he? Was he really? So some woman had bought his painting. Did that give him the right to feel confident? Besides, was confidence what it was all about? He doubted that. He'd never painted out of confidence. It was an obsession with him. Painting cleared his head, took him out of himself. Painting meant he wasn't staring vaguely out of windows. Painting was a way of dealing with the drift. When he felt most alive. That's when living made sense. The rest of the time he was useless, errant. He didn't have the heart to live. He couldn't shake the ordinariness. He lacked Dylan's magic, Lizzie's clear-eyed acceptance of limit. He was a nobody and a fool. Still, at least he wasn't feeling sad. At least he wasn't hung up about being a failure. Well . . . not quite. He figured he'd get through the day just fine. He'd stop in and see Olivieri. He'd contact Phyllis and Bridge.

Stoker paid for his chicken pie, coffee and tart. He chatted to the New Zealanders about Nieu-Bethesda and pointed out some camping sites and hot springs on the road map they had laid out in front of them. It turned out they had seen *Once Were Warriors* and liked it every bit as much as he did. There was talk about the arty opening credits, the fucked-up machismo. Rugby players were nowhere near that psycho, one of the New Zealanders added. Oh yeah? Maybe there was a point here, Stoker admitted. Still, getting an update on *Once Were Warriors* was just fine. Stoker quit. He walked to the pay-phone outside the Spar on Station. No one answered at Blake Street. Stoker dialled Bridge's home number.

'Hello.' It was Bridge.

'It's Stoker.'

'Hello Stoker. It's good of you to call.'

'You okay?'

'The tests were negative.'

'That's good, that's good.'

'By the way, I'm having a party.'

'A party? When?'

'Saturday.'

Stoker didn't know how to ask her what she was celebrating.

'I'm leaving for Turkey,' Bridge said.

'That's great!' Stoker said unconvincingly. Bridge was crazy about minarets and belly-dancing and stuff like that. 'You be gone for long?' Stoker asked.

'A while. I'm flying to Cairo, then cutting through to Alexandria and catching a boat.'

'Sounds great!'

'So, you think you'll come? To the party I mean.' She laughed.

'Definitely.'

'Bring Phyllis.'

'She's working.'

'Tell her to come after work.'

'Will do.'

'So I'll see you Saturday, then?'

'Definitely.'

Stoker wanted to ask about Prue, then he thought it best to say nothing, wait for Saturday. He put down the phone and dialled Phyllis. She wasn't in. He left a message on her answering machine and walked over to see Olivieri at Dominion Hardware.

Olivieri was packing away some paint and a roller. The customer was an elegantly dressed woman in her forties. She was on a cell phone discussing colour swatches with what sounded like her hubby. Olivieri saw Stoker. He was all smiles as the woman thanked him for the purchase. Stoker recognised the woman as someone he'd recommended the harlequin house to. Caught between the cell phone and Olivieri's ministrations, she didn't pay him much attention.

'You need a colour, any colour, you call me,' Olivieri said. The woman left, the purchase in one hand, the other patting her hair. Olivieri stared at Stoker. He wasn't angry, he was hurt, which made it worse. Stoker didn't know how he was going to smooth Olivieri's feathers.

'I trust you and this is what you do to me?'

Stoker was silent.

'Two days, two days you don't come to work, what am I supposed to do? You tell me? You don't call. Nothing. What am I supposed to do?'

'I'm sorry,' Stoker said. After all, Olivieri had a point.

'Sorry?! Sorry?! I'll show you sorry.' Then Olivieri came out from behind the counter, grabbed Stoker by the shoulders, and planted a kiss on both of his cheeks. 'Next time you don't come to work I'll spit on your grave. I call your house. No answer. I call Phyllis, she tells me you are at your brother's in Riebeek-Kasteel. So you see, I know your movements, my boy.'

Olivieri sounded like something out of a Terence Hill and Bud Spencer movie. The fact was Olivieri loved Stoker.

'We're a team. Don't forget that,' Olivieri said.

'I won't,' Stoker said. He was stunned.

'So, how is your brother?'

'He's fine.'

'Why didn't you tell me you have a brother?'

'It never occurred to me.'

'Never occurred to you?! Am I not your friend?'

'Sure you are.'

'Then why don't you tell me? Why don't you tell me about your family?'

Stoker couldn't think of a good reason. Olivieri simply belonged to a part of his life in which his family didn't feature. Olivieri was his livelihood. Olivieri owned the studio.

'What's he like, your brother?'

'He's very quiet,' Stoker ventured.

'He have a family?'

'No.'

'How old is he?'

'Thirty-seven.'

'And he doesn't have a family?'

It had never occurred to Stoker that Dylan didn't have a family. Dylan was immaculate. He didn't even have a lover.

'At thirty-seven a man should have a wife, children. What's wrong with your family? Three of you and no children?'

Stoker was speechless. This wasn't what he'd expected to hear. The fact was Lizzie was sterile, Dylan needed no one, and he, well, he wasn't fit to be a father. Dylan had chosen celibacy, Lizzie had a string of lovers, and he? He had Phyllis who, until recently, he'd planned on dropping. For the three of them the nuclear family was nowhere in sight. Stoker didn't know whether to laugh or cry. He decided to laugh. Olivieri stared at him, his bushy eyebrows meanly furrowed, his heart bursting with love. Once Stoker had started laughing he couldn't stop. In stitches, he held on to the counter for dear life.

'Tomorrow you work,' Olivieri said. He was at a loss as to how to deal with Stoker. 'Come,' Olivieri said. 'I want to show you something.'

Olivieri closed the store and led Stoker upstairs to the studio. Stoker entered. The studio was jam-packed with flowers. Stoker was confused.

'What's with the flowers?' Stoker asked. For a second he'd thought Olivieri had lost his head. Then he thought that maybe Phyllis had bought them in a fit of concern. He hadn't exactly been in the best frame of mind at the Happy Wok.

Then again, there were so many. Too many! He'd never seen so many flowers except at his parents' funeral.

'Some woman came in here. A beautiful woman. Classic. She asks if you are in. I tell her no. I tell her you're supposed to be working but you are in Riebeek-Kasteel. She tells me it is a surprise.'

No wonder Olivieri was so nice to him! He'd clearly been impressed by all the flowers.

'What did she look like?'

'Oh beautiful, beautiful. Classic. Hair like silk. Very expensive. Like a movie star.' Stoker guessed it was the woman at the gallery. Who else could it be? All his friends looked like peasants or extras in a Nirvana video.

'She leave a name? A number?'

'Nothing. She just came with these men.'

'She use a florist?'

'How do I know if she used a florist? She just came in with flowers and more flowers. Why do you expect me to ask if she used a florist?'

Stoker stared at the flowers. The air was heady with a myriad of scents. He'd never received flowers before. What could have provoked her? It had to be her. Stoker was at a loss. His eyes were playing tricks with him, he thought. This couldn't be happening. He picked up a rose, cut it at the stem, snipped off the thorns and placed it in the buttonhole of Olivieri's satin bomber jacket.

'She like you, hah? This woman?'

'Maybe,' Stoker said.

Right then he felt like he was being killed with kindness.

A bunch of red roses in hand, Stoker headed home. He wanted nothing more than to stare out of his loft window and see rooftops. Just rooftops. No windows, doors, backyards. Given the fact that it was impossible to see nothing in Obs, rooftops were a good second best. People rarely loitered on rooftops. Rooftops were where people fixed things. The only people who spent time on rooftops were the ones who lived in songs.

Stoker turned his front door key and entered. It felt like a lifetime had passed since he'd last left. There were no messages. Jay was probably with Dayglo. He hung his duffle-coat on the landing, then changed his mind. Jay would most probably swipe it, he thought, as he climbed the stairs to his loft and opened the door. He half-expected another untoward assault on the senses, some unnerving overkill, but the room was the way he'd left it. The unmade bed. The tacky tin tray. A two-day-old snackwich. An empty mug. The packets of Grand-Pa and Panado. The dried remains of Jungle Oats stuck to the dark inside of the bowl reminded him of a sore. There was a note from Phyllis saying that she wanted her bakkie back. There were lots of criss-crossed kisses attached.

Stoker slipped out of his clothes and padded across his bedroom floor. He put Phyllis's note into a biscuit tin with all the other notes he'd received over the past year and a bit. Then he picked up his toilet bag and towel and padded down to the bathroom.

The bathroom floor was flooded. Phyllis must have used the shower last. Stoker had to tiptoe to make sure he didn't break his neck. For once he was grateful for the wet floor, Phyllis's signature. For Phyllis the bathroom was literally that – a bath room. Water spat through the shower curtain, dripped from her body, overflowed the sink, spilt in sheets from the lip of the bath. According to Jay, Phyllis was a slovenly hippo. In kinder moments he referred to her as a river horse. Jay on the other hand was so neurotic about water and fungal infection that he dusted himself down with talcum powder. And it was this obsession which had spawned the name of Jay's band – Nappy Rash. It was Nappy Rash which had performed live at the gallery opening the night Stoker lost his Doc. Stoker hadn't seen Jay since then and was glad not to see him now.

Stoker could feel the steam peel the smoke off his skin. He found himself scrubbing himself harder than usual. He didn't want to stand under the shower like a hunk of tortured meat, his usual stance when in showers. He had no desire to think about anything. He shaved without a mirror, feeling the shape of his face. He clipped his nose hairs. He shampooed and conditioned his hair, what precious little there was. He soaped the crack of his arse with a modicum of pleasure. Satisfied that he'd cleaned himself, he proceeded to wank. Miraculously he managed to picture nothing and no one. Making sure that he'd left no trace of sperm in the shower he returned to his bedroom, slid into bed and called it a day.

This resolution would entail an embargo on phone conversations. It meant relieving himself in a bottle and pouring it out of the window and letting the rain rinse the roof clean. It meant lots of sleeping, reading, and more wanking. Stoker was going into hibernation. He was cracking up. In effect he would not be working at Dominion for a third, fourth and fifth day. He would not leave the house. His hot plate, kettle and snackwich machine were with him upstairs, as was the portable fridge which belonged to Lizzie. His only occasion to exercise his legs would be to go downstairs and shit. He left a note and the car keys on the hallway stand for Phyllis. The note said that he'd gone on a walkabout and would explain later. When exactly later would be he didn't know. He'd written the note on one of Prue's cards of famous South African women. The card pictured Winnie Mandela in tribal dress. Prue had had to junk her stock since Winnie for some reason was no longer popular. Why, Stoker didn't have the faintest idea. He'd sealed the card along with the keys to Phyllis's bakkie and placed the bunch of roses from the studio beside it. Then he'd walked up the stairs to his loft room and locked the door from the inside.

Stoker had had enough. He'd make Bridge's farewell his gala return to society. To pass the time he'd fulfil his original intention which was to stare at the rooftops facing his loft window. He'd finally get down to finishing Winterston's *Art Objects*, a book he'd borrowed ages ago from Dom. It was all a bit much, the spit and polish and overwroughtness. Still, he'd give it another go. He'd also reread special passages in Patrick White's *The Vivisector*, a book Dylan had given him when he was trying to figure out whether he was an artist or not. Again, way too overwrought. Still, there was more here, he thought, stuff that stuck and bothered you way later.

He'd think about sandsharks, Dylan's book, about the strange coincidence in the titling of their respective works – *Man in a Landscape; Vertical Man, Horizontal World*. He would show Dylan the painting, maybe it could work as a book cover? But then again, the painting was sold. He'd barely had a chance to live with it and it was gone. It hadn't even lived out its run at the gallery! The mystery woman had somehow managed to get the painting then and there. When Stoker had called up and discovered this fact, he'd felt cheated. Somehow bought out. He'd wanted the triumph of selling his first work to govern and define his mood, but the more he'd thought about it, the more angry he'd become. He'd guessed that it was because he was a nobody that the gallery had allowed it to happen. Whichever way he'd looked at it, the deal wasn't kosher. His rights had been taken away. He was being killed with kindness. Precious, you're being precious, he'd said. Nobody plays by the rules anymore. Still, he'd have to find out who the mystery woman was so he could get hold of the painting and show it to Dylan. So the situation was unethical, but it wasn't all bad. The woman had sent him flowers. That's of course if it was in fact her.

The more Stoker reasoned, the more confused he became. Eventually he gave up. His mind stopped drifting and leaping from one connection to the next. Finally he just ate, slept, shat, read. There was nothing sublime about it all. He was just chilling out. Of course, innumerable little activities occurred which proved Dean's point that it was in fact difficult to truly do nothing. Stoker also discovered the root of Dylan's point that no matter how many bridges you burnt, you never stopped needing.

He sorted out his clothes and decided to abandon half his wardrobe. He went through his papers and repacked his trunk. He sorted out his camping gear, the thought of the New Zealanders crossing the Karoo at the back of his mind. He cleared up his room, eliminating all evidence of a pointless existence. He found himself living in his environment as though he were going to die at any moment. He took stock and wrote a will. He left his unfinished paintings to Dylan, three of his best shirts to Dean, his camping gear to Waldo, his snapshots to Lizzie who controlled the family album. He split his books four ways. Joan got all the art books, Dayglo got Huxley's *Doors of Perception* from which all Stoker could remember was the description of the effects of LSD on Huxley's corduroy trousers. Dylan and Dom got the rest of the collection which amounted to fourteen books. He left his snackwich machine and kettle to Phyllis, his leather jacket to Olivieri. As for Jay? There was always the dufflecoat.

Stoker's spring-cleaning and accounting was directly linked to his feeling sick to death with chance. It took him three days to effect some order to his aimlessness. He resolved that he would start afresh if he were not struck dead by chance, as active in isolation, he realised, as it was in any other situation. He wished he could take stock more often. Constantly picking up bits and pieces may be a fact of life, but he'd at least make sure that the bits and pieces made some shred of sense. He realised that the final purpose of the exercise wasn't to resolve the question of who and what he was. That was a lost cause. Still, he'd lay down the foundation of some order. He'd leave behind a life that was legible.

This, Stoker realised, had always been the way of his mother. She was a first-rate accountant of the flesh and the spirit, a visionary when it came to lists. And yet how fragile had been her order! Stoker found himself sobbing, the memory of his murdered mother still snagged in the rubble of his heart.

On Saturday morning Stoker reconnected the phone. Jay hadn't been around to use it. Stoker listened to the click and purr and wondered who to call. He dialled. Lizzie picked up the phone. As always she was downright rude. Lizzie hated the phone, which wasn't surprising given the fact that it was her lifeline for eight hours a day.

'It's Stoker.'

'Where the hell have you been?!'

'Home.'

'The whole world's been looking for you.'

'Well I've been home.'

'Phyllis is pissed off with you.'

'She'll get over it.'

'Incidentally, so am I.'

'You are?'

'Could we meet?'

'Sure. You want to go to Greenmarket Square with me? I have to get Bridge something for her farewell.'

'I'll pick you up in half an hour.'

Lizzie was the first to cut transmission. Stoker was about to call Phyllis, then changed his mind. She'd probably still be sleeping. Besides, he didn't actually want to talk to her, what with going awol. He'd rather wait till she'd left so he could leave a message on the answering machine. He'd heard her enter the house and climb the stairs to his room. He'd stuck to the note and flowers as the point of contact. Now he realised that he still had to deal with the fact that he hadn't answered her knock.

Exactly half an hour later Lizzie was parked outside Stoker's. Lizzie was obsessed with punctuality, a trait which held the rest of the world to attention. Before she could honk her horn, Stoker was on the street and opening the passenger door. He bent over and gave her a peck on the cheek which she accepted with abrupt graciousness. She recognised Stoker's duffle-coat. She also noticed that he wasn't wearing his Docs. Lizzie had a photographic memory when it came to clothes. In Stoker's case it wasn't difficult for her to notice if something was out of the ordinary. Stoker usually wore the same clothes, or slight variations thereof, day in and day out. He hadn't taken his Docs off since Lizzie had bought them for him just over a month ago. He hadn't worn his duffle-coat since he was sixteen.

'I went to see Dylan,' Stoker said.

'And?'

'He sends his love,' Stoker lied.

'Yeah, sure. What's the bastard up to?'

'He finished his book.'

'You're kidding.'

'I'm not. He read the whole thing to me.'

'And?'

'It's brilliant.'

'I suppose it would be,' Lizzie said grudgingly. She wished she could fault Dylan as an artist in the way she faulted him as a brother. 'Is he still a morose little fuck?' she asked.

'He seemed quite chirpy to me. I got the feeling he was ready to reach out. He'd been thinking of me, he'd said.'

'The problem with Dylan is that he does a lot of thinking and precious little doing. You know I haven't heard from him in over a year? You believe that? My own brother lives, what? Two? Three hours away and he doesn't even contact me.'

'I'm sure he's got his reasons,' Stoker said.

'I suppose you just melted when you saw him, didn't you?'

'Look Lizzie, I can't help it if I'm not as pissed off as you are. Besides, Dylan's been doing a lot. You should see the way he's fixed things up.'

'Don't, just don't talk to me about the fucking house. Okay. I don't want to know what that morbid fuck's been up to in our house.' Lizzie looked as though she was about to snap. Shit, Stoker thought. Then Lizzie swerved from the brink on her own accord.

'You tell him I was working? You tell him I've got a job?'

'I did. I told him you were making big bucks.'

'And what did he say?'

'He said he was happy for you,' Stoker lied.

'Bullshit! He probably wondered what the hell I was doing in telesales. You know what a purist he is. Art, art, and more fucking art. I wish he'd just wake up and realise how hard it is just to live. It takes a fuck of a lot more than art and fresh air.'

'What are you shouting at me for, Lizzie?'

'I'm not shouting.'

'You're being shrill.'

'Well it's the weekend. I can afford to be shrill. You have no idea how much energy it takes just to be nice, buttering up some retard client with light chatter, inane jokes, talking about nothing of value just so the bastard can sign on the dotted line.'

'How much you make this week?'

'Six.'

'Six grand? Jesus, Lizzie.'

'I know, it's disgusting. I make so much money I could cry.'

Lizzie slowed down as they passed the game reserve on De Waal Drive. Wildebeest and zebra were grazing close to the wire fence.

The reserve was probably the most precious sight in Lizzie's daily life, Stoker thought. She passed it every day to and from work. She was silent as she drove by, apparently calm, at peace. Stoker was glad for the break but knew it wouldn't last. The reserve was Lizzie's little piece of Africa, cordoned off and un-tainted. In one fell swoop she could erase all the buildings and streets, see sloping green fields filled with buck and arum lilies. She had a powerful imagination. He knew she dreamed of an Africa before empire. Stoker loved this quirk in his sister, her schizophrenic capacity to betray every urban bone in her body. In truth she was no different to Dylan or Stoker. Given half the chance she would tear up the streets to get to the sea. One of her pet hates was the way the city council had decided to light up Table Mountain by night. Can you imagine what those poor animals and plants must be going through? Can you? she'd asked. One night she'd gotten it into her head to destroy the electrical source. She'd wanted Stoker to join her but he'd declined. It's unnatural, it's obscene, she'd said. What's wrong with us? Why do we have to have the whole fucking world visible twenty-four hours a day? Lizzie blamed it all on Edison and post-modernism. She had a point. Still, as far as Stoker was concerned, electricity was a miracle. He hated the way people took it for granted that you could stick a plug in a wall and blow-dry your hair.

Lizzie's Beetle swooped past the reserve and rounded upper Woodstock towards the city bowl. She resumed talking.

'You seen Dayglo?'

'I haven't seen anyone.'

'He say anything to you about us?'

'Like I said, Lizzie, I haven't seen anyone. I've been locked up in my room for the past three days.'

'I could kill that bastard.' Lizzie and Dayglo were lovers. Cape Town was a small town. 'He's turning into an E-head. You know that?' Stoker braced himself, took the flak.

Lizzie hated drugs. She hated artists. She didn't know what she was doing with Dayglo. She loved him and was convinced that he was using her. When Dayglo had met Lizzie three years ago he was a lawyer. He had a vintage Mercedes and managed a bond on a snazzy house. Lizzie and Dayglo were happy then. In those days Dayglo was called Felix. About a year ago Dayglo had quit his job, sold his house and Mercedes, and gone back to his true passion – drumming. He'd worked as a session musician before he'd hitched up with Jay and Percy and started Nappy Rash. Lizzie had fought to stick with Dayglo but it was hopeless. Eventually he'd moved out and installed himself in his music studio. He'd shaved off all his yuppie curls, dropped his suits off at the Salvation Army, and started wearing very bright clothing. He wore bright clothes because they made people smile, he'd said. According to Lizzie, all Dayglo's wardrobe did was give her a headache.

Dayglo had definitely had a vision. He drummed like a man possessed. That's all he wanted to do. Lizzie didn't know what had hit her. Initially she'd tried to adapt. She sat around waiting for him at gigs. She wore herself out waiting for him over cold suppers. Eventually she'd given up. The reason she was so pissed off now had to do with the fact that Dayglo had introduced her to his new girlfriend the night before. Stoker had met Dayglo and Anthea at the Seeff Gallery. He had to admit that visually, at least, they suited each other. They belonged to the same tribe. He vaguely remembered Anthea telling him she was going to live in a pyramid. There was a colony somewhere in the forests of Knysna. Apparently the pyramids had different landings. The bedroom was situated at the apex of the pyramid which, according to Anthea, had something to do with the third eye or pineal gland. Stoker had been too drunk to remember the details. He remembered Dayglo hanging on to Anthea's arm, all ears. Stoker believed they'd be happy, for a while at least. He couldn't say this to Lizzie of course, she'd only bite his head off, or worse, kick him out of her life. When Lizzie got hurt she got very perverse. One had to tread carefully around her at the best of times.

Stoker studied his sister as she swerved the Beetle into the parking lot at the corner of Bree and Shortmarket. Lizzie was a beautiful woman. Probably one of the most beautiful he'd seen in the flesh. She was forty and looked eighteen. She'd always reminded him of Olivia Hussey in *Lost Horizon*, a movie about a Shangri-La in the Himalayas where people remained eternally young. Her face had a symmetry which had escaped Dylan and himself. Her skin was flawless, her eyes possessed a clarity and a forthrightness which, given the circumstances, could scald and melt with equal intensity. She sported a longish black bob and like Dylan, she was dressed in black from head to toe. She wore no jewellery. Stoker pictured her with a gun and smiled. Lizzie couldn't stand the thought of any part of her being pierced. She'd flung and suffered enough slings and arrows to need a physical punchline. Besides, she'd chosen the route of the classic and corporate. Still, there was a buoyancy about her. Lizzie could wear anything and still be beautiful.

Phyllis, on the other hand, was utterly colour-blind. Phyllis mixed and matched her clothes with such vigour, such a pre-

69

posterous lack of style, that she left the viewer with no choice but to weep or yield. Stoker had had to do a lot of yielding. The fact was he'd gotten used to Phyllis's bad taste. It had a ring of truth about it. Phyllis had a pierced navel and a lizard tattooed along her neck. She wore glitter nail polish and had a penchant for things plastic. Phyllis and Lizzie were like chalk and cheese. Still, they got on just fine. Phyllis was probably the only person who could handle Lizzie's erratic mood swings. Stoker either said nothing or lied. Phyllis was straightforward. Lizzie appreciated Phyllis's honesty. It more than made up for her bad taste, she'd said.

Stoker lit a cigarette outside the Magnet on Bree, then he and Lizzie headed down Shortmarket Street towards Greenmarket Square. It was the first cigarette he'd smoked in three days.

CHAPTER TEN

The weather was perversely warm. The city centre was packed. The doors and windows of restaurants and businesses were flung wide open. Stoker regretted not leaving his dufflecoat in the Beetle.

They passed Nino's and Lizzie poked her nose in to see what was what. Nino's was the culinary heart of the city bowl. It catered in equal measure to brunches and fashion. People drank cappuccinos at a rate of knots. Anybody who was anybody usually grazed at Nino's on a Saturday morning.

'You want a coffee?' Lizzie asked.

'No.'

'Come on, Adrian. Have a coffee with me.'

Stoker guessed that something was up.

'I need you,' Lizzie said, her voice marred by a saccharine plaintiveness. 'You see that man over there.'

Stoker looked.

'Don't be so bloody obvious.'

Stoker was enjoying himself. 'Is that the man you've been raving about?' Because, of course, Lizzie may have been pissed off with Dayglo, but this in no way stopped her endless store of amorous fantasies.

'That's him,' Lizzie said.

Stoker stared at a self-composed man in his fifties. The man wore a dark green turtle-neck and professorial-looking glasses. He was reading *The Economist* and sipping a lemon tea.

'Isn't he gorgeous?'

'Isn't he a bit old for you?'

'I'm forty, remember.'

Stoker tended to forget how old Lizzie was. This wasn't surprising. She looked ridiculously young and usually lied about her age, unless the reverse proved more convenient. Lizzie was fickle. Stoker never knew what to expect from one second to the next.

'He's the man who bought the house down the road from me. Isn't he beautiful?'

Stoker had to admit that the man was handsome in a chiselled Mills and Boonish way. He'd most probably be cast as the heroine's dad, someone lonely and protective. Stoker stopped his imagination in its tracks. Lizzie needed cheering up. If it took gawking at someone reading *The Economist* and drinking tea, then fine.

'Okay, I'll stick with you,' Stoker said. He loved his sister best when she was frivolous.

As chance would have it, a table cleared right next to Lizzie's prey. Lizzie ordered a continental breakfast for the two of them, a cappuccino for herself and a Stoney ginger beer for Stoker. Then she pretended to pick up on a burning conversation concerning the innocence of OJ Simpson. She went through coroner's reports, false leads, the question of racism, the ins and outs of wife battery versus murder. Stoker was lost. He knew precious little about the case and what he knew he'd gleaned from Gloria's rack of *You* magazines. He didn't read the papers or watch TV. Lizzie, on the other hand, read *Time* and *The Economist*. It was through Lizzie, via *Time*, that he'd heard about the Khoi supposedly originating from the east, about some linguistic links with Japanese. Stoker hadn't read the article but he found the notion hugely interesting.

Seated across from Lizzie, Stoker guessed that she urgently needed some intelligent response from him concerning OJ. He turned to Lizzie's target next to him, introduced himself, then deferred to the man's higher learning on the matter at hand. You bastard, Stoker could feel Lizzie saying to him. But he was in no mood for the charade. He felt sorry for the man and figured he'd only ruin Lizzie's chances if he indulged her by opening his mouth in some half-baked fashion. It was best to bail out, rope the man in, and see what happened. Stoker was having a good time. And besides, Lizzie had asked for it.

The man lifted his nose from *The Economist*. 'I beg your pardon,' the man said.

Lizzie was floored.

'My sister was just trying to explain something complicated. I figured you'd be able to help.'

The man was staring at Lizzie. 'Do I know you from somewhere? I'm sure I've seen you before.'

'I don't think I know you,' Lizzie lied.

'Of course! You live down the road from me. I live at the corner of Bellevliet and Crown.'

'The dusty pink house that's just been renovated?' Lizzie ventured.

'The same,' the man said. 'My name is Grant, by the way. Grant Klingman.'

'Elizabeth Stoker.'

'You can call her Lizzie,' Stoker said.

Grant Klingman looked at Stoker. He seemed mildly startled by Stoker's presence.

'My brother Adrian,' Lizzie said.

'Stoker. You can call me Stoker.'

'It's the red hair,' Lizzie said.

'How do you do . . . Stoker.' Klingman shook Stoker's

hand. His grip was weighted and strong. It reminded Stoker of Dylan.

Lizzie was radiant. Klingman had recognised her. In the space of two weeks she had colonised his memory.

An awkward silence consumed the air once the introductions were over.

'I don't mean to be rude, Lizzie, but I've got to find something for Bridge.' Stoker turned to Klingman. 'My friend was recently raped,' he confided. 'She's flying off to Turkey and I need to buy her something to cheer her up.' Then Stoker turned away from the baffled Klingman and back to Lizzie. 'You don't mind if I dump you, do you? I could meet you here. I'll leave my duffle-coat if that's okay. See it as collateral.'

Before Lizzie had a chance to reply Stoker had gulped down the remainder of his ginger beer, jammed a croissant in his mouth, and walked across the street into the labyrinth of Greenmarket Square. It would have to be something small, he thought. It would have to be something that brought her good luck. Bridge needed as much of it as she could get.

Stoker wove through the clothing stalls, sifted through the racks of trinkets. Nothing. He realised that he wasn't looking for anything particular. He couldn't predict the outcome of the search. He wished he'd gone through his things in Riebeek-Kasteel. Surely there would have been something special in the house? Something from his childhood. A family heirloom. Then, lost in the imagined drawers and attic of his family home, Stoker found what he was looking for – a yo-yo cut out of a single piece of oak. He placed the yo-yo in the palm of his hand. He imagined the yo-yo in Bridge's palm. The wood was smooth and warm. He liked the fact that it wasn't accompanied by a string. Abstracted, he placed the yo-yo in his jeans pocket, felt it living there, then he removed it and held it in his other hand. This was it, he thought. A stringless yo-yo. This was the gift with which he'd cross Bridge's palm.

Aware that he was being looked at, Stoker stared at the man who he presumed was selling the yo-yo. The man had matted black hair and a full beard, his skin was tawny, his eyes a startling sightless blue. For a second Stoker thought the man was blind.

'You shouldn't be selling this,' Stoker said.

The man grinned and shrugged his shoulders.

'How much?' Stoker asked.

'I don't know,' the man said.

Stoker stared deeply into the man's eyes. What was he looking for? A sign of corruption? A clue to the worth of the yo-yo?

'I'm selling all I have,' the man said. The man's voice was so forlorn it made Stoker's heart twist. He realised that he wasn't trapped in a con. The man clearly had no idea what the yo-yo was worth – at least not in monetary terms. Stoker realised that he had been so focused on finding the right object that he'd forgotten the context. Now he found himself squatting on the cobbled square. There was no stand, no bright array of trinkets. The bearded man was sitting on a backpack. Next to the yo-yo were a pair of hiking boots, two embroidered shirts, a bead necklace, a cluster of nondescript yet beautiful stones. Stoker was moved by a mix of feelings, ashamed for not noticing how hard-up the man clearly was. He felt an urge to protect the man, an impulse at odds with his desire to take what belonged to the man.

'Tell you what . . . I'll give you one fifty for the yo-yo. Fifty now and a hundred later.'

The man looked at him, confused.

'It's like this. There's a party in Obs. The party is tonight at number 16 Norfolk Road. If you come to the party I'll give you the hundred.'

'Why must I go to a party to get the money?'

'Because it's important.' Stoker did not know why it was important, he only sensed that it was. 'My friend,' Stoker resumed, 'my friend, she's been raped, see. So she's pretty freaked. She's having a farewell party and then she's going to Turkey. This yo-yo is for her. I want you to know that because I feel this yo-yo is important to you. I want you to be there when I give it to her. It's a special yo-yo. I can feel it. I want you to talk to her about the yo-yo.'

'This yo-yo was made by my great-grandfather,' the man said.

Stoker cut him short. 'See, there we have it. The yo-yo has a story,' Stoker said. 'I want you to be there to tell her the story.'

'It sounds like a good plan to me,' the man said. 'It is true that I am selling a piece of my heart.'

Stoker wished the man hadn't said that, but the truth could not be avoided.

'So, I will give you fifty now and a hundred later. What do you say?'

The man asked for precise directions to the party. Stoker learnt that the man was a stranger to these parts. He wrote down Bridge's address and phone number on the fifty rand note. 'This way you won't lose it,' he said.

'Thank you,' the man said.

'My name is Stoker, by the way. The girl you will be talking to is called Bridget.'

'Bridget,' the man said, then added: 'My name is Immo.'

'Immo,' Stoker said.

'That's correct,' the man said. He was smiling, his eyes radiant.

Stoker headed back to Nino's. He was in a very good mood. He could feel the yo-yo brush smoothly against his thigh. 'Immo,' he said. 'Immo.'

Lizzie was seated where he'd left her. She was sucking on a peach dessert. Klingman was sitting opposite her. Stoker couldn't see Lizzie's face, but judging from Klingman's they were having a great time. With his granite jaw, greying temples and sensitive-looking eyes Klingman looked more responsible than any bank loan ad. Stoker slid alongside Lizzie.

'That was quick,' Lizzie said.

'I'm sorry,' Stoker bitchily replied.

'You find anything?'

Stoker held the yo-yo between the tips of his fingers. Lizzie took the yo-yo and examined it. She was stumped.

'May I?' Klingman took the yo-yo from Lizzie's hand. Stoker noticed the matter-of-fact way that Klingman touched her.

'It's solid oak,' Klingman said. He let the yo-yo roll across the table, then scooped it up as it tipped over the edge.

'Handcrafted,' Stoker said.

Lizzie was unimpressed.

'It is rather interesting, in the light of the tragedy which has befallen your friend, that you should buy her a yo-yo,' Klingman said.

'That so?' Stoker asked vaguely, scooping up a mouthful of Lizzie's peach dessert.

'Have you heard of Freud's expression, Fort-Da?'

'Can't say I have,' Stoker said.

'Freud speaks of how a baby's identity is constructed in relation to the presence and absence of the mother. Fort! applies to loss, Da! to gain. In Freud's story the baby unravels a reel of cotton, watches in panic as it rolls away.'

'What has this got to do with a yo-yo?'

'A yo-yo leaves, then returns.'

'If it has a string. This one doesn't.'

'And yet it possesses the emblematic power to restore.'

'I guess you can make of it what you will,' Stoker said. He was peeved.

Lizzie picked up the yo-yo with renewed interest. Stoker ordered a coffee. He realised that he was about to explode.

The drive back to Obs was uneventful and strained. Lizzie gazed fixedly at the winding road, occasionally slowing down to admire a patch of vegetation, the sunlight across the factories of Paarden Eiland, the still beauty of the bay, Bloubergstrand in the distance to the west, the snowcapped Hottentots-Holland mountains to the north.

Lizzie had the vivid penetrating look of someone on acid. Everything was too interesting. Stoker shut up. He guessed Lizzie was happy and that it had everything to do with Grant fuckin' Klingman. He'd quite liked the guy until he'd broken off into symbols and theories. Stoker was superstitious. He hated shrinks and psychologists. He couldn't stand the idea of everybody rubbing off their pain onto everybody else. In this respect he and Phyllis were kindred spirits. Phyllis hated having ideas about anything, hated dumping her feelings like they were nuclear waste. Real conversation belonged to amateurs of the heart, she said. He'd always liked the phrase, the sense of being an amateur. Phyllis had a whole store of phrases that kept popping up, then were swiftly forgotten. It was Stoker who'd kept Phyllis's gems alive. He kept them in his biscuit tin.

Stoker battled to set aside Klingman's theory about the emblematic power of yo-yos. It was a fuckin' yo-yo, for chrissakes. What about the weight? The grain? Why did it have to be a symbol for something else? Why did people constantly have to connect everything to everything else? Symbols, theories, metaphors were the culprits. Metaphor was the equating of the unequal, Stoker remembered Dylan saying. The notion made complete sense to Stoker. It was a notion he applied to the workings of his own art. For him painting wasn't an excuse for words, though of course he'd invariably have to say something about what he'd done. For some unfathomable reason people expected the artist to take them on a guided tour. Dangle a carrot and people raved. The fuckin' sloths! Stoker had read *Real Presences* by George Steiner. The book had served as grist for his mill. Steiner wanted to abolish art criticism and get down to the thing in itself, uncluttered by third-rate and third-hand information. This was the way that Stoker saw the world, except of course the world had to have a different idea of itself. The world couldn't make a move without mirrors. And neither, it seemed, could he. Stoker could not escape the fact that he too existed in a labyrinth of associations. Besides, he also worked with references. Who didn't? He just hated having to make a big song and dance about it.

'You want to come over for coffee?' Lizzie asked.

Stoker knew that Lizzie wanted to talk. He didn't. 'No,' he said.

'I'll see you later then,' Lizzie said, slightly miffed.

'Yeah. I'll see you at Bridge's.'

Stoker climbed out of the Beetle. He turned to close the door.

'By the way, Grant will be joining me at Bridge's,' Lizzie said.

'Great,' Stoker said.

As he opened his front door he hoped he'd sounded convincing.

CHAPTER ELEVEN

Stoker entered his bedroom to find Phyllis. She was seated cross-legged, going through his will.

'Howzit sweetheart,' Stoker said. He tossed aside his dufflecoat, then he lay on the bed, gazing at the ceiling. Waiting.

'It's good to know you're worth a snackwich machine and a kettle,' Phyllis said. Stoker was in no mood to be baited. He continued staring at the ceiling.

'I suppose this is what you've been doing? Your so-called walkabout?'

'Uh huh.'

Phyllis set aside the will and stood staring at Stoker staring at the ceiling. 'I missed you,' Phyllis said.

'I missed you too.' Stoker realised that he wasn't lying. 'How did you get in, by the way?' he asked.

'Jay. He borrowed your leather jacket.

'You mind if we don't talk, Phyllis? I'm feeling knackered. I just want to lie down and say nothing. Why don't you come over and lie with me.'

Phyllis walked over and draped herself around Stoker's prone body. They lay together without saying a word. Stoker could feel the steady heaving of Phyllis's chest. He rolled over and moved his thigh between her legs. He remembered how he'd once hated the clamminess of her skin, as he ran his hands along her thighs and gathered the hibiscus pattern of her dress into a bundle around her waist. Without saying a word he entered her, lay with his cock throbbing inside her. Then, slowly, Phyllis started moving, her suckling cunt slipping back and forth. His lust kindled, Stoker started fucking, his movements brief, regulated. He barely breathed, the denim around his crotch soaked with Phyllis's come, his neck to her lips. Eventually he rolled over, his cock still throbbing, then dying as he fell asleep.

When Stoker awoke Phyllis was gone, the light slanting in a new direction. This was always the way he and Phyllis reconverged. A few words, a latent fleeting tension, silence, a fuck. It was the truth of feeling that counted. They trusted their bodies more than their minds, their need for each other like a locking in outer space, a space beyond the room they were in, beyond the city, the world as they knew it. Stoker could slip inside Phyllis as in a dream. She let the boundaries fall away. There were no questions, no recriminations. He could enter her blind and she would help him find a way. If he had a future, it was with her. This knowing was not a conscious thing. It wasn't a contract. Phyllis, he knew, lived in a flawed weak world, in which she lifted when most people crushed, saved when others destroyed.

Stoker knew that he was apt to blow Phyllis out of proportion. There was nothing ideal about her, and it was this that he loved the most.

Stoker lay in bed feeling lucky for the link that bound them. He listened to the stairs creak, watched as the bedroom door opened. It was Jay.

'Howzit bru,' Jay said.

Stoker stared at Jay as he slithered across the floor.

Jay was a snake, a nasty beautiful snake . . . passionate . . . sinister . . . a creature lost in a wilderness clamouring to be heard on terms which were his own. He played without rules, without respect, Stoker thought, watching Jay move towards him. He said one thing and did another. No one trusted him. Still, most people fell victim to his charms in some way. Dom for instance. Himself. Most people. Jay let you know he was a creep, then made you feel it was an achievement to like him.

Stoker hadn't bothered to let Jay know that he was sick to

death of his leather jacket going astray. The only way he could physically stop Jay from having his own way was by killing him. And the last thing he wanted was Jay's blood on his hands.

'You coming to Bridge's tonight?'

Stoker didn't answer.

'Dayglo, Percy and me will be playing.'

'Sounds good,' Stoker said. He'd heard Nappy Rash a thousand times. They were a good enough band but he was tired of hearing them. He wished they'd cut a record and fly off somewhere. LA maybe. Somewhere where he didn't have to see them. The best thing that could happen to Jay was fame. Stoker prayed for everyone's sake it would happen soon. The thing was, Jay was the genuine article, which, Stoker supposed, was why he was such a creep. Who said great people had to be nice?

'You mind if I hold onto your jacket?'

'No problem,' Stoker said. Then, impetuously he added: 'Keep it.' Jay evidently had more use for it than Olivieri.

'You giving it to me?'

'You may as well keep it, Jay. I smell you every time I wear it. If I were looking for a second skin it wouldn't be yours.'

'I take it that's an insult?'

'It's the truth.'

'There's no truth, bru. See it as an insult, it's more honest. You want to hear a song I'm working on?'

'Do I have a choice?'

'You're the best ear I've got, Stoker.'

'I know fuck-all about music, Jay.'

'Sure you do.'

Jay was looking at the rooftops from Stoker's loft window. There was no denying he was beautiful. It was a creepy beauty. His nose like a hawk, his lips always faintly wet, his cat's eyes, the hair like freshly-laid tar, the rippling dagger-like length of him . . . Jay reminded Stoker of Viggo Mortensen in *Indian Runner*, a bad seed with genius. He watched as Jay started to sing, the words coming out with a hiss. He knew that Jay could hear the instruments filling the voice, could feel the voice tear away casually. Nothing was emphasised, nothing done to death. Stoker relented, closed his eyes and listened. He let himself be blown away by the swell, the simplicity, the crux of pain, the craving for love. It would have to take someone as twisted as Jay to work up such hunger and loss, Stoker thought.

'It's called "Dark Age of Trust".'

'It's beautiful, Jay.'

'You think so?'

'It's perfect.'

'I figured you'd like it.'

Stoker hadn't seen Jay since the Seeff exhibition, hadn't heard him sing since the night Jay's voice had accompanied him like a shadow as he veered diagonally into the wasteland of rubble and mud. Stoker suddenly felt the need to be with him. Jay's song had twisted its way into his heart. He was suddenly looking forward to Bridge's party, looking forward to Nappy Rash. Stoker chuckled just thinking of the name. It was a stupid, crazy, puerile name.

Stoker dug the yo-yo from his pocket and tossed it over to Jay. Jay clutched it in the palm of his hand.

'There's energy here,' Jay said.

'Probably because it's been nesting right next to my balls,' Stoker said.

Jay sniggered.

'When did you write that song?'

'A while ago. It's been coming slowly, you know. With the music and everything it runs to ten minutes.'

'It feels like a lifetime to me.'

'Yeah. There's a lot of Dom and me in that song.'

'You two still fighting the big fight?'

'We're too bloody exhausted with it all. Still, we're hanging in there. Who knows. Right now she can't stand me, but it shifts, you know. Love's a fickle thing. What do you say we head down to the Heidelberg, get some burgers and beer? I'm paying.'

'Sounds good.'

'I'll see you downstairs. I need a crap,' Jay said as he turned to leave. 'Thanks for the jacket,' he added. 'You can change your mind if you feel like.'

'It's yours,' Stoker said as he watched Jay leave the room, Jay's voice still ringing in his ears, warming him all over.

Stoker lay on the bed thinking of 'Dark Age of Trust', of Dom and Jay. Things never seemed to be working between them, but still they stuck together. Dom seemed to be the one consistent thing in Jay's heart. She was his anchor and she hated it. Stoker couldn't blame her. Jay was definitely not easy to live with. Fuckin' musos, Stoker mused. They always had one thing on the brain. Music. Dayglo wasn't any different. And he? Stoker felt lucky to have someone as intact and understanding as Phyllis. Still, there was no knowing when his luck would run out.

Stoker got up. He made a mental note to wipe the come stains off his denim crotch as he descended the stairs. In the hallway he saw Jay put down the phone. Jay's face was ashen.

'What's up?'

'It's James, he's dead. The man's dead.'

'James Phillips?' Stoker stupidly asked.

Jay nodded.

'Jesus fuck. How?'

Jay remained seated, freaked. Then he rose and steered Stoker through the front door. Stoker could feel Jay shaking.

The Heidelberg Tavern was across from Gloria's Diner on Station. Jay and Stoker stepped in. Neither said a word. The place was packed with people who had no idea about Jay's grief. And yet there was a sick appropriateness about their going to the Heidelberg, Stoker thought.

Around three years ago, on a day like today, a group of gunmen carrying AK47s had walked in and killed three students drinking beer. Stoker hadn't thought about the murders for a while, except now with James's death the memories started flooding back – the suddenness, the arbitrariness of it all! Stoker and Waldo had thought of going to The Heidelberg on the day of the PAC killings. Who knows? They could have been blown away too. They could have been victims of a cause as pointless.

Stoker didn't know James the way Jay did, but he knew about death, about senselessness, the memory of his murdered parents merging with the Heidelberg massacre. It figured that Phyllis, much as she preferred crayfish tails to flowers, would organise some wreaths in honour of the dead. This was way before he knew her.

As for Jay and James, they'd gone to school together in Springs. They'd played music together. Stoker may not have known James in the same way but the more he thought about it the more freaked he became. The last time Stoker had seen James was about five months ago at the River Club. At the time Phyllis was running the bar in the Water Room. James and Phyllis were old friends. They'd met way back when Phyllis had worked as a waitress in Yeoville, back in the days when she was still an avenging angel, in the days when she could look straight into the barrel of a gun. Phyllis was still as fearless, but she was no ways near as suicidal.

Somewhere along the line Cape Town had softened her. The reason James was at the River Club had to do with a combination of Phyllis and booze. Stoker had walked up to James. James, as usual, had asked him to sit down and have a beer.

'That's a good woman you've got there,' James had said, motioning at Phyllis as she walked away. Stoker had noticed that James's finger was bandaged. 'Broke it playing cricket,' he'd said. 'Can't play right now, music that is.' That was pretty much the last time Stoker had seen James.

Jay walked over with two pints. 'The burgers are on the way,' he said, planting himself opposite Stoker. For a while all they could do was stare at each other. Stoker lit a cigarette.

'Want one?'

'Nah, thanks.' Jay downed his pint and called for another. 'I'd seen him in Grahamstown,' Jay began. 'You know about the accident?'

'I heard.'

What Stoker had heard was that the composer of *Faustus in Africa* had died in a car accident. He hadn't known it was James, hadn't bothered to enquire.

'You know what James said? He said that *Faustus* was going to be the last thing he did.' Jay sat staring at Stoker. Stoker couldn't recall Jay ever studying him so closely. What was he looking for? Stoker looked back, not knowing what to say.

'He'd had this car accident. He was driving back after dropping off a couple of girls. It turns out he was in love. You believe that? James had finally found someone crazy enough to live with him. Driving back he'd crashed the car. It was a crazy stupid thing to drive in the state he was in. Suffered a hairline fracture. He was put in hospital in Grahamstown. After two days the idiot checked himself out. The even bigger idiots at the hospital let him go. Just like that. Then things went from bad to worse. I don't know. There were complications. His liver packed up. Meningitis.'

'What's meningitis?'

'Fuck knows. Something to do with the brain freezing up or something. Does it fuckin' matter?' Jay's beer arrived. 'You sure you don't want another?'

'I'll wait.'

Stoker was picturing James's face. The one he remembered seeing five months ago. It was an eighteenth-century face, he thought. Something out of a Hogarth painting with his mutton-fat curls and long pointy nose like a question mark. The booze-green nicotine-stained eyes. Mostly he thought of James's low gravelly voice, the way James always seemed to be saying something designed specially for the person he was talking to. James had always had something good to say about what Stoker was doing. Come to think of it, he'd always had something good to say about anybody who was fighting to make something out of the country.

'It's a good thing *Sunny Skies* was released,' Stoker said.

'Was it? Who bought the record when it came out? Fuckin' Spliff. They'll probably be milking it for all it's worth now. I remember James telling me how disappointed he was with the distribution. How local music wasn't getting a hearing. And the way he said it – disappointed – I could feel his fuckin' heart was broken, man. Why the fuck does someone have to die so people can hear? It's sick, Stoker. The whole fuckin' disaster. What a waste. What a stupid fuckin' waste.'

Jay sat bent over and freaked. Tears dropped onto the jutting collar of his jacket. Stoker watched the tears as they slid glistening across the cracked leather. He was nervous. Usually Jay could twist his way out of any situation.

Maybe James wanted to die, Stoker thought. Maybe he meant it when he'd said that *Faustus* would be the last. But then, according to Jay, James had fallen in love. He'd found a woman. Stoker was feeling increasingly depressed. He knew that if he didn't leave the Heidelberg soon, they'd have to carry him out.

'James is a legend,' Stoker said. 'He'll keep on being a legend.' The acknowledgement was an obvious and feeble one. It was all he could muster.

Jay wasn't listening. He was far away, lost at high school in Springs. Him and James in high school.

The burgers arrived. Stoker and Jay ate in silence.

CHAPTER TWELVE

Bridge's farewell turned out to be James's. There wasn't a single person who hadn't heard and who wasn't freaked. The mood of the group shifted schizophrenically from tears to reflection to manic pleasure. Everyone knew or knew someone who knew James. Stoker doubted that any other death in the local music world, in the arts as a whole, could have produced the feelings that everyone was feeling. The party felt like a wake, the grief was active, wholesome. The *Sunny Skies* CD was playing. It felt like James was right there with them. Then Stoker realised that James had to be everywhere. He'd crossed the country a billion times, he'd entered the hearts of thousands of people. Everywhere people had to be thinking about James. In bars, living rooms, in lonely alley-ways, in every conceivable pit of hope and despair people were thinking of James.

Way beyond the booze and destruction there was a goodness, Stoker thought. Maybe James just didn't want to live any more. Who knows? Who could speak of the moment of death? No one. Stoker believed that in spite of the talk of medical fuck-ups, the talk of waste, James's death somehow felt right. He was still with them. He was here to stay. There had been nothing point-less about his existence. The dream and the power in the music far exceeded the flesh. 'We pick up the pieces,' Stoker muttered to himself. 'We gather all the scattered pieces. We are never com-plete, never whole. We belong to others the way others belong to us.'

Stoker could feel tears starting to well up. He was starting to choke. He needed to get out of the room, away from the manic despair, the music. He walked out the back door.

In Bridge's garden Stoker lit a cigarette. It was cold. The temperature had dropped radically. Everyone was inside. Sto-ker was glad for his duffle-coat, glad for the cold and isolation. He climbed up the fig tree in the garden. For what felt like ages this was where he sat, high up in the branches, black against the black sky. In the house next door he could see through a bedroom window. He smiled as he watched the two men through the window down below. They were both in bed read-ing books. Stoker struggled to work out what they were read-ing. He couldn't. They were both engrossed, the one with his back to the wall, the other flush. A gentle calm pervaded the scene, one of the loveliest Stoker had witnessed for some time. Two men in bed reading books.

'Stoker!' It was Bridge. 'Stoker!'

Stoker was tempted to reply, but something in him couldn't.

'You see Stoker?' Bridge was talking to Dean. 'If you see him, tell him some guy is here looking for him. Something about owing him a hundred or something.'

'Sure,' Dean said, stepping into the back garden. Dean was clearly not about to charge around looking for him. Stoker watched Dean pissing in the grass, Dean's arc of piss a glitter-ing yellow.

'You been mainlining vitamins?'

Dean looked around. He saw no one.

'I'm up here.'

Dean looked up. 'You been perving?' he asked.

'There's nothing much to see.'

'Fuck you,' Dean said.

'Come up.'

'Do I have to?' Dean asked.

'You've managed to get this far away from your home, you may as well climb up.'

Dean began to climb awkwardly up the tree. 'You expect me to climb all the way up there?'

'As far as you like.'

'It's fuckin' freezing. You should be inside. Bridge's been looking all over for you. There's some guy, I think he's German or something. He can't figure out why everybody keeps laughing and crying. He's sitting on Bridge's sofa drinking himself silly, waiting for you. You owe him a hundred.'

Dean managed to reach Stoker. He stared at the couple down below.

'Pretty sight,' Stoker said.

'Laura Ashley eat your heart out,' Dean said. He lit a joint and stared out across the black sky, past Groote Schuur Hospital, towards Devil's Peak, a giant wedge of rock before them. Dean passed the joint to Stoker.

'Swazi?' Stoker asked.

'Fuck knows. What's this tree we're sitting in?'

'Fuck knows.'

For a long time Dean and Stoker sat in silence and smoked. Then Stoker spoke. 'Those guys down there . . . they haven't said a word to each other in all the time I've been here. They've just been sitting and reading.'

'There's only so much talking a man can do,' Dean said. Just the way Dean said what he said made Stoker think of Dean screaming at his ex at the Lounge some time ago. He could still see the blood of Dean and his ex dripping off the map of the world that hung in one of the rooms. He could feel the lingering desperation in Dean's voice, the hopelessness, the dead space words inhabited when there was nothing left to say and you couldn't stop talking.

'You read, right?' Stoker said, cutting away from the bleakness in his brain.

'You know I read.'

'What happens to you when you read?'

'Is this a trick question?'

'Well?'

'Depends.'

'On what?'

'What I'm reading, you moron. Like dick fiction. Dick fiction's got its own laws. Stupidity is the key to dick fiction. The dick's usually a down-and-out misogynist. There's usually a truckload of mystery and it takes the whole book to solve the mystery. The dick can't be too clever. I like that. The fact it takes forever to work out the clues. Most people are like that. Most people are bad dicks.' Dean stopped. 'What are you asking me this for?'

'Just asking.'

'You bored?'

'Nah. I'm just sitting in a tree with you, Dean.'

'What do you think those guys are reading?'

'The guy with his back to the wall is reading something serious, like a history book. The book's got pictures.'

'Here.' Dean handed Stoker a loupe.

'What's this?'

'A loupe. For seeing things. Take a look.'

Stoker applied the loupe to his eye. 'It's too far away,' Stoker said.

'Here, let me take a look.' Dean held the loupe to his eye. 'You're right. I use it to look at things close up.'

'What for?'

'Just to see. Stuff. A scratch on an arm, a picture in a magazine. Stuff.'

'Have a feel.' Stoker handed Dean the yo-yo.

'It's got a lot of energy.'

'That's what Jay said.'

'Jay's pretty cut up by James's death,' Dean said.

'Your friends don't die on you that often,' Stoker said.

'Don't kid yourself,' Dean said. 'Death's popular these days.'

Stoker relit the joint. He saw that Dean was wearing a LOVE LIFE T-shirt, a flame burning at the fulcrum of a painted heart.

'Dean?!' It was Bridge.

'Yeah?'

'Where the hell are you?!'

'Up here.'

'You see Stoker?'

'He's right next to me. He's been here all the time.'

'Stoker.'

'I know.'

'Would you please talk to this guy? There's a guy here. He keeps talking to me about his great-grandfather. Said you'd give him an extra hundred for talking about his great-grandfather. It's an interesting story and all, but I'd appreciate it if you'd just talk to him. He's nervous as hell.'

'I'll be right down.'

'Well, make it snappy. Who is he anyway?'

Stoker leapt from the lower branches.

'You coming down, Dean?'

'Nah. I'll park off here. It's a kif spot.'

Stoker walked over to Bridge and gave her a huge hug.

'That's nice.'

'Close your eyes and open your hand.' Stoker placed the yo-yo in Bridge's hand. 'It's for you.'

'It's beautiful, Stoker.'

'You really think so?'

'It's absolutely beautiful.'

'I bought it from Immo this morning.'

'Immo? The guy whose been chewing my ear off about his great-grandfather?'

'The same.'

'Who is he?'

'I don't really know.'

'He's gorgeous.'

'You think so?'

'I love the way he talks.'

'You mean you love the way he looks.'

'He's sort of innocent and obsessive, you know? Like that guy in the book Dom gave me to read. Voss. That's it. That's the name of the guy. Some crazy German who dies trying to cross the Outback. It's terribly romantic. There's this English woman living on the frontier of the Outback. She writes all these deeply felt, restrained letters which Voss never receives. It's agonising.'

'Sounds worth a squiz,' Stoker said.

'You should read it. So where did you find him?'

'Who?'

'Who do you think?! Your wild friend from Borneo.'

'He's not my friend, Bridge. So don't get any ideas. I don't know him from a bar of soap. I just met him today. For all I know he's probably as twisted as the tree in your backyard.'

'Ask him to stay.'

'I'll do nothing of the sort.'

'Just tell him to enjoy himself. Tell him it's a special occasion. I told him about James. He didn't know who James was.'

'The guy's only been here a couple of days, Bridge.'

'Then enlighten him.'

'You having a good time?'

'Maintaining, you know.'

'Me too.'

'It's terrible about James.'

Stoker was in no mood. 'What's that line in *Predator II* again? The one the alien keeps saying?'

'Shit happens?'

'Exactly.'

Bridge got the message. 'Talk to Immo, please,' she said.

'Immo, is it?'

'Just tell him everything's fine. He just has to relax. Pour him a glass of wine or something. Here.' Bridge handed Stoker two glasses of red wine. 'Thanks a million for the yo-yo.'

'You should thank Immo. I just paid for it.'

Bridge kissed Stoker full on the lips and walked off. Stoker watched as she glided away in her pinafore, her pigtail bobbing. The test was negative, Bridge had said when he'd phoned her and she'd told him about the party. That's all she'd said about the rape. Could the test be final so rapidly? Death was popular these days, Dean had said. And Dean was right. Still, you had to believe you were exempt. Somewhere along the line you had to kick the fear.

Stoker walked over to Immo who was staring at one of Prue's pictures. He tried to see Immo through Bridge's eyes. He could see what she saw. The compactness, the sinuous strength, the thick black Walt Whitman beard, the crazy blue eyes.

Stoker joined Immo in front of Prue's sepia image of a black man, the man's face criss-crossed with barbed wire, scientific jargon purporting to describe the limits of the black man's brain stencilled into the bolted rusted frame. The image came from a book entitled *Native Life in South Africa*.

'You like it?' Stoker asked.

Immo turned to look at Stoker. He was all smiles, looking glad to meet someone he vaguely knew.

'It is a strong picture, I think.'

'It's Bridge's mother. She made it.'

'Oh? Really.' Immo seemed impressed. 'It is different now, you think? In South Africa?' he asked.

Stoker was sceptical. Still, he was in no mood to be a wet blanket. Immo was so starry-eyed, he'd probably left Munich or somewhere, hitched down through Africa, wanting to see what all the fuss was about in the southern tip.

As it turned out Immo had come from a village outside of Bremen called Stühr. He was a panel-beater. He'd in fact walked down Africa. Stoker was flabbergasted and hugely impressed. He'd never met anyone who'd done anything so insane.

'Why did you walk down Africa?' Stoker asked.

'Anger,' Immo replied. That was it. There was no subtext. No moral. Nothing.

'Anger?' Stoker repeated, wondering if he'd heard Immo correctly.

'Anger,' Immo said, apparently without the faintest inclination to elaborate.

Stoker tried to imagine how angry a person had to be to do something that stupid. He studied Immo's face and couldn't find a trace of anger anywhere. All he could see was someone who seemed gentle and lost.

'You got a place to stay?' Stoker asked.

'Bridget, she say I can stay here.'

'Here?' The conniving little slut, Stoker thought, and smiled.

'Yes. She say I must stay here.'

'You know she's leaving soon. She's going to Turkey.'

'Yes,' Immo said. 'I know she is going. That is why you are all here.'

Bridge had given Stoker no indication that she'd wanted Immo to stay. It was just like her. He guessed she could do what she wanted. It was her house. Besides, it sort of made sense. She could go to Turkey and Immo could look after the place. Still, it seemed pretty sudden to Stoker. Even he didn't have the faintest idea who Immo was. All Stoker knew was that Immo had once been very angry, that he was a panel-beater who came from a village outside of Bremen. Immo could be a serial killer for all he knew. Stoker somehow regretted inviting the bearded crazy-looking stranger to the farewell party. He handed Immo the hundred he owed him. He suddenly felt as though he'd been way too generous.

'Who is James Phillips?' Immo asked.

'A bru,' Stoker said. He was in the mood to use words unintelligible to foreigners.

'Bru?' Immo asked.

Stoker relented. 'A friend. A brother.'

'Sunny skies,' Immo said. His face was beaming.

'Sunny skies,' Stoker said, and clinked his glass against Immo's.

Stoker could feel his gut clench. And then he saw James laughing at him, laughing at the craziness of a lone German walking down Africa and ending up at a party to celebrate his death.

CHAPTER THIRTEEN

When Phyllis arrived the party was in full swing. Nappy Rash were going wild, doing renditions of James's songs. Immo was dancing with Bridge, Immo leaping about like a whirling dervish and making everyone's eyes pop, Bridge swinging and churning at the belly. Dean was doing his slow steady sway, his limbs out of synch. Stoker stood with his back to the wall, his legs crossed, staring at Bridge. He was amazed how vibrant she seemed, her pigtail slashing the air like a whip. She was hell-bent on enjoying herself. Moving on. The rape was a fact she couldn't vault, still, she was going to enjoy herself in spite of it. She had to get her strength from Prue, Stoker thought. He doubted he could marshal resources like Bridge's under the same circumstances. He pictured himself being raped, pictured the hard-on he'd seen on Sandy Bay ramming its merry way up his arsehole. And then he saw Phyllis as she thrashed and grooved across the room, kissing everyone as she wove her way towards him. She wore her tapered brown fake fur, hot pink minidress, gold shoes, and a fat string of green and blue beads. She'd made the necklace herself out of bits and pieces from Dom's bead shop.

Phyllis was laughing loudly, moving wildly. Stoker noticed that the kohl around her eyes had smeared. She drew him onto the floor. He couldn't resist. Pressed close to Phyllis, her crotch grinding against his, he saw her bloodshot eyes. He realised that she needed to hold him and so he let her move him across the floor, Dayglo driving hard on the drums, Percy cruising, Jay howling.

'Hello chooks.'

Stoker didn't say a word. He simply held her, let her release her weight upon him. Phyllis had taken the initiative so that she could fall into his arms, let loose all her pent-up rage and pain. She'd known James longer, harder, deeper. She and James went way back. Stoker knew that the last thing Phyllis needed were words of consolation. He veered away from the tragedy, stuck to details they could chew and spit out.

'How's Frogg?' Stoker could smell the brandy as she breathed against him.

'I quit.' Phyllis was always quitting. Stoker let it slide. 'You?' Phyllis asked with her smeared Cleopatra eyes.

'Spent the afternoon at the Heidelberg with Jay. Then here.'

Phyllis wasn't really listening. 'It was the fucking TV,' she said, sticking to the thought in her brain. 'You believe that? I found out through the TV. I'd gone to get a coffee. You know they've got TVs all over the fucking complex. And there it was. Some fuckwit telling me that James was dead.'

She was sobbing. Stoker could feel her nails digging into him, as though she were holding on to a cliff. He winced, kept holding her. There was nothing he could do, nothing he could say. James's death was bad enough. Finding out through the TV was the pits. Phyllis hated TV. It was the beginning of the end in South Africa, she'd said. He thought of Phyllis's words – all we do is gather up the pieces – words she'd said to him when he'd broken down at the Happy Wok. He let her scream, let her pierce him because it was inside him that she wanted to scream. No one tried to shut her up. Dayglo drove harder. Jay blew every fuse he could blow. Phyllis's screams lifted the night to a different pitch, drawing everyone into the trashed country of her pain and sorrow. Then, just as violently, as abruptly, she stopped, the music falling with her whisperings, then soaring as she broke away from Stoker. She started thrashing and grooving again, her attention directed to Jay, then shifting away from the band to Bridge. Bridge crying and laughing and grooving.

94

Stoker lit a cigarette and walked off the dance floor. Phyllis would be fine, he thought. Bridge too. Everything was going to be fine. Phyllis had performed the exorcism. She was the bimbo-shaman.

Stoker walked through to the kitchen and poured himself a glass of wine. Outside a fire was blazing. Stoker joined Dean and Putter by the fire. Putter was toasting a marshmallow.

'You want one?' Putter asked.

'Wouldn't say no.' Stoker popped the scorched marshmallow into his mouth.

'It's laced,' Dean said. Stoker had never had a laced marshmallow.

'What's inside?' Stoker asked.

'Nexus, Plexus and Sexus,' Putter said. He was giggling uncontrollably.

'I'm looking forward to looking as stupid as you do,' Stoker said.

'You feel like checking up on our couple next door?' Dean asked.

'Think I'll stay on terra firma for a while,' Stoker said.

'It won't be firm for long,' Dean said, and lifted himself into the fig tree with a newfound ease. Stoker watched as Dean rippled up into the topmost branches.

'Just be careful, Dean. The last thing we want is for you to break your neck and ruin the party,' Stoker said.

'We don't even want you to waste our time calling the ambulance,' Putter added.

'Watch out now,' Stoker persisted, listening to Dean tittering crazily.

'Think of the rest of us. We're all too fucked to be worrying about each other,' Putter said.

'They're fucking,' Dean hissed. 'God! What a beautiful sight!'

Putter was suddenly curious. 'Who's fucking?' he asked.

'Some guys,' Dean said.

'How many?'

'Just two, you greedy bastard.'

'Dean's having me on, right?'

'I doubt it,' Stoker said.

'Can you see everything?'

'In fuckin' technicolor, man.'

Putter climbed the tree and joined Dean. In silence they sat and watched the couple fuck.

Stoker sat by the fire and thought about Dylan. Now that Phyllis had quit work they could take time out, a couple of days maybe, and see Dylan. They could leave tonight or start out early in the morning. Phyllis could use some fresh air, space. They could go fishing maybe. He'd have to fix things with Olivieri. There was only so far Stoker could push him.

Phyllis came over and sat beside Stoker. 'Bridget loves the yo-yo,' she said.

'Thought she would.'

'Lizzie's here, by the way. She's just walked in with a dish called Grant something or other.' Phyllis cradled her head in Stoker's lap and stared into the flames.

'They met today, at Nino's. This morning,' Stoker said.

'That's fast.'

'You know Lizzie, she cuts through the crap one time. What with Dayglo fucking out on her and senility creeping in, she wants a man and she wants him now.'

Phyllis chuckled. It was good to hear her chuckle.

'I was thinking maybe we could go away for a few days, now that you've quit Frogg.'

'Where?'

'Somewhere. I thought we could go to Dylan's. We don't have to stay there. We could go on a road trip.'

'What about Olivieri?'

'I thought maybe Immo could fill in for me. He's doing nothing right now.' This was the first time Stoker had thought of Immo in connection to work.

'Immo? You mean that hairy freak Bridget's hanging out with?'

'The same.'

'You know he's going to be house-sitting when Bridge goes away?'

'She's not going away.'

'What?'

'She's cancelling her ticket.'

'You're kidding. Why?'

'You should take a look at Immo and you'll know. Those two are all over each other.'

'Jesus fuckin' Christ. First it's Lizzie and this guy Klingman, now it's Bridge and fuckin' Omo!'

'It must be a full moon rising or something.' Phyllis was giggling. Then sadness once again overtook her. 'Bridget's decided that the party's a farewell for James. Makes sense, don't you think?'

'Right now I'd prefer not to think,' Stoker said. He was starting to feel the effect of the laced marshmallow. 'You mind if we go?' he asked. 'I need to stretch my legs.'

'Alright,' Phyllis said.

'Cheers,' Stoker said to Dean and Putter. There was no reply. They were rapt with attention.

'What are those two up to?' Phyllis asked.

'They're learning about the birds and the bees,' Stoker said.

CHAPTER FOURTEEN
_____

Dawn had broken by the time Stoker and Phyllis finally left Bridge's party. They'd left Phyllis's bakkie on Norfolk and walked. The laced marshmallow had sharpened everything for Stoker. His mind was a river, his body charged with renewed energy. Phyllis on the other hand was dog tired. In the tall grass that lined the Black River she'd fallen asleep. The air was crisp, the grass dry. Stoker covered Phyllis with his duffle-coat, then proceeded to stroll through the long grass. He stopped at the bird sanctuary, then he wove through a warren of nests perched amongst the tall reeds. The bird sounds were exquisite to his laced ear. At a distance he studied the bill formations and colours of feathers. His gut felt as liquid and cold as the Cango Caves. He felt the cramping of his innards, knew the pain would pass. Eventually he settled in the tall grass next to Phyllis and yielded to the river in his mind, Phyllis's breathing heavy yet constant beside him.

He studied the zig-zag of her body, the glistening helmet of red hair, the smudged eye-liner, the full lips faintly parted. Her clasped hands and crossed legs. Her bare shins. Her gold shoes glittering like tinsel in the tall green grass. Then Stoker turned his eyes away in a slow broad arc, devouring all within his vision, the broken arm of river, the highway beyond, the swollen dome of the observatory amidst the low canopy of trees behind him, the madhouse at his back to the left with its eerily still barracks. How often he had walked along the Liesbeek and Black rivers which, like a double stitch, passed the lower boundary of Obs. How eerily still Valkenberg had always seemed to him with its raised windows that defied the prying eye. Here, just beyond his purview, madness was installed. He pictured the smocked patient he'd once seen ascending a freshly-cut field, carrying a water canister. Then, shifting his mind's eye back to the crooked oily arm of river, he thought of the beginnings of things, of rivers and trees and swamp. He wished that the river wasn't polluted. He felt like swimming, yielding to a current greater than himself.

Yes . . . they'd go away for a while. He'd fax Dylan. He'd leave a note for Olivieri explaining the situation, suggest that Immo take over for a few days. He and Immo had already talked about it. A deal was struck. There was just the fine-tuning left to do. Since the bakkie was still on Norfolk, he'd talk to Bridge about looking after Phyllis's cat. For now he'd stay put until Phyllis awoke. They'd pack the bakkie and head north. Phyllis wanted to go to the hot springs in Citrusdal. She had a friend who worked there as an aromatherapist and masseuse. Both he and Phyllis could do with a solid pummelling. His joints were aching and it wasn't just the lingering night chill. After a few days away they'd come back. Phyllis would have to find a new job, he'd have to start painting.

Stoker had been thinking of two-metre-high canvases, a scale larger than he'd attempted before. He'd been thinking of great swaths of earth the size of coffins dislodged through the force of magnetism, hanging charged and suspended above a betrayed and gaping earth. Of nails impaled into the wooden arm of a hammer. Of a Yale lock, a three-pronged plug torn from its mains, suspended above a suitcase. The recurring image he saw was the suitcase. He'd seen an image of a man seated on the suitcase in an open field. He'd realised that the image he'd seen was an adaptation of a Joy Division poster with Ian Curtis seated on a suitcase, his grey flannelled legs folded, his brogues shimmering, the sleeves of his shirt folded at the elbow, his languid fingers clutching a smoking cigarette, his hair cut like an ancient Roman's. As the remembered image surfaced, its protagonist was supplanted. It was not Curtis Stoker finally saw, but himself. In the end only the suitcase had remained – signalling arrival? Departure? Stoker wasn't sure. He saw only a suitcase. He could not determine whether it was full or empty. He could never fathom what, if anything, was inside. Just the suitcase then. And then Stoker had started thinking of carborundum, brick dust, paint. Seated in the tall green grass, immersed in the fullness of a broken dawn, he saw the canvas blazing with reds and ochres. He thought of a working title – *Domestic Baggage*.

A blackbird settled on the grass beside him. Stoker watched as it fluffed its emerald feathers, hovered, then settled on Phyllis's hip. He wondered if he'd tell Phyllis about the bird which had come to her in her sleep. Then Phyllis stirred. The bird remained perched on her hip. Phyllis lay staring at Stoker, her head cradled in the crook of her arm.

'Make us some coffee, would you.'

'We'd have to head home first.'

'Oh,' Phyllis said, staring sleepily at the nature that surrounded her.

'I could head back to the car. Sort things out.'

'You remember Chunky Charlie?' Phyllis was in no mood for reason.

'Who the hell is Chunky Charlie?'

'You don't know Chunky Charlie? Shame on you, Stoker.'

'Please. Enlighten me.' Stoker lit a cigarette.

'Chunky Charlie was a photo strip about a fat black man with a magic coat. He could produce toasters and fridges and three course meals from his coat pocket. The strip was big in the '70s.'

'I'm sorry my duffle-coat doesn't work in the same way.'

Phyllis wasn't listening, entangled as she was in the drowsy web of her own thoughts. 'I used to love Chunky Charlie. It was one of Chan's favourites. He'd saved them for me.'

'It's a bit sick, don't you think?'

'What?' Phyllis asked, veering into the country of dialogue.

'A black guy in '70s South Africa – producing toasters and fridges and pots of espresso from his coat pocket.'

'I didn't think of that. I suppose it is a bit perverse.'

'A bit?!' In Phyllis it had always been difficult to distinguish naivety from innocence. 'Look, what I'll do is head off, sort out Olivieri, pack the bakkie, some clothes for you. You want to go, right?'

'I want to go.'

Phyllis was still dog-tired and drained. Still, she seemed to want nothing more than to go away. Stoker watched as she held out her hand, watched as the blackbird settled upon it, then hopped back to her hip. Phyllis smiled. She glowed with a wan and sleepy radiance.

'I loved Chunky Charlie,' she said. 'Chunky Charlie was better than Kid Colt . . . Lone Wolf . . . Rocco de Wet . . . Grensvegter . . . Die Wit Tier . . . Dokter Conrad Brand . . . Swart Luiperd . . .'

Phyllis had fallen back into a deep sleep. Stoker had to pick the keys from her pocket, the blackbird like a sentinel on her hip.

While Phyllis slept amidst the tall grass beside the Black River, Stoker missioned. He had no trouble packing his own gear since he'd already sorted out the contents of his life. His clothes and toiletries were in order. His camping gear – pots, pan, grid, Cadac – were scrubbed and ready. He would have to think for Phyllis. There was nothing she needed more than to be taken care of. James's death had wiped her out in a way Stoker had never seen before. Beneath the tears, the screaming, the laughter, lay a numb and blighted heart. He pictured her on the water's edge, a discarded doll, a corpse. She would sleep forever if she could, release herself from the waking world, from memory. He'd have to make sure it didn't happen, he thought, as he opened the door to her flat on the corner of Orphan and Long.

Phyllis lived with her cat, Petal. Stoker smiled as he watched Petal brush her arched body against his leg. He scooped her into his arms and closed the door. Then he laid her back on the hallway floor. Stoker was tempted to play his favourite trick, sticking masking tape to Petal's paws and watching her freak out. But there was no time. He worked his way through the flat, gathering up the essentials.

No amount of love, no degree of friendship, could overcome Phyllis's fundamental need to live alone. Petal was no more than an adjunct, the most intimate illustration of Phyllis's aloneness. It was simpler, she'd said. Cleaner. Stoker had always understood Phyllis's drive to be alone, but never her reasoning. He moved from room to room.

She'd need her toiletries, bather, clothes, a book. Her huggable pumpkin globe? Beside her bed he found a copy of *The Waiting Country*, a marker jutted out halfway. Her boots, socks, three dresses, jerseys, overcoat. Even in the country she would need the spectacle of colour, the distraction of detail. Stoker realised that he'd never dressed Phyllis. He imagined what she'd want, not what he desired. Phyllis dressed for no one but herself. Thigh-high suede boots, Nikes and sandals took care of the shoe front. A pink polo-neck, a bright blue cardigan covered with ducks, red jeans, a yellow woollen skirt. Sunglasses. Tapes.

Stoker took one last glance at the bedroom. He checked to see if the answering machine was on. In the kitchen he found a box of rye biscuits, two cans of condensed milk and a can of caramel. He packed a can opener, chopping board, cutlery. In the bathroom he scooped up an extra roll of toilet paper, Phyllis's toothbrush, shampoo and hot oil. Was her period due? He packed everything into a large red suitcase. Lastly, he packed Petal into the cat-box. Then he closed the door and left.

He opened the back of the bakkie and packed Phyllis's suitcase and cat-box. He'd already laid out the mattress and bedding in case she needed to sleep. He realised that he was still tripping, their bodies out of synch, Phyllis closing in on herself, needing the safety of her shell, while he grew raw to the splendour of the world.

'It's okay, Petal. You won't be cooped for long. Bridge will take care of you.' Stoker stared deeply into Petal's unblinking slate eyes. Then he reclosed the cat-box.

Phyllis was still sleeping when he walked through the grass towards her. In his hand he held a flask of coffee and a cup. With a blade of grass he tickled Phyllis's nose. She wriggled, then blearily stared up, her hand shielding her eyes from the sun. Stoker produced her sunglasses and poured her a cup of coffee.

'Thanks, Chunky,' she said.

Stoker bent down and kissed Phyllis. She was willing, yet he could sense that she felt a terror of being overwhelmed. He pulled away, realising that he wanted nothing more than to fuck her. Surely it would be the best thing for both of them? Still, he could see that she was elsewhere, clinging to the space of dream . . . a fat black man with a magic coat stuffed with goodies.

'Everything's ready,' Stoker said.

'You're a darling,' Phyllis said. 'My darling.' She spoke with a deep tiredness, as though she possessed the stamina for love but not the stamina to act upon it. Stoker took Phyllis in his arms and lifted her. In silence they walked to the bakkie.

'You want to sit in the front or back?'

'I'm alright,' Phyllis said. 'I'll be alright.' And climbed into the passenger seat.

Stoker reversed off the gravel drive to the river and headed for the N7. For a long time Phyllis didn't say a word, her eyes blacked out by the sunglasses, her posture oddly erect as though perched – alert yet passive. Stoker drove in silence, the city dwindling as they headed north, becoming a wake of brick and plaster.

'I thought we should go to the hot springs first.'

'That's good,' Phyllis said. There was no enthusiasm in her voice. Yet there was a trust. Stoker would lead the way.

'You want to hear some music?' Stoker asked.

'If you want.'

They drove in silence.

Citrusdal was two and a half hours away. They would get there in time to pitch the tent in daylight. There was no rush. They could take it slow, go off the beaten track if they felt like it. Maybe stop for a picnic. It would be better to see Dylan later. Right now they needed each other. Their own silence.

Stoker had never seen Phyllis so silent, never witnessed a dimension of grief so vast within her. Unwashed, uncaring, she sat beside him, a blade of grass in her dyed hair, his duffle-coat wrapped about her. He noticed that she was no longer staring vacantly before her. He could sense a slow and steady interest as they crossed the surrounding countryside, the chequered fields of hay, the lolling cows beneath a swath of shade, the Piketberg mountains in the advancing distance, the washed blue and the glints of orange of the Cederberg beyond. She had slept long and deeply. The duffle-coat was beginning to fall away, the warmth of the sun playing against the bare flesh above her breasts. Her plastic necklace glittering.

'Could we stop? I've got a fat piss,' she said.

Stoker swerved the car onto the gravel shoulder. He lit a cigarette and watched her step out, remove her fake fur, and stare at the valley below. Then she walked a few feet away and squatted. Stoker discovered the gathered and sheltered remains of a tree and began snapping the dried twigs and putting them into bundles. It seemed to him that for miles around this was the only sound. The snapping of twigs.

'Get the Cadac out, would you.' He needed to delegate. Phyllis needed something to do. 'Check the lower left corner for water, coffee, sugar, Long Life.' It felt strange to list the ingredients for a cup of coffee, as though she were a creature unschooled and alien, a creature who had lost track of what most people took for granted. . . . Long Life . . . The words echoed in Stoker's brain. They seemed to him to echo across the whole valley.

Phyllis lit the gas and heated the water. She sat on the stone wall and looked down into the valley below, down into the distant troughs of shimmering water. She listened to the hiss of the Cadac, the brittle snapping of twigs.

'Kindling,' Stoker said, as if she didn't know. Kindling . . . He was smiling his winning smile as he said the word whose meaning reached beyond the function it was performing. She'd eventually talk, he thought. She'd ease into a more pliant and open register. He was in no hurry. He wanted her to know that. To know that he wasn't dead inside. That he was there for her. She could fall and he would hold her. She could scream inside him and he would echo the pain.

Stoker stacked the kindling into three black rubbish bags. Then he proceeded to hack the thicker branches with his axe. The day glittered with a chilly brightness.

In silence they drank their coffee.

The hot springs were tucked in a wooded vale, sixteen k's from the highway. In the distance the Cederberg stretched up into a clear sky. Stoker parked the bakkie outside Reception and booked in. The camping site cost twenty rand a day.

When Stoker returned to the bakkie Phyllis was gone. She must have headed to her friend Hedda's place. Hedda, the aromatherapist and masseuse. He'd leave her be and sort out the camp for the night.

Driving in he'd noticed that his favourite spot, Site 26, was free. After working out the direction of the wind, he backed up the bakkie so they could face the warm stream. Then he switched on Radio Lotus. A soundtrack for some Indian movie played while he sorted out the fire. More than anything he knew that Phyllis would want warmth. The music snaked through the trees. The couple in the movie would most probably be chasing each other through the trees, Stoker thought. The woman doing a twirl, her sari all aglitter and flowing, the guy in a white shirt and pants with a shitty moustache and too much chest hair and Brylcreem. The two of them singing away – synched of course. The bits in the trees were the best. Before the caste wars and the shitty conflicts. That's Bollywood. Then Stoker chuckled as he recalled Dean's take on the local movie industry. JOLLYGOOD. Trust Dean to come up with such a gem. Tonight they'd have braaied chicken and rice, Stoker thought.

Stoker set up the tent and packed all the perishables inside it. They'd probably sleep in the bakkie. He could feel rain coming. While he had the gap, he concentrated on the coals – he'd need to cook the chicken.

The Citrusdal hot spring was one of Stoker's favourite places in the whole world. As a child his family would come here for day outings, sometimes weekends. Riebeek-Kasteel was a stone's throw away. The springs were more built up now. New chalets were cropping up along the forested slopes of the narrow valley. Still, his favourite spot was untarnished – a clearing beside a stream of steaming water. While the fire steadily blazed Stoker stripped and discreetly entered the warm water. He rested within a narrow crevice of rock, let the warm belching current beat against his neck and shoulders. He ran his hands through the silt and the rich red rank mud along the edges of the narrow stream. Then, slowly, he began to baste himself. Inhale the rich putrid smell of mud.

As children Lizzie, Dylan and Stoker loved to cover their bodies with tribal patterns of red mud and stalk each other through the rocks and trees. Dylan was the natural tracker. Stoker and Lizzie were the hunted, stifling their terrified giggles as they squeezed into concealed spaces – the shaded hollows of rocks, the leafy shelters of trees. Underbrush. Running his hands through the dreadlocked reeds that lined the stream, Stoker remembered how he and Lizzie had squeezed into a narrow hollow within the lip of the bank, the knotted reeds a perfect screen. For what still felt like hours Dylan had searched and searched, obsessively retracing his steps. Stoker could still feel the squelch of Dylan's footsteps, just an inch away from him and Lizzie. In the slivers of light he could still picture Lizzie's startled and excited brown eyes. She had held him, unafraid. The putrid smell of mud had filled the congested space in which they'd squeezed their small bodies. Dylan had been so close, and he hadn't been able to find them. This was their one victory, the first and last time Dylan would fail, the first and last time Stoker and Lizzie would outwit him. Dylan was a born hunter. One day it would be men Dylan would stalk and kill.

Phyllis appeared at the water's edge. Beside her stood Hedda. Stoker was glad to see Hedda. Glad for Phyllis's sake.

'You coming in?' he asked.

'Tonight,' Phyllis said. She was gathering her towel and toiletries. Stoker knew the ritual. For Phyllis the springs meant a swim in the hot pool, a Jacuzzi, a session with Hedda, then another dip in the pool. And then the camp-site.

'You'll eat with us, Hedda?'

'Will do,' Hedda said, stepping down into the water. She was a strong woman who wielded her weight with infinite gentleness. Stoker had never seen a woman more graceful. She pivoted on the mossy rock with complete control and balance. Then she slipped into the water, her long yellow hair fanning outward and quivering in the stream.

'Hedda,' Phyllis said.

'Yeah?'

''Give me an hour. I'll see you at the house.'

'I'm looking forward to it, doll.'

Hedda spoke with a voice at once abrasive and as soft as cotton wool. Phyllis and Hedda were once lovers, Stoker reminded himself. The affair had been brief. Their true journey was one which would be intermittent yet deep. Their lives had continued with the sweet memory of their lovemaking. According to Phyllis, Hedda had needed saving. They'd met at Magrawley's on Long about four years ago, Hedda seated at the bar, Phyllis singing a karaoke. These were their first coordinates. Phyllis had walked up to Hedda and asked her why she looked so sad. Hedda had been taken aback by her forthrightness.

'I'm mourning,' Hedda had said.

'Then I must help you,' Phyllis had replied. 'Come.'

And Phyllis had taken Hedda to her flat.

Hedda's lover had died in a fire. The reason for his death had remained a mystery. For three years her life had been destroyed. She'd walked through the city with a black cloud hovering above her. Phyllis could see the stain of cloud.

'People have colours,' Phyllis had said. 'I will show you how to shine.' Phyllis's words during one of her reflections on past loves. Words Stoker had cherished because they said so much about Phyllis, her way with people, with lovers . . . I will show you how to shine . . . Phyllis's grand legacy.

Stoker watched Hedda as she lay in the water, a beautiful smile upon her face, her sinuous body composed.

The move to the hot springs had been the best thing, Stoker thought. The city was destroying him. Here he could heal himself, and heal others. The sad and the wounded were the ones who came to the springs, Stoker reminded himself. Solemn tragic creatures like his parents, himself. Phyllis. Hedda. The waters were said to have miraculous powers. As a child this had not occurred to him. Then the springs were as miraculous as any natural setting. He had never thought that this was where his parents had come to heal themselves and each other.

Stoker climbed out of the water. The effect of the laced marshmallow was finally wearing thin. The light, he noticed, was glowing with a radiant deep pink. He wrapped a kikoi around his waist and slung on his duffle-coat. Then he laid out a plateau of coals, clamped the chicken to the grid, and boiled the rice.

'You staying long?' Hedda asked.

'A few days,' Stoker said.

'That's good. Could use the company.'

'What's the weather been like?'

'Wet nights. But the days have been grand. You planning on painting?'

'Just drawings. Wouldn't mind walking, though. Thought we could head off Algeria way, camp over at the Forestry Station maybe, move further afield. Head out into the mountains. Nothing's definite. You?'

'Tuesday's good for me. I've got some walks we could do.'

'Looking forward to it.'

'Phyllis okay?'

'She's fucked actually.' Then Stoker told Hedda about James's death.

'Jesus,' Hedda said. 'She loved James.'

Stoker stared into the trees and thought of death, of how everyone was walking towards a death which they could not conceive. The girls murdered at the Heidelberg Tavern. The pensioner he'd read about in *You* who'd been stabbed for a slab of Blossom margarine. His parents. James. Hedda's lover destroyed in a fire. Each death had its pointlessness and its singularity. Never judge a life by the way it ends, Dylan had said to him. There is no real connection. You could anatomise the body, but the spirit? Who can know the spirit of a man? Mystery clings to each one of us. Each one of us moving from day to day. Each with our own hopes, dreams, heartbreak. Dylan had a way with words.

Stoker thought of the incidental moments which had drawn him to James over the years. Somehow James wasn't dead, he thought. No – James was alive. James was with him, with Phyllis, with all those whom he had known and touched. Stoker smiled at James who he saw smiling at him. James was waving the finger he'd broken in a cricket match. The broken finger which had stopped him from playing music during the Christmas of '94. Yes . . . that was it. James had broken his finger. He couldn't play anymore.

Hedda handed Stoker a joint. He could feel her hand around his neck, her chest pounding against his. Nothing was said between them. Then Hedda spoke.

'I'll check you later. Phyllis is probably waiting for me.'

'Sure,' Stoker said. He needed to turn over the chicken. Slice some lemon.

'Hold onto the joint,' Hedda said.

Stoker realised that Radio Lotus had signed off. He noticed that it was dark but for the stars, the gridded plateau of burning coals.

CHAPTER SEVENTEEN

Phyllis and Stoker made love in the warm stream. In the flickering light of candles arranged about them he watched as Phyllis sang softly as she writhed above him, her voice gentle, tugging playfully as she sang the chorus of Robbie Robinson's song . . .

You don't stand a chance against
    my prayers
You don't stand a chance against
    my love
They outlawed the Ghost Dance
But we shall live again, we shall
    live again.

Hedda was seated by the fire, drumming in synch with the beat. Stoker was riveted to Phyllis's face, his hands holding her at the waist, her breasts swaying yellow in the light.

When Phyllis had returned from Hedda's he could see that she'd changed. Her pain had shifted to a deeper, more restful place. It was the old Phyllis he saw now, the old and the new. She had crossed the bridge of weeping. She had been altered by a death which had restored her to the land of the living.

You don't stand a chance against
   my prayers
You don't stand a chance against
   my love
They outlawed the Ghost Dance
But we shall live again, we shall
   live again.

Stoker listened to the low music emanating from the tape deck, to Hedda's steady drumming. He listened to Phyllis's sighs as she came, her sightless eyes lifted to the stars glittering through the trees, a faint drizzle falling upon her face. Stoker held on until she had released and then he came in turn, a low groan his only sound.

Hedda eventually joined them in the water, the candles spluttering then dying in the rain, the night withdrawing a need for eyes. Into the early hours of the morning they talked. Stoker spoke of angels, of how he had never believed in angels until now. Hedda spoke of the wild cats which were being systematically murdered by the local warden. Phyllis braided Hedda's hair in the dark. It felt like Braille, she'd said. My whole life feels like Braille. She wasn't struggling any more, she'd said. The language of darkness had come easily to her.

Neither Phyllis nor Stoker understood the meaning of what they were saying. Theirs was a truth wrapped in words as crunchy and sweet as lettuce leaves. Lettuce leaves wrapped around pieces of sautéed chicken, Phyllis had said, licking her lips and making smacking sounds so that Stoker and Hedda knew what she was doing. And then a silence set in. Their last words washed along by the stream. They lay in a crude circle, their bodies touching, yielding to the slow current, the brushing of limbs. The rain poured down upon them, the cold merging with the warm water whose source was deeper than they could imagine.

Stoker was the first to pull away. The laced marshmallow had finally worn him out. He needed to sleep. Phyllis meanwhile was waking up, becoming alive to the pouring night. While she and Hedda continued, moored yet drifting in the stream, Stoker dried himself under the back door of the bakkie. Then he climbed in beneath the covers. Through the night the rain pounded on the roof. Stoker slept through the storm, his a deep and blissful sleep.

The next morning he washed the dishes from the night before. Most of the work had been done by the rain. The water which he'd caught in a pot now boiled on the Cadac. Phyllis lay asleep. Stoker made two cups of coffee and handed one to Phyllis. Hers, he knew, would be cold by the time she was awake enough to drink it. She'd drink it all the same. Phyllis couldn't live without coffee first thing in the morning, whether hot or cold.

Stoker walked towards the pool, his towel over his shoulder. It was the one he'd received from the woman who'd bought his painting and Doc, a towel once covered in dog hairs. He wore swimming shorts and the gumboots the woman had given him. Walking towards the pool, the gumboots squelching in the rain-sodden red ground, he thought of the woman, of the flowers she'd given him dying slowly in his studio. He sipped his coffee as he walked.

The pool was hotter than the stream. Stoker found the source and slowly moved his back sideways back and forth, the pressure from the source easing the twinges of pain in his shoulders and neck. There was no one else in the pool. It was early, the sky spent and still above him. His glasses fogged, set aside, he persisted in studying the intricate weave of ivy across the curved monastic walls that surrounded the pool. His eyes gladdened by proximate things, he studied an insect stranded and fluttering in the water. With the tip of his finger he scooped up the insect and drew it closer to his weak eyes. He wished he had Dean's loupe so he could see the insect more clearly. He watched the fine wings shake off the water, the flexing of antennae, the 3-D eyes, the articulation of legs like fine lettering. Then he noticed that the creature was wounded. He could not ascertain how or where. He placed the creature on the marble floor of the pool-side and watched its painful gait, watched it rest on the fogged lens of his glasses. He wondered whether the creature was worth saving. Then he felt the water as it lifted and buffeted against him, and saw Hedda's body arc beneath the surface, then emerge. He watched her as she swam back and forth and eventually pause at the other end of the pool. The two of them remained silent in the water, each basking in the heady heat. He noticed that Hedda's hair was braided.

'I'll see you in an hour or so,' Hedda said, as she lifted herself from the water. 'You'll have to wake Phyllis. I've got breakfast planned.'

'Sounds good,' Stoker said, watching the fall of Hedda's breasts, the glitter of wetness across her toned thighs. Then he watched as she disappeared. He thought of Raquel Welch in *A Million Years BC*. For the next hour he remained in the water. He watched his fingertips wrinkle.

'Hedda's expecting us,' he said.

Phyllis was awake, sipping her coffee and reading.

'Make us another, would you. In exchange I'll read to you. There's this bit in *The Waiting Country*.'

'I'm listening.'

'Coffee first.'

Phyllis evidently wasn't suffering a relapse. He was glad that she was focusing on something. She'd been raving about Mike Nicol's book for some time. When Phyllis liked something everybody had to know. When she hated something, the same applied. It was rarely an opinion she gave. Rather, it was an emotion. The brain, like every part of her, was an emotional space. Stoker had read somewhere about 'the structure of feeling'. The words applied to Phyllis. Her life was a structure of feelings.

'I'm listening,' Stoker said.

'Coffee!' Phyllis pleaded and pouted. She was definitely getting whimsical.

Stoker stared at Phyllis tucked away beneath the bright pink blanket, her eyes sparkling above the splayed cover of the book.

'People read all sorts of books, books on spiritual rebirth, self-help and management . . .' Stoker wondered what Phyllis was getting at. 'It's all here,' she said. 'Nicol has it taped. He's seen a way out. Out of the guilt, the vengeance. He doesn't tell you what to do or how to change your life. He doesn't preach. He uses his own life to illustrate things. There's nothing heroic about it. None of Rian Malan's self-promoting anguish.'

'You're on a soapbox this morning,' Stoker said. He hated bitching, no matter how impassioned and sincere. He hated comparison. Nicol was Nicol. Malan was Malan. Judging Phyllis's state of mind, he knew he could afford to be combative. He handed her a second cup of coffee and made himself a rooibos tea.

'Fire away,' he said.

Phyllis was riffling through the pages deciding where to begin.

'It's the bit about the inauguration. It's so beautiful. Nicol goes through Mandela's inaugural speech.'

'Yeah?'

'It's just so beautiful. Did you know that Mandela quoted Ingrid Jonker?'

Stoker didn't.

Phyllis read.

' "The certainties that come with age tell me that we shall find an Afrikaner woman who transcended a particular experience and became a South African, an African, and a citizen of the world.

Her name is Ingrid Jonker.

She was both a poet and a South African. She was both an Afrikaner and African. She was both an artist and a human being.

In the midst of despair, she celebrated hope. Confronted by death, she asserted the beauty of life.

In the dark days when all seemed hopeless in our country, when many refused to hear her resonant voice, she took her own life.

To her and others like her, we owe a debt to life itself.

To her and others like her, we owe a commitment to the poor, the oppressed, the wretched and the despised".'

Phyllis paused.

'Don't you think that's beautiful, Stoker?'

'It's beautiful, Phyllis.'

Phyllis's face was radiant. Stoker realised that it was James she was thinking of. For her James was as real, as true, as great an artist and human being. It was his loss that moved her. James's and Ingrid Jonker's.

'There's a poem. Shall I read it to you?'

Stoker was silent. He was listening, glad to see such buoyancy, such hope.

Phyllis read Jonker's poem.

'The child is not dead
The child lifts his fist against his mother
    who shouts Afrika!

The child is not dead
Not at Langa nor at Nyanga
nor at Orlando nor at Sharpeville
nor at the police post at Phillipi
where he lies with a bullet through his brain

the child is present at all assemblies and law-giving
the child peers through the windows of houses
and into the hearts of mothers
this child who only wanted to play in the sun at
    Nyanga
is everywhere
the child grown to a man treks on through all Afrika
the child grown to a giant journeys
over the whole world
without a pass!'

Phyllis paused. Stoker sipped his tea and stared down at the passing stream. He was thinking of angels, of a conversion, a superstition, a faith, a strange something that was taking him over. It was a feeling, an intuition, which was also over-whelming Phyllis, he thought. Was it simply grief which had produced this new faith? Never before had he and Phyllis fucked so passionately. What was it about? What was he feeling that had changed him so?

'There's a bit here where Mandela responds to Ingrid Jonker's poem.'

Stoker was listening.

Phyllis spoke.

'"And in this glorious vision, she instructs that our endeavours must be about the liberation of the woman, the emancipation of the man, and the liberty of the child.

'It is these things that we must achieve to give meaning to our presence in this chamber and to give purpose to our occupancy of the seat of government.

'And so we must, constrained by and regardless of the accumulated effect of our historical burdens, seize the time to define for ourselves what we want to make of our shared destiny".'

Stoker, usually sceptical, couldn't find the heart to alter a single word. It must be so, he told himself. It must be so.

'There's one final bit,' Phyllis said. 'It's the bit I like best. It's Nicol's response. You ready?'

Stoker smiled at Phyllis glowing expectantly under the pink blanket.

'Here goes . . . "There was an obvious straining for fine language. In the sentences a new rhythm was manifest, and an awareness of words and how they linked to one another and how they stirred in the imaginations of those who heard them. Care was being given to this language. It was being treated as fragile and in need of rejuvenation . . . I felt that in a way Mandela was asking people to reimagine themselves. Perhaps he saw the election days as the beginning of this process and was hoping for a greater change." Isn't that beautiful, chooks?'

Stoker was thinking of Dylan's book, of how much Phyllis would love it.

CHAPTER EIGHTEEN

By the time Stoker and Phyllis reached Hedda's, Phyllis was ravenous. Hedda served a massive omelette, juice and coffee. Conversation passed back and forth in between mouthfuls, with compliments accorded the cook, the Kenyan coffee planters and growers of citrus fruit. Hedda informed them that lemons were rotting by the truckload, thanks to a union strike. Stoker suggested that greed was fucking up the best intentions. Phyllis, tripping on *The Waiting Country*, saw a new spirit overtaking the land. When Stoker suggested a walk in the mountains, Hedda informed him there was a rapist on the loose – a detail she'd forgotten to mention the night before. Phyllis told Hedda of Bridge's tragedy. Then Phyllis returned to the book she was reading and chewed off Hedda's ear while Stoker washed the dishes.

A joint passed back and forth. Stoker retired to the lounge which reeked of aromatherapy oils, sweat and fresh air. He realised that he needed a massage and couldn't afford it. He knew Hedda, but not enough to presume anything of her. Seated in an armchair he stared at a series of black and white photographs of fire attached to the wall. The photos were closely cropped, the flames abstracted, the lack of colour forcing the element to transform, to become something else.

Hedda had never talked of her lover's death, at least not to Stoker. Most of what he knew, he knew through Phyllis. He imagined he saw the face of a man whom he'd never met. He imagined the man trapped. Suffocated. He imagined the man drugged and immune to the tragedy befalling him. He paused, steered away from the flames, sank into Phyllis's reading, then drifted off. He returned to the images he'd seen on the bank of the Black River. A plug ripped from its socket. Why? The wooden arm of a hammer studded with nails. Domestic baggage. He could find no answers. He saw only the images, felt only the urge to commit them to paper, then canvas. Carborundum. Brick dust. Metal. Oils. Surely the fact that he worked in a hardware store was relevant? There lay the clues to the materials, the theme. Well . . . sort of. Still, why a lock? A plug? Klingman would no doubt have a theory about it. The problem with Klingman was he found everything too interesting. Then Stoker thought he was being unfair, and not just to Klingman. Lizzie clearly liked the man, he could tell. Though he hadn't spoken a word to her at Bridge's party, he could tell. Then Stoker found himself switching back to Phyllis's reading, back to the reckoning and the hope . . .

'"We lie to one another. We lie to accommodate. We lie because we believe it does not matter. We lie because we think that in the face of so many years of misery, a lie that is for the good is not a lie at all. And we lie because we have no self-respect. We lie because we are victims. We lie because we cannot imagine ourselves in any other way".'

The words clung and pricked like burrs, turning Stoker's thoughts once again to Dylan's book. Was this not also the source of his brother's outrage? The hypocrisy that afflicted so many in this land? The sickness that dogged all optimism? Ours was still a criminal society, belated in its newfound goodness, Stoker thought. Belated in its celebration of those who were good. James, for instance. Anger suddenly kicked in. 'The bastards,' Stoker whispered, remembering Putter's outcry. 'The bastards.' And then he thought of a plaque he'd seen when he'd gone to an art exhibition at the Castle. The plaque was a dedication to those who fell in the Great War. He remembered being struck by the word 'fell'. One does not die, one falls. Was this true? Did one fall?

Stoker could not understand the restlessness which had overtaken him. His mind was crammed with jarring associations. He could find no through-line, no purpose for it all. This was the restlessness which overtook him when he felt the desire to work. Only painting could still his mind, focused work hold the broken pieces together. And then his attention shifted away from the wall plug which had entranced him in the midst of all his jarring thoughts.

Stoker rose from the armchair and entered the kitchen. Phyllis was talking passionately to Hedda. They were enjoying themselves.

'I need to work,' Stoker said.

Phyllis and Hedda turned to look at him.

'We'll go for a walk some other time,' Hedda said.

Stoker knew he'd not be missed. He bent down and kissed Phyllis on the head. She brushed her hand across his arse. Then he strolled back to the bakkie and unpacked his chalks and paper.

He cleared the surface of the braai area and spread out some newspaper. Then he laid out the drawing paper and lit a cigarette. He was overtaken by an excitement, he could feel his throat clench. Then he proceeded to draw a giant three-pronged plug with its wires cut. A suitcase just below it. The images were precise yet the delineation was rough, the context a smear of lines and smudges. Stoker longed for the colours which he saw. For now he would draft the scale, the position of each object.

The image of the suitcase kept changing. Was it Phyllis's red suitcase? No, it was older, less solid. Again he thought: Was the suitcase full or empty? Had it arrived at its destination or was it just about to leave? Why the breakdown? The suspension? The constant questions?

Stoker packed away the three rough sketches he'd done and boiled some water for tea. He had to see Dylan. That was that. It was pointless trying to find meaning where there was none. It was the application that mattered. The scale. Depth. Matter. Questions were a luxury. They'd stay the day, make the best of it. Go for a walk. Swim. Eat. Rest . . .

Then Stoker undressed and immersed himself in the warm water. He dug his fingers into the putrid mud, studied the colour. Drank his tea.

When Phyllis returned to the camp-site Stoker was stirring a risotto over the fire. He knew that she'd sensed his need to be alone, or at least not with her. Similarly she'd needed time out with Hedda. Phyllis had always been able to recognise the signs of withdrawal in Stoker. The polite conversation. Detachment. The mute enthusiasm. She'd guessed he was working on something. She would wait for when he was ready to talk about it.

Phyllis bent down and kissed Stoker. 'Thanks for spoiling me,' she said.

'You were freaked, that's all,' Stoker said, handing Phyllis a spoonful of sauce to taste.

'Mmmm,' she said. And then she added: 'Death's never felt so close before. I guess it happens to all of us sooner or later. The closeness. You okay?'

'Yeah, I'm okay. Nothing beats cooking over a camp-fire.'

'Tastes good,' Phyllis said, sitting down beside Stoker.

'It's a pity I forgot the sweet basil.'

'I'm glad it's just the two of us for now,' Phyllis said.

'And Hedda?'

'She's doing fine. She's changed. The way her skin glows. She's looking gorgeous these days.'

'It's the place,' Stoker said.

'It's also the fact that she's dealing with others, helping people.'

So Phyllis sensed it too, Stoker thought. The need for bodies to heal. 'I was thinking we should leave tomorrow. Head to Dylan's.'

'Wherever,' Phyllis said.

'You don't mind leaving?'

'I'll be leaving with you.'

Stoker let her words plumb the depths of him. 'Hedda eating with us?'

'If you wish.'

'She may as well. Who knows when you'll see her again.'

'Soon,' Phyllis said.

'Soon?'

'She's having to leave. She wants to.'

'How come?'

'There's the conflict with management, the way the cats are being exterminated, the rapist. You believe that?! So much for fucking nature. Anyway, she's got another man.'

'She has?'

'He sounds really good. For her anyway. Someone she knew years ago in high school. He'd found out where she was working and caught a bus to Citrusdal. He'd walked sixteen k's in the pouring rain. Arrived at her door in the middle of the night. She hadn't seen him in what – fifteen years? And there he was, right on her door step. His name is Theo.'

'Sounds romantic.'

'It gets better. Turns out he was in prison for ten years.'

'You're joking. What for?'

'Fraud.'

'And now?'

'He's a dockworker. They're planning on getting married.'

'Just like that?'

'They've been together for a year. They were childhood sweethearts.'

'No wonder she's glowing.'

'It gets lonely out here, Stoker. There's only so much nature a woman can stomach.'

'Speak for yourself.'

Stoker was glad for the altercation, the concern and the flippancy, Hedda's love-life a peace offering passing between them.

'I'd do it. If you wanted to. I'd do it,' Phyllis said.

'You'd leave Cape Town?'

'What's to leave?'

'Everything. Your whole life.'

'It's just work, you know. A girl's got to live.'

'What are you going to do about Frogg?'

'I'm not going back. I spoke to Dom.'

'And?'

'There's a vacancy at the bead shop. The one on Long Street.'

'What are you going to do?'

'Sell beads. Make jewellery.'

'Should be fun.'

'You think I lack ambition?'

'That's not what I meant.'   ·

'I know it's not. I'm just asking.'

'You lack nothing, Phyllis.'

'Now you're being ridiculous.'

'I'm not, Phyllis. I mean it.'

'Thanks for the certificate of approval.'

'You feel like fighting, is that it?'

'Kiss me,' Phyllis said.

Stoker leant over and kissed Phyllis. He tugged the flesh of her lips, drew in the breath of her. And then Phyllis withdrew. The conversation didn't veer a jot.

'That's what Gloria says. She says I lack ambition.'

'She should talk.'

'What's that suppose to mean, Stoker?'

'Nothing.'

'You can't stand her, can you?'

'No comment.'

'You know you can't. It doesn't matter. She can't stand you either. So. You think I lack ambition?'

Phyllis was definitely game for a rumble. She was enjoying being difficult, Stoker thought. Nothing truly grave was being discussed, yet there remained an undercurrent, a reckoning. Phyllis wanted it that way. This ballet of anxiety, this play-acted doubt.

'What do you want to do, Phyllis?' She could tell him anything and he would listen.

'Make enough money not to worry.'

'Then what?'

'I don't know. Do something.'

'Like what?'

'Something.'

'What?'

'Stoker!' She braved the little storm she'd brewed.

'I'm just asking,' Stoker said.

And Phyllis reached out and ran her fingers across Stoker's face.

'You know why I like you?' Phyllis said. 'I like you because you're obsessed. You've got a single thing in your head.'

'I'm not talking about painting.'

'I'm not talking about what you're saying, Stoker. I'm talking about what you are. This body of yours . . . this temple . . . Everything you've ever made lives inside you.'

Phyllis had moved from an inner restlessness to seduction. To Stoker, it was as if she drifted listlessly between pangs of aimlessness and a vague outward need. Her hand slipped across Stoker's narrow chest as though across a touchstone, some proof to be perceived, a truth connected to the wideness of his reach, the narrowness of its expression. Maybe he was contained, reduced, wittled in a way she could never be. Phyllis was like a vine, entangled, restless, criss-cossed by immeasurable tributaries, areas of drought. Her heart was polluted with too much love, Stoker thought. Her sense of duty to herself squandered. There was nothing Phyllis could ignore, nothing she could shut away. For her there could be no solace in the creation of things, no measure of lasting value accorded to any action. For her life was a levelling, nothing mattered more than anything else. Everything was one, the worst and the best. There was no lesson to be learnt. There was only living to be done. And done again. And it was because of this knowledge that Stoker loved her.

'You'd be different if you weren't painting. You wouldn't be happy,' Phyllis finally said, her lips to Stoker's nipple, her tongue like a seismograph.

'Me, happy?' Stoker replied, perplexed by the journey on which Phyllis was taking him.

Phyllis pulled away from Stoker's chest.

'Yes, you are,' she said. 'You're happy. You don't know it but you are. Most of the people I know, they're not happy.'

122

'And you?'

'I'm fine. You know that. I'm just fine. I've been a misery guts lately, what with James's death and everything. If it was Chan or my mum I doubt it would be the same. You expect your parents to die.'

'Do you?' He didn't.

Sensing Stoker's distress Phyllis corrected herself. 'I'm sorry,' she said. 'I didn't mean it like that. It's just . . . death's so close. To me at least. When I think of all those crazies I had to deal with in Jo'burg, the bloody-mindedness, the stupidity, the sickening carefree murderousness of it all . . . Your parents' death is one example. But it's another kind of death I'm speaking of, something self-inflicted, wanton. Am I making sense? It's just that it's becoming the same with people our own age. If I think about Chan or my mum, they've never talked about dying, at least not with me. It's a generation thing. Nowadays people expect to die prematurely.'

'You mean Aids?'

'It's not just Aids. It's a head thing. Attitudes are different. There's so much sadness. It's so difficult to believe in anything these days. And I suppose what I'm saying is that you do. You've got something to hold on to. A sense of things. A narrow road.'

'I don't know about that, Phyllis.'

'It's the way I see it, Stoker.'

'It's so fuckin' hard just to make sense of things, Phyllis. If you knew what's been going on in my head. The weird shit I've been picturing. Fuck, I don't know. I'm just hacking away, you know. There's no grand plan, none that I can see, not yet at any rate. Like angels, for chrissakes! What am I doing talking about angels? The way I see it now, angels are a cop-out, a sign of stress. Besides, they're too fuckin' fashionable. The point is I'm actually clueless.' Here Stoker paused, broke the flow with an acid laugh. 'Last night you were talking about life being like Braille. Well to me it is, most of the time. Maybe the artist in me wants it like that? You never know with artists, they're a devious and tricky bunch. That's Lizzie's point by the way, and she's probably right.'

'Lizzie's just love-sick at the moment. But you're right. Most artists are as corrupt as the Church. But the point is, I think you're different.'

'Bullshit, Phyllis. You're just horny!'

'Is that a hard-on I see before me?'

'Don't.'

'And why not?'

There was no point in trying to stop Phyllis. Stoker let her suck him off. The night was clearly going to be long and varied. Who knew where the conversation would lead? Everything seemed to hold together through a series of dropped stitches.

'Most people die too late, the few too soon,' Stoker said as Phyllis spat his come into the fire.

'Who said that?'

'Nietzsche, via Dylan.'

'You believe that?'

'I think so.'

'Sounds pretty twisted to me.'

'Maybe I'm twisted.'

'No, you're not. You'd like to think so, but you're not.'

'I couldn't bear the thought of Dylan dying,' Stoker said.

'That animal! He's tough as nails. He'll live forever.' The knowledge Phyllis spoke was mostly rumour, things she'd heard via Stoker. The crackpot brother who Stoker and Lizzie hardly saw . . . the poet, the soldier, living in a house of sorrow. Writing. Writing.

'I think you'll love his book.'

'I'm looking forward to reading it.'

'You know he likes you, don't you?' Stoker lied. Dylan had never indicated any interest in Phyllis's existence.

'I hardly know him, but I feel I can depend on him, just the way you've talked about him. Maybe because he's not so needy. So grasping. Most of the people I know, they take. They're not even aware of how selfish they are. That's what makes it so terrible, Stoker. Like that bitch of a boss at Frogg. Everybody's just holding on. Grabbing. It's just so blind and calculated at the same time. Of course I can't stop them. I can't say no, you can't have this, you can't have that. Besides, these are mostly people I care for! Dom and Jay. Joan always so freaked. Where we live it isn't easy. I guess that's why I want some money. A little space to breathe.'

In the midst of talk of Dylan and art and death and selfishness and blindness, Stoker had watched as Phyllis sucked his cock. He loved being used by her, loved the fact that nothing had crossed his mind as she sucked him off except her. Her lips, hands, the way her fake red hair brushed his body, the way she wiped his come from her mouth with the back of her hand, spat it out. Her crazy belief in him . . . Now we're related, she'd said at the ticket desk the day she'd dyed her hair.

'You think it would be easier if we lived together, Phyllis?'

She let the question linger, let the gravity of it all sink inside her. And then she turned against him.

'You crazy?' she said. 'We're usually broke, both of us.'

'But we'd be fighting to keep each other alive.'

'We'd kill each other, Stoker.'

'You think so?'

He'd thought he could reach that part within her that existed beyond giving, some absolute she'd always evaded, some commitment that was whole. That part of her buried deep inside. The part he loved the most.

'It's scary,' she said. 'You know how we need space. You especially. You'd go mad living with all my shit all of the time.'

'I'm willing to run the risk. Besides, I'll have the studio.'

'The water do something to your brain, Stoker?'

'You're deflecting, Phyllis.'

'The water's definitely done something to your brain.'

'You scared? Is that it?'

'I'm not scared. How could I be scared of you?'

'You're scared.'

'Why? Tell me why it's such a good idea to move in with me, or me to move in with you?'

'It's not an idea.'

'Then what is it?'

'It's a feeling.'

'A feeling. I suck you off and you want to move in with me.'

'For chrissakes. You know that's bullshit!'

'Is it, Stoker? Is it really? So I'm fuckable, I know that. Just because you can sink your cock inside me doesn't mean we can live together. Just the other day you were crying because you were confused. Remember the mystery woman?'

'That was then, Phyllis.'

'Now who's bullshitting who?'

'Look, the woman has fuck-all to do with it. I'm talking about now, this second.'

'Well as far as I'm concerned she's around, buzzing away in your brain. You were thinking of leaving me, remember?'

'I told you that it was a stupid idea. I told you I loved you.'

'And I know you do. You think I'd suck your cock off if I didn't? I may be stupid, but I'm not that stupid.'

'You going to think about it at least?'

'No, I won't. Right now we're good for each other, Stoker. Right now there's no one else I want to be with. But I want you to be free. I don't want to come home and expect to see you.'

'You afraid?'

'I'm just not ready, that's all.'

'What's that supposed to mean?'

'I don't know. I've lived alone for too long. It's been me for too long.'

Just the way Phyllis said it made Stoker's heart twist.

'We could change that,' he said. 'You're crazy about me, Phyllis.'

'Am I?'

'Well, aren't you?'

Stoker was hurting. The conversation had taken a direction he couldn't have predicted. He was lost in the wilderness of his love, his belief in their togetherness.

'Well?' Stoker repeated.

'Yes I am,' Phyllis said. 'And I want to continue being crazy about you.'

The situation was hopeless. Stoker accepted that he'd overstepped the mark. It was pointless having what was not his to have. Phyllis was Phyllis. All he could do was love her, accept the drift, the isolation, the fact of something which could never be whole.

'You're right,' Stoker said. 'Maybe it's the water. You think we should wait for Hedda?'

'You eat. I'll wait.'

CHAPTER TWENTY

Stoker and Phyllis spent two days and two nights with Dylan. He'd been expecting them. Stoker had faxed Dylan from the hot springs. Typically, the reception was reserved. Dylan nodded, shook Phyllis's hand. This was their first meeting, Stoker realised.

'We couldn't afford much in the way of food and stuff, but we've brought enough,' Stoker said.

'Allow me,' Dylan said, removing the package of food from Phyllis's hands. Then Dylan turned and walked into the kitchen. Stoker followed with the rest of the stuff.

In the hallway Stoker paused and watched Phyllis as she moved through the living-room, then stopped in front of Dylan's desk. Phyllis hadn't been to Stoker's family home before. He watched as she flipped through the titles of a small pile of books next to a ream of A4 paper, a jamjar filled with pens, a portrait of Stoker's parents. Other than the desk and its contents there was little that indicated Dylan's presence, Stoker realised. Dylan's handiwork remained invisible, existed solely in the maintenance of the structure as it was. It was as though nothing had changed, everything fixed in time. Lizzie was probably right about what she'd considered Dylan's morbidity. Lizzie never wanted to hear about the house because she knew that nothing had changed. Then, out of the blue, Stoker heard Lizzie's excited and frantic screechings as she clattered down the stairs in her school shoes, the slipstream of air as Dylan slid down the banister about to swoop upon her, then letting her go. Leaving just enough room to heighten the pursuit.

'She's a fine catch,' Dylan said to Stoker. Dylan's heavy arm around his shoulder, shaking him. Together they watched Phyllis as she studied the portrait of their parents. Had Phyllis seen what he had always seen? Stoker wondered. The father composed and direct, the mother withdrawn and hurt. Dylan like the father, Lizzie and Stoker a blur between the mother and father. Lizzie's beauty as brittle and sheer as the mother's . . .

Dylan broke away, walked up to Phyllis. 'Could I get you anything?' Dylan asked.

Phyllis swerved to face Dylan.

'I didn't mean to startle you,' Dylan said, a grin breaking his pitted face.

'No. Thank you,' Phyllis said.

'Stoker told me about James in his fax. I'm sorry,' Dylan said.

Stoker moved from the hallway to the stairs. He'd intended moving his and Phyllis's belongings to his bedroom. On the stairway he stopped, found himself unable to tear himself away from Dylan and Phyllis's conversation. Their voices rang low, the clarity reaching him unstaunched. Again Stoker flashed back to when he was a boy. He remembered watching Dylan. Dylan's hands and ear flush against a papered wall, tracking Lizzie's thrilled and fearful breathing on the other side.

'Thank you for having us,' Stoker heard Phyllis say.

'It's good for me to have people around. I haven't, you see.'

'I know.'

'Stoker been telling you about me?' Dylan asked.

'Not much,' Phyllis lied. 'You know Stoker, he doesn't talk. He has told me about your book. He's very excited.'

'Ah yes, the book.'

'I'd like to read it,' Phyllis said. 'If you don't mind?'

'I can't see why not.'

'I've been reading a wonderful book. It's called *The Waiting Country*.'

'Ah yes, Nicol's book.'

'You've read it?' Phyllis asked excitedly.

'Not yet.'

'Well I've almost finished reading it. You can borrow it if you want. Stoker's not about to start. He's not really a reader, you know. In fact he suggested you should read it.'

'Thank you.'

'Stoker said you were going to publish your book.'

'Perhaps. Perhaps not. You like fishing?'

'I've never fished before,' Phyllis said. 'It's odd that I haven't, come to think of it. My stepfather's a seaman. Well, he used to be.'

'We should all go fishing,' Dylan said.

'Where's the toilet?'

'It's right over there. To the right, down the corridor.'

Stoker listened to Phyllis's footsteps as she walked away. He heard the bathroom door open and close. She'd be alright, Stoker thought. Dylan was doing his best to make her feel welcome. Other than himself, Stoker doubted that Dylan had any visitors. Phyllis's presence, sad as she was, was a blessing of sorts. Stoker set down his and Phyllis's belongings, then sat on his old bed. Light streamed through the curtains, through the rows of painted racing cars. And then, again, a nagging flash cut through him.

Maybe Phyllis couldn't deal with Dylan's presence? She didn't know Dylan the way he did. Just the way the conversation had shifted. The way things had been touched upon, nothing held . . . there was an awkwardness. Phyllis had never had any problem dealing with strangers. And yet . . . Maybe it wasn't such a grand idea, him and Phyllis being here. What was the point? So she could meet Dylan? What for? So she could see the house, see the tragedy of it all written over Dylan's face, over each and every object untouched, unchanged? Nothing had been taken except for the lives of their parents. It was crazy being here. It was stupid. Lizzie was right, the whole situation was morbid and depressing.

Stoker sensed he was being watched. He turned to find Dylan standing by his bedroom door. Stoker realised that he was caught between a past he couldn't shake, a present that was somehow fraught. He should never have told Dylan about James, never attempted to relate Phyllis's sorrow. Then again, Dylan would have found out soon enough. Dylan could break the skin of any disguise.

'I presume you've been listening in on my conversation with Phyllis?' Dylan said. 'There's nothing to fret about, Adrian. Merely civil banter.'

And then Dylan relayed the conversation with startling precision, the tone shifting with each brief movement. Dylan was a writer, Stoker reminded himself. Dylan preyed on little things, involuntary twists, the shimmer of possibilities. Fuck you, Stoker thought. He knew that Dylan was fucking with his head. Somewhere along the line this was the situation they always reverted to, the situation Dylan stalked, the situation Stoker couldn't quite escape. Fuck you, Stoker thought, as he watched his brother grin and walk away.

'We go away to calm down and it doesn't really happen.' It was Phyllis talking, tugging at his thoughts.

Stoker looked up from the bed where he sat, light pouring through the room. He was fucked if he knew how to navigate the turmoil in his brain, the turmoil between them. He and Phyllis were caught, Stoke realised. Nothing was certain between them. The conversation at the hot springs had proved that. 'Give it time,' Stoker limply said. 'Things won't change overnight.'

'There's too much happening, Stoker. Don't you think so?' Phyllis sat beside him.

'That's why I locked myself away,' Stoker said.

'Locking yourself away didn't change anything.'

'I guess not.' Stoker was glad that Phyllis didn't decide to confront him. It still bugged him that he hadn't spoken to her the day she collected the car keys, the roses and the note. He'd felt disconnected. He still did. He'd never had Dylan's spooky centred calm. He'd always been fearful. He was broken at the core, Stoker thought. His life was rubble. It didn't in fact surprise him that Phyllis was sceptical about their moving in together. The plug torn from its mains . . . the hammer studded with nails . . . pretty much summed up the mess he was in. Stoker realised that he couldn't quite blame Dylan for what was going on inside him. He held Phyllis's hand.

'Living can be so crazy sometimes. Just talking to someone, having a conversation can screw you up,' Phyllis said, her hand in turn gripping Stoker's.

'You talking about Dylan?' Stoker ventured.

Phyllis looked at Stoker warily. Stoker smiled.

'Dylan told me he thought he'd upset you. Don't worry. He's used to it,' Stoker said.

'Remember how upset you were? About Bridge? About feeling dead inside? About not being able to help anyone?'

'I remember.'

'You still feel that way?'

'Yes.'

'Me too,' Phyllis said.

'I guess that's why I made that silly proposal about us moving in. I know now, it's silly. We'll have to get used to ourselves before we can get used to others.'

'It'll never happen. Not like that, Stoker.'

'You're sad right now, Phyllis. Probably sadder than you've ever felt before. Me, I'm sad most of the time. Not like you. You're different, Phyllis. I think you're feeling what most people feel all the time. This sadness. But you've got a light few people have. I haven't got it. Dylan doesn't. Nobody I know really has it, except you.' Stoker could feel Phyllis shaking in his arms. He didn't know what else to do or say.

'You think Dylan will let me read his book?'

'He said he would.'

'He tell you everything he and I talked about?'

'I guess.'

'Why?'

'Why what, Phyllis?'

'Why did he feel he had to tell you?'

'That's an odd question.'

'It seems odd to me that he and I should talk, and then when I'm having a shit he should tell you everything we talked about!'

'It wasn't much, Phyllis.'

'I just think it's odd, that's all. He could have talked about something else. Moved on.'

'People don't.'

'People don't what, Stoker?'

'People don't just move on. It's all instant replay. Just now you were harping on about Bridge, about how I was feeling. It's because it doesn't go away. Nothing goes away. You adjust, that's all. Dylan was probably adjusting to you. He doesn't know you, remember. Not well. He's probably letting me know that you and he are finally talking. Relax, Phyllis. There's no need to be so worried.'

Phyllis abruptly broke her hand away. Stoker was as lost away from her as he was holding her.

'I'll need to start working when I get back,' Phyllis said.

'You serious about working for Dom?' Stoker was glad for the change of subject.

'I'll be able to make lots of jewellery,' Phyllis said.

'Should be fun,' Stoker reiterated with all the enthusiasm he could muster.

'You?' Phyllis asked, her eyes rooting him to the point where he stood.

'I'll be back at Olivieri's – if he'll have me. Then I've got to start this new series of paintings. I've got a pretty good picture of what they look like. I can see them clearly. Feel them. I can't wait to start.'

'You tell Dylan about them?'

'Not yet. But I will.'

Stoker lay on the bed. Phyllis lay beside him. She gazed up at the ceiling, at the different colours Stoker had marked on the plastic globe above her. With her painted toe outstretched, Phyllis twirled the globe.

'Murmansk,' Stoker muttered to himself, and fell asleep.

In his dream Phyllis was driving. He was in the passenger seat. She kept looking at him and laughing. Then she crashed into the wall of a tunnel. Then the dream cut to Stoker being catapulted in his seat. The roof of the tunnel grew taller and taller as he hurtled up through the air. I am going to die, he thought, I am going to die, as he held on to the seat for dear life.

When Stoker awoke he was alone in the bedroom.

CHAPTER TWENTY ONE

Dusk had fallen. In the living-room by the fire Phyllis was reading Dylan's manuscript. Stoker entered the room. Phyllis lifted her gaze from the page. Stoker bent down and kissed her. Then he sat down. Exhausted and silent he stared into the fire. He was thinking about his dream. He wondered whether he had been saved in the dream or whether he had died. He realised that on both occasions that he had slept at Dylan's recently, he'd woken up startled. Afraid. He thought of the dream of the sandshark brushing his shin, of Dylan's remark that he needed to see the differences in things that seemed the same. He thought of a whirling globe, Phyllis's glittering toe outstretched, then hurtling through the air holding on to the seat, the bakkie in flames far below him. Was this an image he could paint, a man trapped in mid-air, about to die? Was it James's death which had provoked the dream? Stoker was glad for the warmth of the fire.

'The responsibility for a funeral is not perpetual,' Stoker said to himself.

Phyllis lifted her head. 'What was that?' she asked.

'Nothing. It's nothing,' Stoker said.

'I thought you said something.'

'I did. It's nothing. Just mouthing off, you know. I was just thinking of a phrase I read in a drawing by William Kentridge.

Something I saw at the Irma Stern. It happens to be a West African proverb.'

'What is?'

'"The responsibility for a funeral is not perpetual".'

'I should hope not,' Phyllis said. 'We'd be a miserable bunch if that was the case.'

'I had the weirdest dream about you and me. You were driving. We were going down De Waal Drive at full speed. I'm sure that the dream was set on De Waal Drive, except that we were suddenly in a great cavernous tunnel. Something like the Du Toitskloof tunnel except taller, darker. You kept laughing and then the car spun out of control and hit the wall. The next thing I was hurtling through the air in one of those ejector seats, holding on for dear life. The roof of the tunnel kept retreating, me hurtling higher and higher then, miraculously, landing on one of the ledges high up, like the ones in cathedrals, the gargoyles squatting on them, peering down. I could see the bakkie below in flames. I was glad to be alive, but you were dead.'

Phyllis stared at Stoker. She didn't say a word.

'I've been sitting in front of the fire thinking that maybe the reverse is true. That maybe it's you who's alive and me who's dead. You know how everything reverses in your head? You're actually dead, but you think you're alive? Stuff like that.'

'I don't know, Stoker. It was your dream.'

'I guess so. Maybe it's this house. I have the weirdest dreams in this house.'

'Dylan seems to be going through similar stuff.'

'You mean the book?'

'It's odd, don't you think?'

'I guess it's what you make of it.'

'It just hits you. It's just there. Everything. You get the feeling he's picked himself clean. Every word is a shining bone.'

'Incandescent?' Stoker added.

'It's frightening though. The way he seems to have let go of personal pain. There's no anger. No need to explain anything.'

'I hope it does well.'

'Stoker.'

'Yes?'

'Don't be afraid.'

Stoker was silent. He was afraid. Enmeshed. Confused. Too much had happened too soon. Little seemed to endure. There seemed to be no footing, no certainty. The mystery woman in the gallery. Who and where was she? Why the flowers? All the dead flowers. They seemed to embody the vivid yet fickle nature of his life. The splendour and the waste. The lost Doc. The rape. James's death. He could see a sequence but no connection. He realised that he had never had much of a sense of humour. What little humour he had he had lost. Then, for no apparent reason he saw a rusted green tap bandaged to a brown cough-mixture bottle. All he saw was a tap, a bottle, knotted together. He vaguely considered that perhaps he was losing his mind. And then he thought: Isn't this what we all go through? This constant bombardment of images and associations? This makeshift suturing?

Phyllis had resumed reading. Stoker had continued staring into the fire. Neither had uttered a word. When Dylan entered the room Phyllis was deep in thought, her finger travelling across a page of the manuscript. Stoker was smoking.

'The two of you remind me of a scene in a nineteenth century novel,' Dylan said.

Stoker turned to look at Dylan. He was flushed and cold, his hands pressed into his overcoat. Then Stoker turned to Phyllis. She was gazing intently at Dylan's flippant grin. Was she trying to discover the man who had written the book? Could she see that there was more than one Dylan? The one who could communicate his soul on paper, the other diffident and intimidating. How many Dylans were there, Stoker wondered.

Dylan knelt before the fire, his back to Phyllis and Stoker. Was he expecting Phyllis to say something? A normal person would have expected something. But Dylan was calm, unaffected. It was as though he had done Phyllis a favour by giving her his book, Stoker thought.

Stoker watched as Phyllis studied Dylan's sallow and pitted profile. Then her attention shifted to Stoker.

The next morning Stoker and Dylan went fishing. They'd left early for the coast, Dylan driving the family station-wagon, the boat hitched to the back. Phyllis had decided to stay at the house. She needed to rest. She'd said she'd use the time to finish reading *The Waiting Country*, Dylan's book.

Dylan had motored into the middle of the bay and dropped anchor. The water was surprisingly shallow. Stoker stared at the gaping mouth of the bay that led to the Atlantic Ocean. Dylan unwrapped the left-over chicken from the night before. His fishing rod, already cast, languished at the side of the boat. Stoker sipped a cup of coffee, smoked a Chesterfield Light.

The night before Stoker had been unable to sleep. Phyllis had retired. Stoker had stayed and kept the fire going. Dylan had had to wrench him away in order to go fishing. That's usually how it was – Dylan dragging Stoker. Dylan organising the worms.

'You want a bite?' Dylan asked, handing the chicken sandwich to Stoker.

'Too early,' Stoker said. He was staring at the still water. The flamingos in the distance. Then Stoker turned to Dylan.

'What you going to do now? Now the book's finished?'

'What I always do, I guess.'

Stoker didn't enquire. He kept staring at the water. He watched a sandshark sway past and smiled.

'You?'

Stoker turned to face Dylan.

'What are you going to do?' Dylan insisted.

'I've got some paintings in my head.'

'Like what?' Dylan knew that Stoker needed to talk. When Stoker was silent the way he was, he needed to talk. This was the one opportunity, right here in the heart of the bay. Just the two of them drifting, like in the old days. This was where the first visions had started. This was where Dylan had showed Stoker his first poems, where they'd spoken about women. Where they'd learnt about silence, the way the currents shifted below.

'I feel like a stuck record saying this because it's in my head all the time,' Stoker started. Dylan listened. 'I've got this picture of things being useless, things no longer attached to functions. Everything floating like this, like you and me, just floating, waiting, drifting. Nothing seems to be making sense to me these days.'

Dylan lit a cigarette.

'What was it really like, Dylan? Seeing people die in front of you? I haven't, you see. I haven't really been there. Inside the situation. I haven't seen someone's eyes just die before me.'

Stoker didn't really want to know about Dylan's war experiences. Stoker was just warming up. Finding a way to reach what he wanted to say.

'I see this image of a plug ripped from its mains. A three-pronged plug with the wires cut, like a gash, a torn artery. The plug hovers within an electrified space, the prongs alive. There's just this huge plug hovering over a suitcase. There's nothing else, nothing definite. Just all this immense energy. The paint is crawling with energy. Quivering particles of colour, metal, earth. I don't know. Stuff. Just stuff floating and all I can see is this suitcase and this useless plug.'

'What's the connection?' Dylan asked.

'Between the plug and the suitcase?'

'No. Between the vision and the fact that you haven't known death, seen someone's eyes die in front of you?'

'The uselessness of things, I guess. The fact that everything has an expiry date. Things. People.'

'James?'

'Yeah, James. He was thirty-six, for chrissakes. He hadn't even started. Things were just beginning.'

'Maybe they weren't. Maybe he knew it was over for him?'

'Who the fuck knows anyway. No one. No one fuckin' knows.'

'You can't justify a life by the way it ends, Adrian. That's all I know. For what it's worth.' Dylan paused. 'Have you read *In the Country of Last Things*?'

'No, but it's a beautiful title . . . *In the Country of Last Things* . . .'

'You should read it. It may be of interest to you.'

'Who's it by?'

'Paul Auster.'

'The guy you told me about? The one who's obsessed with chance?'

'The same. *In the Country of Last Things* is one of his better works. Auster's an opportunist at heart, but when he nails something he nails it.'

'What's it about?'

'Last things. There's a woman called Anna. I think it's Anna. She's living in New York after the big bang, an apocalyptic fall-out of some kind. Industries have shut down. There's no food. Libraries have become squatter camps, books burnt to keep the squatters warm. In your current state of mind you'll love it. Anyway, the heroine lives in a library. She finds a job as an object collector.'

'A what?'

'An object collector. She collects objects. Things people throw away. Useless things.'

'And?'

'The point is that her job is to find what remains useful in useless things. When something breaks or falls apart there's always a little piece of it that still works, that could be re-used. Everything doesn't die at the same time. There are parts.'

'What are you trying to say?'

'Read the book. See if it's worth it. Everything isn't over yet, Adrian. Not by a long way. Things may have fallen apart for you, but the centre's holding. You'll just have to trust me on that score.'

Dylan was grinning. Even Stoker managed a smile. That day they didn't catch a single fish. Mostly they talked, polished off the chicken and the coffee. Dylan even broke a rule and had some whisky. Stoker told Dylan about the mystery woman. He told him about the crazy German who'd walked across Africa because he was angry. They talked about Phyllis.

'She's one in a million,' Dylan said.

'You really think so?'

'You can tell she's real. Which I guess is why she's perverse enough to dress the way she does.'

'She doesn't like you, you know that. She thinks you're Frankenstein.'

'I wish I was Frankenstein – the creature, that is. I'd have no excuse for being who I am.'

'And what's that, Dylan?'

'Mean.'

'Yeah, sure,' Stoker said.

'You don't believe me?' Dylan asked. He was grinning.

'You're just trying to make me feel better, that's all,' Stoker said.

'I wish that was the case.'

'It is.'

'What if I decided to fuck Phyllis? How would you feel?'

Stoker was silent.

'I'm asking you a question, Adrian. How would you feel if I fucked Phyllis? Would you think I was mean?'

'What are you talking about, Dylan? You shouldn't be talking like that. What the fuck are you talking about?'

'I'm talking about Phyllis. I'm talking about fucking her.'

Stoker was shaking. Dylan was grinning.

'I just don't want you to think everything's fine, Adrian. No one is allowed to cocoon themselves in misery, or joy for that matter.'

'That's a shitty thing to say, Dylan. It's beneath you.'

'It's beneath no one. You know why Phyllis is afraid of me? She's afraid because she likes what she's feeling. She can't pin it down.'

'You mind if we head back? I'd like to get back.'

'Sure, Adrian. Whatever you say. Just read *In the Country of Last Things*. You might feel better. You might stop feeling sorry for yourself. You might start addressing what's happening around you. You might learn to care instead of whining about feeling dead inside.'

Stoker swung his fist in Dylan's direction. Dylan caught Stoker's fist and held it in his powerful hand. Dylan was still grinning when he rewound the fishing rods.

'I guess no one wants to be caught today,' Dylan said. He started the engine and headed for the shore.

CHAPTER TWENTY THREE

Stoker didn't breathe a word when they got back to the house. Dylan packed the fishing gear in the shed. Stoker walked into the living-room. Phyllis was sitting by the fire. She'd just finished reading Dylan's book.

'It's brilliant,' she said.

'Get your things. We're leaving,' Stoker said.

'Right now? What about the fish?'

'We didn't catch a thing,' Dylan said. He was standing on the threshold, cleaning his nails with a flick-knife.

'I've finished the book,' Phyllis said.

'And?' Dylan asked as he peeled away from the threshold and walked towards her.

'It's beautiful,' Phyllis said.

'You think so?'

'It's incredible. The way it all hangs together. What can I say?'

'You don't have to say anything. Not to me, at least. But I think Adrian's got something to say to you.' Dylan smiled at Stoker. Then he turned and left the room.

Phyllis stared at Stoker. She could see he was mad as hell. She walked up to him.

'Just leave me be, okay,' Stoker said, pulling away.

'What happened?'

'Nothing I care to talk about. Just leave me be. I'd like to just sit here. I'd like to be alone.'

Phyllis refused to leave. 'Stoker,' she said, bending down to hold him. 'Stoker.'

'Don't forget this,' Dylan said.

Phyllis swerved around. Dylan stood before her, the fake fur in his hand.

'You an animal lover, Phyllis?' Dylan asked.

Dylan was baiting Phyllis, Stoker thought. He was baiting both of them.

'I guess you aren't then,' Dylan said. 'Sorry about the fish. We could use a fish right now. A festive meal to tide us through.'

'Why are you doing this?' Phyllis asked.

'What may I ask am I doing?'

'This.'

'You'll get used to me. Adrian overreacts sometimes. Isn't that so, Adrian?'

Stoker rose to face his brother, his hand finding Phyllis's as he did so. He said nothing.

'You know how precious you can get,' Dylan resumed. Then, turning to Phyllis, Dylan continued. 'He's a bundle of nerves, is our Adrian. Most of the time he feels that nobody likes him, or understands him. Well you don't have to worry. He'll be okay. He's just a little afraid of me right now. He'll get over it. It's the way things are between us. I had to frighten him a little. Frighten him so he can see. I just paid you a few too many compliments, Phyllis. You know how it is. You like someone, you go overboard explaining how much you like them. That sort of thing. Why don't I give you some space – presuming of course that you need some space. Do you? I don't know, you see. I don't know.' Dylan withdrew.

Stoker's heart was pounding. Still, he could not speak, could not act.

'I'm ready to leave if you are,' Phyllis said to Stoker.

Stoker left the room, collected their belongings and descended the stairs.

'Are you sure about my keeping *The Waiting Country*?' Stoker heard Dylan say to Phyllis.

'Keep it,' she said.

Stoker packed the bakkie, climbed into the driver's seat and waited for Phyllis. He watched her as she walked towards the bakkie, watched Dylan standing on the veranda, his body blocking out the door. Dylan was waving.

Stoker didn't bother returning home. At the bottle store on Lower Main he stopped the car, got out, and removed his backpack and drawing materials.

'You can hold on to the camping gear for now,' he said.

Phyllis looked at him imploringly. Neither had said a word since they'd left Dylan's. Phyllis let him go, then she slid into the driver's seat and drove off. He assumed she was heading back to her flat on Long.

Stoker bought a pack of Chesterfield 30s, a litre of Coke and a bottle of La Rochelle brandy. His money was running out, he realised, as he crossed the street and opened the door to his studio. Dominion Hardware was closed.

He entered the studio. The flowers were still there, the scent thick in the air. Who needs the fuckin' countryside, he asked himself. He placed his drawings on the table. Then he flipped through his tapes and found The Pardon Beggars. He lit a cigarette and started dancing. He had an awkward way about him as he moved across the paint-splattered floor. Then he stopped, and stared out of his studio window. All he could see was himself. What had happened? Over and above the lurid fact that Dylan wanted to fuck Phyllis, what had happened? Was it all just a game for Dylan? Dylan seemed to suggest it was. Was he too self-involved? Was that why Dylan went on the way he did? There was technically nothing new in what happened. Things always turned out badly between him and Dylan. Stoker guessed that he'd been fooling himself about them finally getting it together with no static. Maybe Dylan was bored? He was a bastard when he was bored. Or maybe he'd meant it about

Phyllis. And if Dylan did? What was he supposed to do? And Phyllis? Surely it was up to her? Before Dylan had even opened his sordid mouth Stoker had sensed something was going down, except he was too self-involved to do anything except fuck off like a spoilt brat. Maybe he'd just overreacted? He realised he'd have to call Phyllis, sort things out.

In the Country of Last Things . . . that's what Dylan was talking about. Stoker worked the phrase over in his mind.

Nothing is destroyed completely, Dylan had said. There were always parts that kept working. You just had to find them. The plug, the suitcase, the lock, the tap bandaged to a cough-mixture bottle – these were the clues to his life, the part of it, at least, that he had to paint.

Stoker flipped the tape and got out his staple gun, scissors, saw and measuring tape. He built a two-metre-long frame, cut a bolt of canvas, focused on the tension, then he stapled the canvas to the wood. He poured himself a stiff brandy and Coke, opened a can of PVA and primed the first of a series of canvases he'd call *In the Country of Last Things*.

The air was heady with the smell of fresh paint and stale flowers. He bent down and stared at some faded purple petals lying on the floor. Maybe he'd start painting tonight, maybe tomorrow. He'd have to start soon and he'd have to sell. He was running out of cash. In fact he had just enough for a spicy beef pita and a couple of beers at Lawrence's.

He took a swig of brandy and stared at all the flowers. He realised he hadn't told Phyllis about the flowers. He hadn't told anyone. Why? It was the sort of thing people talked about. But he hadn't. Anybody in their right mind would mention an event as crazy as this. What had he done? He'd walked out of Dominion and locked himself away for three days. Fuck-all had changed by the time he'd stepped out on parole. He'd been his own jailer and he'd learnt nothing except how to keep his house in order. So what? You can't keep your life in order – not physically at least. Shit happens. And it happens constantly. People die, get laid, quit work and do a million other stupid little things which there was no point thinking about.

Now that the spree had ended, now that he could feel the change clinking in his pocket, it was time to start grafting. He'd have to give his notice, discuss things with Jay. Living in the studio wouldn't be all that bad. He had a Cadac, a mattress, running water. There was a toilet out back. At the rate he planned on working he may as well. Besides, much as he liked Jay, the man got on his nerves. Stoker guessed that anyone would after a while.

Phyllis was right. It was a crazy idea, them moving in together. What for? So he could feel secure? Who was he kidding? No one. He certainly wasn't kidding Phyllis. Or Dylan either. Dylan was right – he probably was an indulgent little fuck. But so what? As long as he had a roof over his head, so long as he could paint, he would be just fine. He'd call Phyllis and apologise. He might even fax Dylan, even things out. Right now he'd have three or four more brandies, then head to Lawrence's, have a bite, see people.

CHAPTER TWENTY FIVE

Lawrence's was situated on Trill off Lower Main, a stone's throw away from Stoker's studio. A double storey affair with a bar, two eating areas and a salon, Lawrence's was top of the pops for Stoker. In Lawrence's words the place was post-Shirley Bassey. Red velvet wallpaper, lots of fake gold and shining wood. For Stoker the place felt like the inside of a toaster. When he stepped in, Peggy Lee was singing. The place was packed. Stoker expected he'd see someone he knew. He relaxed and ordered a Windhoek and a spicy beef pita. Lawrence appeared. He usually did. He owned the place. He was part of the furniture.

Stoker loved Lawrence. Like Phyllis, like Olivieri, Lawrence was one of those people who caught his imagination. He was a tallish elegant man in his fifties. A former drag artist, wig master and antique dealer, Lawrence was now a successful publican. Stoker and Lawrence usually met under circumstances such as these – on Lawrence's turf. Stoker couldn't picture meeting Lawrence anywhere else, though he remembered those chance meetings long ago when he'd done some set painting for Capab. That's when he'd seen Lawrence's drag show. Him and Lizzie. Lizzie and Lawrence went way back.

'Lizzie's here,' Lawrence said. 'She's with some rather elegant gentleman.'

'That's good,' Stoker said. Lizzie was always at Lawrence's. Lizzie loved Lawrence's as much as he did, except she had to ruin it all by saying it was the closest thing to Europe in this godforsaken hole. Lizzie had lived overseas for too long. Stoker was convinced it had affected her in a rather unpleasant way.

'I suppose she's introduced you to her new beau?'

'But of course,' Lawrence said. 'He's moved down from Durban. Recently divorced. Starting up a new practice.'

It didn't take Lawrence long to get anyone taped. 'What do you think of him?' Stoker asked.

'It's not for me to say,' Lawrence tactfully replied. When it came to the crunch Lawrence would side with Lizzie before he'd side with Stoker, and it wasn't just because Stoker rarely had the bucks to grease his till. Lawrence had always taken him with a pinch of salt. Like most people, Stoker supposed. Still he loved the pants off Lawrence.

Jay entered the bar. Now here was someone less likeable than he was, Stoker thought.

'Howzit Jay.'

Jay was pissed off.

'What's up? You need a beer?'

'Yeah, I need one. You'll never fuckin' believe what just happened.'

'What just happened, Jay?'

'You see the film made on James? It was aired two days ago.'

'James is on film?'

'Yeah. Alex and Melinda got it in just in time, I guess. You know Alex? A Jo'burg connection of mine?' Stoker didn't. 'Anyway it was on *Collage* last night.'

'So?'

'So Dayglo's watching it, see?'

'Yeah?' Stoker took the beer from Lawrence and passed it over to Jay.

'So anyway, James is going on about how fucked up the music industry is, right. How if musicians had any sense they'd catch the next flight out of here.'

'That's a provocation, of course. I mean James stayed. James was talking about people having to stay, surely? I didn't see the programme so I can't say. But you know how cynical he could get. Who could blame him?'

'Whatever. The point is Dayglo – the fuckin' E-head – has decided to take James literally. He's bought himself a ticket for London. Dayglo's out of here and I'm out of a drummer.'

'He's leaving?'

'You deaf, Stoker? The bastard's fucking off. Nappy Rash's just gotten started, for fuck sakes. You know what a good drummer he is.' Jay was beside himself.

'Have a swig,' Stoker said, slipping the brandy into the inside pocket, the only functional one in the leather jacket he'd given Jay. 'Surely you can talk Dayglo out of it? You could explain that James probably meant the reverse. Pressure makes people say the weirdest things. You say one thing and feel another.'

'James fuckin' meant it, bru. I saw him in Grahamstown before, I know. He was up to here with the music industry. The thing is Dayglo's leaving. He met some guys from San Francisco or somewhere. A bunch of surfers who happen to be pretty shitty musicians. They came over to surf, Jeffrey's Bay way, told Dayglo – he could easily get work. You know how susceptible he is. Tell him something promising and he'll leap at it.'

'Speak of the devil,' Stoker said.

Dayglo entered. He was grinning from ear to ear, dressed in bright green jeans, an acid pink sweatshirt with a giant fuzzy red worm writhing across it.

'Howzit bru,' Dayglo said.

'Howzit,' Stoker said.

'You have a good trip?'

'So so,' Stoker said. 'Went to the hot springs Citrusdal way, then over to Dylan's.'

'Sounds cool,' Dayglo said. No matter how hot anything was, it was still cool for Dayglo.

'If Dom comes over tell her to wait,' Jay said. 'Tell her I've gone over to the Ruby to organise things. I'll be back. Maybe by then this fuckface will have caught his fuckin' plane to nirvana.'

'Spoilsport,' Dayglo said, grinning as he watched Jay leave.

Tonight was definitely not the night to talk about moving out, Stoker thought. The way Dayglo was smiling he may as well have been on the airport runway waving everyone goodbye.

'So you heard,' Dayglo said.

'I heard.'

'So?'

'Buttons,' Stoker said. He didn't feel like getting into the nitty-gritty. Dayglo was keen.

'People come and go all the time, Stoker. It's the way of the world. It's about tribes now.'

'What does Anthea feel about your leaving?'

'She's cool. She doesn't own me. Besides she's off to live in some pyramid in Knysna. She told you about it, didn't she?'

'She did.'

'And you? Tell me about the trip. You have a good time?'

'I guess.'

'The springs are trippy. Phyllis here?'

'No. But Lizzie is.'

'Oh shit,' Dayglo said. He was grinning. 'I need some water.'

Dayglo was probably on E, Stoker thought. Dayglo returned, holding the glass of water before him.

'There's energy here,' Dayglo said. 'You can see the particles. You're a painter, right. You should be able to see things like this. Like Van Gogh. Van Gogh was definitely high as a kite. He could see things. Movement. Colour.'

Dayglo gulped down the water, smacked his lips, paused, then said: 'When you drink water you bask in your addiction.'

Stoker was in no mood to follow through what Dayglo had said.

Dom entered.

'Howzit Stoker. Dayglo.'

'Howzit Dom.' Stoker bent over and kissed her.

'You see Jay?'

'He's over at the Ruby. He'll be back soon.'

'Phyllis here?'

'Nah. She's home.'

'She wasn't when I called,' Dom said. 'You know if she wants the job or not?

'She does.'

'If you see her, tell her she starts tomorrow. I've left a message on her answering machine.'

'What are you having,' Stoker asked Dom.

'A glühwein,' Dom said, removing her gloves. 'So you have a good time?'

'Yeah, Phyllis needed to chill out.'

'I'm sure. It's weird seeing her so depressed. It's not like Phyllis. She's usually hopping about like Dayglo here.' Dayglo grinned.

'So I hear you're leaving,' Dom said to Dayglo.

'Yeah, I'm leaving.'

'I hear James inspired you. Something about the TV.'

'Yeah. It's the TV,' Dayglo said. 'Everything you want to know is on the TV.'

Dom rolled her eyes. She was a strange bird-like creature. A long hooked nose, thin lips, high cheek-bones, deeply-set green eyes. Her hair fell in wisps like feathers.

'It's shitty employing friends,' Dom said. 'But Phyllis doesn't have to stay if she doesn't want to.'

'She's dying to make jewellery,' Stoker said.

'It's like a madhouse in there. You've been there. Those huge trays of different coloured beads. All you do all day is sift. I should be employing someone from Valkenberg.'

'Believe me, Phyllis is from Valkenberg.'

Dayglo laughed.

'No kidding,' Stoker said, warming up. 'Phyllis has to be the craziest woman I know.'

'You see that programme on the TV about Valkenberg?' Dayglo asked. Neither Stoker or Dom had. They allowed themselves to be distracted. 'It turns out most of the people you see walking around Obs are out-patients,' Dayglo said.

'Phyllis is better off crazy than depressed,' Dom said, resuming her conversation with Stoker. 'The state she was in at Bridget's, I could die. It's a good thing the two of you went away. Unlike Dayglo here, James's death had a totally different effect on Phyllis.'

'I think she's over the worst,' Stoker said. 'Hedda helped her. And, believe it or not, a book by Mike Nicol called *The Waiting Country*.'

'I can believe it,' Dom said. 'It's my book. She finished it yet?'

'Yeah. She's lent it to Dylan, by the way.'

'Your brother?'

'The same.'

'I've never met him but I've read his poetry. What's that famous one again?'

Stoker knew the drill. ' "The Ballad of Koos Malgas",' he said.

'It's a great poem.'

'He's just written his first novel.'

'What's it called?'

'*Vertical Man, Horizontal World*.'

'That's deep,' Dayglo said.

'What's it like?' Dom said.

'You'll see. It's hard to describe. It's not as though there's a story or anything. It's more like painting, I guess. I don't feel like talking about it.'

'That's fine,' Dom said. 'How's Hedda?'

'As sexy as always. You know she's moving back to Cape Town?'

'No!'

'Turns out things aren't as rosy as they should be in Citrusdal. There's a rapist running loose, and some maniac who's killing all the cats. At any rate she's planning on getting married.'

'Hedda getting married?'

'It happens to the best of us, I guess. Some guy called Theo. He's an ex-con, dockworker.'

'I can't wait to see Hedda. It's been ages. I've been thinking a lot about her. She still drumming?'

'She is.'

'So Hedda's getting married . . .'

'What's the name of that book again?' Dayglo asked.

'*Vertical Man, Horizontal World,*' Dom said, slightly exasperated by having her line of thought broken.

'No, the other one,' Dayglo said.

'*The Waiting Country,*' Stoker said.

'That's a great name for a band,' Dayglo said.

Jay entered. Dom's glühwein arrived.

'You hear that, Jay? The Waiting Country. Isn't that a great name for a band?'

'Fuck off, Dayglo,' Jay said.

'There's no need to get nasty, Jay,' Stoker said, finding himself defending Dayglo.

'Fuck you too,' Jay said, and ordered a beer.

Stoker was glad to be back in Obs. Glad for the company. He liked his friends most of the time. He needed another drink and remembered that Lizzie was upstairs. He'd tell her nice things about the trip, Phyllis, about what a shit Dylan turned out to be. She'd like that. He'd be nice to Klingman. He'd ask Lizzie to spot him fifty right there in front of Klingman. She'd have no choice but to revert back to being Sister Mary Agnes, her childhood heroine, an Irish nun who'd run the primary school that the three of them had attended. Knowing Lizzie, if he caught her in a good mood he'd probably be able to score more than he bargained for. One hundred rand? Two? Once she'd handed over the money he'd inform her that Dayglo was downstairs, freak her out a little.

Then go for the jugular and tell her that Dayglo was leaving for London.

Stoker smiled as he headed upstairs. He fancied himself a nasty little piece of work.

CHAPTER TWENTY SIX

One thing led to another that night. Lizzie held on to Klingman and gracefully said her farewells to Dayglo, except, to rub it in, she called him Felix. As far as she was concerned he was just a fucked-up lawyer with a drug problem. Dayglo meanwhile grinned from ear to ear and kissed Lizzie's cheek for old times' sake. Stoker wondered how in hell they could have been together in the first place.

No sooner had Lizzie and Klingman split when in walked Dean. He was wearing a pair of sunlight-yellow pyjamas, ratty bedroom slippers and a black leather jacket. A postcard poked out of his pocket. He'd popped in to buy a pack of cigarettes.

Needless to say Lawrence liked Dean. Everybody liked Dean. He was your friendly agoraphobic. If he chose to alight at your door it had to be a miracle. Dean never went anywhere. He watched SKY-TV, read magazines. Bridge's party was an exception. Now this. Maybe Dean was finally stepping out of his shell? It had to happen sooner or later, Stoker thought. The heart breaks, you crawl under the carpet feeling like a criminal, then sooner or later you're up and about. By default a certain peace comes to the most hard-core of lovers.

'Howzit Stoker.'

'Howzit Dean.'

'I've got a card from Waldo, said I'd keep you posted,' Dean said. He placed a bright pink card on the table in front of Stoker. On the pink card was a blue god with ten arms and a snake curled about him. Neither the snake nor the god seemed to be fazed.

'What does it say?' Stoker asked, unwilling to turn the card around.

'He says he's missing you all. He wants me to transfer some more money. He's staying a while longer.'

'How long has he been out there?'

'Six months.'

'When's he planning on getting back?'

'He's not planning a thing.'

Stoker flipped the card. That was it. Waldo was missing everybody but he wasn't coming back. The sentiment made sense to Stoker. There was no good reason why Waldo should head back. He'd quit his teaching job in Guguletu. He and Joan weren't hitting it off. Besides, she was in New York and they needed to be apart. Stoker wondered why people had to be so literal about separating. He knew that Joan would be back soon, she'd written to Phyllis. It was one of those letters full of tears and outrage and sublime depictions of the weather. Basically, according to Joan, women had to band together and protect themselves from the men. There was talk of spirits and fire goddesses and women who ran with wolves. All Stoker could say in Joan's favour was that she wrote well.

'You staying for a beer?' Stoker asked Dean.

'You crazy?'

'So you're not having one, then?'

'Sure,' Dean said.

Dean loved contradicting himself. It kept him alive, he'd said. For instance he'd walked in to Lawrence's to buy a pack of cigarettes, but he was strapped up with nicotine pads and doing a damn good job of quitting. He needed to continue tempting himself – there is none so pure as the purified, he'd said. In support of his rationale Dean had quoted Emerson about consistency being the hobgoblin of small minds. And, to clinch his scintillating display of reason, Dean had argued that Emerson had to be making sense because his name was also Waldo.

That was Dean, Stoker thought. Facile and brilliant.

Jay and Dom had split after Lizzie and Klingman. Jay was

still in a bad mood when he'd left. If he'd hung around much longer he would probably have killed Dayglo. He'd had enough of Dayglo's grinning. By the time Stoker had broached the issue of moving out, Jay was so angry he didn't care.

'You have a good trip?' Dean asked Stoker.

'That laced marshmallow of Putter's was something.'

'Wasn't it just. Putter and I were up in that tree forever. Those guys wouldn't let up. They fucked all night. It was an incredible privilege.'

'It's good to know that something on this planet still interests you, even if it was virtual.'

'Virtual my arse. You should have been up there with me and Putter. This was live. It wasn't some frozen hackneyed picture of lust. It was interesting. I learnt a lot.'

'Is that why you're out and about in your pyjamas?'

'Who knows? I'm feeling different though, I must admit. I think I'm getting over it.'

'It' was Dean's ex. The fire of his loins. Dean was still being nuked by paralysing flashbacks. Still, Dean was definitely happier.

'So tell me about the trip.'

'It was okay. Clean air, you know. Phyllis is feeling better. You know how cut up she was about James.'

'Well she's in for another surprise, I suppose.'

'What's that supposed to mean?'

'Haven't you heard? Petal's been shot.'

'Petal? You talking about Phyllis's cat?'

'You know another Petal?'

'I left her at Bridge's four days ago. She was fine then.'

'That's the thing about time, Stoker. It changes things.'

'What do you mean about Petal being shot? People don't shoot cats in the city.'

'Well, she's been shot is all I know. She's okay though, just in case I forgot to mention that bit. Talk to Bridge. She's freaked, I can tell you. Don't blame her. She's supposed to be responsible for Petal, her and Immo. You believe that? The woman gets raped, plans on fucking off to Turkey of all places, meets a crazy German, changes her plans, and spends the next three days at the vet dealing with an assassinated cat.'

'Petal's dead?'

'I told you, she's fine. You should believe me sometimes, Stoker. Turns out the bullet went right through her. Missed the heart. You know a cat's heart is right next to the stomach? I didn't. Bridge told me. You should talk to Bridge. I tell you the rape's nothing in comparison to what she's going through now. She doesn't know what to tell Phyllis, what with the way she's feeling. The incident's only going to push her over the edge.'

'Stop being such a heartless fuck, Dean. Phyllis doesn't know? She must have gone straight home after dropping me off. I figured she'd pick up Petal tomorrow. She was freaked when we left Dylan's.'

'How come?'

'It's a long story.'

'I've got the time.'

'Well I haven't,' Stoker said.

'You can tell me, Stoker.'

'Fuck off, Dean.'

Dean had a creepy ability to pick up on anybody's anguish. He'd trained in shiatsu, he could pick up things. He just had to look at the lay of a body and he could tell. The way a shoulder sloped. The way an eye moved. Conversations. Dean could figure out a person by who they were talking to. He could break the code. No wonder he always seemed to know so much. No wonder people came to him.

'I've got to call Bridge,' Stoker said.

'It's three in the morning. She and Immo are either fucking or sleeping. It's Immo's fault.'

'What's Immo's fault, Dean?'

'That Petal got shot.'

'What's that supposed to mean?'

'If Immo wasn't around constantly cuddling Bridge, she wouldn't have been caught off guard.'

'Sometimes your logic astounds me, Dean.'

'What logic? There's no logic. Life's lateral, man.'

'People die, Dean. Cats get shot. People grieve.'

'So?'

'Forget about it. It's pointless talking to you. I've got to call Bridge.'

'Wake up the whole world, Stoker. Go ahead, be my guest.'

'You can be such an arsehole, you know that?'

At which point Bridge and Immo entered Lawrence's.

'Ah, the guilty party,' Dean said.

Bridge stared at Stoker. She looked guilty as hell. Immo held on to her. She walked towards Stoker as though she were walking a gangplank.

'I'm sorry, Stoker.'

'Look, it's not my cat, Bridge. You'll have to talk to Phyllis. You call her?'

'I tried but she wasn't in.'

Where the fuck was Phyllis anyway? Dom had tried to get in touch with her hours ago. No luck. Now Bridge. Where the fuck was she?

'I've been trying for the last three hours. I bumped into Jay earlier, outside the Ruby. He told me you were back. I was terrified of seeing Phyllis. I thought she'd be here. Jay said she wasn't. That she'd gone home. So I called. I could have left a message on her machine but I couldn't tell her like that. You know how freaked she gets about the twisted intelligence of machines? Finding out about James's death on the TV for instance. The way she never stops harping on about TV coming to South Africa right before the Soweto riots and screwing up the truth, breaking up whole families. She'd kill me. She's going to kill me. I know she will. I've been calling and calling. Nothing. I figured you'd still be here. I figured it would be easier talking to you.'

'I'm not playing messenger, Bridge. Petal isn't my cat. I've got fuck-all to do with her.'

'You're the one who left her with me, Stoker!'

'So I left her with you. What's that supposed to mean? That I'm responsible? You said it was okay, Bridge. You said it.'

Bridge was sobbing. Immo was consoling her. Dean was mightily amused. And Stoker was wondering where Phyllis was, and why cats were being shot at all.

'You call her mother?'

'I spoke to Chan. You know the way he talks. You can't understand a word. And he rambles on so. But I did manage to find out that she wasn't at her mum's. But the point, Stoker, is that it wasn't my fault. How was I supposed to know there's a psycho running around Obs shooting cats?'

'I can't believe this! I can't fuckin' believe this! Isn't there any fuckin' peace around here?!' Stoker's outrage had very little to do with Petal narrowly escaping death.

Dean was giggling hysterically. Bridge was still sobbing, Immo calming her down. Stoker, his eyes lifted to Lawrence's velvet ceiling, eventually sighed.

'At least Petal's alive,' Bridge said.

'No real damage?' Stoker asked.

'Nothing. It's amazing.'

'The bullet bypassed all the vital organs,' Immo said out of the blue.

Stoker glared at Immo. 'I hope I've still got a fuckin' job,' Stoker said with pointless ruthlessness. Immo bugged him.

'Oh yes, oh yes. Olivieri, he misses you,' Immo said.

'He treat you okay?' Stoker asked apologetically.

'Yes, he treats me okay. Every day he wants to talk about the Rome-Berlin Axis. You know he's a fascist?'

'Olivieri? A fascist?'

'He's a fascist.'

'Bullshit,' Stoker said. As far as he was concerned a crazy German accusing an Italian of being a fascist was like the pot calling the kettle black.

'Come to think of it, Olivieri probably was a war criminal,' Dean said.

'You're full of shit, both of you,' Stoker said, and turned to Bridge. 'You said Phyllis wasn't home? You've been calling her for the last three hours and she wasn't home?'

'No.'

'She's probably headed back to Dylan's,' Dean said.

156

Stoker turned to Dean. He felt like punching him. It was the very idea he had in his head. Dean was probably right, Stoker thought. He'd better clam up. He didn't want to think or talk about it. And Dean was in a mood to stir shit. For a second Stoker wished that Petal had died so he could shove her inside Phyllis's freezer as a 'Welcome home' present. Where was she? On this one godforsaken occasion Dean couldn't have his finger on the money. He couldn't! Why would Phyllis drive back to Dylan's? Why? It was absurd. The whole thing was absurd. Stoker decided to order another round. By the time he left Lawrence's he didn't care about where Phyllis was. He didn't care about Petal. He didn't care about anybody.

CHAPTER TWENTY SEVEN

Stoker stayed awake through the dregs of the night. He couldn't sleep. Back at the studio he stretched two more canvases and downed the remaining three quarts of brandy. The only way he was going to clear his head was by drinking and working. Everything around him was unstable, it was pointless pretending it wasn't. There was no point in going back to the fraudulent order of his loft. It was pointless waking up in his bed. If instability was what he was feeling, then instability was what he had to work with.

He laid out the drawings he'd made in Citrusdal and studied the series of plugs he'd drawn. What was the motif? A concern with power? The disturbance of the flow of energy? As he stared at the blurring series of plugs he thought of mass production, of how things were designed to have a short life, how things burnt out and had to be replaced. Resourcefulness. Life was about resourcefulness. It was about not being dependent on objects, on anything. Nothing lasted. Nothing.

The last of the brandy sliding down his throat, Stoker started soaking a raw canvas in red paint. In the wetness he sketched the outline of the plug and the suitcase with a stick. The suitcase, he finally realised, was not Phyllis's red suitcase but the one in his studio. The one that contained his hammer, nails, drill and painting brushes ranging from two millimetre to household proportions. A simple brown cardboard suitcase.

Stoker had told Dylan that he'd found a language. What he'd really meant was that he'd found a way of working. *Man in a Landscape* was a beginning, the fruit of a series of failed experiments. His was a laborious process of obliteration and revelation. He estimated that it would take him months to finish a canvas. He didn't have the time.

Stoker looked down at the wet red canvas, the plug and suitcase cut across it. He thought of discarded things. Of the brick-dust he'd scraped out of the kilns of a brick-field in Paarden Eiland. He'd mix the brick-dust with acrylic the way he'd done in *Man in a Landscape*. Later, much later, he'd work in the carborundum. He still had a sack of it. He loved the sound of the word. The dull silvery effect reminded him of granular mercury.

Obliteration and revelation . . . the thing beneath the thing . . . a stripping and layering of surfaces that could go on forever . . . Stoker wanted nothing more than to disappear and find himself again, to lose and to find, over and over. This was going to be the single most important process in his life from now on. Fuck the world at large, he thought. Fuck the rent, fuck Phyllis, fuck everybody. He was going to live with his paintings. If people wanted to see him they'd have to see him at his counter at Dominion. He wasn't going anywhere. He wasn't calling anyone. He was going to stay right where he was. He was going to enter the country of last things.

BOOK
TWO

CHAPTER ONE

In the three months it took Stoker to complete the cycle of paintings, he lived above Dominion Hardware. He worked on *Last Things* by night. During the day he ran the hardware store. Olivieri had agreed to let him work from nine to five plus half-days on Saturday. The job was relatively easy and brought in just enough for Stoker to feed himself and paint. He was glad for the routine – the stocktaking, reorders, inventories. He'd organised a sharpening service for knives, scissors, hedge shears, lawnmowers, saws. The service was called Cutting Edge. It was corny, he knew. Still, given the influx of aspirant low-lifers hell-bent on gentrifying Obs, the phrase worked. His most prized innovation was the weekly dust-up and restyling of the display windows which hadn't received much in the way of attention for over a decade. There were paint brushes on display which had lost their bristles, whistling kettles which no longer whistled, Tupperware faded by the sun, tools poised for immediate use which had long lost their gleam, dusty Cadac boxes and paint tins speckled with mouse turds. No wonder people hardly came to buy anything. Olivieri's display windows had the appeal of a rotting mouth.

Stoker had always loved hardware stores. He'd once said that if anyone felt like fulfilling his ultimate wish, they should write out a blank cheque and drop him off at a hardware store. Given the fact that the wish hadn't been granted, it was fitting that he should earn his living by working in one. Then again, Dominion was no ordinary hardware store. And because it was nothing like Hawkes and Findlay down the road, Dominion posed no threat. Olivieri had invested in all sorts of junk and it was largely the junk which sold – porcelain dolls, plastic bubbles made in Taiwan containing fake snowscapes and tropical fish, hideous brass and gold-plated paraffin lamps, lurid fruit bowls. Dominion was the home of the cheap birthday present. Stoker had given Phyllis a heart-shaped paraffin lamp for her birthday, 'You're all heart' painted on the side. At any rate, the occasional practical sale did occur and Stoker had to be ready to sell tools and cleaning products. Thanks to his efforts there had been a noticeable increase in sales which, to smooth Olivieri's ego, Stoker attributed to the new blood that was flowing into Obs and the increase in house sales.

One of Olivieri's newfangled conditions of employment concerned a standard floor-cleaning product which he'd decided to stock. Stoker's job was to recite Olivieri's ad for the product to all prospective customers and whenever Olivieri rocked up to check on Stoker. With a trip of the tongue and a wink of an eye, both of which Stoker had thoroughly rehearsed with Olivieri, he'd have to mouth Olivieri's appalling sales pitch: 'We carry the full range of Nova floor treatment and home cleaning products, says the boss o' Nova.' Having regurgitated Olivieri's copy, Stoker would punctuate the pitch with a flourishing gesture that directed the hapless customer to a portrait of a seedy grinning Olivieri in his pink satin bomber jacket, a Camel plain tucked behind his hairy ear. People had done worse, Stoker reminded himself each time he undertook the chore.

Olivieri was pleased with Stoker's efforts and particularly proud of Stoker's rendition of his one claim to literary fame. As far as Olivieri was concerned the boss o' Nova witticism was the high point of his intellectual life and his finest invention. Off and on Olivieri would rock up for spot checks and Stoker would have to kick into action with a trip of the tongue, a wink of an eye, the tap of a heel, and a click of a finger. Invariably Olivieri would burst into uproarious laughter and slam the counter with his fist. Then, finally, he'd calm down, appraise a new display, go through the reorder sheet. Then he'd pop open the till, pocket some bucks and split. According to Olivieri he was enjoying an early retirement. As far as Stoker was concerned there was nothing early about retiring at ninety. Still, it was a fine thing that Olivieri was enjoying himself.

Thanks to Stoker business had improved slightly. Olivieri

was able to buy a new hairpiece – one that blended more convincingly and had a better grip. Olivieri's taste for porno magazines had been supplanted by the influx of video. He'd spend ten rand and lock himself in a video porn bunker on Long, or splash out on the more lavish strip shows and live sex shows at Heaven. And heaven was what Olivieri was after.

Stoker was perversely pleased by Olivieri's regular spot checks and company. No one humiliated, infuriated or fascinated him more. Olivieri was his personal hell. Stoker couldn't imagine two people better suited for Sartre's *No Exit* than he and Olivieri. He pictured himself condemned to dispensing hardware, condemned to the endless re-enactment of Olivieri's putrid boss o' Nova ad while Olivieri cracked up laughing for no good reason. At least he was amusing another human being, Stoker thought. If Olivieri's heaven was Stoker's hell, then so be it. Worse things had happened to people.

Stoker watched as Olivieri drove off in his aubergine Beetle, the silencer rattling like crazy. He was probably heading off to a porn bunker on Long. It was three in the afternoon. Stoker had two hours before closing. Needless to say, his resolution to isolate himself from the world was more easily said than done. He could lock himself away for three days, but three months? The point was not to quarantine himself but to isolate and focus on what needed to be done. On the night of his resolution he'd been drunk and confused. Thanks to Dean he'd gotten it into his head that Phyllis had driven back to Dylan's. The fact was she had gone to Gloria's. She'd been in a state and the only person she could think of talking to was Gloria. She'd been upset by the turn of events at Dylan's, upset with Stoker, with herself. The fact was she actually did find Dylan attractive. The fact was she didn't want Stoker to move in with her. The fact was she was pregnant and the baby's father was Stoker.

Phyllis had realised for some time that something had changed inside her. She'd been eating more than usual. The fact she'd puked in the middle of *Pulp Fiction* had nothing to do with the movie. And her Betty Blue tummy was no fashion statement. It had become increasingly clear to her that she didn't want to have an abortion, and she refused to use the baby as a way to keep the relationship with Stoker going. The fact was she did end up fucking Dylan. So Dean was technically right after all. It was through talking with Hedda and Gloria that Phyllis had reached a decision to break up with Stoker, though neither party had actually suggested she do so. Her reasoning wasn't clear. There was too much happening inside her. The baby, James's death, Dylan, work. There were too many conflicting sensations. She too had felt the need to isolate herself.

Stoker had wanted nothing to do with Phyllis or with Dylan, or with the fact that Dylan was fucking the woman who was carrying his baby. Did he in fact think of the baby as his? He wasn't sure. The situation was too surreal for words. He felt as though he was caught up in *Loving* or some other stupid afternoon soapie. Gloria would pop in every now and then with updates. She'd never particularly liked Stoker, but she liked the fact that Phyllis was fucking Dylan even less. Stoker was the father of Phyllis's baby which gave him rights, according to Gloria, rights which Stoker in fact didn't want. Phyllis was confused, Gloria said. She didn't know what she wanted. Stoker wasn't sure if this was Gloria's interpretation or the facts. Then Gloria handed him a note. Stoker had received quite a few of these notes. He'd put them all in his biscuit tin. This one read: 'Margaret Drabble lived in a different house to her husband. They'd meet on weekends. I don't think that works for me. There's so many moments which people need to share.'

'Who's Margaret Drabble?' Gloria asked. It was just like Gloria to sneak a peek.

Stoker looked at Gloria with her Cleopatra eyes and giant hairdo and thought of Phyllis forty years from now. 'I don't know,' he said.

'We'll have to find out,' Gloria said. 'It could be a clue.'

A clue to what? Stoker asked himself. He wished Phyllis would stop sending him messages via Gloria.

'She's realising that she can't live without you,' Gloria ventured.

Stoker was sceptical. At least Phyllis had the good sense not to walk into Dominion, he thought. He was glad for the up-dates on her health, the baby. He didn't want to know a thing about Dylan.

'She still working at Dom's Bead Shop?' Stoker asked.

'Yes.'

'How are things going with you? The angina?' he added, needing to steer Gloria away from his love-life.

'Comes and goes,' she said.

When it came to talking about herself, Gloria was always both neutral and vehement. When it came to him and Phyllis, she was an overworked carrier pigeon in the middle of a war.

'I've got to close shop,' Stoker said. He didn't feel like being reminded of his feelings, and neither did he feel like chiselling away at Gloria's sob story. If it wasn't angina it was bound to be something else. Disaster dripped from Gloria's fingertips. She was a geriatric *femme fatale* with a heart condition and a burning social conscience. A deadly combination if Stoker cared enough to get roped in.

Gloria handed Stoker a Tupperware container. Inside there was a chicken pie, chips and salad.

CHAPTER TWO

Stoker was grateful for the chicken pie and chips. Coming from someone who had never offered credit the chicken pie meant a lot to him. Feeling a trifle shitty he made a mental note to be a bit nicer to Gloria when next they met.

Stoker ate the pie and chips with relish, the windows of his studio wide open, the evening air balmy. He thought of what he could do for Gloria in turn. Then he thought of Phyllis's note, of all the notes she'd written to him. Who was Margaret Drabble anyway? There were so many moments which people need to share, the note read. For a split second Stoker thought that these were Dylan's words. Maybe they were? Maybe the note was the outcome of a conversation between Phyllis and Dylan? Who could say where one thought began and another stopped? Wasn't there an origin and intention to every conversation, every rumour? Maybe Drabble was a writer?

Then, needing a shift in focus, Stoker thought of Putter and the Locker Room Project. It had begun – what? three or four months ago? with a card. In that time Putter had been able to generate a degree of involvement and interest unsurpassed in the Cape Town art world. Stoker hadn't needed to leave Dominion to learn this. Just about everyone who popped in to visit him talked about the Locker Room Project. What had started out as a question had become a widespread affirmation. Posters and flyers riddled the city. Putter had produced a booklet that ranked in popularity and portability with the pocket books which Penguin had put out to celebrate its sixtieth anniversary. At the core of Putter's booklet lay a celebration of the idea of Queer.

Stoker stared at the booklet lying on the table where he ate his chicken pie, chips and salad. It was Dom who'd stopped over to give him a copy. On the cover was the question he'd asked Putter at the Seeff Gallery: What is the Locker Room Project? Stoker lit a cigarette and opened the booklet. According to Putter and his cronies the Project was to be 'a mega deluxe ultra vivid lush galore fancy-dress sporty art party designed to showcase Queer culture in the Mother City'. Stoker flipped through the pages of text and black and white images, lingered over a graphic depiction of buggery, the attendant words 'Insert and Play', then read: 'Now is the time to celebrate! We are living in extraordinary times here at the tip of Africa. For the first time it's possible to express and enjoy our differences without apology or fear. Our new freedom is underwritten by the most open and tolerant constitution in the world.' There were precedents – San Francisco, London, Sydney. Now it was Cape Town's turn to stage its Queer event.

Stoker doubted he had anything to celebrate. While Putter was talking about group events, about the death of the art gallery and the beginning of the art party, questioning the conventions of cultural dissemination, finding creative alternatives to things people took for granted, all Stoker could think of was the solitariness of his life and his endeavours. There was no doubt that Putter's armoury of ideas appealed to him. Still, the fact was he'd always been detached, sceptical of public events. Even Dylan had questioned what he'd called Stoker's solipsism. Then again, Dylan should talk. Dylan was even worse. Well, he used to be.

According to Lizzie, things had changed for Dylan now that Phyllis was in his life. Lizzie, needless to say, couldn't believe her eyes. She'd bumped into them at The Last Days of Siam, a Thai restaurant. She and Klingman had ended up spending the evening with Dylan and Phyllis. She'd never seen Dylan so perky, she'd said. Dylan perky? The word somehow didn't seem to fit Dylan, but that's the word Lizzie used. Perky.

Lizzie was ecstatic about Phyllis's pregnancy since she herself was sterile. Lizzie was the mistress of the family album and dead keen on having another Stoker. Still, though she was amazed by Dylan's transformation, she couldn't for the life of her understand what Phyllis was doing with Dylan. The whole thing was a bit sordid, she'd said. It reminded her of *I Claudius*, a TV series she'd seen years ago in England, about a bunch of Romans fucking each other over and killing each other off. It was all a bit too close. Still, the fact that Phyllis was pregnant and hell-bent on keeping the baby meant more to her than the fact that Phyllis was playing ping-pong with her brothers. Besides, who exactly was right or wrong, Lizzie had asked Stoker. Only those involved could be the judges, she'd said. And then she'd retracted and qualified her statement by saying that she doubted either party actually could judge.

Initially she'd felt pity for Stoker, outrage, concern for Phyllis, but these conflicting emotions had fallen along the wayside. She had seen Dylan transformed, Phyllis radiant, Stoker unmoved as though he had somehow willed the separation. Basically there was little Lizzie could do except brief Stoker on the developments. As far as she was concerned, a breakup between Phyllis and Dylan seemed unlikely. Stoker thought of

Phyllis's note. Perhaps the so-called moments which she'd needed to share with him concerned their baby and nothing more?

Stoker turned the pages of the Locker Room Project booklet. He uttered the word Queer. Yes, that was the connection. His life was queer. But so was everyone else's. The difference was Putter wasn't getting strung out and upset, he was celebrating the queerness of things. Stoker resumed reading the booklet: 'People – hetero and homo alike – are waking up to the fact that their sexual identity will always defy neat labelling. Although most Queer people are homosexual, not all homosexuals are Queer. In fact, some straight people are Queerer than some gay people. QUEERNESS IS AN ATTITUDE.'

Everyone Stoker knew was queer in one way or another. Queerness was tied to the instability of things, the crazy happenstance way the world seemed to be working. Nothing made sense until it happened. And when something happened the sense changed. Which was why grudges seemed so crazy, Lizzie had finally concluded. We feel them all the same, but they're still crazy. She was talking to Stoker about Phyllis, but she was also talking about Dayglo.

Stoker suddenly missed Dayglo and wished he was still around. The last he'd heard, Dayglo had left London and was living somewhere in San Francisco. Stoker had received a card from some place in the Nevada Desert. Dayglo had cycled from San Francisco to attend some death and rebirth ritual somewhere in the desert. The ritual happened every year and involved the burning of a forty-foot man. Fireworks exploded from the head and hands of the Burning Man. The whole event was mindblowing, Dayglo said. He wished that everyone he almost loved was there.

'People come and go,' Stoker said to himself. 'People come and go.' He was remembering Dayglo's words to him at Lawrence's, the night he'd heard that Petal had been shot, the night everything had come to a head.

Joan was finally back from New York. Waldo was still somewhere in India. According to Dean, Waldo was scheduled to return in a couple of weeks. Stoker wasn't going to hold his breath. Things were never definite with Waldo. As for Immo and Bridge, they were somewhere in the Karoo. Bridge was most probably still recovering from Phyllis's cat getting shot. For weeks after the shooting she'd talked of nothing else. Stoker hadn't forgotten Hedda talking about cats being shot in Citrusdal around the same time some crazed neighbour of Bridge's had decided to shoot Petal. Because, as it turned out, it was Bridge's crazy neighbour, a Mrs Robinson, who'd pulled the trigger. Why, no one knew. The woman had snapped and Petal happened to be in the way, merrily pissing all over Mrs Robinson's hydrangeas. The case was closed, no charges were laid. Mrs Robinson footed the medical bill. Big deal. At any rate, Immo and Bridge were in the Karoo. Bridge wanted Immo to see as much of South Africa as possible. Besides, she'd planned on going to Turkey. Why not cross the whole of South Africa? Stoker was envious.

Jay and Percy had started a new band. Through Percy's connections they'd found a drummer called Phil and taken up Dayglo's idea for the name – The Waiting Country. Nappy Rash was infantile anyway, Jay had said. Nowadays people had to think big. The whole country was poised for something big. Oh yeah? Stoker had responded. The Waiting Country had a virtual feel about it, Jay continued. Which just about summed up the way things were across the board, Stoker said – virtual. At any rate Jay had moved in with Dom. The move didn't seem to be doing either of them much good. Dom felt stifled and for some obscure reason Jay felt castrated. Still, the feeling was clearly doing his art a lot of good since he was composing furiously, Dom said. She also downloaded updates on Phyllis and the baby. Phyllis had found out she was having a girl. There was talk of calling her Mira after Stoker's mother, or Nellie after Phyllis's mum. Phyllis wanted to know if Stoker had any ideas. He had none.

Stoker closed the Locker Room booklet and stared at the six paintings at various levels of completion lining the room. The surfaces glittered in the dying light. There was a queerness in them that was distinct from Putter's vision, Stoker thought. Staring at the paintings he failed to see any of the hope readied on the lips of his friend. He was lost, he realised. Lost and alone in his world of broken things. Then, out of the blue he recalled the events of New Year's Day. It all seemed so long ago, and yet . . .

Stoker, Phyllis, Waldo and Joan had gone to a massive dump site in Strandfontein. The idea was Joan's. She was looking for the right rubbish to exhibit in the transparent resin frame she'd planned for a pastel drawing she was working on. The drawing was of Percy as a cross between a corpse and a mannequin discarded on a dump site, his body severed at the arms and waist, the parts still linked but twisted ever so slightly. There they were, the four of them, hung over, strolling through the acrid rotting wasteland, Joan and Phyllis collecting specimens of plastic waste with yellow rubber kitchen gloves. That's what he was doing on New Year's Day – strolling through a wasteland of rubbish. Was Joan's inspiration somehow his own? Stoker wasn't certain. There were definite links between them, but the expression was different. Joan's drawing was meticulously detailed. Morbid. It was the texture of things rather than the texture of pastel and paint that drew her. As darkness poured through the gaping windows of his studio, Stoker felt that he had never left that wasteland. The acrid smell of burning waste lingered still. He realised that he could resume work on his paintings. He couldn't sleep.

CHAPTER THREE

'Cape Town's a soap opera,' Dean said.

He was talking to Stoker over the counter at Dominion. It was Saturday and Stoker's half-day. Perdita was sniffing through the musty boxes on the lower racks while Dean followed Stoker as he locked the security gate from the inside.

'You know the picaresque adventure story?' Dean asked.

'No,' Stoker said. 'What's that?'

'Don Quixote, Tom Jones, stuff like that. That's soap opera.'

'I thought Don Quixote was about a crazy guy chasing after windmills?' Stoker asked.

'Isn't that what love's about?' Dean asked.

'Speak for yourself,' Stoker said.

'Okay, fuck Don Quixote. What I'm trying to say is that everything is happening so fast. People keep moving. There's a constant turnover of events. Everything's action from start to finish. There's no room for quiet reflection.'

'Oh yeah, since when?'

'Just let me finish, will you?'

'What's to finish, Dean. You're talking shit.'

'I suppose you know everything about shit, right. You're the king of shit.'

'Okay Dean, just get it out. Talk. I won't stop you.'

'What are you so peeved about anyway?'

'You tell me Cape Town's a soap opera, then you go on about Don Quixote and a Welsh singer.'

'I'm talking about another Tom Jones, you dickhead.'

'I don't give a flying fuck about what you're talking about. I'm just trying to lock the fuckin' door and get out of here.'

'Anyway,' Dean said. He was unfazed. 'Whether or not you agree with me, Stoker, and I think you do, the point is there's no time for quiet reflection anymore.'

'What have you been doing for the past zillion months, Dean? You been stuck in your room having a party?'

'I've clearly chosen the wrong time to talk to you, Stoker. Let's just skip it.'

'Skip what? Go on Dean, I'm just fuckin' tired, that's all. I can't sleep. My painting is driving me crazy.'

'My theory is this, Stoker. Reflection belongs to the nineteenth and early twentieth centuries. Now we're right back to the eighteenth. We're back to spectacle, back to surfaces. You can't dig too deep any more.'

'Says who, Dean, says who? Some arsehole who thinks he can

turn whole centuries into a package deal?' Stoker locked the shop door and stepped into the corridor that led to his studio.

'I'm telling you this so you can chill out,' Dean said.

'Quite frankly I don't know what you're talking about, Dean. And I don't care. Haven't you heard? It's easier to give advice than to take it. Just because you're not heartbroken anymore doesn't mean you can shove your half-baked opinions down my fuckin' throat.'

Perdita raced up the stairs. Stoker opened the studio door. Dean entered. In silence Dean studied Stoker's paintings while Stoker gathered his things in his backpack. They were heading off to the Rhodes Mem Dam.

'So? What do you think?' Stoker asked Dean.

'I'll tell you later. You got everything? Right now I think it's best to follow the example of our four-legged friend and shut up.'

In silence they drove to the dam. Dean parked his Beetle – his was blue. They trundled down the rocky path.

It was illegal to swim at the Rhodes Mem Dam given the death toll – a corpse a year. Still, it was a rule worth breaking. The water was chilly and fresh, the summer heat in abeyance. Stoker stripped and waded into the water. This was his first swim of the season and one of the first outings he'd had in ages. He swam towards a drifting log. Dean and Perdita followed.

Getting out of Dominion and away from painting was a good idea. Dean and Stoker straddled the log at either end and drifted. The dam was empty but for the three of them. The first spring buds shone against the grey branches. Stoker momentarily thought of floating in the bay with Dylan, fishing outside Riebeek-Kasteel, of sandsharks. Dylan. He let the memory slide. There was no real animosity here, he thought.

'You won't need me to frame those paintings you've been doing,' Dean said.

'I guess you owe me fifty then,' Stoker said. Though he was curious as hell to know what Dean thought, he preferred not to think of work. It was good just drifting in the freezing water, the mountain water pouring down the rocky gully. Just the clear sky, the greening trees, the water.

'I've been offered a job,' Dean said.

'A what?'

'You heard me.'

'You, Dean?'

'Things change. Besides it's time to move up the food chain.'

'What are you going to do?'

'Take pictures.'

'For who?'

'The papers.'

'Sounds good.' The fact that Stoker couldn't stand the papers was beside the point. Dean was doing something.

'I get to write as well. Get to talk to someone by the name of Andries van der Merwe who caught this big fish somewhere on the West Coast, Saldanha way. That's my first assignment.'

Stoker laughed. The thought of Dylan and himself in the bay came back – the fact that they hadn't caught a fish.

'It's odd how the mind works,' Stoker said.

'What's odd?'

'The way one thing leads to another.'

'It's a total mystery. Like I was saying earlier about the eighteenth century. There's a connection somewhere to do with speed and surfaces – not holding onto things.'

Stoker wasn't sure if he understood or agreed with what Dean was saying. He couldn't fit all the talk of speed and surfaces with the situation they were in – the way the water rippled in the wind, the drifting log, Perdita edging up to a family of Egyptian geese and freaking them out.

'So what do you think of the paintings?' Stoker finally asked.

'You know I love your work.'

'So?'

'Words fail me, bru.'

'Bullshit, Dean. Tell me. Tell me what you think.'

'You want me to be honest?'

'No, lie. Lie to me!'

'Well I think they're fuckin' incredible is what I think.'

'You lying or being honest?'

'You tell me.'

'They're the best things I've done. Ever,' Stoker said.

'Well most of your work's been shit so far.'

'Fuck you, Dean!'

Stoker and Dean were grinning from ear to ear. In synch they back-flipped into the water. Perdita barked as she paddled to the shore. She could see Joan and Putter descending the slope. Stoker and Dean surfaced. Together they swam to the shore.

Stoker walked over to Joan and gave her a wet kiss. He hadn't had a chance to talk with her since she'd got back from New York.

'You coming in?' Dean asked Joan. He was still lounging at the water's edge, his skin puckered with goose bumps.

'In a while,' Joan said. She was planning to stay the whole day. She'd been back for two weeks and had spent most of it readjusting, talking to friends, trying to get her focus back. At least, that's what she'd said. Stoker hadn't expected to see her, and neither had Dean. It made sense they'd meet at the dam. For Stoker and his circle the Rhodes Mem dam was a mecca as far as watering-holes went. Once, in the middle of winter, Stoker had come to the dam on his own. He'd heard the laughter of his friends from the summer before, Joan's shriek in particular, lifting off the icy surface of the water.

Putter was Joan's closest friend. They always did things together. He adored her and lusted after her but he preferred boys. Joan had a look that could be mistaken for a boy. A flush chest, strong back, a broad face with the definition of a woodcut. She was handsome, brash and loaded with energy.

Putter was in an unusually contemplative mood. No one paid him much attention and vice versa. He sat staring into the water.

'What's up?' Stoker asked Putter.

'This and that,' Putter said.

'When you get into the public eye, you become as vague as Putter,' Dean said.

'Politic, cautious, meticulous and a bit obtuse,' Joan added.

'People don't seem to understand what I'm trying to do,'

Putter said, responding to the bait. 'Like this whole Queer culture thing. Some gay friends of mine think I'm stealing their fire by applying the term to any sexual preference.'

'Fuck them,' Dean said.

'The whole thing's turning into a nightmare,' Putter said.

'I thought it was suppose to be a party?' Dean asked.

'It will be by the time we're done with redesigning the River Club. That's where it's finally going to happen, by the way. In good old Obs. It's appropriate, don't you think? A late colonial building . . . Queer culture in the heart of Empire . . .'

'As far as I'm concerned there's nothing queerer than Empire,' Dean contested.

Putter laughed. It was a relief. He was run down. A cold sore flared just off his upper lip. He looked like an inmate at Treblinka or Belsen with his shaved head, round glasses and his black and white striped denim jacket he'd bought at Greenmarket for a hundred.

'Putter wants all of us, every artist in Cape Town, to help redesign the River Club. The theme is sport, the take Queer,' Joan said.

'What are you going to do?' Stoker asked Joan.

'I don't know yet. Something hyperreal I suppose. That's what I do best.'

'How about a sword fight?' Dean suggested. 'Two huge cocks socking it to each other?' Dean was amused. No one else was. Disappointed with his friends Dean swam back to the drifting log. Putter stripped and followed him. Stoker stared at Putter's cock and smiled. He'd seen over fifty plaster replicas of Putter's lopsided cock. Putter had them lined along the municipal-green kitchen wall of his dingy flat in Mowbray.

'So what's it like being back?' Stoker asked Joan as they watched the swimmers.

'Nothing's changed and everything's changed,' Joan said. 'New York was great, which is to be expected.'

'Is it?' Stoker asked. He felt like bugging her.

'There's just so much, you know. Here everything is so tiny.'

'It's a question of scale?'

'Yes. There was so much happening I found it paralysing. I kept wanting to talk to people. In the end I guess I just wanted to be alone. Just me, you know? I've never been alone. You believe that? It's always been me and Waldo. For the last ten years. I was always the one who did the following. In the end I couldn't stand it anymore. The peer pressure. The ideal couple bullshit. I love him but I just can't live with him any more.'

Stoker was silent. He'd heard variations of this story off and on for the past three years. No one knew what was going to happen. Waldo had left for India to think things through. If Joan was just as confused, then Waldo was just as convinced that they had to stick together. The whole situation was depressing. No one in Stoker's circle had experienced the pressure of sticking together the way Waldo and Joan had. Joan in particular was sick to death of living up to the pressure.

Reading Stoker's thoughts Joan said: 'Egyptian geese mate for life, which is more than we can say for people in Obs.' Stoker chuckled. 'He'll be back soon. Dean tell you?' Joan asked.

'No.'

'He's decided he's going to use his fixed deposit and start a restaurant.'

'Sounds good.'

'You really think so?'

'Waldo's not a social worker. It's crazy to think of him going back to teaching in Gugs. The way I see it the best thing that could have happened to Waldo was the bike accident. Sounds sick I know, what with his arm fucked up the way it is, but at least he got to milk the bastards for everything it was worth.'

'Everything?'

'You know what I mean, Joan.'

'You know he's been painting too?'

'I know.'

'He's apologised for not writing to you by the way. You know how he hates writing.' Stoker chuckled. For a teacher Waldo was a shitty writer.

'It's funny . . . ' Joan said.

'What's funny?'

'I told Waldo I'd leave him if he started painting. Isn't that just sick?'

'You're not the only bitch in the art world, Joan.'

'It's not that. It's the way he does it. There's so much light!'

'Which is more than I can say for you and me,' Stoker said.

'I went to the studio the other day. It was terrible seeing what I was making. Emotionally *Coastal Resort* is over for me, yet I still feel like I'm killing something. The drawing's taken so much energy out of me, and it's not over yet!'

Stoker had always recognised the misery and the austerity in Joan's art. The combination was unavoidable. She'd tried to flee into the cosmetic but the lesions kept breaking through. She'd always been drawn to the ugly, the vulgar, the exquisite pain of situations she could only control in art. Stoker wanted to veer away from the darkness that had snagged both of them.

'You bring anything back from New York?' Stoker asked.

'These.' Joan stuck out her Docs. Stoker studied the white stitching against black leather, the elevation. Which led Stoker to the story of how he'd lost his Doc outside the Seeff. He concluded the story with the vision he'd had of Joan, Waldo and Dayglo stealing through the power station in their wetsuits. Stoker could see that for Joan the image brought back a flood of emotion. It spoke of magic and daring and youth.

'Dean told me you sold a painting,' Joan said.

'Yeah. Some woman bought it. The same one who bought my Doc. Still haven't found out who she is. I need to get a slide of the painting for a possible cover for Dylan's book. You know about the book?'

'Phyllis told me. She and Dom and I went out the other night. Shot some pool.'

'How's Phyllis?'

'She's looking great. She still loves you.'

Stoker didn't know what to say. The fact that Phyllis looked great, that she still loved him, the loss . . . all of it left him quivering on the rocky bank of the dam. Joan reached out and held him.

'It was so sudden,' Stoker eventually said. 'That's what I can't figure out. How sudden it was. It wasn't as though we'd fought. There were differences, but we'd never fought. Maybe things were just cracking invisibly. Things do. I know that. I just didn't see it coming. Maybe it's just vanity to think you can control a breakup. You can't. At least I don't think so. Ah, fuck it!'

'How long's it been going on?'

'Three months or so.'

'You hear anything from either of them?'

'No. I get news from Gloria and Lizzie. Lizzie's been talking to Dylan, you believe that?'

'Do you feel out in the cold right now?'

'I've been working so hard I haven't been able to feel anything which wasn't connected to the paintings. That's the strangest thing. I'm so raw inside. I'm hurting all over. But nothing is breaking in me. When I think of what Dean went through, all the pain and destruction, when I look at him now . . . it's strange, the way things heal. Except in me I can't feel a healing. I'm like an animal in my sorrow. There's no room, I won't make room. I can't forgive, forget . . . I won't suffer. I'm hurting, of course I'm hurting. But I won't suffer. I can't. Does that make sense to you?'

'I don't know, Stoker. I think so. Everything's more on the surface with me, you know. I don't know . . . I'm sorry.'

'Don't be. Maybe I'm just being vague. Maybe I don't know what the fuck I'm saying anyway. I'm splitting hairs. I'm being stupid. Fuck knows what's happening. I don't. I feel numb and I'm working like a demon. Well, at least I'm fuckin' working.'

'I must come and have a look.'

'Do. I need to know what you think. After all, you're the star around here.'

'Fuck off, Stoker.'

Stoker and Joan hugged each other and laughed. It was good for both of them to speak the way they did.

'I'll need some idea of where to exhibit them,' Stoker said. 'Right now I'm too exhausted and I can't stop. I've got this new idea for the cycle I'm painting – to do with the back of a ripped-open radio. The inside of the radio is like a city.'

'That's New York,' Joan said. And laughed.

CHAPTER FOUR

Joan stayed at the dam with Dean and Perdita. Stoker drove back to Obs with Putter. Though still troubled, Putter was much revived by the swim.

As the Citroën hit De Waal Drive, Stoker spoke.

'For what it's worth, it's a great thing you're doing,' he said.

'You mean giving you a lift?'

Stoker smirked. He liked Putter most when he was bitchy.

'I guess,' Putter said, picking up on Stoker's question. 'It just can't be done on the smell of an oil rag, that's all.'

Stoker laughed. He was glad that he had work at Dominion to keep him going.

'When does the revamping of the River Club start?'

'Yesterday,' Putter said.

'You want me involved?'

'I need everybody involved, that's the problem . . . getting everybody involved. I'm sick to death of great ideas going nowhere. The only party Capetonians know is a slumber party. Everybody's locked into themselves. Me, me and more fuckin' me. This is supposed to be the '90s. It's the age of the pack, the terrorist cell, the hydra-headed god with a million hands. We need a Baader-Meinhof of the art world.'

'What's that?'

'Sometimes I wonder what planet you're on, Stoker.'

'I'm just asking. There's no harm in asking.'

'I'm talking about a group of hard-core civic-minded types using art instead of bombs. Healing instead of destroying. It's the energy I'm talking about. The Baader-Meinhof were a group of young German intellectuals unwilling to accept the lies of post-war Germany. I'm talking about finding a graphic means to alert a whole nation to hypocrisy and ethical sloth. It's not war I'm talking about, it's art crime. Fuck it! I'm not in the mood right now. Yeah, I need your help – when you've got it to give.'

'I'll help,' Stoker said.

There was a pause.

'You heard the one about Capetonians going to Jo'burg?' Putter asked.

'No.'

'When a Capetonian goes to Jo'burg he asks: Where do you go? A Jo'burger asks you, What do you do? All we're ever into here is what's to see. The city's so beautiful, it's killing me.'

The Citroën passed the zebras and wildebeest grazing on the arum-lilied slope of Devil's Peak. Stoker watched as one of the wildebeest broke into a gallop. The others would follow, he knew. Putter turned into Obs.

'Everybody's talking about the Locker Room Project,' Stoker said.

'I should hope so.'

'You've designed a whole new profession for yourself. The maker of the Art Party.'

'The question is, are we Queer enough? Can we do something that will change this city? The whole fuckin' face of southern Africa. Retards like Robert Mugabe aren't helping one bit.'

'You're tapping into what people want, which is fun,' Stoker said.

Putter laughed, his laughter acrid. 'The very thought of fun makes me puke,' Putter said. 'The whiteness of it all. The sunny skies, the braaivleis.'

'The Citroën,' Stoker added.

'Fun's where it's at. True. It's all about the pleasure dome. What most people don't realise is that fun is a matter of discipline. Ethics. Art. Fun is politics.'

'You better watch out, Putter. You'll end up being mayor.'

Putter chuckled. 'You know how this whole thing started?' he said.

'I don't think you did either. I remember asking you at the Seeff and you couldn't come up with an answer.'

'Remember Craig Darlow?'

'The guy you were so cut up about? The one who died of Aids?'

'That's why. Because of Craig. Because of the millions who are going to die of Aids. Maybe me. Maybe you. Half our fuckin' friends. That's what the Locker Room Project is for me. It's about thriving in the midst of death. About celebrating life for what it's worth. Waking up this syph city.'

Putter was crying by the time they turned into Lower Main and parked in front of Dominion Hardware.

'I'm sorry, Stoker. I'm just a little worn out. I'll get over it.'

'Don't,' Stoker said, wrapping his arm around Putter. 'Don't ever get over it.'

Stoker and Putter looked into each other's wet eyes. In synch they grinned and gave each other an Eskimo kiss.

'You want to come in for some coffee?' Stoker asked.

'Nah, I'll be fine. I've got to sort out some shit at the River Club.'

'You should pop one of those laced marshmallows. You could use one,' Stoker said.

Putter laughed. 'I'll come over and check out the paintings some other time. Promise. Oh fuck, yes!'

'What?'

'I nearly forgot.'

'What?'

'Bianca asked me to ask you to call her. Here's the number.'

'Who the fuck is Bianca?'

'The woman at the Seeff. Remember? The woman who bought your painting.'

Stoker was thrown. 'How did she get in touch with you?'

'She recognized me at some launch. She's a curator or writer or something. She's been in the country a while. Just came back from Jo'burg. She's collecting for some art gallery in Italy. You know Europeans, they're always collecting. Call her up. She needs to talk to you.'

Putter drove off. Stoker looked at the card Putter had given him. It read Bianca Buonacuore, Galleria dell'Arte Moderne Frassini. The address was Palermo, Sicily. There was a printed phone and fax number, and a local number handwritten at the bottom in green ink.

Stoker remained on the pavement on Lower Main for some time. He couldn't believe what had just happened. Until he'd spoken to Joan about the woman who'd bought his painting, he'd barely given her a thought. She'd been finally docked as a chance acquaintance, an apparition, a strange encounter long ago. So much had happened in between. The breakup with Phyllis, the baby, Dylan's book, James's death, a host of events which had driven him into isolation – into the country of last things.

Bianca Buonacuore. He could barely pronounce her surname. He hadn't realised she was Italian. To him she was Slavic. So much for being able to figure out nationality!

Bianca Buonacuore . . .

Stoker opened the door to his studio. He was glad he didn't have a phone or a fax machine. He laid the card on the table and switched on the kettle. The roses which she'd sent him had long dried. They hung from their stems above the table.

Bianca Buonacuore . . .

Stoker made himself a cup of coffee and stared at the transistor radio which he'd found in the street. He stared at its ripped-open back, sank into the intricate blocks of blasted machinery, the labyrinth of pathways, the blaze of wiring. He laid down a sheet of drawing paper and sketched a grid with black chalk. Into the night he drew a series of patterns. He was searching for the right position from which to paint the torn innards of the radio. By the fifteenth drawing he had some sense of where he was going.

That night he dreamt of a sea of flowers. Of a woman he did not know.

Sunday was Stoker's day off. He lay inside his sleeping-bag, his eyes wide open. He studied the length of the paint-splattered floor, the motes of dust in the sunlight, the smoke from his cigarette curling upwards. He found himself recalling the mock wedding ceremony which he and Phyllis had performed. Phyllis had recited the litany. When it came to the matter of the ring, Stoker had blown a perfect smoke ring. Phyllis had reverently inserted her finger into the ring. Stoker thought about Phyllis, about Dylan. He thought about Bianca Buonacuore. He wondered whether or not he would call her. Sunday was as good a day as any. It would be stupid not to call her. He could show her the cycle of paintings, take the slide of *Man in a Landscape*. Who knows? The radio painting would be the last in the series of *Last Things*.

Stoker rose, slipped on his black jeans, and stepped onto the balcony. Lower Main Road was still. Above the rooftops, in the blue distance beyond, he stared at the snowcapped Hottentots-Holland mountains. He let the spring sun pound against his scrawny chest. He smelt the heat and the sweat of his body. It was time for the annual shaving of his armpits, he thought. He'd go over to Lizzie's for a shower and shave. Maybe she'd be gracious enough to offer him some breakfast. Klingman was probably with her. They'd been spending a lot of time together. Or maybe she was at Klingman's. Lizzie and Klingman commuted. Stoker had the keys to Lizzie's place on Crown.

Stoker stepped back into the studio, grabbed his towel and toilet bag and slipped them into his khaki backpack across which, at the age of sixteen, Dylan had penned the legend WHATEVER DOES NOT KILL YOU MAKES YOU STRONGER. Then he picked up Bianca's business card, exited the studio, and stepped into the blazing spring light.

Lizzie lived in lower Obs, on the other side of the railway line that linked the city bowl to the Indian Ocean. Stoker crossed Lower Main and strolled down Trill. He passed through the subway that linked upper and lower Obs. The walls of the subway exploded with giant painted daisies, the kind found on tissue boxes.

Lizzie was alone when Stoker arrived. She was glad to see him. Unlike Stoker or Dylan, Lizzie had always had an instinct for family. She longed to have both her brothers in the same place at the same time. With this thought in mind she handed Stoker the invitation to Dylan's launch of *Vertical Man, Horizontal World*.

'Don't tell me you're not coming,' Lizzie said.

'I wouldn't miss it for all the world,' Stoker said. It sounded as if there was a trace of malevolence lurking beneath his remark. There was none.

'The shower's free. Grant's still sleeping.'

'Thanks,' Stoker said, and walked towards the shower.

By the time Stoker had showered and shaved his face and armpits, breakfast was ready. Klingman was laying the table. Lizzie was opening a bottle of champagne.

'What's to celebrate?' Stoker asked.

'Life,' Lizzie said. She was ridiculously in love. And love was a good thing for Lizzie. It made her generous, open, it ironed out all the crabbiness and brought out her exquisite beauty.

Klingman was one lucky man. Stoker had to admit that much as he didn't like Klingman, he couldn't actually fault him. There was an openness and an honesty about him. Stoker respected the fact that Klingman had never adjusted his behaviour to suit him. Klingman was a happy, good-looking, lecherous bastard.

'Your sister and I are getting married, by the way,' Klingman said.

'That's odd,' Stoker said.

'Why's that?' Lizzie asked defensively.

'Oh nothing. It's great you're getting married. Somebody has to. It's just that I was thinking of marriage this morning. It's just odd that you think of something and next minute somebody else is talking about it. Like marriage, for instance.'

'What were you thinking of?' Klingman asked.

'Oh . . . smoke rings . . . nothing really. Just the idea of getting married with smoke rings.'

'Stoker, really!' Lizzie often wondered whether or not Stoker was mentally defective.

Klingman, thankfully, didn't bother to expound on a theory of smoke rings. They were clearly too interested in each other to pursue the matter. Stoker dug into his scrambled eggs, salmon and bagel.

'Dylan suggested you exhibit your new works at his book launch,' Lizzie said. Stoker was silent. He continued eating. 'He said that in the light of your last conversation, your paintings and his book might work well together.' Stoker was amazed that he wasn't losing his appetite. 'What do you think?'

'I'll think about it,' Stoker said. 'You mind passing me the salt, Grant.' Klingman stared at Stoker. Stoker stared at Klingman. 'You mind passing the salt,' Stoker repeated.

'That's the first time you've ever spoken my name,' Klingman said as he passed the salt.

'Is it?' Stoker asked. The observant fuck. Klingman had a way of unnerving him. The way he noticed things. His directness.

'Thank you,' Stoker said. He realised that he actually meant it. 'So, when's the wedding?' Stoker asked, shifting the conversation.

'We want to get it over and done with,' Klingman said.

'That's an odd way to treat a wedding,' Stoker said.

'Well, the wedding's immaterial,' Klingman said. 'It's just a procedure. We're planning on adopting, you see. As soon as possible.' Stoker looked at Lizzie. She was beaming. 'The wedding will be something special, of course. You'll be the best man. There'll be a big party. But the fact is we want to adopt a child.'

'That's fantastic,' Stoker said. He thought of Phyllis's baby, of his own lack of enthusiasm starkly contrasted with Lizzie and Klingman's excitement. He realised he couldn't have found a better place to spend a Sunday breakfast. He poured three glasses of champagne. 'Cheers,' he said. Being with Lizzie the way she was right then had to be one of the finest moments of his life.

There was talk of the three of them spending the day together, maybe going to Scarborough. Klingman was a surfer, which explained why he was in such a fine shape at his age. Stoker declined. It would have been a good day, he knew, but Bianca was uppermost in his mind.

Stoker picked up the cordless phone and dialled.

'Hello?' Stoker recognised her voice.

'Hello, it's me. Adrian Stoker. I got your number from Putter. You gave him your card to give to me. Apparently you wished to talk with me?'

'Yes, I do,' Bianca said. 'Are you free today?'

'I'm free.'

'Would you mind if I came over to your studio at say . . . three?'

'That should be fine,' Stoker said.

'I'm so glad you called,' Bianca said.

'Three then.'

'Three it is. Goodbye.'

'Goodbye.'

Stoker clicked off the phone. He realised he was sweating.

'Who was that?' Lizzie asked, curious as hell.

'Oh, some woman.' Stoker enjoyed the fact that the conversation had been a complete mystery to Lizzie. What Lizzie didn't know was that the whole thing remained a mystery to him as well.

CHAPTER SIX

At three precisely the doorbell rang. Stoker walked onto the balcony and looked down. 'Catch,' he said, and tossed the key into the street. He waited. Listened to the footsteps as she ascended the creaking stairs. She stood in the opened doorway and smiled. She was as calm and assured as always.

'So, we finally meet again,' the woman said. She walked over to Stoker and planted a kiss on his cheek. Stoker realised that he still preferred to think of her as *the woman*. No name could compete with the mystery of that word . . . Without further ceremony the woman removed her jacket, set aside her transparent handbag, and lit a cigarette. This time her lighter worked. She stood staring at the six canvases lined along the wall.

'Could you make some tea?' the woman asked. 'I'm parched.'

Stoker obeyed. He was glad for her naturalness, her focus. It was clearly the paintings which were drawing her. Still, his vanity was a trifle dented. He would have hoped for a burning gaze, a lingering touch. Neither was forthcoming. He was suddenly ashamed of his fantasies. In silence he made tea.

'Would you prefer to sit outside?' Stoker asked.

'No. I would prefer to stand right here.'

Stoker sat down on the single chair and studied her as she studied his paintings. There was so much he wanted to ask her. Where she'd been. What she was doing in South Africa. Putter had mentioned curating and some book. Then there was the business card with the words Galleria dell'Arte Moderne Frassini, Palermo, Sicily. Staring at her Stoker realised that she was oblivious to the attentions of men. She must have been raped visually her whole life, he thought, running his eyes along the curve of her legs, her full hips, the narrowness of her waist, her strong arms, her neck a flick of pale flesh beneath her black bob.

'These works command attention,' she finally said. 'The depth of labour is obvious . . . the eye can track and dart across shimmering semi-precious surfaces, sink into vibrating nooks and crannies.'

'At times I had to stand outside on the balcony to get some perspective,' Stoker said. 'It was never clear when to stop.'

'I see a counter-process to the media image,' the woman said. 'I see Anton Tapies, Anselm Kiefer. Which of course does not mean that I find the work derivative. I don't.'

'It's the relationship with matter,' Stoker said. 'That's the link, I think.'

'Yes. Yes, it is. I love the materials you are using. The reds and ochres. The glitter of carborundum, the grit of brick and coal-dust. The nails, hessian, wire.'

The woman was running her fingers along the surfaces of the paintings. She moved from one painting to the next with a breathtaking fluency, her naked arm outstretched. Then she stopped, sipped her tea, and smiled.

'The content of your paintings subverts narrative, don't you think?'

Stoker was silent.

'The plug torn from its mains,' she ventured. 'The handle of the hammer studded with nails. A giant lock bereft of function. Is there some irony here in these beautiful, roughly-hewn, useless objects? Or rather a pathos?''

Stoker remained silent. He was disturbed and excited by the canny similarity between her interpretation and his understanding of what he was trying to do.

'Narrative can deviate,' Stoker said. 'It can take away from what the work is about.'

'Sometimes that is true, yes,' the woman said. 'A lot of South African art suffers from an overdose of narrative. It's all about telling stories. To make it pass as art it has to be accompanied by some justifying text.'

'That's unavoidable, don't you think? People search for meaning everywhere. It is the disease of our time.'

'Yes and no,' the woman said and laughed. Then she lit another cigarette.

'We want convenient crutches,' Stoker continued. 'We want to open simple windows and say – that's the answer.'

'And you?' the woman asked.

'I guess the past is embedded in each one of us,' Stoker mused. He realised he was being baited. In a nice way. But baited all the same.

'A lost, broken, beautiful past?' the woman enquired.

'To me these works belong to the present,' Stoker countered.

190

'Is this how you feel? Lost. Broken. Useless. Beautiful?' the woman persisted.

Stoker was feeling increasingly embarrassed. He was convinced he was blushing.

'I see I've upset you,' the woman said. She didn't miss a thing.

'No,' Stoker said. 'It's just . . . you know . . . I haven't had a talk like this before. Not about my work.' Stoker realised that what he'd said was the truth. He'd talked to loads of people off and on, friends mainly, but he'd never felt so pinpointed.

The woman saved him from stumbling by enquiring about the unfinished canvas lying on the floor. Stoker showed her the gridded series of drawings he'd made of the gutted radio.

'Here,' he said, handing her the actual radio. The woman peered inside.

'Did you know there is a poem written about the broken inside of a radio?'

'No,' Stoker said.

'I think it was an Irish poet. I think the poem was about Belfast. I remember reading the poem years ago when I was at school in England.'

'That's interesting,' Stoker said.

'That I went to school in England?' the woman teased.

'That too, but no, the bit about Belfast.'

Yet again Stoker had been struck by the way the woman could read his imagination, find words to describe it that made sense to him. Belfast, or parts of it anyway, was the embodiment of the gutted city.

'The drawings are powerful,' the woman said. 'You must exhibit them with the paintings. You must give your audience the process – as much of it as you can. And please, you must triple your prices at least! Come, let's go to the balcony and sit in the sun.'

Stoker picked up the chair and followed the woman onto the balcony. For some time they were silent, the woman sitting, Stoker standing. Stoker waited for the woman to speak. She had put on her sunglasses. The sun blazed across her face and

191

neck. Her arms. Her legs. Stoker couldn't see her eyes, which unnerved him even more. He watched as a smile crossed her face, then blurred into something more enigmatic. He was at a loss in terms of what to say. He wanted to enquire about *Man in a Landscape*, about his Doc, about what she was doing. Reading his thoughts she spoke.

'I am a curator as I'm sure your friend Putter has told you. I am also a writer. We have lots to talk about, you and I. For now I want only to let you know that I admire your work greatly. I like it not because it is original. I doubt such a thing exists. I like it because of the feeling it gives me. There is a pathos in your work that is ancient. It is humourless and it is sad. This, I suppose, is the weather of your work. It reminds me of the flickering remains of a winter hearth, of a desolate sunset, the colour of your hair.' And here again she smiled. 'You have every right to be sad, of course. Sadness is not a crime. It is what one makes of one's sadness that matters. Just as it is what one makes of one's delight. That is what binds you and your friend Putter. Irrespective of the application, there's a shared intensity. You want to know why I bought your boot? I bought it because it was a sad boot – a lonely boot. I bought it so I could turn the sadness into magic, turn a certain loss into gain – into a little story you could remember. I bought it so you would remember me.'

Stoker was unable to speak. He did not want to. He wanted to listen to her for ever. To listen to the lyricism of her voice. He wanted to be seduced.

CHAPTER SEVEN

That evening and night Stoker saw no one. Once the woman had left he had returned to the balcony and occupied the chair in which she'd sat. He watched as the sun slowly set, the image of her remaining vivid in the encroaching darkness. They would meet again, she'd said. Soon. He did not have the courage to enquire where he could find her. It was he, it seemed, he who must be found. It was she who had said these words, and she had uttered them with an urgency and a passion which had awakened all his hope. He had believed her as he watched her drive away in her rented blue Golf. He believed her still as he watched the setting sun. And then he had risen, switched on the studio light, and begun work on the last in the cycle of *Last Things*.

Stoker worked through the night, incapable of rest. Never before had he experienced such passion in a stranger, such passion for his vision, though it seemed to him that she lived in a brighter, happier world than his. Still, she understood him. She did not condemn him. Instead she celebrated his limited vision. She not only saw merit, she saw a certain grace in his endeavour. She had seen something miraculous in his beautiful useless things.

He had blushed at the mention of the word beautiful. She had applied the word to his grim images and, by association, to him. He had never thought himself beautiful. He was always too self-involved, awkward, detached, unable to truly reach. The word possessed a quality which was alien to him. Stoker popped in a tape by Björk. Now there is beauty, he thought. There is the sublime. There is an art utterly modern, utterly incandescent. Immersed in the strains of Björk's voice, Stoker cut the intricate image of the gutted radio into the wet grey canvas. He drank in Björk's words, pictured her as she walked towards the edge of a cliff, as she hurled car parts, bottles and cutlery over the edge. Then he thought of the poem the woman had mentioned about war-torn Belfast. He thought of the sadness of his images. But there was a resourcefulness, he countered. There was hope. Surely there was hope? He sang along with Björk – 'I go through all this before you wake up so I can feel happier to be safe again with you.' He pictured Phyllis standing on Chapman's Peak throwing car parts and cutlery into the sea below. It was the sort of thing Phyllis would do. Then he thought of the plea he'd come across on a wall: ONLY

CONNECT. Was this what he was asking for? In the midst of all the broken pieces of a life, of all our lives, was this what was needed? Some connection? Some beauty? Some crazed act of love?

Then he thought of a sculpture he had seen months ago, drifting in the moat of the Castle built by the Dutch East India Company as a way-station between the Cape of Good Hope and the East. The sculpture was of a giant broken jug, its neck and mouth unfurled like a loud hailer, a gramophone. Made of mild steel, stitched plastic canvas, and painted with blue and white banner paint suggesting a Delft pattern, the jug drifted on a wooden raft. The jug was broken, its life-giving properties forever lost, and yet it continued to speak – of hope? Of connection? Some unbroken reservoir? Of a dream of unbroken jugs? Then Stoker thought of sound, of the jug's unfurled mouth, of how sound became pristine when cast across water. Yes, that was the jug's true meaning, its residual function. The jug spoke to all the thousands that passed its mouth. It spoke of the importance of speech. Words were a form of sustenance. Then Stoker thought of the giant whistles which were being made by the same artist for the Locker Room Project. Giant whistles calling all to attention. The name of the artist was Kevin Brand. He liked the name. It had the same fiery quality as his own . . .

Stoker stopped and stared at the gutted radio he had drawn into the wet grey canvas with a stick. The lines resembled the ploughed tracks of a wintry field. The head did one thing, the hand another. He could be a bleak bastard, Stoker thought.

CHAPTER EIGHT

The Monday at Dominion Hardware was uneventful. Stoker sold a toilet brush, three cans of white PVA, an A4 notepad, a candle holder. Olivieri popped in for his boss o' Nova fix and hung around a little longer since he hadn't seen Stoker since Friday. Stoker informed Olivieri that he'd finally met the mystery woman. And? And? Olivieri wanted to know more, but Stoker decided to be casual about the whole thing so as to increase Olivieri's exasperation. The pleasure did not lie in information. Rather, Stoker enjoyed Olivieri's excitement. It kept Bianca alive, kept her real. If Stoker needed a half-day off during the week – anything – he just had to inform Olivieri. A beautiful woman was a matter of national importance, Olivieri said. Stoker was not averse to sexism when it was in his favour. And as far as Olivieri was concerned, women on or off screen, clothed or unclothed, were the be- and end-all of life.

'Tomorrow,' Stoker said. 'I'll need the whole day off.'

Olivieri glowered, checked the till, pocketed some cash. Then he shook Stoker's hand in agreement and turned to leave.

'She's called Bianca Buonacuore,' Stoker said. In the face of such generosity Olivieri deserved some information.

'Ah, buonacuore, buonacuore,' Olivieri said. 'Bianca the Good-hearted.' Then Olivieri winked and left. Stoker doubted he'd ever be lucky enough to have a boss like Olivieri again.

Dean popped in to inform Stoker that he'd fucked up on his first assignment. He was in a state. He'd driven out to Saldanha to photograph Van der Merwe's zillion ton fish, except the pictures had vanished in the developing process.

'The fish's most probably eaten and shat out by now,' Dean said. He was mortified. He didn't know how he was going to tell Andries van der Merwe that there was no record of his giant marlin or whatever the fuck the fish was. It turned out that Dean had spent the entire morning contacting every angling magazine across the country, faxing a statement of confession explaining that Andries van der Merwe had in fact caught the zillion ton fish, and that, on the strength of his statement and the absence of photographic proof, the sceptics would just have to believe him.

Stoker was amused. Dean's disaster had brightened up his day. He suggested that he and Dean meet for a Burger Special at the Planet if Dean was keen.

'Okay,' Dean said, with a deathly expression on his face.

Once Dean had left, Lizzie called to remind Stoker of Dylan's launch and her wedding preparations. She needed some ideas. Stoker didn't have any.

Joan called to say she was freaked out about Waldo's impending arrival. Stoker suggested she meet him and Dean at the Planet. He was sure Dean had a story that would cheer her up.

Then Gloria popped in. She was furious and Stoker didn't know why.

'I've just spoken to Olivieri,' Gloria said.

'Yes?'

'He says you've been dating some Italian woman.'

The bastard, Stoker thought. The bastard. Didn't Olivieri have anything better to do than to misinform the whole world?

'Well, what's this about an Italian woman?' Gloria asked.

'It's nothing,' Stoker said. 'Just some art dealer. She's interested in my work. There's nothing to it.'

'Olivieri tells me you've got the whole day off tomorrow. He tells me you and this woman are going to Sandy Bay! He tells me she sends you lots and lots of flowers! And I thought you were such a good man, Stoker!'

Stoker couldn't believe his ears. Maybe Dean was right, maybe this fuckin' town was a soap opera!

'You believe Olivieri?' Stoker asked Gloria. 'Well you shouldn't. It won't help your angina any.' Stoker was pissed off. 'I asked for the day off because I wanted to work on a painting, that's why. I used the woman as an excuse. He wouldn't give me two seconds off if he knew I was painting a radio.'

'You're painting a radio?'

'It's a long story, Gloria.'

'Why are you painting a radio?'

'Why not?!' Stoker could no longer contain his outrage. Just when he was feeling lucky Olivieri had to stick in a dagger. Either he was a very interesting subject of abuse or Olivieri was a very bored and very addled old man. Fuckin' geriatrics,

Stoker thought. They live longer than they deserve, then they proceed to screw up everyone else's life.

'I hear Lizzie's getting married to someone twice her age,' Gloria said.

'No she's not, Gloria. She's getting married to someone ten years older. I guess Lizzie hasn't told you she's forty, has she?'

'Lizzie's forty?'

'Yes, Lizzie's forty.' Stoker hoped that this fact made Gloria feel shitty about looking like a wreck at her age. This wasn't quite true, of course. With her hairdo you could hide a toaster in and her Cleopatra eyes, Gloria looked great. Still, to rub it in Stoker informed her that Lizzie had never had a face-lift in her life. She was just very blessed. Gloria was suitably miffed.

'I suppose you told Phyllis that I'm seeing another woman, right?'

'I didn't say anything of the sort. Why would I?' Gloria lied.

'Why indeed . . .' Stoker mumbled under his breath. He suddenly felt an acute pang of loss. He wished Phyllis would walk in with her crazy gold shoes and radiant smile. Either he was very horny or still very much in love. Right then he couldn't say for sure. He hadn't seen Phyllis in – what? Three months? She was – what? Six months pregnant? She was probably being carted around on a fuckin' stretcher! She probably couldn't fit through the fuckin' front door! Stoker was so pissed off he was glad to be locking up, glad that Gloria hadn't rocked up with another Tupperware container filled with chicken pie and tipsy tart and god knows what else. He didn't want to be spoilt by a nosy witch. He wanted to be left alone to carry on as he wished. He didn't need Olivieri fucking with his head. He'd be seeing Phyllis soon anyway. Dylan's book launch was on Saturday. Between now and then he'd try and erase Phyllis from his brain. Having Gloria around didn't help.

'I have to close shop,' Stoker said, and proceeded to bundle Gloria out of the store. Motioning her out from behind, Stoker remembered the article he'd read in *You* magazine about some Cuban women smuggling domestic appliances in their headgear. The article had been indelibly printed in his imagination.

That's where the toaster idea had come from. Gloria could do it, Stoker thought. Her permed hedge was thick and daunting enough to elude any customs officer. Then Stoker pictured Gloria screaming down Lower Main with her hairdo on fire. It was the most heart-warming thought he'd had all day. He put on his jacket and strolled round the corner to the Planet.

Stoker never ceased to be amazed by the effect of leaving the confines of Dominion Hardware for the outdoors. Inside the store five million things crowded in on one. Stoker was convinced that someday a customer, or himself, or hopefully Olivieri, would be seriously injured by a collapsing shelf and all its contents. The fittings were riddled with woodworm. Someone could probably sink a hand right through the wood to get something from the other side. Maybe he could arrange for Olivieri to walk past the paint section and accidentally on purpose arrange for ten tons of paint to crash on his hairpiece. Why not? The bastard deserved it. Besides, he'd lived far longer than it was healthy! Stoker doubted Mrs Olivieri would miss him. He doubted anyone would. By the time Stoker reached the Planet he hoped that Olivieri would live to a hundred.

Joan was on her second brandy and Coke by the time Stoker sat down across from her in the dingy room. He hadn't had much of a chance to talk to her, except for the travel blurbs she'd given. Their conversation at the dam was the first, and besides, she wasn't in much of a mood and neither was he. With Joan conversation was usually a lopsided affair. Words failed her at the best of times. When she spoke the brain seemed to be the last point of contact before her voice reached the light of day.

Stoker drank his beer and waited. For good measure he lit a Chesterfield Light, making sure that the smoke didn't travel in Joan's direction. While he waited Stoker took in his surroundings. The Planet was probably one of the tackiest bars in the universe. Nothing gelled. The walls were bland, peppered with a random combination of retro posters – Joy Division's *Unknown Pleasures*, a still from *Clockwork Orange*, a massive and odd blown-up image of St George's Cathedral, its parishioners a monotonous serialised cluster of bald and neutered window dummies. The selection of images seemed so arbitrary, monochromatic and unalluring, and yet Stoker and his circle had persisted in turning the place into a mecca. It was probably because the place was so devoid of care, Stoker thought. Because it was a shell and nothing more. The place said nothing. Any meaning that could be found had to be scavenged. The very effort to interpret the Planet had to be a sign of boredom or fatigue. Stoker withdrew from the dull dilapidated surroundings and ordered a Burger Special. This was a staple for Stoker and his friends, two for the price of one the burgers came in a pita bread.

By way of an introduction Stoker started talking about art. This was their shared territory, except that Joan was pretty successful. She always had more commissions than she could cope with. She usually hated them, but she did them all the same – which was how she'd been able to afford to get to New York. She'd painted a Rousseauesque jungle scene for a couple of toucans housed in a ritzy house in Fresnay, a Renaissance mural for a theatre on the Waterfront, a bunch of very slick oil paintings for a German art dealer, a sketch of Table Mountain for some rich aunt. The painting looked just great against the Morkels lounge furniture, Joan said. She wasn't particularly impressed with herself. What she loved doing nobody wanted to buy – which was her pastel series of meticulously detailed drawings, mostly of Percy in various stages of agony and undress. Percy stark naked and writhing effeminately, his lips parted breathlessly, a cock-ring floating above his head like a halo. Percy in a red leather jacket with his cock strapped with masking tape, against a neon cityscape. Percy dead in a trash heap – Joan's current drawing. She'd had a three month break and was slowly and painstakingly trying to get back to work. It wasn't easy, and as Stoker soon discovered, the reasons weren't as obvious as he'd thought.

Joan had met Percy about a year ago when he, Jay and Dayglo had started Nappy Rash. They'd gotten along just fine.

When Joan had decided to shift away from using media images and taking her own photographs for her drawings, she'd chosen Percy for her model. The choice was obvious. Percy had precisely the gorgeous seedy blue-collar inner-city edge Joan was looking for. She'd started taking pictures. Percy was happy to strip. He showed her his S&M gear. It was his cock-ring that emerged transfigured in her reworking of Michelangelo's *Dying Slave*.

The problem was that Joan had started fucking Percy, which as it turned out was why she hadn't been available for any real conversation since she'd got back. Stoker stared at Joan. She was clearly distraught. She couldn't quite make sense of it all. It was all new to her. And she was clearly not interested in keeping the affair under wraps. Joan was a Plumstead girl, privileged and honest. Percy clearly mattered to her. It wasn't a question of Percy versus Waldo. That wasn't the point. She knew it was crazy to break up a ten-year relationship. Still, she needed to change. Percy was offering her what she needed – less light and a lot of darkness. Growing up in Plumstead had turned her into a stupid spoilt grub, she'd said. She needed to change, and she needed to change fast. New York was the beginning. Stoker stared at her as she talked. She was so clear and straightforward and freaked. Stoker hoped that Dean would be late. He didn't know how Dean would handle Joan's news. Then again, it had fuck-all to do with Dean, or himself for that matter.

As it turned out, Dean didn't rock up till much later. It was just him and Joan. Stoker doubted that it was advice Joan was seeking. She usually did what she felt like. At least that's the impression she gave off. Now a different scenario was being played out, one in which Joan was always giving in to peer pressure. This wasn't surprising. Relationships as long-standing as hers and Waldo's were rare. They belonged to a virtually extinct species. Nothing lasted these days unless you were desperate to make things last, and then the desperation eventually fucked things up.

The thing about Stoker and his circle, Stoker realised, was

that they were never desperate enough. People fell in and out of each other's arms like there was no tomorrow. One would never guess that this was the '90s and the Age of Disease. Big fuckin' deal. Was there an age that wasn't? Whatever . . . still it could be said that Stoker and his friends were the emphatic representation of the '90s with all the risk that came with a passionate commitment to adventure and self-discovery. At least, that's the way things looked in a certain section of Cape Town. Like Joan had said, Egyptian geese mate for life. Humans were another story. Stoker couldn't begin to count the number of stories he'd heard of condoms fucking out.

'We decided to separate, right,' Joan began. 'Which was why Waldo left for India and I fucked off to New York. The idea was we'd get back. But I can't see us getting back. Not the way it was. It was hell, Stoker. Nobody really saw it. Nobody wanted to know. I love him so, but if he'd only learnt to put his cock away it would have been another story . . .' Joan trailed off.

Stoker pictured Joan's telling image of Percy with his cock strapped up in masking tape. Then Joan started crying. It wasn't a pretty sight. This was definitely not the moment for any snide remark. Besides, whatever he said that was vaguely cynical would probably wash over Joan. As she'd once said to him, she couldn't debate anything because she wouldn't have a leg to stand on. It was a trait she shared with Phyllis. A sort of exquisite cluelessness. Stoker wasn't much better. But he had a vague inkling of how things worked. He wasn't sure if it was a handicap or a talent. Still, like Joan and Phyllis he hated discussion. Most people's points of view were canned, anyway. Besides, what Joan and Phyllis had, which counted for a whole lot more in Stoker's book, was a straightforward honesty. They were both obsessed with the truth. They both hated having to scratch around trying to get at it. Lies fucked you up in the long run, they'd both said independently of each other. Stoker begged to differ, but the Planet was not the right place to get into it.

'When exactly is Waldo coming back?' Stoker asked.

'Soon,' Joan said. 'He's used up all the money he was going to. He's coming back soon.'

Stoker wondered why Joan had decided to start an affair with Percy just when Waldo was returning. Then he realised he was being too rational. Maybe she needed to do something cruel just to get herself off the hook.

'He'll just have to live with it,' Joan said.

'Who?'

'Waldo. He'll just have to deal with it when he gets back. Both of us will.'

'You need another brandy?' Stoker asked.

'Why not,' Joan said.

Stoker and Joan ended up spending the rest of the night at the Planet getting plastered. Dean eventually arrived with Putter. They talked about the Locker Room Project. They talked about Lizzie's wedding. About adoption. About Phyllis and Dylan. About Waldo. Eventually everybody cracked up over Dean's disaster at work. They all concluded that it was a sad thing that Andries van der Merwe's fish had not been caught on camera. Putter stated that he was glad that Dean's disaster had happened. We need to restore the power of print, Putter said. A fish which has been written about was as real as one that had been photographed. Dean's decision to publish his statement of confession meant a new era in the annals of angling magazine history.

Stoker had thought he could get away without mentioning Bianca. He was wrong.

'How was your meeting with the Italian curator?' Putter asked.

'What Italian curator?' Joan asked.

'The woman who bought your Doc?' Dean added.

So Stoker informed everyone that the woman was crazy about his paintings. Joan admitted that she was jealous. Putter wanted to know if she could donate some bucks to the Locker Room Project. Stoker said he'd find out, but he didn't know when he'd next see her. He told nobody that he had Tuesday off. He wasn't sure if he'd call Bianca Buonacuore, or whether he'd paint.

The following morning Stoker was amazed to discover that he didn't have a hangover. He awoke early and resumed work on the radio painting. In the afternoon he stopped over at Farber's for a steak roll and a Stoney ginger beer. There was no way he was going to stop over at Gloria's. While eating he realised that he was walking to Prue's on Blake Street. Stoker hadn't seen much of Prue since Bridge's rape. According to Putter she'd just come back from Graz where she'd sawn up some chairs and rebound the mismatched halves with organza, the stuff used for wedding dresses. The piece was called *For Better or For Worse*. Apparently she was back.

Prue opened the security gate and let Stoker into the Blake Street studio. Prue was clearly glad to see him, but she was also in a bad mood.

'I've just been thinking of you,' Prue said.

'You were?'

'Actually I was thinking of Dylan. I don't suppose you have a copy of his poem "The Ballad of Koos Malgas"?'

'No, I don't.'

'A pity.'

Stoker was curious.

'I've just received this troubling circular from the Brethren of the Owl House. I'm preparing a response on the future of their restoration project.' Prue paced the room waving a printed document. 'It's just awful . . . the callous and insensitive way in which Koos has been held up to public scrutiny by those who claim to be acting in his best interests.'

Stoker was pleased to find Prue outraged. It was always a good sign when she was upset by something connected with art.

'I've got Dylan's fax number. You could ask him to send a copy of the ballad to you. Either that, or you could see him on Saturday. He's having the first launch of his new book at Lawrence's. You could speak to him then. What's this with Koos and the Owl House?'

'This,' Prue said, once again waving the document at Stoker. 'According to the Brethren Koos is a drunk who lacks motivation and needs informed and sympathetic supervision. The report goes on to contradict itself by arguing that Koos is motivated by profit for himself – God forbid! and that his traffic in cement sculpture has produced a slew of minor problems.'

'What's that supposed to mean?'

'It gets worse,' Prue continued, ignoring Stoker's question. 'It seems that Koos is not suitably grateful to the Brethren either. It seems, I quote, that his sixty rand food allowance per week from the shop goes nowhere, not stopping to reflect that it was merely instituted to avoid his spending all his money on drink, and was never intended as the only food for an extended family of ten. Perhaps it is human nature to complain for with all his other expenses and a substantial drinking habit, Koos has managed, in the last year, to pay off a new TV set.'

Prue turned from the page and looked at Stoker. Then resumed: 'If one did not know better, one could be forgiven for assuming that these were extracts from a colonial diary of a different era – not a period when South Africa is trying to rid itself of the colonial mentality which these sentiments represent.'

Stoker sat down. He lit a cigarette and listened as Prue returned to the document.

'In spite of all the problems and misgivings about Koos Malgas, the Brethren concede that Koos does have his uses. He is an added attraction for visitors. Also irreplaceable is his knowledge of the Owl House as it was in Miss Helen's lifetime.' Prue paused, then qualified. 'What seems to have been sidelined by all these revelations about Koos and his private life is the fact that virtually every statue in that garden was built by him. It is true that the creative process was an interactive and dynamic one. A process in which Koos and Helen worked together. But he was more than merely her labourer or her handyman. The sculptures in that garden would not have taken the form they have without his particular input. As I see it the relationship between Koos Malgas and the Brethren is one of manipulation and control. It seems to have very little to do with Koos's needs or agenda and everything to do with the agenda formulated by the Brethren. In short they seem to be of the opinion that whoever pays the piper owns the tune!'

There was more.

'The way Koos Malgas is discussed is so insulting as to take one's breath away!'

The doorbell rang. Stoker went to open the security gate. Two black women with the compressed dignity of civil rights workers handed him a begging letter. He handed the letter to Prue.

'Hand the women five rand, would you. There should be enough in the cash box.' Then Prue walked over to her new Canon Colour Copier and photocopied the letter. By now Prue should have over three hundred begging letters, Stoker thought. Documentation was her addiction, the source of her discursive art. Stoker returned the letter and five rand to the women.

'Read this, would you. I'll make some coffee,' Prue said.

She had written a lengthy response to the Brethren's report in which she emphatically claimed that Koos Malgas did not need a forced retirement package but a good lawyer. Stoker smiled in the face of Prue's tireless and often witty vigour. Listening to her rant was just the break he needed. She handed him a cup of coffee.

'You hear from Bridge?' Stoker asked.

Prue showed Stoker a photograph of Bridge and Immo bungee-jumping into the Victoria Falls. Stoker felt queasy just looking down at the crazed grins on Bridge and Immo's faces, the sharp drop into the mist and spray.

'Who needs to bungee-jump when you can risk a taxi into town,' Stoker asked.

Prue chuckled. 'I hear you've been painting,' she said.

'You should come over and have a look,' Stoker said. 'Remember the piece I exhibited at the Seeff?' Prue nodded. 'Well these pieces are a development. They're massive. I'm looking for the right place to show them.'

Prue was just the person to talk to about the actualities of art-making. She was a veteran. She always had time for others, and she had good ideas.

'You should try the African Studies Department at UCT. I'm sure they'll have space. What are the works about?'

Stoker gave his spiel.

'Rather gloomy,' Prue said.

'Well I'm feeling rather gloomy. I guess nothing is really working for me, you know.'

'Putter tells me Phyllis is pregnant.'

'Six months.' Stoker wondered if Prue knew about Phyllis and Dylan. He wished he hadn't told her about Dylan's book launch. But then again, if she didn't already know she'd find out soon enough. Dean was right. Everyone knew the days of everyone else's fuckin' lives.

'What do you think of Immo?' Stoker asked.

'He reminds me of Bridget's father,' Prue said. It was enough. Prue was divorced. She'd long ago stopped calling Bridge's father by his name.

'Bridge is crazy about him,' Stoker said. Prue smiled knowingly. Stoker changed the subject. 'You doing anything for the Locker Room Project?'

'How could I not?' Prue asked. 'With our civic-minded friend breathing down our necks.' Prue adored Putter. In many ways Putter was continuing an art tradition championed by Prue. The application was different, of course. Times were different. Well, sort of. Begging letters looked like they were here to stay.

'I'm thinking of reworking one of Muybridge's series of a naked woman throwing a ball. It's all I can think of right now. You?'

'I don't know yet. I'm too locked into what I'm working on right now. It's a painting of a gutted radio. But I'm sure I'll get around to it. You mind if I use the phone?'

'Go ahead.'

Stoker produced Bianca's business card and dialled. Amazingly she was home. Amazingly she agreed to meet with him.

'Give Bridge my love when you speak with her,' Stoker said to Prue. Then he kissed her and departed. He walked to Main Road and caught a taxi into town.

CHAPTER TEN

The taxi which supposedly seated twelve was crammed. Stoker counted twenty bodies excluding his own. As the taxi sped and zigzagged down Main, Stoker stared at the toothless Dracula mouth of the money-collector yelling at the passing trade. The taxi squealed to a halt, a body was ejected, a new one injected.

With half of his arse seated on thin air, Stoker thought of hard-core dental surgery. The removal of the upper and lower front teeth was high fashion on the Cape Flats. The fashion turned on the avid pursuit of the better kiss, the better blow-job. Ghastly as the visual was to Stoker, its effects were proven. He himself had once been the jolly recipient of a tooth-less blow-job. No matter how hard he tried Stoker couldn't picture the face of the girl who'd sucked him off so long ago in the parking lot outside the Galaxy Club in Rylands. He could still feel his cock inside the buffered flesh of her mouth.

All the way into town Massive Attack blared on the stereo. Stoker listened to the excruciatingly detailed and perfected seduction of the sound. He felt numb. His friends were definitely suffering from a musical drought, he thought. The year had produced no anthem worth mentioning, except for Nusrat Fateh Ali Khan's *Dum Must Must*. Then Stoker reminded himself that Bowie and Eno had a new CD that was due for release. It would be their first collaboration since *Heroes* and *Low*. Stoker was looking forward to it. He stared at the careering world outside and thought of Koos Malgas, Dylan's poem, Prue's despair. Then he thought of Bianca. He realised that he only had fifteen rand on him, enough for a sandwich and beer, the taxi-fare home. He realised that he hadn't changed his clothes in a while, that he wasn't wearing any underwear. He concentrated on nuking his hard-on.

The taxi arrived at the terminus. Stoker stepped out into the throng of hawkers. He walked past racks of cheap gaudy dresses and thought of Phyllis, of the hibiscus dress he'd bought her at Truworths. He stopped at a rack of cheap sunglasses. It was pointless even thinking of buying a pair since he was blind as hell, and contacts were out of the question. Like Lizzie, Stoker wasn't into having his body messed with at such close range. He bought a packet of roast peanuts and munched all the way to Greenmarket Square. He'd agreed to meet Bianca at Petit Paris, his favourite city bistro. Petit Paris was a third of the size of Nino's. Stoker had the idea that the occupants had egos which were equally modest. It was an illusion of course, but it was one he cherished. He ordered an Emmenthal sandwich and water. He'd save the beer for later.

Petit Paris was a glass box that overlooked the cobbled heart of Cape Town – Greenmarket Square. It was a few doors down from Nino's where Lizzie had met Klingman. No thanks to style and commerce, Petit Paris had revamped itself to favour expensively dressed and good-looking people like Lizzie and Klingman. Across from Stoker a man was talking into a cell phone. Further down a woman was reading *Business Day*. A lurid collection of interior designers? clothing designers? were smiling at each other. It looked at though they were high as kites. Stoker appreciated the fact that all the waitresses were young and gorgeous. They were dressed as tackily as he was.

Bianca stepped in looking as rich and successful as most of the people in the bistro. Stoker gawked at her as she advanced towards him, wearing an infectious smile designed to shred every ounce of cynicism lingering inside him. She kissed him on both cheeks and sat down.

'So how's my poor artist?' Bianca asked.

'Poor,' Stoker said. Bianca laughed and ordered a beef sandwich and white wine for herself, a Windhoek for Stoker.

'You like this place?' Bianca asked.

'I feel like I'm in a movie,' Stoker said.

'That's where we all are, not so? In the movies.'

Stoker felt a terrible urge to kiss Bianca. She had the kind of lips that looked like they were injected with silicon. He knew that she knew what was going on in his head. She was the sort of woman who was used to being desired. She had a way about her of feeling very lucky. Stoker doubted that she'd had to fight for anything in her life. He wondered what she was doing with him.

Bianca's sandwich arrived. Stoker watched her eat, the slices of beef and pickle red and green against her large peach lips. To pass the time Stoker told her the sad story of Koos Malgas. She was, surprisingly, very interested and remarkably informed about Koos's relationship with Helen Martins. She even knew of Dylan's famous ballad. For some reason it hadn't occurred to her that Dylan was his brother. Then again, why should she? His family didn't exactly own the name.

'Greatness runs in your family,' Bianca said, picking up the thought in his brain.

Stoker had the sickening feeling that she meant it. He told her about Dylan's launch, asked her if she would accompany him.

'Yes,' she said.

Stoker may as well have been proposing to her, such was the emotional frenzy coursing through him. She, in turn, responded as lightly, as flippantly, as naturally as she always did. Stoker could sense no emotional turmoil within her. He was at once gladdened and saddened by this.

Bianca finished eating her sandwich. 'I suppose you want to know what I'm doing here,' she said.

Stoker was silent. He hoped she'd profess undying love. Her response was more secular.

'As I've said before, I am a writer. I write about art. I also collect for an important gallery in Italy. Which is why I can afford to buy your paintings.'

'Paintings?' Stoker asked, stressing the plural.

'Yes. I would like to buy the new cycle when it is finished. I also wish to set the price at something suitably astronomical.'

'You wish to buy all of them?'

'It is a series, is it not?'

'Yes . . . but . . .'

'You think I am a neocolonialist? Is that it? A European who has come to steal the best and take it home to her native land?'

'It's not Putter you're talking to, okay. It doesn't matter to me who sees my paintings. They must be seen.'

'Don't forget that Putter has a point, however.' Honesty seemed to be the game Bianca was playing. 'We have travelling shows,' she said. 'We can arrange exhibitions of your work in different countries. Northern Ireland, for instance. Belfast.'

'But why me?' Stoker asked. He was flabbergasted.

'Why not you?' Bianca countered, then teasingly added: 'Are you ashamed of success?'

'You do realise that *Man in a Landscape* is the first painting I've sold? I'm a nobody.'

'Then you will be a somebody,' Bianca said.

'I wish to have an exhibition here, in my country,' Stoker said. He had never spoken with such a keen sense of place before. He had never valued South Africa with such earnestness. He wondered why.

'Where would you like to exhibit your work?' Bianca asked.

Stoker mentioned the African Studies Department. Bianca suggested the wasteland surrounding the Seeff Gallery. She pictured the paintings hanging in the unfinished empty spaces of a building under construction. Stoker was both awed and alarmed by the daring of Bianca's suggestion. Stoker hated provocation. That was Putter's way. The way of the Situationists. The risk of a new and unusual environment frightened him. Bianca's idea was seductive, but its enactment was daunting.

'Tell me about your writing,' Stoker said, wishing to shift the limelight away from himself.

Bianca spoke as effortlessly about herself as she did about others. In fact her sense of self, her sense of her function as a writer, was deeply enmeshed in the lives and efforts of others. At the root of the book she was writing lay the riddle of South Africa. She was keenly aware of South Africa's current fashionability. She wanted to get beyond what she perceived as the ruinous recent legacy of The New. South Africa was afflicted with a preoccupation with newness and yet, she countered, this obsession with the new was in fact an obsession with what was old elsewhere. She saw the new democracy as a variant of fascism, another means whereby a country would be held back. Democracy was a kind of camouflage. A global hallucination.

'The fact is, people can't stand freedom – it's too scary,' Bianca said. And here she laughed. 'No one in fact wants freedom. They merely want a more genteel and less vulgar form of enslavement.'

Stoker was all ears. Whether or not he agreed was not the issue. He enjoyed the playful way in which Bianca couched her earnestness.

'But I'm running ahead of myself,' she said. 'What in fact am I writing about?'

Stoker waited.

'Have you read the poetry of Lionel Abrahams?'

Stoker admitted that he had not. He admitted that in fact he didn't know who Lionel Abrahams was.

Bianca spoke:

'Stay quiet a while.
Let words
rinse clean,
dissolve.

Squat amid potsherds,
scrape your scales.
Let opinion
fall away.

Bear to be numb and dumb,
void of judgements.
Allow a waiting emptiness
of which none knows.

Silent a while
on a margin,
give no name or shape
to expectation.

Let indifferent time,
random flickers of the air,
ungathered dust
bring some instruction.'

Bianca paused, let the words hover. Tether. 'That is why I
write,' she said. 'To give no name or shape to expectation.'
Then solemnly added: 'Do not prohibit that which cannot be
named. George Steiner.'

Stoker thought of the book by Steiner which he'd read and
thought about a while ago. What Bianca had said made sense to
him. He thought about Abrahams' poem, about the way the
words had popped from her mouth like charged and tremulous
sound bites. He watched her as she removed her Gold Card
and paid the bill.

Though he more or less understood what Bianca was trying
to say, he still wondered whether she was being obtuse. Was
she trying to fob him off with poetry? He wanted to know
much more about the book she was writing. He sensed that she
would have told him, but that the situation was not right. He
anticipated another time and place. Then he anticipated absolutely nothing. Gazing through the window of Petit Paris
onto the cobbled square he saw Phyllis, then Dylan. They were
both laughing. They were holding hands. He realised that he
had never seen either of them so radiant, not even Phyllis. No
remembered expression of wonder and joy could compare with
what he was seeing right then – the way Phyllis smiled, the way
she and Dylan looked at each other, the light sure clasping of
their hands . . . Phyllis wore an orange midriff and a short
skirt. Her hair, he noticed, was blond at the roots, tapering to
the colour of strawberries. Her swollen stomach blazed in the
spring light.

Bianca must have noticed the sudden shift in Stoker's expression. He had opened himself up to her. Now she saw a withering, a deathly pallor overtake him. She turned and followed his gaze. Then she placed her hand upon his.

CHAPTER ELEVEN

Stoker was not prepared for such a harsh visual update. He'd mentally prepared himself to meet Phyllis and Dylan at the book launch. Seeing the two of them amidst all the passers-by, watching them as they laughed, as they moved, as they basked in each other's company, had left him utterly shocked. Was it envy he was feeling? Despair? Stoker wasn't sure. At the core he had always considered himself selfish. Self-centred. He had told himself that he loved Phyllis, that he needed her. He had thought of leaving her. He had thought of moving in with her. It was she who'd sensed that neither of them was ready for the commitment. In one of her cryptic notes which Phyllis had sent via Gloria she'd talked about finding a home of one's own, about never sitting on the edge of another man's nest. The words were in quotation marks. They were Turgenev's.

Was that what he was trying to do? To sit on the edge of her nest? If he'd never felt comfortable inside his skin, how could he feel comfortable anywhere? Phyllis had always been independent. No one had ever paid her way and no one ever would. She had her flat on Orphan and Long, she had Petal, Dylan. A job. There was nothing squalid, errant or confused about her. Phyllis maintained in ways Stoker never could. She engaged the world on terms which were her own. Watching Phyllis and Dylan disappear Stoker realised that her decision to leave him had proved convenient. Her decision had dovetailed with the plot of his life. She had freed him to enter the country of last things.

Stoker winced at the thought of last things. In the three

months in which he'd immersed himself in his paintings he had enacted the finality he'd wanted to achieve. His broken life . . . his broken paintings. There was a definite connection. He'd never wanted to resolve the breakup, he'd wanted to push it further. If he was heartbroken now, so be it. How many lives were being broken every second of every day! If it was jealousy he was feeling, if it was envy, then it was the jealousy and envy of one who enjoyed the acrid taste of loss.

Stoker was not impressed with himself and he didn't care. He held the instant of Phyllis and Dylan's disappearance in the field of his gaze. Then he let the image slip away and yielded to a benign and peculiar joy. The radiance of Phyllis and Dylan had relieved him from the burden of finding alternatives, some way of redressing the balance. What for, and why? Stoker realised that it did not matter that he was the father of Phyllis's child. By this he meant that it did not matter that he was not with her. Dylan was clearly doing a fine job as a surrogate father. Dylan seemed happier than Stoker had ever seen him before. Of course Stoker could never know the basis for Phyllis and Dylan's joy. Who could say what went on in the lives of lovers? No one. Stoker could only guess. He had a certain advantage, but advantages too extinguished with time. He was confident that they were living a fine life together. Beyond conviction, he decided not to pursue the matter any further.

When Stoker turned to face Bianca he realised that she was still holding his hand. He didn't know whether to laugh or cry. Bianca Buonacuore . . . Bianca the good-hearted. As he turned to face her Stoker realised that he did not desire her, not sexually at least. He was glad for her presence, glad for her friendship. He realised suddenly that he felt incredibly tired. He realised that all he wanted to do was to go back to his studio. He wanted to be alone. He wanted to sleep. To paint.

Stoker studied the woman seated in front of him. How easy it was to make a fetish of a human being, he thought. How easy it was to conjure mystery. True, she was beautiful, talented, articulate. But these were not measures of her value. He imagined her as someone who bore an uneasy relation to her

214

beauty, her talent, her articulacy. As he steadily resumed his composure he realised that he was grateful for the time she had given him. He had found a new friend. And that, he understood, was all he needed. A friend. Someone with whom he could talk, to whom he could listen.

Stoker watched her light a Gitanes. She would not enquire into what had happened. It was none of her business. In fact it was none of his. He suddenly felt light and buoyant. The peculiar suddenness of his breakup with Phyllis no longer puzzled him. Things changed at every instant. Why search for a definitive meaning in endings when things ended and started all the time? Was he truly a heartless cuckold, or was he conducting himself in the only viable way? It is the ideal that destroys, Stoker thought. If nothing is ideal, if everything changes, if no one is able to judge and define the life of another, then how could people allow themselves to undergo the absurd melodrama of loss? His separation from Phyllis was finally painless. He still loved her, and he was sure that she still loved him. There was nothing left to do, he realised, but to get on with his life.

Bianca ordered another beer and a glass of white wine. Stoker lit a cigarette. And then he smiled. He was glad to feel as small, as incidental as he felt in the larger scheme of things. He was glad that someone had valued the scraps he had salvaged – his few paintings. He was glad for the day off and glad for the work at Dominion. He looked forward to seeing Phyllis and Dylan. Maybe he was just too young for Phyllis? It was true that she was even younger physically than he, but she was older. She was an old soul. He could just about look after himself, just about cope. And the fact was that he enjoyed the meanness of his existence – that he could just about afford the roof over his head, the food he ate, the money for paints and materials. He'd never really asked for much. He'd never painted because he thought he could earn a living doing it. He'd done it because he had to. He didn't have much of a choice. What else could he do?

'About your writing,' Stoker said, sipping his beer.

Bianca smiled. She seemed happy to resume a conversation which earlier, ironically, she had not wanted to pursue.

'Ah yes, the writing,' Bianca said, then continued. 'How can one write about art in South Africa today? All the restrictions are gone. There is nobody to be angry with . . .'

'You really think so?' Stoker asked.

'What do you think?' Bianca replied.

'I think there are still restrictions. I think the fight is never over.'

'Ah, the Romantic,' Bianca said.

'That's just a convenient and false term,' Stoker said. He had a feeling she was baiting him. He let himself be baited. 'The way I see it, we're still fucked,' Stoker said. 'Go to the townships. See for yourself. But I'm not really talking about the fact that people are still starving, the fact that we need more houses, more jobs, and the fact that we don't have the resources to satisfy these needs. I'm talking about art. The foreign market has this idea of who and what we are. Take Willie Bester, for instance. He hit the jackpot with the cover of *Vogue*. His work sells like hot cakes. Now I'm not knocking the work. The fact that I don't particularly like what he does is beside the point. The point is that's what the world wants, that's what it sees as South African art. Crude serialised depictions of trauma. We're still stuck with a bunch of neocolonialist art curators both inside and outside this country.'

'Like me,' Bianca said.

'Perhaps,' Stoker replied. 'As far as I'm concerned the West has to start looking after itself instead of going around playing Father Christmas.'

Bianca chuckled, lit a cigarette. 'It's very difficult to change people's opinions,' she said. 'Perhaps it's South Africa's role to help the world to change its mind. Perhaps South Africa has to reimagine itself.'

Stoker thought of Mike Nicol's book. 'Have you read *The Waiting Country*?' Stoker asked. 'I haven't. I've only heard bits. I think you should read it.'

'I have,' Bianca said.

'I suppose you would have,' Stoker said. He wondered if he was the only person on the planet who hadn't.

'*The Waiting Country* is the answer to *My Traitor's Heart*,' Bianca said.

Stoker remembered that this was roughly the point which Phyllis had made in Citrusdal. At the time he wasn't into making comparisons.

'What do you mean?' Stoker asked.

'Well, *My Traitor's Heart* is a study in bile, in treachery and revolt. It is the work of an apostate. *The Waiting Country* is the long-awaited equaliser. It is the work of the good son.'

Stoker listened. Bianca continued.

'Nicol's book manages to sneak out of the dualism of action-reaction. It doesn't set out the terms. It works like the poem I quoted earlier. It asks us to stay quiet a while, let opinion fall away. Nicol's waiting country is Abrahams' waiting emptiness of which none knows. In your paintings I see the same suspension . . . the suitcase . . . the hammer studded with nails . . . the plug torn from its socket . . . the breakdown of the certainty and flow of action . . . power. These tactile and graphic images are, for me, emblematic of a state of hovering, of being between things. They suggest a space neither of doubt or of hope. Bear to be numb and dumb. Those are Abrahams' words. Words which I think describe the shape, the spirit of your paintings. We are living in uncertain times. Either we fall into the abyss of equivocation or we find new ways in which to act.'

Was that what he was, Stoker asked himself. Was he numb and dumb? Was that why he had felt so little pain on seeing Phyllis and Dylan? Was that why he could sit opposite Bianca and hold this conversation without a feeling of heartbreak?

Stoker was glad for Bianca's interpretation.

That day Stoker did not go home as he had intended. Instead he chose to spend the rest of the day with Bianca. No actual decision was made to this effect. They simply left Petit Paris and found themselves strolling through the city centre. It was a balmy spring day. They wove through the stalls on Greenmarket Square. Stoker thought of his chance meeting with Immo, the yo-yo, Immo's collection of stones which he'd picked up on his walk through Africa. On Church Street they stopped outside African Image to examine a series of township barber-shop signs. While Stoker toyed with an old copperplated compass at one of the second-hand and antique stalls, Bianca entered African Image to arrange a purchase and time of collection.

This was followed by a visit to the Association of Arts. There was an exibition of pastel drawings. Stoker was struck by the difference in application and intention between the drawings he saw and those of Joan's. Here he found serenity and light, a goodness that felt insipid to him. He thought of Bianca's notion of treachery and duty, of stepping beyond both dynamics. The pastels he saw looked like they'd settled into a groove too soon. They were nothing more than soulful parables which amounted to good taste. Or were they? Stoker realised that he couldn't quite get a handle on what he was seeing. They were beautiful, true. But something in him rejected what he saw. Maybe it was because he felt that he hadn't been taken beyond what he already knew? Then again, was it truly the job of the work to do so? Surely it was up to him? Stoker couldn't figure it out. He found himself both rejecting and yielding. He felt pissed off by the turmoil inside him. It wasn't a turmoil about anything real, he thought. The whole thing was about taste. Fuck taste, he thought. Though he knew that that was where everything was going. These days it was all about taste. There were no absolutes. Or were there? He finally came to the conclusion that he didn't like the pastels he saw. Nothing had really moved him beyond the restlessness in his mind.

Eventually Stoker and Bianca quit the Association. They found themselves strolling along the tree-lined Government Avenue.

'This is our Tuilleries,' Stoker said. This wasn't his own description but one he'd heard before. It came with the role he'd assumed as friend and guide.

Bianca pointed out a squirrel only to discover that it was a rat. Then they entered the lush labyrinth of budding flowers. Stoker realised that he had never mentioned the flowers which Bianca had sent to him. He felt compelled to speak, then chose not to. There are no words for certain deeds, he thought, as they stopped in front of the giant statue of Cecil John Rhodes. Rhodes's handlebar moustache seemed to quiver as he gazed fixedly towards Cairo, his felt hat clutched in his right hand. Birds twittered in a sanctuary nearby. There is nothing queerer than Empire, Stoker recalled Dean saying. He smiled wryly, and plucked himself away from Rhodes's undeflecting gaze. He stopped a few metres away at his favourite spot in the city centre – a glaucous green pond filled with massive koi fish, their fluid sluggish bodies splattered and dappled with pinks, whites and oranges.

'It is a curious thing,' Stoker began. 'I have always loved fish.'

'And why is that?' Bianca asked.

Stoker let the question slide. 'Once I found a great big snoek lying dead along the beach,' he said. 'The snoek was lying on its side. Through the torn flesh I could see the beginnings of bone. What struck me most were the wedged patterns of bird feet that veered to and from the dead fish like a fan.'

'It did not matter that the fish was dead?' Bianca asked.

'No. And that's the peculiar thing. My love of fish has never had anything to do with whether the fish was alive or dead. There is a market in Salt River that I frequent. It's a large chilly warehouse. There are racks and racks of fish packed in ice. Like diamonds. And to me the fish are jewels. The colours have always enthralled me. The purples, greens, blues. In some ways I've always thought the Salt River Fish Market was the finest art gallery in Cape Town.'

Bianca chuckled. She was charmed.

Stoker was struck by his sudden compulsion to speak of fish. It was a passion dear to him. He wanted Bianca to see beyond the apparent morbidity of his vision. They were both staring intently into the green pond flickering with sluggish colour.

'I have a sister,' Stoker resumed. 'Her name is Lizzie. You will meet her if you come to the book launch.' He was inching towards what he had come to believe was the source of his passion for fish.

'Many years ago, when I was little . . . nine years old . . . my sister and I were detained at Nairobi airport. We were en route to England. The reason for our journey is not important. We never got to England. In fact, as it turned out, I've never left Africa. Lizzie has, she spent many years in England. Anyway, for forty-eight hours we were not allowed to leave the area in which we were detained. I don't remember the details as well as Lizzie. She is older. According to Lizzie we were not allowed access to food or a toilet in all the time we were detained. Apparently I was impossible. Lizzie had to look after me. And this is where the fish come in. There was a pond filled with goldfish in the courtyard adjoining the room in which we were detained. It seems that was where I spent almost all my time while we waited for the plane that would take us back home. It was the goldfish pond that helped me. What is odd is that I remember being detained, but I don't remember the pond or the fish. Lizzie swears by it, and I believe her. Lizzie's story has helped me make sense of a love for something which for years I never understood. Isn't that curious?'

'I was just picturing you as a little boy with your pale freckled face and red hair under an African sun.' Bianca ran her hand through Stoker's hair. The impact was glorious. 'Have you always worn glasses?' she asked.

'I'm blind as a bat,' Stoker said. And Bianca laughed.

They left the green pond behind them and came upon a rose garden. Weaving through the beginnings of roses, through thorny grey stalks and mounds of wet grey earth, Bianca resumed the topic of fish. She informed Stoker of the global increase in the sales of fish tanks. They were becoming as permanent and essential a fixture as TV. Well, not quite, but Stoker understood the exaggeration. Then she shifted to a recent visit to the aquarium on the Waterfront. She'd discovered that the aquarium was the first in the world that had managed to house and keep snoek in captivity. The experiment had initially failed, then borders had been painted to designate a feeding area for snoek. Since snoek were temperamentally difficult to transport they had to be anaesthetised and delivered on stretchers. The experiment seemed to have succeeded, she said.

Stoker listened, entranced by the vision of anaesthetised snoek on stretchers. Then they stepped into the Natural History Museum.

Bianca was thrilled as they travelled past glass cabinets containing convincing replicas of a tiger, a seal, a host of animals, birds and reptiles, each caught in convincing facsimiles of natural settings. They saw a graphic depiction of a giant lizard whose bloodied flesh was being torn apart by smaller lizards. Stoker and Bianca studied the artwork, the renditions of flesh, blood, the geography of a prehistoric jaw. They passed a reproduction of a Bushman in the process of making a fire. The Bushman's flaccid body was crossed by the shade of a mud hut, a painted scrub landscape stretching into the distance beyond, reminding Stoker of a Pierneef painting.

Here all of Africa was contained, named, held before the viewer in all its deathly naturalistic splendour. Here, beneath the flickering fluorescent light existed an Africa of which Stoker rarely thought. The Africa of Rider Haggard and Cecil John Rhodes. The Africa of Empire. Here each and every animal was lovingly reproduced. Frozen in time and place. Stoker felt the same thrill he had felt as a child. Passing through this theme park of dead and half-remembered things – a fake elephant, a stuffed hyena – Stoker felt neither loathing or shame. Here the once living and now dead blurred into that which looked real but was thoroughly synthetic. There was a certain poetry, Stoker thought, in the fastidious blurring of the

221

real and the artificial. After all, isn't this what was happening everywhere in the modern world? This systematic and gorgeous fakery?

'Every wild creature I kill crosses the boundary between wilderness and number,' Bianca vaguely said, tugging at Stoker's thoughts. They were standing before the suspended bones of a whale. The air pulsated with a sonar squawk.

From the Natural History Museum they passed the Paddock, an outdoor theatre. Bianca was discussing the question of whether or not Saartjie Baartman, the Khoisan woman known as the Hottentot Venus and preserved in a muséum in Paris, should be returned to South Africa and buried. As she detailed the delicious perversions of nineteenth-century ethnography, the anatomical links that were drawn between the bloated arses of Khoi women and European prostitutes, Stoker suddenly broke into laughter. He was struck by the delirious screechings of children emanating from The Paddock. Bianca broke her monologue. Together they drank in the wave of gasps and screams. The children in The Paddock were watching a dramatisation of a Grimm fairy tale. Stoker pointed out the sign for The Paddock – a two-dimensional cut-out of an ark on a storm-tossed wave. The ark was suspended in a tree. In the portholes, bulwark, stern and deck of the ship appeared an array of twinned animals, each with a distinctively childlike aspect.

From The Paddock Stoker and Bianca passed into the National Gallery, drawn by a criss-cross of red ribbon fluttering above the entrance like a wish. After a cursory examination of the new acquisitions they entered the photographic exhibition entitled *Positive Lives*. A candle burnt in the centre of the room. It was here, amidst the living eyes of the dead, that Bianca informed Stoker of the death of her brother. A chill had overcome her, a chill of loss, of a shared life remembered. Stoker hadn't stopped to think that Bianca had a family. So amputated had been his vision of her! So pristine and unnatural! The photographs drew each of them singularly. The exhibition demanded an eye for an eye. There was no room for commiseration or pity. Stoker felt his heart stop as he faced the eyes of a man his own age. Their dates of birth were exactly the same. The man's date of death his own. Stoker recalled Putter's outrage as they drove away from the Rhodes Mem dam. He thought of the impact of Craig Darlow's death on Putter, of how Darlow's death had become the key to the Locker Room Project, the source of outrage, hope and fearlessness. Darlow was what? Twenty-four when he died? And Bianca's brother? Then Stoker recalled his conversation with Phyllis in Citrusdal. She had never felt so close to death, she'd said. Her mother and Chan had never entertained thoughts of their mortality. Was this true? And did it matter if it was or wasn't? Phyllis's point still contained a bracing truth. In an Age of Disease no one was exempt. For Stoker's peers life was a matter of timing, of ethics and mathematics. Error reigned. The knowledge of a premature death stalked his generation.

Stoker studied Bianca as she moved slowly from image to image. He wondered to what degree it was art she saw, or life. Then again, Stoker thought, in the presence of art one was also in the presence of death. A life was lived both inside and outside a canvas. An accretion of moments were captured, a tracing of a story etched. Stoker could not ascertain the state of Bianca's mind. He turned away from all the faces he saw, faces that reflected his own. It was not fear that drove him away, but a sense of familiarity, of vulnerability. He felt no more alive than the countenances of the dead that faced him at every turn. He moved into the next room.

The room was filled with another sequence of ghostings. All about him stood the sculptures of Jane Alexander. Bianca joined him. Neither spoke as they moved in reverse directions across the room. Alexander's most well-known work, the *Butcher Boys*, was absent. Stoker could still picture their haunting presence, seated in a row with their unwavering sightless yet penetrating eyes, their spines tearing through flesh, their mantels of horn. The loss of the *Butcher Boys* was the gain of the Venice Biennale, Stoker reminded himself. Alexander's mutant sculptures were burnt into his imagination. He did not miss the grim spectacle because he would never forget it. At that very moment in time the *Butcher Boys* formed part of a pageant of gripping depictions of the human body over the last century. Stoker had seen images in a catalogue which Prue had shown him.

Stoker was struck by a marked shift in Alexander's vision. Gone was the brutal atavistic beauty. In its place was a quieter yet still unnerving calm. Stoker stood before a sculpture of a black man in a black suit. The man was seated in a black chair, a briefcase at his feet. The man was staring at a white television. On the screen a white man was moving nervously, repeatedly straightening his tie. The whole conveyed a mood of anticipation, but also of anxiety. The piece was called *Integration Programme: man with TV*.

Stoker turned to find Bianca. She was staring at a figure of a naked woman, her arms thrust over a metal stand. A filigreed lace cloth travelled in a neat arc across the collar-bone. Like weeds the lace and flesh had interwoven, merged, becoming almost indistinguishable. The whole was a disturbing fusion of the real and the fake, the human and the doll-like. The woman was clearly dead, a vertical exhibit in a mortuary. The woman seemed eerily calm, as if to say that she had finally quit a living world that had not been good to her. And yet, and yet, was there truly peace here? In the midst of ruin? Stoker wasn't certain. He discovered that he was having difficulty breathing. He left the room with the intention of returning on another day.

Passing through a labyrinth of rooms that shifted in historical period and medium, Stoker exited the gallery. Outside he drank in the screeching sounds of horror and delight emanating from The Paddock. Seated on the stairs of the National Gallery he lit a Chesterfield Light. In the distance he could see the copper-domed roof of the library, the tree-lined ridge of Signal Hill beyond. He thought of why people made the things they made. He thought of Dean's remark about how difficult it was to do nothing. He'd end up rushing to the nearest paint brush, Dean had said. And it was true. There was nothing to do but to act. The question was why? And how? He too was implicated in a madness. There was no reprieve. Sculpture was not his medium. He sought relief in two-dimensional surfaces.

Bianca sat down beside him and plucked the cigarette from his hand. Stoker enjoyed the familiarity, the ease with which she could adjust herself to his presence. There was nothing forced between them. No ulterior motive – at least none that he could sense. He was happy to have spent the afternoon with her. Happy for the uproar of children in the near distance.

'Do you remember Augustus John's painting of TS Eliot?' Stoker asked.

'But of course,' Bianca said.

'Did you know that the painting is housed in the Durban Art Gallery?'

Bianca did not.

'For some reason it is not exhibited. Isn't that depressing?'

'Yes,' Bianca said.

Together they watched the late afternoon sun sink behind Signal Hill.

'Let's stick together for the rest of the day,' Bianca said.

Stoker could find no reason not to.

CHAPTER THIRTEEN

That evening Stoker and Bianca dined at Pickwick's on Long. Stoker half-expected to see Phyllis. Long Street was her turf and place of work. Stoker saw Dom's black Beetle drive past. In the passenger seat was Jay. It seemed odd to see familiar faces. The day, though beautiful and warm, was strangely desolate. He had spent it in the company of a stranger. A stranger who was growing increasingly less strange. A funereal scent had clung to Stoker. In the midst of a newfound communion, he and Bianca had passed through a pageant of sorrow and death. Stoker could still see the instant at which Phyllis and Dylan had passed from his sight. It was an instant as precisely etched within him as all the faces he had seen at the *Positive Lives* exhibition. There was Phyllis and Dylan's laughter. There was the raw exchange of glances between himself and the man who shared his date of birth. So much had happened, so much that filled him, so much he could not contain. Misery tugged at his heels. He was glad that Bianca had surfaced relatively unscathed.

Pickwick's was her favourite eatery, she said. The closest thing to places she remembered elsewhere – Montreal . . . Perhaps Pickwick's was where she could find herself again? Perhaps she too was lost? Alone?

Bianca went on to reflect on the blurred sense she had of place. She spoke of having always moved, having always lived out of a suitcase. She had bought three bottles of red wine and together they had driven to her rooms at the Peninsula Hotel in Sea Point.

Her balcony window overlooked the sea. Stoker watched a passing ship, flush against the horizon. He drank his wine, listened to the sound of the shower. He heard the shower stop. He tried to imagine Bianca's method of drying herself. He wondered what she would be changing into. And then she appeared beside him in silk pyjamas. He breathed in the smell of her as he offered her a glass of wine. She took it from his fingers without touching him.

'I've made your bed for you,' she said. 'Do you have to be up early?'

'I start work at nine,' Stoker said.

'In that case I'll drop you off first thing in the morning.'

And then she leant over and kissed him, not twice this time but once. She left him no time to respond. Stoker watched the shimmer of her as she padded to her bedroom. For hours he drank and stared out to sea. The vision was, for him, a luxury. Eventually he showered and went to bed.

The night was peaceful. No dreams awakened him. In the morning he sat bleary-eyed at the kitchen table eating a bowl of Weetbix. Bianca was downing four Guarana tablets with a glass of tomato juice. They drove in silence back to Obs. Nothing was said of a future meeting. There were no fond recollections of the day they had spent together. Stoker hoped she would remember Dylan's launch without his having to remind her. He hated remembering things which the whole world had forgotten.

Stoker watched Bianca's rented Golf as it sped away. Then he opened the security gate to Dominion Hardware. He felt as he entered the store as though he had left a Club Med experience for a Dickens novel. He stared at the cluttered dingy room. This was where he spent six days of every week. This was his reality. It felt just fine to him. He had had his spree. He wasn't greedy. At Dominion Hardware he had some control. He was the manager of his own time.

For starters Stoker dusted down the display window. That way he could begin by watching people pass by. In another life he was probably a window-dresser, he thought. He certainly took inordinate care to make sure that the windows suited his sense of balance and proportion. Stoker loved to rearrange the paint tins in particular. He created new constellations. He thought of the paint tins as gymnasts caught in some intricate manoeuvre, the weight centred, the focus clear.

Once the windows had been tidied and rearranged, Stoker stepped indoors, sat back, and waited. Time passed without the blare of a radio, the distraction of a newspaper. Unlike Lizzie, Stoker found little merit in knowing what was happening around the world. Irrespective of his knowledge events occurred, he'd said. In his daily life he unwittingly experienced more than enough visual and aural bombardment. According to Dean, who was apt to have facts at his fingertips, the average amount of information an average human being ingested amounted to 5 000 bytes. Whatever Dean meant by this it sounded awesome.

Stoker couldn't understand what Dean saw in working for the papers. Still, at least he was doing something and enjoying it. Dean's slacker days were over and he didn't mind. He was charging all over the place in his blue Beetle, meeting, talking, photographing. His years of sitting around and staring at images had come in handy. Dean knew how to take a picture and it showed – whenever he didn't fuck up on the developing process. Stoker smiled as he thought of the fish that got away.

The postman arrived with a bunch of brown envelopes with windows. There were also two postcards – one from San Francisco, the other from Karala. The postcards were from Dayglo and Waldo. Stoker thanked the postman in a manner that was more than seemly. Then he tossed a coin into the air. Dayglo won.

According to Dayglo life was grand. He'd started a band called Butchers of Distinction – the byline for Farber's Meat Market. They were doing covers and the band liked the idea of being named after a butcher shop in Obs. Other than playing covers, which took care of surviving, Dayglo was auditioning for loads of bands, checking out the scene. He fitted in just fine, he said. He didn't actually miss anyone. There were so many people in the world, there was no way that he, Dayglo, would miss anyone. All the same he sent his love to everyone – to Jay and Lizzie in particular. Could Stoker please make sure that both parties received his love? The bastard, Stoker thought. Three months down the line Jay and Lizzie were still pissed off with him. In the middle of the postcard Dayglo had taped a salt sachet with the legendary McDonald's logo. If this was a joke Stoker wasn't amused. The sick fuck!

Waldo informed Stoker that he hadn't drunk a beer in months. That the sacred cows in India lived on plastic bags and cardboard boxes and still produced pretty fine milk. And that he was smoking more dope than he'd ever smoked before – which added up to an unreckonable amount. Karala was great. He was painting loads – sweetmeats, gods and a host of other finicky things like the fall of light on a sandal. He was also drinking loads of tea. Could Stoker please send his love to everyone – to Joan and Dean in particular. At the bottom of the card Waldo informed Stoker that he was going to start a restaurant as soon as he got back. Joan had already informed him of this. Waldo was clearly on a roll.

Stoker doubted that Joan had told Waldo about Percy. How could she? Waldo had no contact address. He kept moving all over the show. According to Dean, Waldo had spent some time in Bombay with a Kenyan drug dealer. He'd spent time on a camel in a desert up north. Now he was in Karala, somewhere in the south drinking tea. Waldo had been in India – for what? Eight? Nine months? This was Stoker's first postcard, which made it special. He flipped the card over. The card was lurid and glittery. It depicted some Indian god painted blue. The god had an elephant's head and four arms. When Stoker twisted the card it gave off a light that made him think of an acid trip.

Well, at least his friends were having a great time. Stoker laid the cards on the wooden counter and stared at them. He reread the words, then flipped them back over. The postcards were a hell of a lot more pleasurable than the newspaper, he thought. He enjoyed the fact that his friends could barely string a sentence together.

The day would have been a coup as is, what with postcards from opposite ends of the world. That is if Olivieri hadn't rocked up and decided to die laughing.

Olivieri had stopped in as he always did. He was as chirpy as ever. No mention was made of the shit he'd caused with Gloria. But, just to get the story straight, Jay had arrived prior to Olivieri. Stoker, having exhausted his meditation on the postcards, was sitting behind the till thinking of nothing in particular. He hadn't received a customer all morning. This wasn't uncommon. Sometimes hours would go by without a peep. A bright yellow morning light poured through the window and doors, bounced off Waldo's card, giving the dingy cramped interior an electric glow. The edges of the cardboard boxes shimmered, the wooden floor beamed, metal objects glittered. Stoker's red hair beamed against the wooden panelling behind him. Light bounced off his thick lenses.

Adrift upon a current of unconnected thoughts, his eyes unseeing, Stoker eventually sensed Jay's presence. He couldn't say how long Jay had stood in the doorway, his leather-clad figure glistening in the pouring light.

'Howzit Jay,' Stoker said, his words low and sleepy.

Jay stepped into the store with an aimlessness that counter-pointed Stoker's. They were both doing time. Stoker was glad that Jay had thought of stopping in. They hadn't seen much of each other since they'd cancelled the lease. Last Stoker had heard, Jay had moved in with Dom and started a new band. The Waiting Country.

'Saw you yesterday. Driving past on Long. You were with Dom,' Stoker said.

'Fuck Dom,' Jay said. Clearly nothing much had changed in that quarter.

'You want some coffee?' Stoker continued. He didn't wait for an answer before turning on the Cadac positioned on a small counter behind him. Then he opened a packet of Eat-Sum-Mores and arranged them on a plate. Jay said nothing. This was going to be a good one, Stoker thought. Whenever he and Jay had nothing to say it was always a good one. He was about to tell Jay about the postcards he'd received, but Jay had already picked up the card from Dayglo and was reading it. Stoker didn't say a word. Jay read in silence, then he flipped the card around and stared at the picture of San Francisco which was pretty bland. Jay lit a cigarette. Stoker joined him.

'I was driving down Durbanville way,' Jay began. 'Went to see my folks. There was this traffic jam. Thought there'd been an accident or something. The cars were so jam-packed you couldn't even fart without feeling like you were disturbing the peace. It turned out people were lining up bumper to bumper for over six hundred metres just for one of those burgers. It's crazy if you think about it. Fuckin' Dayglo.'

'You stop for a bite to eat?'

'What for?'

'People are lemmings,' Stoker commiserated.

'I wish,' Jay said. 'The nice thing about lemmings is they rush headlong into the sea and fuckin' drown. The problem is people are getting shitfaced on Macburgers but no one's killing themselves.'

'Like I've always said, Jay, we need a system of tariffs.

Boycott the fuckers. You'd think that by now we'd know enough about deprivation to figure out not everything's worth having, but oh no . . .'

'Sounds like Dayglo's doing well though,' Jay said. Jay being gracious was a bad sign.

'The Butchers of Distinction,' Stoker said. Jay attempted a laugh. He could tell that Jay was feeling shitty.

'Times is few,' Jay said, his voice low. 'Dayglo did the right thing leaving.'

Stoker was surprised. Jay's tone was genuinely conciliatory. He had to be feeling truly shitty to be so fair, Stoker thought.

'You think so?' Stoker asked, egging Jay on.

'At least he's doing something. Making sense of things.'

'You?'

'Me?'

'Yeah you, Jay.'

It was one of those stalled moments in a conversation when everything was repeated. As though every word was being heard for the first time and flipped over-easy like an egg, like the way the light reflected and bounced off things in the room.

Jay wasn't ready to talk. Stoker pointed out the card from Waldo, but the card didn't mean much. Jay and Waldo weren't so close. Well, not before Waldo left at any rate. But things were changing because the way people felt about each other kept changing. Because of Percy, Jay was seeing more of Joan, and one thing led to another.

'Waldo's in for a surprise,' Jay said. 'Joan tell you?'

'She has.'

'Percy can't believe his luck.'

That's all Jay said on the matter, but Stoker knew what he meant. Joan was something special. She was a grafter with a strong heart, not a big one, but a strong one. She gave sparingly of herself, but when she did she gave a lot. Percy happened to be the lucky beneficiary. Percy who was nothing like Waldo. Percy who was somehow a catalyst for a need that Joan was feeling.

Stoker remembered what Joan had said at the Planet about

having to fall prey. That's what she needed. She'd experimented with her dark side but she hadn't really lived it. Through Percy she was aiming to live it. Good-looking sleazy Percy with the drug habit and the street cred. Percy who came from the same neighbourhood as Phyllis – Brooklyn. Or the Bronx as those in the know called it. It was the sort of place you'd expect Edward Hopper to paint and Tom Waits to sing about. A place filled with accidental genius, drop-outs, losers and lovable creatures. Stoker remembered the words he'd seen on a wall in Brooklyn when he'd stopped over for supper at Chan and Phyllis's mother's place: SOMEBODY HELP ME. In a sense it could have been Percy's plea. Percy had needed the sanity, the graft, the belief of someone like Joan. A girl from Plumstead. At any rate, that was Stoker's point of view. Like Phyllis, Percy was strong meat. Other than that, Stoker was clueless.

Stoker was glad when Jay spoke. It helped him knock the itch of Phyllis aggravating his mind. Phyllis and Percy . . . childhood buddies . . . white trash . . . heartbreakers . . .

'We're playing at the Magnet tonight,' Jay said. 'Could use the company.'

'Can't see why not,' Stoker said. 'I haven't heard the new band.'

'Sounds shit,' Jay said. Which was fine. Jay needed to be hard on himself.

'You need any bucks?' Stoker asked.

'Could use twenty.' Stoker opened the till and took twenty from the float. Jay didn't comment.

The water had boiled. Stoker made coffee.

'You miss James's benefit concert at the River Club?' Jay asked.

'Yeah. I've been locked in, you know,' Stoker said.

'It was worth it.'

'Dom said so.'

'You been talking to her?'

'Not much. Now and then, you know.'

'Her dad's gone in for a prostate op. She and Phyllis have

been working like dogs. It's crazy, we live together and hardly see each other. I don't know what it is about that woman, Stoker. I love her, you know. But just trying to talk to get . . . just trying to get through . . . I don't know. She's on this whole spiritual pluck. If it's not meditation then it's Tai Chi or African drumming. She's trying to clean up her act – which is fine. Somewhere along the line we both have to. I just don't know why she has to be such a bitch about it.'

Stoker had heard this story a thousand times. He wasn't in the mood.

'Who was playing at the benefit gig for James?' Stoker asked.

'Kalahari Surfers, Springbok Nude Girls. The concert was a way of paying off James's hospital bills.'

'That's what I heard,' Stoker said, handing Jay his coffee.

'You'd figure that it'd be over when someone dies. But it isn't. There's so much shit that has to be swept under the carpet. It never fuckin' ends.'

'The Valiant Swarts?' Stoker asked.

'Yeah?'

'They play at James's benefit?'

'Sometimes I think that's the only band you fuckin' care about, Stoker.'

'Well?'

'No.'

Stoker and Jay were drinking coffee when Olivieri rocked up. Stoker could hear Olivieri a mile away. Olivieri's silencer was fucked. With the usual rattle and clatter Olivieri parked his Beetle and stepped into the store.

'Howzit boys,' Olivieri said. He was chirpy as hell. As usual he was wearing his signature pink satin bomber jacket, a Camel Plain tucked behind the ear.

Olivieri slapped Jay on the back. Jay squinted down at Olivieri and manufactured a fat grin.

'So how's life on the farm? Kif and dandy?' Olivieri asked.

Kif and dandy? Stoker thought. He'd never heard these two words used in the same breath before.

'No sales,' Stoker said.

'But they will come, they will come. People always come. There is always something that needs fixing. The whole world is falling apart! The whole world needs a hardware store!'

Olivieri had a point, but right then Stoker didn't share Olivieri's twisted optimism. He looked at Jay. Jay just stood around making no comment. Jay was enjoying himself.

'So, how was your date?' Olivieri asked.

'Date? What date?' Jay pitched in.

'Stoker here is a regular Valentino. You don't know that, Jay? Oh yes, Stoker's the one they like. Behind those serious glasses of his lie the eyes that will make a pussy melt.'

Jay guffawed. Stoker stared into the vague distance. He kept reminding himself that Olivieri wouldn't be around for long. At the moment of this realisation Stoker was clueless about how prophetic his wish actually was.

'So, tell me. How is she?'

'She's Italian. From Palermo,' Stoker said, grudgingly doling out info.

'From Palermo! That's where Mrs Olivieri comes from! It's a small fucked-up world, hah?' Stoker and Jay were mum. 'From Palermo! Ah, beautiful Palermo! That is where I first meet Beatrice.'

'Beatrice?' Jay asked.

'Mrs Olivieri.'

It was difficult to imagine Mrs Olivieri with a first name, let alone one as beautiful as Beatrice. According to Olivieri she had all the fine qualities of Dante's Beatrice – wisdom, grace. She'd probably have to have both in truckloads just so she could deal with Olivieri's shady dealings. She was the bosom of atonement, Olivieri said. His confessor.

Yeah, sure.

Jay, standing behind Olivieri while he raved about Mrs Olivieri being one of the seven wonders of the world, was directing Stoker's attention to Olivieri's hairpiece. Working his hand like a crane, Jay pretended to lift up Olivieri's hairpiece. Stoker tried to keep calm. Olivieri, oblivious to what was happening above and behind him, signalled to Stoker to begin

his boss o' Nova routine. Stoker had never done it when anyone who qualified as a friend was in the store. But then Jay
clearly needed cheering up, and Stoker didn't actually care.
People sold themselves for a lot less.

Like an impresario Olivieri informed Jay of the proceedings,
then waited. And then Stoker began. With a click of a finger,
the wink of an eye and a stomp of a foot on the wooden floor,
he let the words roll and bounce off his tongue: 'We carry the
full range of Nova floor treatment and home cleaning products,
says the boss o' Nova.'

Then Stoker flicked his arm in the direction of the framed
photograph of Olivieri that hung just above and behind him,
before turning back to his audience and winking.

As always, possessed by the genius of his copy, enamoured
by the seedy double of himself hanging on the wooden fitting
on the wall, Olivieri burst into laughter, slammed his fist on
the counter, clutched his chest, and promptly died.

Before either Stoker or Jay had realised what had happened,
they had a corpse to deal with.

CHAPTER FOURTEEN

The rest of the day was a wash-out. Death had a way of screwing things up. Stoker had seen enough movies to know what to
do, yet for a long time he remained standing, unmoving,
staring at Olivieri's dead body. Jay was as silent as he. Both
were fascinated by the sudden turn of events. Then Jay bent
down and rearranged Olivieri's hairpiece which had flown in
the direction of the skirting when his head hit the floor. In
unison Stoker and Jay lit cigarettes, both drawn instinctively
to the imitative world of the living.

One minute Olivieri was laughing his head off, the next he
was dead as a doornail. It was the sudden shift which threw
Stoker. Olivieri was lucky, he thought. Olivieri was very lucky.

To be swept away so easily! Without a struggle. To die laughing! Who could ask for more? For Olivieri's sake Stoker was relieved. Olivieri had lived a hell of a lot longer than he deserved. What's more, he'd had a great time. Still, Stoker wished that the death had occurred elsewhere, in the middle of a porno flick for instance. He wondered whether dying coming was better than dying laughing. An ejaculation somehow seemed less attractive, more messy. Stoker realised that he was splitting hairs as usual.

At this point in the stream of his thoughts Stoker noticed that the bowels did in fact discharge in the moment or thereabouts of death. He called the swab team at the Groote Schuur Hospital which, conveniently, was just up the hill. He debated whether or not to call Mrs Olivieri. Or Phyllis for that matter. He decided not to. Not yet at any rate. Jay decided to stick with Stoker. He had nothing better to do. Stoker was glad for the company.

They stood outside the store, away from the stench, smoking cigarettes and waiting for the ambulance. It was a beautiful day. Through the door Stoker stared at Olivieri's contorted grinning body. He thought of the paintings of Robert Longo, of all the dead bodies he'd seen in the movies. He thought of the fact that he'd be out of a job. He got it into his head that he was somehow responsible for Olivieri's death. The thought cut through to the quick. His conviction was obtuse enough to make sense. After all, it was he who had enacted Olivieri's stupid precious boss o' Nova ad. It was the ad which had killed Olivieri. Wasn't it his mouthing off, caught between boredom and a dry conviction, which had always resulted in one guffaw after the next? If he hadn't done his stupid show Olivieri wouldn't have laughed, slammed his fist on the counter, and dropped dead.

'It had to happen some time,' Jay said, lighting another cigarette.

'Yeah sure,' Stoker said.

'The guy was what? Seventy? Eighty years old?'

'Ninety,' Stoker said.

'Ninety?! You're joking,' Jay said.

'I tell you he was ninety.'

'Bullshit,' Jay said.

'Check his ID if you don't believe.'

'What's the point?'

'You feel like getting us some steak rolls while I wait? Get me a Stoney. On second thoughts, get me a beer. Feel free to get what you want. The till's yours.'

Jay stepped over Olivieri's body, moved round the counter, took what he needed, and went shopping. Buying things was a big thing for Jay since he never had much money. He especially enjoyed pushing the shopping trolley on Mondays when Dom shopped for the week at Pick 'n Pay.

The ambulance arrived along with the style council from Human and Pitt, the funeral parlour in Woodstock. They work in teams, Stoker thought, like the cops and the towing companies. Stoker watched as they carried Olivieri's body out on a stretcher. He wished he'd removed the hairpiece. It was bound to come unstuck and fall in some stupid direction. Since Olivieri was thoroughly dead Human and Pitt assumed the helm. Clad in dignified black, they informed Stoker that the deceased would be happy to see any mourners in two hours or so. For some reason he couldn't fault their sense of humour. He'd expected a backlog of corpses. Still, as far as speed, they were a pretty industrious bunch. He took the business card containing the details of Olivieri's whereabouts, then he dialled Mrs Olivieri. She was clearly deaf. Stoker didn't like the idea of shouting on the phone. He told Mrs Olivieri he'd come over, waited for Jay, and closed shop. But before he did so, he decided to call The Bead Shop. Dom picked up the phone. Stoker was relieved. He told Dom to tell Phyllis that Olivieri was dead. Then he gave Dom the directions to the funeral parlour. He said that he and Jay would meet Phyllis there if she was keen. Or Dom, for that matter.

By the time Jay arrived with two steak rolls, a six-pack of Windhoek, a pack of Chesterfields, Lexington tens and a bottle of La Rochelle Cape brandy, the store was closed. They climbed into Dom's black Beetle and drove to Mrs Olivieri's house. Stoker had never seen Mrs Olivieri before. He doubted he'd fail to recognise her. Geriatrics weren't that common in Obs. Most of them had been farmed off to frail centres in the southern suburbs.

Mrs Olivieri lived on Lower Wrensch, down from the Model Café on the corner of Crown where the first Obs movie had recently been shot. According to Dean, Stoker had appeared in the footage. The camera must have caught him on the way back from Lizzie's. The movie had eventually ended up on TV, except Stoker wasn't in it. He'd ended up being edited out. Figures, Stoker thought. Jay parked Dom's Beetle outside Mrs Olivieri's house.

The house looked like it hadn't been painted in over fifty years. It was slate grey with a beige tinge and some nifty touches of bleached Macmillan green. It looked like something you'd see in the country. Very old world. Different to most of the houses in Obs with their glossy bright colours and revamped fittings.

Stoker knocked. Waited. Knocked again.

'Knock knock,' Jay said.

'Who's there?' Stoker replied.

'Knock,' Jay said.

'Knock who?' Stoker asked.

'Knock knock,' Jay said.

Stoker grinned in disgust. The door opened. Somewhere slightly above the door handle Stoker spotted a tuft of lilac hair.

'Mrs Olivieri?' Stoker asked.

Mrs Olivieri nodded and smiled. She reminded Stoker of the old lady he'd seen in *Drugstore Cowboy*. The same one he'd recently seen in *The Professional* by Luc Besson. She had the same butterfly spectacles with popping radiant eyes. She looked more like Olivieri's grandmother than his wife.

Stoker didn't know what to say to her. She seemed so chirpy and kind as she opened the door and let them through. Stoker had the feeling that she recognised him. Maybe Olivieri had

238

mentioned him to her. It was possible. People talked about other people all the time. At any rate she was not put out by their presence.

Stoker and Jay followed her down a long dingy corridor. The place was packed with things. Old Get Well cards pinned to the felt interior of a glass box, sepia photographs dating back to the beginning of time, stuff and more stuff. Stoker felt like he was walking through a badly-lit museum.

At the end of the corridor they came to an eau-de-Nil and sunlight yellow kitchen. On a '50s fridge door Stoker spotted a photo of himself and Olivieri taken outside Dominion Hardware. The photo was stuck to the fridge door with a lemon magnet. Phyllis had taken the photo over a year ago. He'd wondered where it had disappeared to. Stoker was a little more than disconcerted when he saw the photo of Olivieri stark naked, standing next to an equally stark naked Phyllis with her Dulux dog hairdo. Stoker couldn't remember taking the photo. It must have been taken before he'd entered their lives. So. Mrs Olivieri must have had a pretty good idea of Olivieri's dealings. The photo of Olivieri and Phyllis clearly didn't faze her as much as it did him. So much for knowing what's what, Stoker thought.

Stoker and Jay sat down at a blue Formica table. Mrs Olivieri poured the tea. Stoker and Jay inhaled the smell of cookies in the oven.

'So he's dead, is he?' Mrs Olivieri asked.

She was chirpy as hell. Either she was a retard or very perverse, Stoker thought.

'He must be dead. Otherwise why do you come here? Why do you look so sad?'

She was a detective to boot! A regular Ms Marple.

'It must be Mario's heart,' Mrs Olivieri said. 'He had a bad heart.'

Stoker wasn't sure if this was a medical diagnosis or something more personal.

'So we finally meet,' Mrs Olivieri said, smiling away.

The situation was so painless there was really nothing Stoker and Jay could do but relax.

'Beatrice,' Mrs Olivieri said, holding her hand out to Jay. Jay introduced himself then kissed Mrs Olivieri's bony knuckles. What a jerk, Stoker thought, and shook Mrs Olivieri's hand. She didn't seem that keen to see her husband.

Stoker watched as Mrs Olivieri padded down the hallway in her slippers. Then he looked at Jay. Jay took a swig from the bottle of La Rochelle and passed it to Stoker.

'What do you think?' Stoker asked.

'She seems fine,' Jay said.

'Wouldn't you be a bit surprised if Dom dropped dead?'

'Not if she was ninety,' Jay said.

'I guess not,' Stoker sighed as he watched Beatrice reappear. The quirkiness of her behaviour had forced him to stop thinking of Olivieri's old lady as Mrs Olivieri.

In her hand Beatrice had an envelope. It was addressed to Stoker.

'Open it,' Beatrice said. She was keen as hell.

Stoker opened it.

Inside there was a long letter from Olivieri which, as it turned out, Beatrice had written and Olivieri dictated. The gist of the letter had to do with the fact the Olivieris had never had any kids and that this had to do with Mario Olivieri's low sperm count. Given the absence of progeny Olivieri had decided to give Stoker the hardware store, the studio, his porno collection and his Beetle. Stoker was flabbergasted. Beatrice hovered over him excitedly while he took a very large swig of La Rochelle. In the event of Olivieri's death Beatrice would hold on to the house and their combined savings, which came to quite a lot. Well, given the fact that Beatrice was pretty ancient, it was a lot of money to plan a future with.

'You happy?' Beatrice asked Stoker. Stoker didn't know what to say, he was blown away. He handed the letter and the bottle of La Rochelle to Jay to ensure that he wasn't hallucinating.

'The devil!' Jay said. He was laughing his head off. 'This is incredible,' he continued. 'You get the store, the studio, the Beetle. What's this about a porno collection?'

'Oh, Mario loved pornography,' Beatrice piped in. 'His whole life he loved pornography. Naked women. That is how we met.'

Oh yeah? Stoker thought. He and Jay looked up, burning with curiosity.

'Oh yes, I was quite a stripper in my day. I had a beautiful body. Beautiful, beautiful. *Bellissima*. I show you.'

Beatrice padded off. Jay passed the brandy back to Stoker.

'Take the biscuits out of the oven,' Beatrice called as she disappeared.

Jay moved the biscuits out of the oven and left them on the stove surface to cool. Beatrice reappeared with a box of photographs.

The photographs seemed to date back to the '20s. They were all of a dark-haired woman with a very beautiful body. Contrary to Stoker's idea of the goings-on at the time, the pictures were pretty explicit. Beatrice had arranged the images so that they mounted in intensity. For starters there were shots of her sporting a feather boa, carrying a milk pail, against a fake mountainside by a fake stream.

'Beautiful, no?' Beatrice asked. She was definitely not interested in criticism. Stoker and Jay nodded in agreement as they silently riffled through more than a hundred images of Beatrice swooning, pouting, being fucked from every angle and in each and every orifice by marauding priests, crusaders and a host of other classic pillagers.

'It is a pity that I didn't have a daughter as beautiful as me,' Beatrice said. 'You can each keep one if you like.'

Stoker and Jay looked at one another, then each slipped a photo into their pocket.

'So you accept Mario's proposal?' Beatrice asked Stoker. Stoker was silent.

'He loved you very much, my Mario. He said . . . Stoker . . . He is the smartest boy I know. The apple of my eye. He did not like your paintings, I must tell you that. They were too modern, Mario said. But he liked you very much. He said, Stoker is my true son. That is what he said.'

Stoker saw a tear fall from Beatrice's eye. A single tear. Then he folded her in his arms. This small old bony woman who had once been so beautiful and so fuckable.

CHAPTER FIFTEEN

Beatrice had packed Olivieri's Henry Fonda gear, Jay had packed the biscuits. Stoker had driven the three of them to Human and Pitt. At the entrance to the red brick building with its tinted windows Stoker had stopped Dom's Beetle. Beatrice asked Stoker and Jay to wait for her. She wanted to see Mario Olivieri alone. Stoker and Jay agreed and stood outside, Jay munching a biscuit, Stoker smoking a cigarette and polishing off the remainder of the brandy. There were still the beers to get through.

During Jay's tenth biscuit Dom and Phyllis arrived in Phyllis's bakkie. Stoker was struck, as he always was, by their contrasting physiques. Dom tall and skinny with her bird-like head, Phyllis now bloated in the middle like a cartoon. Stoker was glad for the fact that there were more significant things to deal with, such as Olivieri's death. He hadn't talked to Phyllis in over three months.

Phyllis hugged Stoker. Dom hugged Jay. Then they swapped.

'Beatrice asked us to stay outside and wait,' Jay said.

'Who's Beatrice?' Dom asked, cracking open a Windhoek.

'Mrs Olivieri,' Stoker said.

'What's she like?' Phyllis asked.

Like you, Stoker wanted to say. Like you.

Yes, Beatrice reminded Stoker of Phyllis. That's why Olivieri was so attracted to her. Perhaps Olivieri saw Phyllis and himself as youthful versions of he and Beatrice? Perhaps . . . Stoker realised that he wouldn't get the opportunity to find out.

'Feel,' Phyllis said, taking Stoker's hand and placing it on her exposed stomach. 'You can feel the heartbeat now.'

Stoker looked at Phyllis as he placed his hand on her stomach. He was overcome by her unnerving directness. Her expression was open. Clear. Stoker could locate no pangs of regret. No untoward longing.

Neither Stoker or Phyllis felt like broaching the past. What was done was done. Holding his hand to Phyllis's stomach he realised that she wanted him to know that he was still inside her. That it was their child and not Dylan's she was carrying.

It all seemed appropriate somehow. The funeral parlour, the pregnancy. No one truly felt sad. There was no reason. Olivieri's death was no tragedy. Stoker realised that he hadn't even shed a tear. He realised how alone he felt, how remote he was from the child in Phyllis's belly. Was he cold? Was he dead inside? No, he thought. He felt alive. He was immersed in the intricacy of a new day.

Stoker had not seen Phyllis in ages. You could log it in months, but it wouldn't clarify the nature of the time which had passed, the distance. He had not wanted to see her. She in turn had not wanted to see him. And now? Now that she was standing in front of him, his hand on her stomach? It was as though little had changed. Of course this was not true. Their lives were different. And yet something had remained. Something which would never change between them. Something Stoker had no words to explain.

'Stoker just inherited Dominion Hardware, the studio, Olivieri's Beetle and porno collection,' Jay said. He was unable to resist a chuckle when he mentioned the porno collection.

'Makes sense,' Phyllis said as she swigged a beer, her voice knowing yet vague.

'That's incredible,' Dom said.

'He deserves it, don't you think?' Jay asked Phyllis, as if to say that Stoker had suffered enough.

Stoker was embarrassed by the attention. It felt rotten.

'Yes, he does,' Dom said, giving Stoker a kiss on the cheek and biting his ear.

'Ouch!' Stoker cried. Before he knew it Phyllis had planted a fat lingering kiss on his lips.

A flood of desire rushed through him. He could suddenly feel Phyllis, the uniqueness of her. Her flesh. Her exquisite lechery.

Then Phyllis pulled away and gazed into the sun as though nothing significant had happened.

Stoker realised there was nothing he could do about his desire for her. He realised that he hadn't fucked in over three months. He also realised that he was probably solvent for the first time in his life. It wasn't much in the larger scheme of things, but the hardware store, the studio, the Beetle, even the porno collection, meant everything in the world to him.

Stoker lit a cigarette, cracked open a beer, and waited for Beatrice, his lips still throbbing with Phyllis's kiss. Life was twisted and there was nothing he could do about it. He watched Dom and Jay as they cuddled against Dom's Beetle and spoke in whispers. He watched Phyllis seated on the sidewalk in her orange halter-neck, pink hot pants and gold shoes. And then Beatrice appeared. She was sad yet radiant. Phyllis walked over to Beatrice and gave her a big kiss. Beatrice drew back, measured Phyllis's shoulders, and handed her Olivieri's pink bomber jacket. It suited Phyllis to a T. Then it was Jay's turn. He kissed Beatrice on both cheeks. He was getting to like her a lot. Beatrice scratched her bony fingers in Jay's hair, then she handed him Olivieri's comb, hairpiece, and Zippo lighter. Dom for no apparent reason found herself gladly accepting Olivieri's dentures. Then Beatrice handed Stoker Olivieri's car keys, the holder emblazoned with The Virgin Mary on one side, a large-breasted redhead on the other.

Dom climbed into her black Beetle. Jay climbed into the passenger seat. Stoker climbed into the passenger seat of Phyllis's bakkie since Beatrice insisted on climbing into the back. The vehicles split in different directions.

First Phyllis dropped off Beatrice on Lower Wrensch, then she drove to Lower Main and stopped outside Stoker's studio. For a brief while they sat in silence, the engine idling, Phyllis's belly jammed against the steering wheel. Stoker wanted to ask Phyllis to come up for tea, but he couldn't.

'I'll see you at the launch,' Phyllis said. Stoker was silent. Phyllis ran her fingers through his red hair. 'Thanks for phoning me,' she said. 'It meant a lot that you thought of me, but then it was an obvious choice, wasn't it? It was Olivieri who brought us together.'

Stoker did not feel like talking about the past or the present.

'He was a decent man after all. It's funny. You know how pissed off I got about how he tricked me, how he'd rub his bony chest against me . . . now I miss it. I miss it so much.'

Phyllis started crying.

Stoker was terrified to ask her what she really missed. He thought of the note he'd received via Gloria. The note about Margaret Drabble and her husband living in separate houses. How no good could come of that. How all the special moments had to be shared. If this was what Phyllis wanted then why, in the midst of tears, did she remain so cool, so detached? Why was she crying? Stoker held Phyllis tightly in his arms. He wished they could remain like that forever.

'I've got to go,' Stoker said, his words a calm yet violent contradiction of his feelings. 'I'll see you at the launch.' Then he bent over and kissed her.

As he opened the passenger door Stoker realised that he hadn't driven in Phyllis's bakkie in ages. He realised that what was once a common and shared space was once again hers, and hers alone. Or was it? He pictured Dylan seated in the place where he had sat. Dylan driving, Phyllis seated.

Only objects stay the same, Stoker thought, as he walked towards his front door. Or did they? Surely people changed inanimate things? Surely people fused things with their spirit, their auras? Then Stoker felt the keys to Olivieri's Beetle. Later he would go for a drive. For now he wanted to dwell on the auras of objects.

As he turned the key to his front door he heard Phyllis's bakkie pull off. He could not bring himself to turn around and watch her fade away. He felt an irresistible urge to resume work on his radio painting.

For hours Stoker worked on his process of obliteration and revelation. He worked carborundum into the wired interior of the radio, deepened the crevices, smoothed the surfaces, broke then restitched a section of canvas with scooby-doo wire. He vanished into layers of paint and brick-dust, glanced across surfaces of steel. In the midst of working on his radio painting he began to mourn. His shifting mood steered the process.

The gutted interior of the radio had become his heart. A heart disconnected, dysfunctional, yet a heart that continued to beat. He thought of Beatrice's bravery in the midst of her sorrow. He laughed a drunken laugh as he pictured her gifting of alms – the dentures, the jacket, the hairpiece. All the integral properties of Olivieri's life had been cast like ashes, set to embark on new and strange journeys. Perhaps Olivieri's dentures would remain with Dom all her life? Perhaps unwittingly she would find herself consciously losing them in a field of grass? Nothing that is given is given for all eternity, Stoker thought. Objects moved from life to life like wind. Stoker wished that he could find a way to record these strange details. If he were Dylan perhaps he could have written it all down. But he was not Dylan. Like most people he did not have the tools to record his life.

Stoker stared at the canvases and paints that surrounded him. This, he thought, this was all he was able to muster. These were his tools, his means of speech. A speech that did not belong to words but to colour, to matter. The objects he had selected were so few. How many more would he incarnate, reshape? How many paintings were there left to do? He had always been slow. Nothing ever came easily to him. His journey was a dogged one. He could not excuse himself from the labour that awaited him.

By nightfall he was exhausted. He had completed another stage, created another opening. He set aside the tools, prepared a snackwich and coffee, and lay down in the darkened room, the red tip of his cigarette and the blue flame of the Cadac the only sources of light. The streetlights on Lower Main had failed to appear at their appointed hour. Was this too a sign of mourning? Stoker asked himself. He wanted to sleep, remained restless. He thought of Olivieri's will. Of the love that Olivieri had expressed in his letter, transcribed and perhaps worded in part by Beatrice. He was Olivieri's true son . . . Was that why Olivieri had always given him a hard time? Because he loved him so? Stoker had thought of Olivieri as his hell, he as Olivieri's heaven. What a neat yet feeble conceit! Callous too! Still, it was too late to rearrange the past. Olivieri had always pissed him off. And yet he had cared for him.

Tomorrow he would resume work at the store. Tonight he was going to get up, get out, and get thoroughly pissed. He needed to shift the pressure in his brain, move Phyllis away from the little light that remained – light she was consuming. He wanted to hate her, and couldn't. His lips, he realised, still throbbed with her kiss. He stubbed the cigarette onto the studio floor, unzipped his jeans and started to wank. He saw Phyllis. He saw himself fucking her against Dom's black Beetle outside Human and Pitt. He saw Beatrice in the photograph she'd given him. He saw himself licking Beatrice's tits, sinking into the oil slick of her young eyes. He saw Bianca as she appeared before him on the balcony at the Peninsula Hotel. He slowly unbuttoned her silk pyjamas. He pressed himself against her on the metal railing overlooking the Atlantic Ocean, a passing ship flush against the horizon. The ocean drowning their sighs. He wiped the come off the hollow of his stomach with the edge of his sleeping-bag and lay, sighing, still. Then he zipped up his jeans and rose.

The snackwich had burnt. The coffee was still unmade. Stoker closed the studio door, descended the stairs, opened the side door to Dominion and took fifty from the till. Then he crossed a blackened Lower Main, turned into Trill and entered Lawrence's. Dean was at the bar. He was playing chess with himself, toying randomly with the pieces. Stoker ordered a Windhoek and four Panados.

'I received a card from Waldo today,' Stoker said. He could

247

hardly believe that it was still the same day. 'I got one from Dayglo too. Waldo's been gone now – what? Nine months? Fuck knows. Finally I get a card. Turns out he's drinking way too much tea in Karala, he hasn't had a beer in ages, he's smoking up a storm, and guess what? Cows in India eat plastic bags and cardboard boxes. You can get milk from scrap!'

Dean was grinning from ear to ear.

'What's so fuckin' funny, Dean? It's true!'

Dean kept on grinning.

'Okay, Dean. It's funny. But it's not that funny!'

Dean started laughing. Stoker downed his beer and ordered another.

'You know something Dean, you can be such a moron. You know that? If you don't I'm telling you. You're a moron.'

Dean was howling with laughter.

Stoker suddenly remembered Olivieri's crazy laughter and clammed up. He wasn't going to say a word, provoke another death. He was just going to sit and drink his beer.

'Howzit Stoker.'

Stoker swung around. Right in front of him was Waldo. Stoker was stunned. Dean couldn't stop laughing.

'I just . . . I just got a card from you today. Today. I got a card from you. You're supposed to be in India. You're . . .' Stoker trailed off. Something . . . everything was starting to warp. He felt as though he was about to faint.

'Time's a relative thing,' Dean said.

'Fuck off, Dean,' Stoker said. Dean didn't.

'I get a card from India and right in front of me stands the man who sent it.'

'Now isn't that strange,' Dean piped in.

Stoker realised that Dean was even drunker than he was. He suddenly expected to see Dayglo before him. But Dayglo was nowhere to be seen. Instead Stoker felt Waldo's hand press on his shoulder. For good measure Stoker placed his hand on Waldo's shoulder. Together they stood, the pulse of life one upon the other. And then they hugged each other and broke into uproarious laughter.

'It's good to see you,' Waldo said. 'Dean and I came over to Dominion this afternoon but the place was closed.'

Stoker looked at Waldo. He noticed that Waldo had lost a lot of weight. He noticed that Waldo wasn't looking very good. He saw that Waldo's eyes were as red and stoned as they had always been. He felt Waldo's stubble as he resumed hugging him.

'What's that smell?' Stoker asked, sniffing Waldo's hair.

'Almond oil,' Waldo said. 'My hair's been falling out. I'm using almond oil to strengthen it.'

'Beatrice should have given you Olivieri's hairpiece,' Stoker said.

'Who the fuck is Beatrice?' Dean asked.

Stoker explained. He retold the day – the postcards, Jay, Olivieri's heart attack, Beatrice's porno career, the funeral parlour, Dom, Phyllis, and the bit about the hairpiece, the dentures, the satin bomber jacket.

Dean and Waldo listened in stunned silence, occasionally breaking into mild laughter as Stoker detailed the quirkiness of his day.

'So the lucky bastard dropped dead laughing,' Dean said. It was natural for him to find the good things inside the sad.

'It must have been weird, you and Jay having fun at Olivieri's expense and then having him drop dead right in front of you. It must have been weird. I should have been there. I should have recorded the whole thing.' By way of a response to a missed opportunity Dean started taking photos of Stoker and Waldo.

Then Stoker told them about the will. About the hardware store, the studio, the Beetle and the porno collection. Dean and Waldo were as gobsmacked as Stoker had been earlier in the day.

'You couldn't stand the bastard,' Dean said.

'I probably got the wrong end of the stick,' Stoker said shamefacedly, and ordered another beer.

'What a day! What a tragedy! What a fuckin' coup!' Dean said. 'We have to celebrate. There's no two ways about it.'

Dean ordered three triple whiskies. Stoker stared at Waldo disbelievingly. They were both grinning from ear to ear. Stoker wondered where Joan was. Waldo had clearly heard nothing about her and Percy. Either that or India had turned him into a Taoist or something.

For the rest of the night Stoker and Dean listened to Waldo's tales about India. About the deserts in the north, the tea plantations in the south, the constant bartering, the chillum smokers and dealers he'd hung out with in Bombay, a laced green bhanglassi, a lethal yoghurt concoction he'd drunk – after which he'd collapsed on the restaurant floor, his rupees flying all over the place. Neither Stoker or Dean could believe that a drug existed that could floor Waldo. He talked about the heat, the attitudes toward rest, the chalks and gouaches he'd done on the Spoornet train tickets he'd primed and taken with him. He was looking forward to showing off his wares.

In the midst of Waldo's unending story Joan appeared. It turned out she and Waldo had spent the day together and that she'd told Waldo about Percy. It turned out that Percy wasn't going to arrive till later. Waldo and Joan were so happy to see each other that neither felt inclined to cause shit. The facts were on the table.

Eventually Waldo started talking about the restaurant he wanted to start. It would work from three to three and function as a tapas diner. He'd kept the dream alive since his days in Barcelona. The restaurant idea had altered since being in India, become more hybrid. Waldo saw something that was a cross between Spain, India and South Africa. He was especially struck by Ganesh, the god of wisdom and wealth. In every shop in India there was a Ganesh, Waldo said. He'd thought of maybe calling the restaurant Café Ganesh. Who knows? It was just an idea.

After about the fourth triple whisky Stoker opened his mouth. 'Why don't you take over Dominion Hardware?' he said.

Everyone, including Joan who by that point had been clued into Stoker's day, seemed to think it was a fine idea.

Joan was waiting for Percy when Dean, Waldo and Stoker walked over to Dominion Hardware. Waldo was keen to see the space.

'The store's been going since the '30s,' Stoker said drunkenly as he fumbled for the right keys for the alarm and security gate.

Waldo peeped excitedly into the darkened display window while Dean pretended to be the look-out for a burglary.

Eventually they entered the store. Stoker switched on the lights. The fluorescent bar flashed, darkened, then quivered like a disco strobe. Dean moved to the music in his head. The lights soon resumed their full glow. Everyone was silent. Stoker and Dean watched Waldo as he moved through the cluttered room, rearranging the space in his mind. Once again Stoker was struck by the surreality of receiving a postcard from India on the same day that Waldo had returned. He was struck by Waldo's footnote saying that he wanted to start a restaurant, struck by the odd timeliness of Olivieri's death, the will which had left the store to him. Yes . . . it was appropriate that Waldo should have the space. They could work out a fair rental. Stoker could continue living upstairs. Life could go on.

'We'll have to keep the place almost exactly as it is,' Waldo said. Stoker and Dean listened, confused. 'We can't clear out this place. We've got to keep most of it as it stands. People could buy hammers, nails, toilet brushes, whatever, between three and three. We could include it on the bill. Tortillas, chips, salad, a toilet brush.'

'Cool,' Dean said.

'Food and hardware,' Waldo said. 'That's what we all need.'

Dean was grinning. Stoker was mulling over the concept, recalling the fact that Olivieri had said pretty much the same thing just before he died.

'Food and hardware,' Stoker said to himself. It made sense. He pictured people walking by, stopping at the display window to look at the price of enamel paint and seeing tables, candles, people seated for supper. The vision had a certain appeal. Olivieri would surely be pleased. The hardware store would continue virtually unchanged. Stoker realised that he'd probably have to assume responsibility for the hardware sales. Something would have to be worked out between him and Waldo. But the idea definitely appealed to him. It was the '90s after all. All over the world spaces were being shared. The most arbitrary combination of businesses seemed to be working successfully. The combination of a club, eatery, clothing store and hairdresser on the corner of Shortmarket and Loop, for instance.

'Dominion Food and Hardware,' Stoker said.

'Dominion Food and Hardware,' Waldo echoed.

They were both glowing with the prospect.

'How about a party to finalise the idea?' Dean suggested. 'We could move some of the stands into the storeroom, make space for tables and chairs. Move in a sound system. We've already got a Cadac. We could get in a couple more. The bottle store's across the road. There's Farber's Butchery, the vegetable stands on Station. We could organise something for Saturday. What do you think, Waldo?'

Waldo was silent. He was mulling over Dominion Food and Hardware versus Café Ganesh. He was thinking of displaying a Ganesh in the window, working in a water feature.

'It's Dylan's launch on Saturday,' Stoker said.

'That's fine, that's perfect,' Dean said undeterred. 'It's happening at Lawrence's, right?'

Stoker nodded.

'So, everyone can move over after the readings and stuff. Waldo can prepare the food. I'll work on the drinks. We've got a till. We could work on some menus.'

Dean was excited, and it wasn't just the whisky talking. Stoker and Waldo had the same feeling. Bureaucratic complications aside, the whole thing was starting to make sense. No one had the vaguest desire to talk about health inspectors, extractor fans, toilets, grease traps and the general nitty-gritty of setting up a restaurant in a so-called civilised world. They'd open informally.

Stoker looked at the seedy grinning portrait of Olivieri hovering above the till . . . Olivieri was happy as hell, Stoker thought. In the morning he'd make a rosary of plastic carnations and hang them around the portrait. He'd select some black cloth from Olivieri's range of diaphanous materials and drape it across the display windows. He'd toss plastic carnations onto the cloth. Saturday would be Olivieri's night. He'd drag Beatrice over. Maybe she could say something. Yes. The whole thing was making sense.

Stoker realised that he was exhausted. It had been a long and eventful day. He needed to rest. He saw a yellow police van stop outside the store. He walked over to speak to the policemen. They had every right to be suspicious. What were three drunken louts doing in a hardware store in the middle of the night? Stoker explained that he was the new owner, and that Waldo was his future business partner. Businesses were changing hands all the time in Obs. Dominion Food and Hardware was the latest in an endless relay. Stoker watched the van drive off. He was glad to have provided the police with an opportunity to act out one of their good behaviour classes.

Stoker returned to the store and ushered Dean and Waldo out. He locked the store from the inside. Before switching off the light he stomped his foot on the wooden floor, clicked his fingers, twirled, and like an ice skater stood with one foot suspended, his hand graciously pointed in the direction of his benefactor. Then he set the alarm, switched off the light, climbed the creaking stairs to his studio, and fell into a deep sleep.

CHAPTER EIGHTEEN

For the next three days Stoker and Waldo scrubbed and cleaned. They bought some second-hand tables and chairs from Munro's down the road. Waldo restructured the counter into a cooking area, with a hot plate, two Cadacs, some chopping boards, Lizzie's portable fridge, a rented freezer and two extra fridges. Stoker cleaned out the toilet and papered the walls with selected images from Olivieri's porno collection. Waldo fixed the wiring and installed some extra light fixtures. Stoker painted in the words FOOD AND where the sign read DOMINION HARDWARE STORE. Waldo drafted a menu and Prue did a design and layout on her colour copier. Dom fitted some glittering beads to the new lights. Jay worked on some live music. Dean, when he had the time, took photos of the changes in process. Phyllis, Dom, Jay, Waldo and Stoker took time out to join Beatrice on Sandy Bay where she scattered Olivieri's ashes into the sea. Bridge and Immo arrived back from Zim in time to help out. They were both broke and would end up helping Waldo in the kitchen and serving when Dominion Food and Hardware eventually took off.

By Saturday Stoker and Waldo were knackered, but they were charged all the same. They'd reshaped the hardware store for a party. This was uppermost in Waldo's mind. The rules and regulations involved in getting a long-term project on the go were another story. Just the idea of starting a restaurant, having the pretext for a party and an existing space which could be revamped was enough. Preparing for Saturday was the best thing that could have happened for both of them. Stoker and Waldo's eyes shone with pleasure. The best part was stocking up on booze, meat and vegetables – compliments of Olivieri. Tired and sweaty they seated themselves and cracked open two beers. Waldo lit a joint. A soothing silence prevailed. Outside, beyond the sun-threaded black cloths draped across the windows, they could hear the belch and stream of traffic.

Waldo was probably Stoker's closest friend. It was a closeness that wasn't easy to locate. Stoker had known Joan longer but somehow the passion that glued people together had come unstuck. Still, between Joan and Stoker there remained the bond of art. With Waldo it was different. There'd never been an immediate fascination the way there was with Joan. Waldo was just there. Stoker's relationship with Waldo had never needed much in the way of words. Neither was a talker. Waldo had a way about him which had never needed mirrors. Most people needed to be seen to be doing something before the action had meaning. Waldo wasn't like that. He wasn't vain or weak. He fucked forward in his own quiet way. And it was this that Stoker had always admired and grown to love. Waldo wasn't a slave to fashion or taste. He did what he needed to do and he didn't make a song and dance about it.

Dean and Joan had taken time out to help frame Waldo's chalk drawings and gouaches. Stoker was staring at them, his eyes travelling in a steady arc from image to image. There were sixty of them, each the size of a train ticket. Framed with slats of tomato crates and perforated aluminium, cushioned in silk, they hung from the wooden panels that separated the storage areas. The images were vivid and sumptuous, amidst the boxes of implements, Tupperware, rows of gardening and carpentry tools. Stoker was struck by a series of sweetmeats in blues, pinks and yellows. An array of glittering gods and goddesses, a pair of gold sandals, Waldo's yellow tackies with elaborately criss-crossed shoelaces.

Waldo had always had an eye for light and detail. Like Dean with his loupe he'd always been obsessed with the smallest of things. Scale was a cultural thing, Waldo had said. Everything about him was contained, restricted. Though he'd always considered space to be infinite, it had never been his for the taking. Stoker marvelled at the economy, the compressed focus in each miniature. He pictured Waldo alone, at peace, oblivious to the torrent of noise pouring through the windows of his rented rooms in Bombay, Karala, the remote villages in the north and south untouched by the advance of capital. He pictured the steadiness of Waldo's hand as he shrank the details of his life. For Waldo nothing was other than what it was at each moment. And it had always been beauty which Waldo had courted. The life, the light, the wondrousness of everyday things. To see life so directly! To find a way of carrying things! To know one's limits, one's strengths!

All this, it seemed, had always been Waldo's province. Stoker thought of Joan's words about killing something that was already dead. How morbid he and Joan seemed in comparison to Waldo! How forlorn! And then Stoker smiled, the solemnity of his thoughts brushed away by the panoply of brightly coloured pictures which Waldo had drawn from his journey. How splendid they were against the cluttered heaviness that surrounded them! The fact that Waldo's miniatures had been painted on the backs of used train tickets made them all the more precious.

Stoker recalled the day he and Waldo had gathered the used tickets from the baffled collector at the central station in town, the day Waldo had decided to do something about all the tickets he'd bought when he'd travelled between Obs and Gugs as a teacher. Stoker imagined all the other journeys hidden beneath the wash of colour, the dates and times, the names of suburbs. One day, he thought, one day some restorer would discover the hidden history of movement. The traffic of bodies. What would the restorer think? And then Stoker chuckled. Waldo's works were runes, he thought. They were tracings of a commuting that was routine and magical. One day the magic beneath the magic would be known to the world.

Exhausted and smug Stoker studied Waldo seated across the table, the smoke travelling across his smiling and equally exhausted face. Dean's crazy suggestion that they pull the whole thing together was just the impetus both of them had needed. Waldo – more than he – had needed to find a focus. Joan had not recanted on her decision to stick with Percy. Restarting a life was a hell of a lot better than starting a scene. Besides, Joan was immersed in the completion of *Coastal Resort*, her pastel of Percy dead and discarded on a dump site. The meticulous detailing which the drawing demanded had obsessed her. It had become her avenue of coping. Stoker noted that Waldo hadn't once mentioned the break with Joan. She was still around. They were still friends. There was a similarity, Stoker thought, between his breakup with Phyllis and that of Joan and Waldo. What had always mattered between them would never change.

Waldo broke the silence and the drift.

'It's all about control,' Waldo began. 'You can't let anything break you. Dominion Food and Hardware is the beginning of the new me. You make your own rules. The way you look at me – I can see the way you think you know me. I've changed, Stoker. You may as well know that. I've got things to say and I'm going to say them. No one's going to walk over me any more, no school principal, no bank manager. I've let things slide for too long, but all that's over. I'm in an aggressive phase. You don't believe me? Well I am. India did it to me. The amount of bartering I had to do, you wouldn't believe. People are like zombies here. It's all about handouts and fair play. Even belief in this country is a kind of slavery. In India belief is active, there's a craziness to it all, a surreality that blows away all the systems we've tried to set up. In India things change perpetually. Belief is water. Control is movement. You know how I've always wanted a piece of land? A homestead? I've always wanted to start an olive farm. Five hectares. I could do it if I wanted to. The bike accident's made it all possible. But now I'm not so sure. The pioneering instinct doesn't hold me the way it used to. I'm thinking about containers now. Trading. A kind of radical informal sector. Containers are where it's at. You can live in a container, ship stuff, organise exhibitions. Anything's possible. You've just got to keep moving. Changing.'

Waldo passed the joint across and lit a cigarette. Stoker found it strange to see him smoke. Waldo had quit years ago. Now he was smoking. It was odd the way Dean had quit and Waldo had started. Maybe he didn't know Waldo anymore? Stoker thought. He wondered if he too had changed in Waldo's eyes. In the gloom, the joint passing between them, Stoker flashed back to the last road trip they'd gone on together. It had been Waldo's idea. Their destination had been the weather station in Sutherland, the coldest spot in the Karoo. They had never reached Sutherland. By nightfall they'd found a deserted two-man shack. There was wood, a brazier. Stoker recalled the gutted dried tortoise he'd found. It was a sign to take it slow,

Waldo had said. Slow . . . For three days and three nights they'd stayed at the shack, rotated the cooking, the search for water. Not a single other human presence had broken the stillness. There was just the two of them, the sky as bright and hard as metal, the stars. They'd both drawn, gone on hikes. They'd hardly spoken. Slow . . . Yes, that was then. And now? A fervour seemed to have gripped Waldo. The magic was still there, the light. But there was a forthrightness which Stoker couldn't recall. Everything seemed to be about mobility, deeds. There was nothing to be waited for, depended upon. Waldo had fallen, and in falling had bloomed.

CHAPTER NINETEEN

In the past Dylan had read his poetry at Lawrence's. The place wasn't new to him. Dylan suited Lawrence's. He had that bulky brooding quality that worked well against the red velvet walls, embroidered divan and flickering candle light. His voice was low, evenly paced, the sentences filtering unbroken into the breathing bowl of silence.

Stoker watched his brother in action, the heaving of his words like the heaving of stone. There was not a shred of nervous energy inside Dylan. Stoker doubted that Dylan had been even remotely anxious about his impending arrival. He measured the crass brutality of their conversation in the boat against his memory of Dylan laughing in Greenmarket Square. The latter was the mood which had survived. Stoker studied Phyllis seated beside Dylan, her mind tangled in the web of his. He remembered how much Phyllis had loved Dylan's book. It was a love which could not be fixed to words. Then Stoker smiled as he recalled a favourite saying of Phyllis's. She'd lifted it from a Dirty Harry movie: 'Opinions are like arseholes. Everyone has one.' Smiling still, Stoker realised that this was Phyllis's way of getting out of the obligation to remark

258

on anything she liked. Now he measured the crudity of these remembered words against the unwavering and exquisite balance of Dylan's prose. He too felt no inclination to interpret what he heard. He let the words sink inside him, pausing only to observe how everything he had heard on that misty morning in Riebeek-Kasteel had remained utterly clear. Fresh.

Then Stoker turned his gaze to Bianca seated beside him. She was still. Attentive. Smoke trailed from her lips. She had remembered his invitation. She was there beside him. His new friend. Stoker smiled as he watched Lizzie fidgeting slightly. She had her hand in Klingman's. Smiling still, he looked at Beatrice with her rapt glittering eyes. On either side of her sat Prue and Dom. Waldo was over at Dominion Food and Hardware preparing for the party. With him were Bridge and Immo, Jay, Percy and Phil, the drummer from The Waiting Country. Joan was still grafting at her studio in the Bo-Kaap. Stoker wondered if Dom had Olivieri's dentures in her pocket. It was the sort of thing Dom would do. Then his mind slipped back to Dylan's novel.

After the reading a dignified-looking literary figure extolled the virtues of Dylan's novel, of the way Dylan had resolved a love of poetry with the demands of prose. She spoke of a dawn long broken in South African fiction. Of the bright light of day that bathed Dylan's words. There was no darkness here, she said, no anger and bile. No stuntedness or deformity which had characterised South African fiction since its inception. The walls had fallen away, all compulsion to defy or react had been vanquished. Here, she said, here the poet and novelist walks over giant plains, stopping to observe, holding memory in one hand, forgetfulness in the other, like a blade of grass, a swath of sand. Stoker enjoyed the obscurity of the literary figure's words – her refusal to explain Dylan's book. In her favour she had remained true to Dylan's equation – *Vertical Man, Horizontal World*. Stoker stared at the cover of the book he held before him. It was the image of a headless horseman moving through a desert. The image was a sepia collage set against the striated yellow of plywood, and was by an artist he'd always admired.

Lien Botha. Still, he regretted not showing Dylan an image of his painting, *Man in a Landscape*. Perhaps, he thought, perhaps if the book were successful and found a foreign distributor, perhaps Dylan would choose to use his painting?

The formalities were finally over. Dylan was surrounded by journalists who were gathered for the occasion. Stoker would find the time to speak with Dylan at Dominion Food and Hardware. For now there was Lizzie, Phyllis, Bianca.

'Thank you,' Bianca said, as she turned to face him. Her gratitude was thick, her voice hoarse. Stoker had never seen her so moved. He was glad to have made this opportunity possible for her. But then it was really she who had made it possible. It was she who had broken the fabric of his life, she who had approached him with her conviction of his worth. It was she who understood the worth of things.

Phyllis appeared beside them. She was radiant. Stoker introduced her to Bianca. This, he realised, was their first meeting. Stoker watched with interest as they spoke. The mood was amicable, gracious. He watched as Bianca placed her pale white hand against Phyllis's belly. He listened as Bianca confessed her ignorance when, as a student of sculpture, she'd chosen to sculpt fertility goddesses. At the root of her flawed execution had been her failure to understand the workings of the navel – how the navel sometimes turned outward and seemed to vanish during pregnancy. Stoker watched as Bianca lifted Phyllis's top to demonstrate the workings of the navel, her youthful mistake. Did she know that he was the father? Stoker wondered.

Beatrice was the next to appear. Bianca discovered that Beatrice was also from Palermo. It was the only word Stoker could recognise in their conversation.

'You must feel proud of your brother,' Phyllis said.

Stoker was struck by the words Phyllis had chosen to use. Was this an injunction? Was it pride he was feeling? Stoker wasn't sure. He was once again struck by the ease with which Phyllis presumed his acceptance of her relationship with Dylan. At every turn she would trump his resistance. Confound his envy and regret. She would leave him no choice but to live. To endure. And so he would. Perhaps he too would learn to walk across giant plains, clutching memory in one hand, forgetfulness in the other.

Lizzie appeared and hugged Phyllis. Lizzie was in awe of her future niece. She and Phyllis talked about babies and adoption.

'It's a strange thing, adopting,' Lizzie said. 'One has an idea of the ideal baby, and then you see all the infants without homes.'

Lizzie and Phyllis talked about babies with HIV. They talked about street children. Klingman, to his credit, had wanted to adopt one of the street children he'd seen on the Foreshore on his way to and from work. But Lizzie wanted a baby. It did not matter what the colour of the eyes were, the colour of the hair. She was becoming ambitious and wanted more than one. Klingman smilingly accused her of suffering from a Mia Farrow complex. Basically, it seemed as though Lizzie could do whatever she wanted. Klingman was game.

Yet again Stoker was amazed by how well Lizzie and Klingman got on. He wondered how one ever found the right person. He doubted he ever would. Connections seemed so arbitrary. If Klingman hadn't moved in a few doors away from Lizzie, she would never have known of his existence. Or would she? Would they have met each other if the circumstances were different? Perhaps, Stoker thought, perhaps things were always meant to work out for Lizzie. There was no denying she deserved it. Then Stoker realised that he was feeling wrecked and hopelessly sentimental. A good night was being had by all, and it was by no means over.

Stoker and Dom were the first to decamp. En route to Dominion Food and Hardware they met Putter. He was a lot less strung-out than on the last two occasions Stoker had met him. Putter's cold sores had vanished. The Locker Room Project was on track. Putter had raised the funding he needed to revamp the River Club. All the artists were pitching in. Stoker sheepishly informed Putter that he'd been hectically busy.

'You, Joan and Waldo will have to do something, there's no getting out of it,' Putter said.

It was pointless telling Putter how hard each of them was

working. Selfless pursuit was key for Putter. It was the group which counted. Putter was only partially right. Joan had to finish *Coastal Resort*, he had to finish the radio painting, and Waldo, well Waldo had a shitload on his plate.

Then Putter informed Stoker of his brilliant idea – an idea which would end up shaping the life of Stoker and his friends for the next two months.

'The theme is sport, right?'

Stoker nodded.

'The theme is a Queer take on sport. So, how about everyone coming in teams? Say a team of weirdly-clad golfers, or tennis players, or . . .'

Putter proceeded to reel off a list of sports as though Stoker and Dom had descended from another planet and didn't have the faintest idea of what he was talking about.

'Imagine the night,' Putter said. 'When you drive through the gates, you'll go platz! There'll be scoreboards made of sequins, pink and mauve floodlights, a choice of fourteen fabulous party playgrounds under one roof!'

Stoker and Dom eyed each other as Putter raved on.

'In the lovely long jump lounge a team of leaping latex lesbians will lick lashings of lugubrious liqueur. In the Ra-Ra-Rugga-Bugga Bar moffie mountaineers will mingle with gorgeous goalkeepers and terribly terrific tennis-players, while outside the raving rollerbladers will race raucously round and round and round and round.'

Stoker could just about swallow Putter's appalling alliteration. It tasted as bitter to him as a Grand-Pa headache powder. He pictured a demented copywriter trapped in a thesaurus and chasing his tail. He'd recognised Putter's allusion to *The Adventures of Priscilla, Queen of the Desert*. He pictured two drag queens in feather boas, chiffon and hiking boots, gazing into the sprawling nothingness of the Australian Outback. He recalled the line, his favourite: 'That's just what this country needs . . . a cock in a frock on a rock.'

As far as Stoker was concerned the words were the cornerstone and the anthem of the Locker Room Project. He'd seen the movie with Phyllis. They'd both raved about it, Phyllis in particular. She'd wondered if South Africa would ever produce anything as zany and uplifting.

Stoker had to admit that Putter's idea was appealing. The team concept with the Queer take was just what the city needed. People were way too fascinated with themselves. It was the pack that counted, he remembered Putter saying. The hydra-headed god with a million hands. As always Stoker was struck by Putter's wacky collective energy. How different it was from the solitary journey he was undertaking, how different from Dylan's book! Stoker was convinced that Putter would be remembered for his madcap grandeur, his sense of the epic in a town riddled with small minds and bloated unearned egos.

When Stoker, Dom and Putter entered Dominion Food and Hardware, Nusrat Fateh Ali Khan's *Dum Must Must* was blaring on the stereo. The heady mix of world music, shot through with a voice that embraced and soared beyond each and every contradiction, seemed to raise Putter's vision one notch higher.

'Yes,' Stoker said. 'Yes.'

CHAPTER TWENTY

Within minutes Putter had blitzed Dominion Food and Hardware with his new directive on Queer team dressing. Stoker ordered a Windhoek for himself and Putter, an Ignition for Dom. Immo was behind the bar, Bridge and Waldo were relaxing around a pot of waterblommetjie bredie. Jay, Percy and Phil were sorting out sound. The sounds of *Dum Must Must* effortlessly contained the band's discordant sound check.

Two people whom Stoker didn't know from a bar of soap but whom he liked the look of were listening with rapt attention to Putter's brief.

'So the whole idea is to fuck up the dress code?' said the first bar of soap. She had her back to Stoker, her hair piled up and wrapped in a brightly coloured cloth.

'It's not necessarily that negative,' said the other bar of soap, a hefty man with thick glasses and grey hair. 'The emphasis is excess. We could come as ping-pong balls. Lots of them.'

'How do we do that?' the first bar of soap enquired.

'We could get, say, sixty ping-pong balls each. We could tie them with wire. We could shave our heads, dust them with talcum powder, then strap the balls to our heads,' the bar of soap with thick glasses ventured.

'What about the rest of the body?' the first soap asked.

'You're the one with the body, you think of something,' the second said, digging his fork into the bredie.

'Cheers,' Stoker said, handing Putter his Windhoek.

'Cheers,' Putter said.

'Looks like you've got people talking,' Stoker said.

'I want the whole city talking,' Putter replied. 'Imagine if we could get the whole city grafting on a fancy dress ball. Anyone anywhere could think up what they want to wear. The only rule is that it has to be Queer.'

'What's Queer to you?' Stoker asked.

'Unusual . . . playful . . . extraordinary . . . productive . . . off the wall . . . pleasure-loving.'

'Nauseous,' Stoker added.

'That too,' Putter mused. 'I'm just trying to activate some kind of alternative expression. We figured we could get ten thousand into the River Club.'

'You're kidding. That's bigger than Sting, bigger than UB40.'

'It's just some home-grown chaos,' Putter said knowingly. 'It's an art party. You can celebrate yourself.'

'That sounds cheesy,' Stoker said.

'Only if you're cynical. I can't afford to be. In fact I don't think anyone can. We need time out from cynicism. Like this place. Dominion Food and Hardware. This feels like time out to me. You see Waglays? On the corner of Trill and Main?'

'No,' Stoker said.

'Waglays has had a makeover. They're selling exhaust-pipes now. You can go in for a pack of cigarettes, a carton of milk, and come out with an exhaust-pipe. Or think of the Caltex petrol station on Main. The attendants are running a shebeen. Now that's Queer to me.' Putter trailed off. Stoker got the point.

He was thinking of what kind of a team he'd like to belong to. The ping-pong idea appealed to him. He turned to reappraise the couple who'd talked to Putter. At that precise moment the bar of soap who'd had her back to him looked in his direction. Stoker saw that it was Hedda, Phyllis's friend and ex-lover, the aromatherapist and masseuse from Citrusdal. The hefty man with the glasses and grey hair had to be Theo, her ex-con dockworker lover.

'You talk to that Italian woman, what's her name?' It was Putter resuming their conversation just as Stoker was about to walk over to Hedda.

'Bianca,' Stoker said to Putter. 'Yeah, I've talked with her. She's coming over tonight. You should talk to her about the Locker Room Project. You know she's writing a book on art in South Africa?'

'Art's dead,' Putter said.

'Fuck off,' Stoker said. He had an unnerving feeling that Putter meant it. The point was taken but it wasn't shared. He would have preferred to find out what Hedda and her beau were up to. Putter continued to chew his ear off.

He'd stopped exhibiting, Putter said. He wanted to redesign environments. He saw life as a series of transformations of existing spaces, a.k.a. finding creative alternatives. Stoker couldn't quite buy the idea. It sounded too much like ad talk. But that's what Putter wanted to get into. He wanted to collapse the divide between commerce and art. He was sick to death of artists constantly being suckers, always grateful for hand-outs, always fucked over by galleries. He wanted to take art to the people. Grafting on one's own fancy dress was an obvious way to reach people. Everyone loved being silly – didn't they? People were craving for the right excuse, and Putter was providing the excuse.

'You see the new graffiti on the Station Road bridge?' Stoker asked.

265

'Yeah. How does it go again?'

'FUCK ALLEGIANCE. ART IS THE EYE OF THE NATION.'

'Make sense to you?' Putter asked.

'Yes and no. More yes than no,' Stoker replied.

'Most people are still walking with their tails between their legs. Doing the right thing. Mixing in the right proportion of guilt and grace. It's a bullshit alchemy that's flying around if you ask me.'

'What do you mean?' Stoker asked. He was lost.

'Like I said, everyone's looking for the gap. There's so much backslapping it's sickening. You'd think Mandela had just been released, the way people talk. The braaivleis is over, it's the art party now!'

'I'll drink to that,' Waldo said.

Stoker was grateful for Waldo's interjection. Putter was starting to irritate him. He was thinking of Hedda and Theo.

Putter's enthusiasm was enough for Waldo. Waldo never needed to know the nitty-gritty of things to enjoy himself. His passion was like a blur. Nothing fixated him for too long and everything mattered – not for what it was but for what it brought out in people. Waldo picked up on moods. Like Dean, though less acutely, Waldo could pick up on moods before most people. And he was usually right. Stoker attributed this sixth sense in Dean and Waldo to the fact that they'd never been able to live down the national influence of their father, a rugby sports commentator and legendary bore. As far as Dean was concerned his dad needed to be fucked up the arse just so he could loosen up, become a little more human. Waldo probably knew that Stoker was getting tired of having his ear chewed off by Putter.

'How's things, Waldo?' Putter asked.

'Cooking,' Waldo said. Putter laughed. He hadn't seen Waldo since his return from India. They had a lot to catch up on and very little time. Stoker left them with the intention of talking to Hedda. He didn't get beyond Bridge and Immo.

'So what's bungee-jumping like?' he asked Immo as he ordered another Windhoek. Immo smiled his deranged and blissful smile.

Stoker still couldn't believe that Immo had actually walked down Africa.

'Different strokes for different folks,' Immo said.

Stoker was slightly thrown by the reply. It seemed to apply less to his question and more to his thoughts. Stoker guessed that if someone couldn't speak English properly, they'd have to speak in shitty proverbs.

'It was good,' Immo resumed, pausing to roll a cigarette. 'It was Bridge's idea. She is not frightened anymore. You know that? She says it is the rape. After the rape she is no more afraid. Me, I was very afraid.' Immo chuckled as he ran his tongue along the sticky side of the Rizla paper. Then he sealed the cigarette and popped it into his mouth. 'Walking is different to falling,' Immo said as he inhaled.

Stoker waited for Immo to continue.

'When you walk you stitch the whole world together. When you fall . . .' Immo seemed not to know what to say next. And then: 'Me and Bridget, we fall in love, you see. We have to fall because we fall in love.'

Stoker found Immo's last remark both obtuse and literal. That was Immo, he thought. Obtuse and literal. There was clearly something compelling about him – the compressed rock-like energy, the Walt Whitman beard, the crazy piercing eyes, the inner calm. It made sense that Bridge had fallen for him. Stoker remembered the first time he'd seen Immo at Greenmarket Square, seated on his backpack, peddling what little he had – a yo-yo, some beadwork, a couple of shirts, boots, a clutch of stones. He found himself hoping he'd get to know Immo better. Immo and Bridge were the right people for Dominion Food and Hardware, Stoker thought. There was nothing desperate about either of them. They seemed to work like osmosis, or like a Venn diagram – connecting and leaving a lot of space for discovery.

'Saw Prue at the reading,' Stoker said to Bridge. 'She okay?' he added, thinking about the Koos Malgas incident.

'She's okay,' Bridge said. 'You know how focused she can get about things she hates. She's needed to focus in order to hate efficiently. She would never have gotten to where she was if she hadn't. Yeah, she's okay. She's taken to Immo.'

'Who wouldn't,' Stoker said. Bridge smiled.

'It was incredible, Stoker,' Bridge resumed. 'The whole trip. There was so much to see. You read *The Waiting Country*?'

At the mention of Nicol's book Stoker realised that he was definitely dealing with an epidemic. Phyllis had talked about it. So had Dom. Dylan had most probably finished reading it. Jay had named his band after it. Now Bridge. Considering the relatively low reading power of his friends, *The Waiting Country* definitely amounted to an epidemic.

'No,' Stoker said. 'I haven't read it.'

'In the book there's this poem by Jonker in which she says something like the children will become giants and trek across Africa, across the whole world. Well, that's how I felt. Like a giant. It was different with people like my mum, like Nelson, or Ingrid Jonker. We've never really had to fight, you know.'

Stoker was sceptical. The way he saw it he had always had to fight. The difference was a matter of interpretation. There was more than one war. But there was always war. This was where he and Putter differed. Putter preferred to think of art crime. Or the politics of fun. This was also where Stoker and Dayglo differed. Dayglo was on some global peace initiative. Fuck that, Stoker thought. Fuck peace. As far as he was concerned the world had a hell of a long way to go before it could earn some peace. Besides, he'd have more than enough peace when he was dead, and even then he doubted it.

Listening to Bridge all wide-eyed and bushy-tailed Stoker realised that he was a miserable sod at heart. He watched Immo and Bridge cuddle. Their intimacy was like Braille. They were learning about each other. And he? What was he learning? Stoker wondered. He'd faced the fact that he was alone. Ordering another Windhoek he recalled Dylan's words about burning bridges, about the fact that people never stop needing. Being alone didn't mean he didn't stop needing. But he wasn't clear about what exactly he needed.

Stoker noticed that one of the plastic carnations had fallen from the wreath he'd made for Olivieri's portrait. Then he turned and saw Bianca and Beatrice step into the store. They were raving in Italian. Right behind them were Lizzie and Klingman. They had a way about them that made Stoker think of bright sunny days and chapels. Dylan and Phyllis were still nowhere to be seen. He realised that he'd lost the inclination to talk to Hedda and Theo.

CHAPTER TWENTY ONE

Stoker ordered a plate of waterblommetjie bredie. He needed to sit down and eat. He needed the world to come to him. It wasn't as though he was feeling alienated. He wasn't. He felt as though he was sitting in his own kitchen. It was just that the pressure of engagement was slightly overwhelming him. He needed to talk to Dylan. He didn't know what he was going to say. He wasn't even clear about what he was feeling. It wasn't anger. It wasn't wholesale respect. At that moment life and art were definitely not the same thing.

The food tasted good. Stoker appreciated the way the vegetables announced themselves. With each mouthful a new taste emerged, took a bow, then drifted into a medley of tastes. He thought of Dylan's remark about how he always had to locate the differences in things that seemed the same – how he saw gradations in a blur. He realised that Dylan was on his mind and that he couldn't shake him. The whole thing between Dylan and Phyllis had happened so fast. There had been nothing clandestine, nothing drawn-out about the connection. One minute she hardly knew him, the next she was fucking him. Then Stoker stopped to remind himself that the exact same thing had happened to him and Phyllis, Immo and Bridge, Lizzie and Klingman, to millions of people all over the world. That's what people did – they fucked. Then Stoker paused, isolated a certain taste in the bredie, and held it at the tip of his tongue.

Was sex the issue? Stoker wasn't sure. He didn't know what the issue was. The whole thing had happened so smoothly. Or had it? Phyllis still missed him. She'd said so. Still, what did it mean to miss someone? Missing didn't change anything. Missing was as natural as breathing. It was something unavoidable which didn't change things. Phyllis was with Dylan. The situation was clear. She'd made her choice and she was sticking with it.

Watching Hedda seated across the room, Stoker recalled her first meeting with Phyllis at Macgrawley's. He pictured Hedda sitting at the bar getting drunk, Phyllis doing a karaoke and as usual, making a spectacle of herself. Phyllis walking over to Hedda and asking her why she looked so sad. Hedda saying she was mourning the death of her lover. Phyllis helping Hedda to smile. Phyllis taking Hedda to her flat across the road on Orphan and Long.

Had something similar happened between Phyllis and Dylan? It could have. They could have met in the city ages ago. Dylan had told him that he'd come in to see his publisher. He and Phyllis could have met. They could have fucked. Why not? Phyllis could have been drawn to Dylan's brooding silence, he to her vivacity. It was possible. They could have fucked long before seeing each other in Riebeek-Kasteel. How was she to know Dylan was his brother?! Stranger things had occurred. Otherwise why was Phyllis so anxious about knowing whether or not Dylan had relayed their conversation to him? Why had Dylan talked to him in the boat about fucking Phyllis? It wasn't a possibility, it was a fact! They'd just decided to keep it a secret, that way they could blunt the pain they were sure he was feeling. The whole thing made sense to Stoker. Still, he couldn't reconcile the deceit with Phyllis's honesty. If she'd fucked Dylan before, she would have told him. Or would she?

By this point Stoker couldn't separate fact from fiction. He needed to believe in some clandestine tryst so as to deal with the suddenness of it all. Still, though his deductions made sense to him, he finally recognised them as more fictive than factual, the stuff of novels rather than life. Shoving aside the ghost of treachery and deceit, he looked around him at all the composed and smiling faces. He let his heart and mind bathe in the delirious whirl of Nusrat Fateh Ali Khan. Olivieri would be proud of the lot of them. There was no doubt about that.

Bianca sat opposite him with her half-eaten plate of bredie. She bore an expression that seemed to say – talk to me. You can talk to me. Stoker couldn't think of anything to say. He watched her shimmering black hair as she bent down to eat. He realised that he loved to watch her eat. He pictured the slices of beef and pickle she'd eaten at Petit Paris, her swollen peach lips. He realised that he was getting a hard-on. He was glad that his cock had a mind of its own. He felt his jeans stretch. He brushed his hand across his cock, then shifted it back to his cold beer.

'You should talk to Putter,' Stoker said.

'There's time,' Bianca replied. 'Right now I'm wondering if you want to make love to me, or get rid of me.'

'Both, I guess.' Stoker didn't mind admitting his feelings. He was lonely, he was horny, he was confused and needed some attention.

'You like?' Stoker asked, alluding to the Dominion Food and Hardware make-over.

'Food's good,' Bianca said. 'I think I need some more.'

Stoker watched as Bianca walked over for a refill. Something about her drabness that night appealed to him. There was nothing tarty about her, not then. She wore no make-up. Her skin had the sheen of crystal. He liked her drab brown cardigan, her loose grey trousers. She wasn't for sale. Watching her Stoker realised that the hard-on was a passing indistinct urge. He didn't actually want to fuck her. He didn't want to fuck anyone. He was turning more and more into a wanker, which was fine for now. Celebrate the self, Putter had said. Sure. There was no denying that bodies had their appeal, but right then Stoker realised that he didn't actually need the solace of another human touch. His body was adjusting to the isolation.

'You like her, don't you?' It was Dom.

'No I don't,' Stoker said. Did he mean what he said? Of course he liked her, but he doubted that was what Dom meant.

'Do you?' Stoker asked Dom.

'She seems very interesting. She's certainly not from here.'

'And where's here?' Stoker asked.

Dom paused. 'Here's South Africa,' she said. 'Here's Obs. Here's a dot hardly worth noticing.'

'You're cheerful tonight.'

'Jay's pissing me off, actually.'

'Oh.'

'Forget about it,' Dom said, and left the table.

Stoker hadn't realised that Dom was as upset as she was. He looked at Jay who was sorting out some cables. Jay seemed fine. Then again he had trashed Dom's flat and she had arranged a restraining order.

Stoker suddenly felt compelled to get into a good mood. A number of people were streaming into the store. Most, it seemed, wanted to remain in the presence of Dylan who'd entered with Phyllis. Stoker remained seated. He watched Phyllis and Hedda embrace, cheeks brushing, arms softly folded. Dylan walked towards Stoker and sat down. Neither spoke. Their eyes were locked, a shared lifetime compressed in their lingering gazes.

'Thank you for coming,' Dylan said.

'Thank you for writing your book,' Stoker replied.

'Let's hope it makes some money,' Dylan said.

Stoker doubted that Dylan actually cared about the money. Just to have written it was enough. Besides, Dylan had said this to him before, and he hadn't believed him then.

'Would you like a drink?' Stoker asked.

'I'll have one of those smart drinks they're serving these days.'

'You'd better watch out. You'll end up saying something clever,' Stoker countered. He wasn't sure if he was being insulting. Dylan seemed unfazed.

'Phyllis tells me you've nearly completed your cycle of paintings.'

'Almost,' Stoker said. He couldn't recall having said anything to Phyllis about his work, but then she had her ways of finding out things.

'You're calling the cycle *In the Country of Last Things*, I hear.'

'Fitting, don't you think?'

Dylan didn't rise to the bait.

Stoker could still hear Dylan saying Phyllis's name. He spoke it with a fullness, an affection, which Stoker could not deny. He wanted to mention that he'd seen them in Greenmarket Square. What was the point? The reckoning was now. Here. Stoker flinched as he recalled the way that Dylan had caught his fist as he reached to punch him. He could still feel the humiliation, the shame of his outrage. His melodramatic and feeble attempt at power.

'I behaved stupidly,' Stoker said.

'So did I,' Dylan replied.

'You were right though . . . It wasn't Phyllis's honour I was protecting. It was my own.'

'Honour,' Dylan sighed. The word seemed absurd, empty to him.

Stoker felt as though he would never say anything right, anything fitting. No words could resolve this moment. Emotions seemed to alter with such rapidity. A gesture, a word, a feeling, each seemed to cancel out the other. Stoker felt that Dylan sensed this. That was why Dylan seemed so calm, he thought. It was the futility of understanding that drove him. A showdown seemed as absurd as any decorous and politic resolution.

Then Stoker recalled the words Bianca had spoken to him . . . *stay quiet a while, let words rinse clean, dissolve* . . . Yes, that is what he would have to do. Stay quiet a while, let the night unlock its own riddle. He would not anticipate. He would not shape. No, he would live in the midst of things.

CHAPTER TWENTY TWO

The night passed with an unwavering good will. Jay sang songs Stoker had never heard before. 'Remember Scratch' and 'Pam Golding Properties' were two of them. The first was

273

gorgeously nostalgic, the second plain bitchy. Both songs reminded him of Morrissey. These were followed by a rousing gospel tune called 'Golly Golly Golly Golly Golly Jesus'. Jay insisted that if the song was worth mentioning, all five gollys had to be included. The set ended with a haunting ballad called 'History Gives Too Soon into Weak Hands'.

Beatrice danced with Phyllis. Dylan and Bianca conversed. Stoker could not think of a more precise word to describe their dialogue – the measured exchange, the depth of mutual enquiry.

Joan eventually appeared. She was exhausted, having spent the last eight hours trying to draw sand. *Coastal Resort* was driving her crazy. She and Stoker talked about art, their one abiding link.

'Sometimes it feels so stupid,' Joan said.

'I suppose there's nothing more obsessive than drawing sand,' Stoker said. Joan laughed.

'Just getting the texture, the light! Sometimes I feel as though I'm drawing myself into a corner.'

'Maybe you are,' Stoker replied.

Joan was looking over her shoulder. Stoker turned and saw that she was looking at Percy. This was the first time he'd seen Joan, Waldo and Percy in the same room. Stoker realised that *Coastal Resort* was probably Joan's only space of true calm. No matter how angry she got, no matter how she battled, at least the ongoing war was her own. In the case of her pastel drawing she'd chosen her own difficulty.

'How was the launch?' Joan asked.

'Exquisite,' Stoker said.

'You talk to Dylan?'

'Not really.'

'You going to?'

'What's to say?'

Joan recognised the futility of the situation. The impasse. Stoker and Joan turned to look at Phyllis as she danced with Beatrice. Then, in unison, they turned to look at Dylan. There seemed to be nothing cloying, nothing stated about Dylan and Phyllis's relationship. The one seemed to orbit the other. Stoker realised that Phyllis and Dylan did not form a Venn diagram. There was no point of intersection, and then a space of discovery. Phyllis and Dylan coexisted. They remained independent. Intact. This, Stoker realised, was what Phyllis had always wanted – a relationship in which she would always remain singular. It was certainly the way Dylan conducted himself. How different they seemed to Immo and Bridge, to Lizzie and Klingman! But then again, Stoker corrected himself, there was no certain way in which lovers behaved. Things changed constantly. Perhaps this was what Phyllis and Dylan had always understood.

'Do you think I'm making a mistake?' Joan asked Stoker.

'Yes,' Stoker said. He was surprised by his directness. He realised that his conviction did not stem from the fact that he cared for Waldo.

'I'll have to continue making my mistakes then, won't I?' Joan said. Stoker remained silent.

'You feel like seeing my paintings?' Stoker asked. He did not want to get embroiled in human intrigue and doubt. He wanted to address Joan on terms which both of them could understand – terms which had a shape, a clarity, that was solitary.

'That would be good,' Joan said.

Stoker led her up the stairs to his studio.

For a long time Joan was silent. Stoker lit a cigarette. Waited. He did not realise that Joan was crying. When she turned to face him he saw the tears. Without a word he folded her in his arms. They stood together in a silence broken by Joan's stifled sobs.

'I know that I seem to be destroying what's good for me. I know. I love Waldo. He is inside me.' Joan drew away and turned her tear-filled eyes to Stoker. 'When I was in New York I was feeling quite down,' she said. 'I felt so alone, closed in by the city. And then the most incredible thing happened.' And here Joan smiled. 'There was a thunderstorm. It was incredible. The city became so warm and sensual and open. People's bubbles burst.'

Stoker let Joan speak without saying a word. He was thankful to be able to help, to be there for her, for someone.

'It's funny the way things happen. I didn't think I'd cry. I didn't think I'd remember the thunderstorm. It's funny.'

Stoker let Joan drift in his arms.

'They're beautiful,' Joan said, as she left his arms and turned back to the paintings.

'What I'm doing is easier,' Stoker said. 'Mixing media I can get an effect that you'll battle for months to create.'

'It's silly, don't you think? Working the way I do? It's so old-fashioned.'

'You're a punk Pre-Raphaelite photo-realist,' Stoker said.

Joan laughed. 'You just make that up?' she asked.

'I wish. It's something I came across. I've been meaning to tell you.'

'I like it a lot.'

'Thought you would.'

Joan paused, then resumed the conversation. 'In New York art is so technological. There are TV screens everywhere. Photographic exhibitions. We're such a poor small country in comparison. But you know, I'm happy to be back home. To look at me you wouldn't think so. But I am. I'm glad for the smallness. The narrowness. I took photographs of the storm from my window.'

'I haven't had a chance to see your photographs,' Stoker said.

'Most of them are just research. The colours of things. Textures. Everything was so big and fast it was hard to find a focus. It was good for me to be alone, away from Waldo. I'm learning about myself, Stoker. You have to believe me.'

'I do,' Stoker said.

'The paintings are great,' Joan said.

'Bianca wishes to buy them for some gallery in Italy. What do you think?'

'They've got to be seen. And you need the money. You know that only foreigners are buying these days? All our major galleries are closing down. Soon we're not going to have much space to show and sell.'

'That's Putter's point,' Stoker said.

'Well, he's right. All the best work is leaving the country. We're going global.'

Stoker laughed.

'What's so funny?'

'I was just thinking about something Dom said, about Obs being an insignificant dot.'

'You know Dom. Whenever something isn't working she can be a miserable bitch.'

Stoker didn't comment. He was glad to see Joan perking up.

'What's this global thing anyway? What the fuck does it mean?' Stoker asked.

'You know.' Joan didn't feel like following a train of thought that was self-evident to her.

'Bianca suggests I exhibit the cycle in one of those buildings under construction on the Foreshore.'

'Sounds good to me.'

'Don't you think it's a bit showy?'

'Didn't you hear me? The galleries are closing down. We've got to create our own spaces. Like Waldo showing his work downstairs. It's as good a space as any.'

'For someone who hasn't gone to art school I can be pretty narrow-minded,' Stoker said.

'You're just frightened, that's all.'

Stoker realised that Joan was right. He was scared. No amount of passion and dedication could stop the fear. He thought of Immo's words, about Bridge no longer feeling scared. Perhaps that was why he'd chosen isolation? It was safer. Art was his excuse, his way of getting out of himself. Was he stopping himself from living? Stoker looked at Joan and thought about what she'd said about having to fall prey, make mistakes. He thought of his process of obliteration and revelation. Art was his country of errors. Art was the incarnation of everything that was broken inside him, everything that was lost. Was it his paintings which had sparked Joan's tears? Before Stoker had a chance to ask her, she was gone.

Stoker remained in the studio. He could feel the floorboards throbbing beneath him. He stared at the radio painting splayed on the floor, still incomplete. This one he would keep, he thought. This one he wouldn't sell.

CHAPTER TWENTY THREE

When Stoker rejoined everyone in the store the party showed no signs of ending. The band had taken a breather. Portishead was playing. Stoker overheard Waldo talking to Beatrice and Bianca about seasonal vegetables and cooking.

'Cooking is like art,' Waldo said. 'There's no end to what you can learn. There are so many layers, so much depth. I wonder if I'll ever be a great chef. I always read the recipes.'

Stoker listened to Beatrice's cackle, watched as Waldo held out his palm for Beatrice to slap, then he passed Bridge. She was talking to Phyllis, Hedda, Prue and Putter about when she was a little girl. About rape.

'I thought rape was taking off someone's clothes, until I heard on the radio about someone who was raped three times. Then I figured it out.'

Stoker continued moving. He didn't know where he'd finally stop. He passed Immo, Jay, Dom and Hedda's beau Theo. They were discussing the Locker Room Project. Dom suggested they use the stock at The Bead Shop and come as marbles. Jay wanted to go as a hot-air balloon. Dom thought it was fitting. Jay accused her of being a bitch. Theo stood by, quietly interested. And then Immo butted in with his theories of walking and falling.

Stoker moved on. He passed Joan and Percy. Visually they fitted together, he thought. They both wore glitter nail polish on their toes and fingers. They were both decked out in a remix of retro-punk garbage chic. Like Anthea and Dayglo they belonged to the same tribe. The same video. He didn't want to know what they were saying to each other.

Then Stoker stopped at the table where Lizzie and Dylan were sitting.

'Where's Klingman?' Stoker asked.

'I wish you'd call him Grant,' Lizzie said. Dylan smiled wryly. 'Anyway he's gone. He's tired.'

Stoker sat down. He realised that this was the first time in ages that he'd sat at the same table with his sister and brother. He sensed that they were all thoroughly aware of the fact.

'We were talking about babies,' Lizzie said.

Stoker thought this rather a tactless subject under the circumstances. He didn't say a word. Lizzie had her own agenda.

'What do you think?' Lizzie asked.

'About what?' Stoker said.

'What do you think?! Babies. Babies. Dylan suggested a girl so your daughter could have a sister to grow up with.'

Stoker was struck by Lizzie's phrasing. He thought it odd that Dylan should be speaking about his daughter. But then, why shouldn't Dylan? Dylan's concern was matter of fact. It suggested a line of least resistance.

'So, what do you think? A boy or a girl?'

Stoker had no opinion on the matter. He had no opinion on anything. He realised that he had crushed a vigorous conversation. He had nothing to say on behalf of himself, his siblings, or his progeny. He simply sat between his brother and sister and lit a cigarette. Again he stopped and pondered over the new signage that dominated the pack of Chesterfields he bought on a daily basis – DANGER: SMOKING CAUSES HEART DISEASE. Inhaling, he resigned himself to the death of an outlaw, and most probably a fool.

Why was everyone so calm? Stoker asked himself. Why were Lizzie and Dylan getting along so well? Dylan had always been scathing about Lizzie. And Lizzie in turn had always thought of Dylan as a stuck-up bastard. And now?

Now Stoker wanted to get the hell out of Dominion Food and Hardware. He wished he could do a Klingman and retire. He wanted nothing more than for Lizzie and Dylan to resume their initial presiding calm – without him.

'You going to show us your paintings?' Lizzie asked.

'The studio's open,' Stoker said. 'Feel free.' Then he got up, forced a convivial smile, and moved to the bar. He knew that neither Lizzie or Dylan had been fooled.

The best thing to do would be to get drunk, Stoker thought, as Waldo handed him a Windhoek. Stoker stared blankly at Waldo.

'It's like separating the white from the yellow,' Waldo said. 'It's not easy.'

'What are you talking about, Waldo?'

'Eggs. I'm talking about eggs. Try to separate the white from the yellow, you'll see.'

'Why you telling me this?' Stoker asked.

'Because someone has to. You think I'm not hurting?'

This was the first time Waldo had talked to Stoker about his feelings for Joan.

'You can't separate things so easily,' Waldo continued. 'Don't try to. Let things be.'

Stoker lit a cigarette. Then he polished off his beer and ordered another.

'By the way, we've sold three soup spoons and bowls, a drill, a couple of candlesticks, three of my Indian gouaches. Not bad.' Waldo clinked his bottle of beer against Stoker's.

'It doesn't have to be a sad night,' Waldo said. 'Change the music if you have to. Enjoy.'

In fact, thanks to Waldo, Stoker was enjoying himself. He was listening to the lyrics of his favourite Portishead song. In his head he sang along: 'Give me a reason to love you, Give me a reason to be a woman.'

'Where's Dean?' Stoker asked.

'There's been an explosion at Howell's Garage.'

'Howell's down the road, Lower Obs way?'

'Yeah. Turns out a Beetle or an Audi caught fire or something. Some idiot was welding dangerously close to an oil slick. The Beetle caught fire, exploded. Next thing every Beetle, Audi and Combi in the place got cremated. The place is a right mess, apparently.'

'Could be an insurance scam,' Stoker said.

'Either that or bad karma,' Waldo said.

It suddenly dawned on Stoker that only a few days ago Olivieri had dropped dead right where he was standing. So much for karma! He thought again about how good it must be to die laughing. Then again, was Olivieri actually laughing at the instant that he died? Stoker could still picture the way Olivieri suddenly clutched his chest, buckled, fell crashing to the floor. The way Olivieri's hairpiece went flying. The way his face froze. Stoker wasn't sure if it was laughter or terror he'd seen cut indelibly across Olivieri's face. Maybe it was a bit of both?

'What are you thinking about?' Waldo asked.

'Olivieri,' Stoker said. And ordered another Windhoek.

CHAPTER TWENTY FOUR

The party folded at four. Everyone had gone except for Immo, Bridge, Waldo and Stoker. Once they'd cleaned up Immo and Bridge left. Waldo hung around for another drink and a joint, then split. He was staying with Dean for the time being. Dean's housemate, fat Flox's dad the body-builder, was in Sun City showing off his brawn. He was working as a P.E. instructor or something. Battling with other people's flab.

Stoker was glad for the peace and quiet, glad that the night hadn't exploded into a sordid scene. It could have. If he'd felt like it, he could have shat on Phyllis and Dylan from a dizzy height. He could have said something nasty just because it felt good. But what was the point? He was sick to death of the charade, sick to death of the deadness he felt inside him. He wondered if he'd actually ever loved. He doubted he had. It had always been other people who'd broken into his life, never the reverse. He was the one who had always been taken over . . . by Phyllis . . . Bianca. He was just as easily left behind.

Still, he maintained, and he maintained because he didn't know what else to do. He never seemed to have the right words. His actions worked against his feelings. He was split like a puzzle that could never be put back together again. There were pieces missing – a piece of sun, a window, the bit with the door handle painted on it. The desolation Stoker was feeling made him scared. There was nothing heroic, nothing noble about his conduct. He was simply confused, afraid he'd lose his footing. Afraid of a pain thrashing inside him. He kept hearing the lines from the Portishead song: 'Give me a reason to love you, Give me a reason to be a woman.'

To Stoker they were a judgement.

Tired, incapable of rest, Stoker decided to go for a drive. He had Olivieri's keys in his pocket. His keys. He'd never had a car before.

Stoker gathered his sleeping-bag, a six-pack of Windhoek, the Portishead tape. He locked the store behind him, set the alarm, and climbed into Olivieri's Beetle. He started the engine, let it idle, then he ejected Olivieri's Charles Aznavour tape and replaced it with Portishead. Olivieri had a jacked-up sound system with perfect pitch. Stoker cracked open a beer and drove.

He had no idea where he was going. He simply knew that he had to get out of Obs, away from anything and everything that felt familiar. He found himself crossing the Station Road bridge. In the distance to his right the brilliant floodlit glare of the new Hartleyvale Stadium incinerated the night. The brightness was odd at such a late hour. Then again, the stadium was still under construction. At the bottom of the bridge Stoker turned right into Ossian. He stopped outside the charred remains of Howell's Garage.

The place had been cordoned off with danger tape. The tape shone red and white in the glare of the stadium lights. Stoker sneaked through. Under a full moon and the towering glare it was easy to decipher the domino effect of the explosion. Hours later the place was still smouldering. He peered through shattered glass at the gutted upholstery, watched the paint as it blistered still. This was the landscape of his radio painting, he thought. Stoker lit a cigarette. At close range he studied the effects of the explosion – the seared wiring, the colours the scorched bodywork assumed, the snake-like crepuscular surfaces.

With the dank acrid stink of burnt oil, paint and upholstery still lingering, Stoker left the garage. He found himself driving down the Liesbeek Parkway in the direction of Muizenberg. The suburbs were dead, the streets empty. He drove through red robots, keeping a sharp lookout for cops. He was in no mood to be interrogated, and neither was he in a mood to stay true to the law. Dawn was creeping up as he stopped at the Muizenburg beach. Stoker cracked open another beer and strolled down to the ocean. In the distance he could see the first surfers. He thought of Joan, Dayglo and Waldo heading for the biggest wave of the outside set. For years the dawn train ride from Plumstead to Muizenberg had been their heart line. Stoker stripped, removed his glasses, and walked into the ocean. The water was cold, but so was he. He let the waves break about him as he floated. He realised that deep down he was happy. He watched the blur of sky curve in flames of red and purple. This was where the whales gathered to mate, he thought. This was where things began. He realised that he didn't have the faintest desire to do away with himself. He let himself enjoy the breaking of a new day.

From now on money wasn't going to be as scarce as it used to be. What he had wasn't much, but it was more than enough. He wasn't going to bother restocking on hardware. He'd sell what was left to sell. The rest he'd keep as is. It would take years for the existing stock to dwindle visibly. Waldo would have a small rental to pay, nothing much. They'd manage. He could use a road trip. Everyone else had come and gone to somewhere special. America, India, Zim. As for Olivieri? Stoker hoped he'd gone somewhere special. Staring up at the exploding blur of sky he pictured Olivieri dressed in his Henry Fonda gear, minus his dentures and hairpiece, tuning his harp.

'Thanks,' Stoker said. 'Thanks a lot.' Then, without thinking, he drolly added: 'We carry the full range of Nova floor treatment and home cleaning products, says the boss o' Nova.'

And in saying this, Stoker understood that he'd have to continue keeping certain things in stock.

EPI-
LOGUE

It took Stoker just over a month to finish the radio painting. The execution had been harder. The details he'd seen at Howell's had sharpened the vision. When he'd finally put a stop to the process he was convinced he'd found the combination of ruin and hope he was looking for.

Lizzie and Klingman had married and settled on a baby girl. Contrary to their original plan the marriage was a biggish affair. Lizzie had her heart set on the ceremony being conducted at the family house in Riebeek-Kasteel – the location was clearly a sign that things were changing in a big way for her. She'd arranged for a priest, a screamingly camp friend of a friend, to conduct the ceremony on the porch. Just about everyone in the book was there. With regard to the naming of the baby there was much debate. It was finally agreed that Lizzie and Klingman's daughter would be called Nellie, after Phyllis's mum, and Phyllis and Stoker's daughter, Mira, after Stoker's mum. Lizzie and Klingman did not deviate from the initial proposition they'd made to Stoker the day he came round for the annual shaving of his armpits. He was stuck with the chore of best man.

It was in her seventh month that Phyllis quit Dom's Bead Shop and moved in with Dylan. The move made sense. Dylan was around. And there was a midwife on hand, a spooky knowing crone who happened to be a childhood acquaintance of Stoker's mum. As it turned out they'd never particularly liked each other. Stoker's mum was always too cold and stuck up, the crone had said. The fact that the crone's animosity hadn't faded one jot didn't faze Phyllis. Let bygones be bygones, she'd said to the crone. They were getting along just fine.

Hedda, Phyllis's friend and ex, moved into Phyllis's flat on Orphan and Long with her ex-con dockworker lover, Theo. It was by chance that Stoker had seen them the night Dominion

Food and Hardware opened. They'd happened to pull in. Hedda didn't expect to see Phyllis. She'd finally quit the hot springs in Citrusdal. She and Theo still hadn't married. They were staying at Theo's mum's place, Goodwood way. That night they were out on the town. They'd spent the day checking out houses for sale in Obs. All the ones worth living in were out of their price range. They were thinking of renting.

Jay had pulled out of Dom's place. She finally needed him out of her hair, she'd said. Jay was crashing at Bridge and Immo's, rotating shifts with them at Dominion Food and Hardware. His tips went into Bridge's cookie jar. The fact that he couldn't pay for the roof over his head was fine with Bridge since the same applied to Immo. Besides, the house on Norfolk was big enough. Thanks to a kind dead granny, Prue's aunt, the house had been given to Bridge. As far as Bridge was concerned she had a legacy of generosity to keep up. Bills were another issue. She had a card phone. Jay paid for the digits he punched in. The electricity and water were split three ways.

Joan had finally finished *Coastal Resort*, her pastel of Percy as a corpse on a dump site. It wasn't easy, but then it never was with Joan. The trash she'd bottled in the clear resin frame worked like the clues to an investigation – a railway ticket with a computer-generated listing of the place and time of departure and arrival, a shoe string, a strapless watch with a smashed glass and a missing hand, a bright green chewing-gum wrapper, an aspirator, four strands of blond hair, and the shredded traces of larger things, like a slice of skin or the button of a shirt. Joan was still seeing Percy and, as she'd put it, making her own mistakes. One night she'd returned from clubbing at the Gel with Dom, Bridge, Phyllis and Lizzie. En route back to Obs she'd run over a drugged-out jaywalker. The injuries incurred weren't serious, but Joan was convinced she was hexed. She'd spent the next day in bed reviewing her life. She still hadn't resolved her connection with Waldo or Percy.

With the assistance of Klingman, Beatrice had sold her house on Lower Wrensch and moved back to Palermo. For a brief while there was talk of Hedda and Theo buying the place.

The idea had appealed to Beatrice, but there was a limit to how low she would go. She had a retirement package to think of and life in Palermo didn't come cheap. She trusted Klingman to strike the deal that would guarantee her comfort. Since property sales were down it took Beatrice a while to strike gold. When she did she promptly left. However, before doing so, she gave a set of nude photographs to Joan. She'd been hugely impressed by *Coastal Resort* and thought that at least one of the two hundred images of herself would inspire Joan. The whole lot did. As far as Joan was concerned Beatrice's staggering gamut of expressions and positions of fuckability was the antidote to all her mistakes. She never ceased to marvel at the whore inside the geriatric.

Stoker had received a postcard from Bianca informing him that Beatrice was well. They visited each other often. Beatrice was keen on art and Bianca was keen on stories. Italian pornography had become a burning issue. With the aid of a rechargeable dictaphone, a notepad and pen, and a truckload of archival data, Bianca was writing a biography of Beatrice's life in between drafts of her book on art in South Africa. Olivieri was a major player, but Beatrice was the star. As far as Bianca was concerned the antics of Jeff Koons and Cicciolina had nothing on Olivieri and Beatrice. The rest of the card informed him that *In the Country of Last Things* had been well received at Galleria Dell'arte Moderne Frassini. She had arranged an exhibition of his works at a sister gallery in Belfast as promised. She'd concluded the card by asking Stoker to write and tell her about his new work, if any. To date Stoker hadn't.

Lizzie had received a postcard from Dayglo saying that he missed her a lot, was glad they'd split up, glad that she was getting married. He'd quit Butchers of Distinction and was no longer doing covers. As for finding the right band – that was a lost cause. Instead he'd found a studio, was producing his own sounds, and playing live at raves with two other drummers. He was having a good time and earning mega-bucks. He doubted he'd be back in quite a while. The drumming ensemble was called The First Supper.

Putter had moved into the final stages of the Locker Room Project. Bookings at fifty rand a shot were flying in. The takings, which went into the thousands, were funnelled back into the project. The ramifications which needed to be dealt with were endless. Putter was at the end of his tether and having a ball. Think big, think cheap, think myth – these were Putter's driving tenets. Joan and Waldo had painted the outside wall of the Zambezi Room at the River Club an acid green. All the rooms at the club were named after rivers. Over the green they'd painted lurid shuttlecocks and cricket balls. The idea was perfunctory and largely cosmetic, but the execution was meticulous and vivid. As a tribute to the survival of Phyllis's cat, Petal, Stoker had contributed an orange wall. In jagged angles across the wall he'd added twenty cats in various degrees and attitudes of panic and terror, dodging a hail of bullets. At the source of the hail was a shotgun caught in a blur of motion. Holding the shotgun was a visored and murderous-looking geriatric in a chequered gingham apron – none other than Mrs Robinson. Putter was a trifle confused, but then he did have a load on his mind. Stoker finally convinced him that a Queer take on sport was blazingly evident.

His radio painting completed and his responsibility to the Locker Room Project and Lizzie's wedding accounted for, Stoker had decided to leave the city for a while. Before doing so he'd had Olivieri's silencer fixed. By that time Waldo was thoroughly immersed in Dominion Food and Hardware. Waldo had had to deal with a host of legalities: install an extractor, go on a sanitation course, junk the system of Cadacs for a three-phase electric stove, etc. By the time that Stoker left, Dominion Food and Hardware was up and running. The liquor licence was still pending.

Stoker had travelled towards Knysna along the coastal road. He'd spent a couple of days and nights in the pyramid colony with Anthea, Dayglo's ex after Lizzie. It turned out Anthea wasn't joking when she'd told him at the Seeff that the sleeping area was positioned just below the tip of the pyramid. Anthea was having a great time. She didn't miss Cape Town or Dayglo one bit. She was hooked on permaculture and proudly guided

Stoker through the labyrinth of bizarrely cross-hatched seeds and vegetables. He was struck by the aberrant logic, the collapse of obvious divides. The basic model was the wilderness, Anthea explained. Plants that grew low were planted under shrubs that grew next to creepers that climbed saplings that patiently waited for trees to die out so they could grow. In a veggie garden Stoker found basil growing next to tomatoes for easy picking, with carrots in between using the root space. Fennel was planted on the outskirts to attract pests and keep them away from the other plants. The old mealies he saw had beans climbing them and pumpkins creeping between the stalks. Fruit vines covered the north-facing aspect, shading it in summer, losing leaves and allowing sun in winter. He was particularly struck by the totemic herb spiral. The quirky combinations were endless. Nothing was queerer than permaculture, Stoker thought. Nothing made more sense. He made a mental note to talk to Putter about permaculture.

The colony was an eye-opener. Stoker wanted to stay but he also needed to leave, move on. From pyramid country he headed for Dweza, a nature reserve in the Transkei, where he spent a week. There he languished undisturbed, spotted game and swam. Then he'd travelled back up through the Karoo into Walter Meyer country. He'd camped over in Graaff-Reinet, visited the Valley of Desolation, then stopped in at the Owl House in Nieu-Bethesda to see if Koos Malgas was still okay. Koos was pissed as usual. Stoker was glad to discover that the Brethren hadn't succeeded in destroying his unsung hero's lifestyle.

From the Karoo Stoker headed west into the Cederberg where he'd spent three weeks tucked away in a valley belonging to the Nieuwoudts. The camping site cost him fifteen rand a day. It was here that he finally found the peace and quiet he had longed for. He bathed in the icy water of the Kromrivier, a few steps from his tent. He stored his provisions in the boot of Olivieri's Beetle which, he discovered, served as a perfect kitchen surface. He finally read *Vertical Man, Horizontal World* and discovered the pleasures of reading instead of listening to others read. Dom had also given him a set of Penguin pocket books filled with gothic tales, high romances and sordid psychodramas. These he read at a leisurely pace beside the fire, under a brilliant canopy of stars. Unschooled in astronomy he'd failed to decipher the riddle. What he did see on gazing up into a startlingly clear sky amounted to a shopping trolley, a dumb-bell, a hinge, a crowbar, and a sliver of a moon just visible beneath a drooping eyelid.

On an early evening when the dry heat had begun to cool he'd go for long walks along steep slopes and valleys where, it was said, leopards still roamed. He saw a klipspringer, some wild cats and a dassie. For three weeks he spoke to no one, his only gesture of communication a nod of the head or the wave of a hand to the farm labourers. Sated and drunk, he slept soundly. At six every morning he would be wakened by the pounding hooves of horses as they galloped past his tent into the mountains. Hung over and at peace, the pounding of hooves in his head, he would trundle down to the bank and begin the day with sweet river water and a Grand-Pa. For Stoker life was perfect, the city a distant memory. Not once did he think of drawing or devising future paintings. The radio painting was the last in the cycle. Only one image continued to compel him, though it would remain unexecuted. It was the image of a man gripping the passenger seat of a bakkie, the seat hurtling up towards the dome of a blackening tunnel, the flaming bakkie in the accelerated distance beneath him.

On the twenty-first day of his stay at the Nieuwoudt farm, a few days before the Locker Room Project, Stoker solemnly packed the Beetle and returned to Obs. En route he stopped at an outcrop of giant red rocks and caves once occupied by Bushmen. The cathedral-like splendour of the setting, the beauty of the worn red rock paintings he saw of elephants and eland made a mockery of Desolation Valley. On a promontory overlooking a trackless expanse of undulating stone, once the floor of an ancient ocean, Stoker ate the last remains of his food – a Marmite snackwich, a naartjie and an apple. His vigil finally completed, he drove along fifty-seven k's of corrugated dust road, through the Long Valley with its plains of purple and giant rocks that seemed to have fallen from the sky, through the Uitkyk Pass, mountain water spilling off its sheer face, through the Algeria Forestry Station. Here, amidst the tall pines, Stoker took a last icy dip, and refilled his water bottles. In the blazing heat he crossed the Olifant's River, the rattle of gravel shifting with abrupt fluency to the purr of tar. The rest of the journey was undertaken on the N7 which stretched from the Namib to the Cape of Good Hope.

Back in Obs, installed in his studio, Stoker caught up on all the developments while he had been away. The Waiting Country had finally folded because of too much infighting and a lack of shared vision. Jay had decided to take an involuntary sabbatical from Dom and music. In addition to working as a waiter he'd started taking acting classes. Stoker was convinced that Jay was on the right track.

Percy and Joan had split up. There were too many subtexts, too much pain, Joan had said. She wanted out. She needed to be alone. The air had thoroughly cleared between her and Waldo. Desire lingered unabated and unfulfilled. She threw herself into commercial work and spent most of her time with women.

Percy in turn had also decided to quit music, Joan, and the world of an artist's model. Together with a friend – Phil, the drummer from The Waiting Country – he'd resumed his career as a mechanic and opened a Moffie Workshop. The tools were pink, the overalls were pink. Percy's speciality, according to Percy, was the four-stroke machine: the suck, squeeze, bang and blow machine. The first stroke was inlet, the second compression, the third ignition, the fourth exhaust. It was at the Moffie Workshop that Stoker arranged to have Olivieri's Beetle serviced when he returned from his road trip.

As for Phyllis, when Stoker saw her she had been thoroughly panel-beaten from the inside and was fit to burst. She was exhausted and content. They conducted a sober exchange, enquired after the other's health. Stoker described his road trip and Phyllis talked of life in Riebeek-Kasteel. Dylan had resumed writing poetry and was drafting a possible book on his parents' murder. The pretext for Phyllis and Stoker's meeting had been the remote-controlled boat he'd made as a boy, the one he'd seen languishing in the bottom of his cupboard when he'd slept over at Dylan's. The one he'd named after his mother. While seated on a rock in the Kromrivier he'd thought of the boat, thought of navigating the waters. He'd faxed a request to Dylan. Phyllis had appeared at his door with the boat. She'd popped into town to see her mum, Chan and Gloria, and to discuss the Locker Room Project. Standing at Stoker's front door holding his boat, she'd said she was killing a lot of birds with one stone. Stoker had no qualms about being a stoned bird among many. In the driver's seat of Phyllis's bakkie, Stoker saw the crone.

While Stoker was away the group had decided, after much debate, to come as hermaphrodarts. This, Phyllis explained, entailed silver helmets with absurdly long points suggesting Teutonic helmets and hypodermic needles. The helmets were to be made of paper, glue and spray-paint. Then there were the aerodynamically designed feathers for the darts which involved the refashioning of metal coat hangers so that the waists of the darts looked like propellers. From this jutting structure reams of toilet paper, spray-painted red and black in keeping with the Teutonic helmets, were cut into strips and pasted to the wires. The strips of toilet paper swayed beautifully in the breeze, Phyllis said. The overall effect had succeeded in conjuring the feathers of a dart. To complete the illusion the group would have their faces, hands and feet covered in a metallic hue. What did Stoker think? He was happy that the decision had been made for him, he said.

When Stoker stopped in at Bridge, Immo and Jay's place on Norfolk to get himself fitted for his costume, he discovered a hubbub of frenzied sewing, spray-painting and gluing. The posse of hermaphrodarts was larger than he'd expected. There was Dom, Jay, Dylan, Percy, Joan, Waldo, Lizzie, Klingman, Immo, Bridge, Prue, Hedda, Theo, Gloria, Chan, Phyllis and Phyllis's mum Nellie, all of whom had to be kitted out for the occasion, all with different sizes and slightly different accessories of a Queer nature. Only Dean, perverse as he was, had decided that he wouldn't participate. Everyone had accused him of being regressive. Eventually he'd agreed to go. After all, he'd said, it was his job to take photos of people making idiots of themselves.

The fact was Dean's mind and heart were elsewhere. While Stoker was away Dean's ex had come to see him. It turned out his ex couldn't bear living without him. He wanted to move back in with Dean. Dean had casually said it was okay. In fact Dean was so ecstatic he couldn't think straight. The rekindling of his great love was the talk of Obs. Dean doubted that a queerer thing could ever happen to him. As a consequence he never got measured and kitted out. On the night of the Locker Room Project Dean came dressed as he always did, carrying a camera with a zoom and a ratty placard with the legend YOU'LL NEVER WALK ALONE. The other member of his team was Perdita. As for Dean's ex, he was flamboyantly and ruggedly decked out as a Ra-Ra-Rugga-Bugga.

Putter, who naturally had his own agenda, appeared in ten inch silver-spangled heels that put Phyllis's gold shoes to shame. He also wore a sequinned wig that bore a striking resemblance to candyfloss, a silver tennis outfit with an enormous bust, and an eighteenth-century pancake face riddled with beauty spots. He tottered and towered over everyone else, regally swatting the masses with his silver-spangled tennis racquet.

Over six thousand people arrived on the night of the Locker Room Project. There were indeed pink and mauve floodlights. People streamed down the long driveway to the River Club in a dazzling array of costumes. Stoker saw a team of day-glo mountain-bikers, a team of parachutists with the parachutes miraculously floating above them like knowing clouds. There were hairy pom-pom girls, two lecherous geriatrics decked out in togas and purple grapes and gauges for measuring cocks. There were a group of buoyant balloonists, a gamut of aquatic sportists and, in a ditch alongside the rosy pink and mauve lane, a couple of fist-fuckers fist-fucking. The assailant wore industrial strength rubber gloves. Both the victim and the assailant wore T-shirts advocating safe sex. In a clump of bushes further along, Stoker spotted a young man skin-clad from head to toe in pink plastic. The man was amorously sucking the pectorals of a blow-up doll. The overall effect was startling yet chastening.

Stoker had never seen so much urban wisdom and colour, so many preposterous and dazzling extensions of selves. A group passed him wearing giant golden galleons on their heads. A TV crew wielding cameras and microphones appeared before the hermaphrodarts. The crew, who'd modelled themselves on the assassins at the Munich Olympics, were dressed in ominous black and acid yellow armbands with the words ART ATTACK. The hermaphrodarts faced the cameras as they rolled, the absurdly elongated points of their helmets bobbing. Chan and Phyllis's mum Nellie, startled out of their brackets by what they had already witnessed, clung to each other as though on the deck of a wrecked ship, while Gloria glowed beside them, a gutted toaster glinting in a hedge of freshly-dyed red hair. Hedda, her oiled and naked *Million BC* body screened intermittently at the crotch by swaying strips of coloured toilet paper, draped herself on a hefty bespectacled and flabbergasted Theo. Dom and Jay stood casually erect and separate, arrogant, wounded, and gorgeous. Bridge bobbed and swayed, the whiplash of her pigtail glittering with sequins, the words QUEER GIANT – in celebration of Ingrid Jonker – painted in green on her silver stomach. Wild-eyed bearded Immo, a dog's bone strapped beneath his nose, his sinuous arms and fingertips rippling, whirled about Bridge as though about a leaping fire. Dylan and Prue stood sombre and quietly absurd. Joan in her Docs with her woodcut face formed the centre of a triptych, with Percy in pink to the right and Waldo in green to the left. Then there were Lizzie and Klingman, the bells of chapels still ringing in their heads, Lizzie bewitched by the thought of fifteen seconds of fame, Klingman content to fall to the cutting-floor, neurotic visions of murderous babysitters uppermost in his mind. Stoker, at odds with the crowds and attention, marvelled at the spectacle that Putter had engineered. With silvered face and perplexed eyes concealed behind thick glasses, he receded before the glare. Dreams of mountains and valleys, eland and buck, of river-water sweet and cool washed through and carried him. It was Phyllis, pure and fearless, always wakeful to the moment, who guided the group through the gauntlet of cameras and microphones, her giant belly like a prow, unaided by artifice. Together and alone they lost themselves in the swelling stream.